ALSO BY DAVID SHIELDS

Heroes

Dead
Languages

Dead Languages

a novel

DAVID SHIELDS

ALFRED A. KNOPF ⚒ NEW YORK 1989

THIS IS A BORZOI BOOK
PUBLISHED BY ALFRED A. KNOPF, INC.

Portions of this book were originally published in substantially different form in the *San Francisco Chronicle* (under the sponsorship of the PEN Syndicated Fiction Project), *South Carolina Review, Turnstile,* and *Four Quarters.*

Library of Congress Cataloging-in-Publication Data
Shields, David.
Dead languages.
I. Title.
PS3569.H4834D4 1989   813'.54   88-13444
ISBN 0-394-57388-9
Manufactured in the United States of America
FIRST EDITION

The author would like to express his gratitude to the New York Foundation for the Arts and the Ludwig Vogelstein Foundation for fiction grants; and the Corporation of Yaddo, MacDowell Colony, Bread Loaf Writers' Conference, Ragdale Foundation, Virginia Center for the Creative Arts, and Cummington Community of the Arts for residency fellowships.

A NOTE ON THE TYPE

The text of this book was set in a film version of a face called Cheltenham, designed by the architect Bertram Grosvenor Goodhue in collaboration with Ingalls Kimball of The Cheltenham Press of New York. Cheltenham was introduced in the early twentieth century, a period of remarkable achievement in type design. The idea of creating a "family" of types by making variations on the basic type design was originated by Goodhue and Kimball in the design of the Cheltenham series.

Composed by Creative Graphics Inc., Allentown, Pennsylvania
Printed and bound by R. R. Donnelley & Sons, Harrisonburg, Virginia
Designed by Iris Weinstein

FOR MY FAMILY

Are not our lives too short for that full utterance which through all our stammerings is of course our only and abiding intention?

JOSEPH CONRAD, *Lord Jim*

Dead
Languages

1

I UNDERSTAND that whenever Demosthenes got a little tongue-tied he'd leave Athens to camp out on the Mediterranean coast where, with pebbles in his mouth, he'd rehearse his oration against the sound of the Aegean Sea until his rather unGreek diffidence ceased and words became waves within him. Then he'd return to Athens to deliver a very authoritative, unhesitant speech which always concerned the sanctity of the Greek city-state and never received anything less than unrestrained applause from the rude multitude. The trip to the Mediterranean, the swim at sea, the favorable reception in the senate: it's a delightful tale complete with moral in tow. And yet there are those—surely, Sandra, you are one of them—who will want to insist that Demosthenes, forced to flee Athens and lecture inattentive fish every time he was scheduled to speak about the city-state, should have drowned himself at high tide, whereas I'd want to emphasize that Demosthenes never left the coast until he was speaking so loud he could no longer hear the Aegean arriving on the rocks.

The big city boy, who hates the city, leaves the city to perfect a speech in praise of the absolute supremacy of the city. The audience, impatient to applaud, doesn't perceive that the greatest orator in Western civilization often speaks with seaweed sliding out his mouth. Why would someone for whom talking was torture want to talk all the time before thousands of Athenians? Because otherwise he'd have drowned himself at high tide. My sister—so shy, so sincere—once wanted to be an actress. The best jazz drummer I've ever heard had only one arm. We all choose a calling that's the most radical contradiction of ourselves.

And what's my calling? I am not a postal clerk. All I've ever had are memories; metaphor is only an escape from error into elegance.

No imagination, only memory. More specifically: Lido Isle the summer of 1960. I remember Father reading about the Rosenbergs in a wooden chair chained to a steel stake in the sand; Mother sitting at her black typewriter in her ugly black swimsuit, inhaling Kents and exhaling black smoke while writing a retrospective on the Hollywood Ten for *The Nation* ("Perhaps the whole intent and purpose of the loyalty orders was merely to collect evidentiary leads—like a boy collecting wads of string in the hope that someday he will have enough for a noose"); Beth, too fat to have fun, never failing by lunch to complete the crossword puzzle; the hideous sand dunes in the distance, slime mold clinging to the four legs of the dock, the muddy shore at morning, but all that recedes and I see myself, absurdly small, seated in a white rowboat that later is to become much photographed by Father because it's the source of all mystery. It's the source of all mystery because, although it's without oars or owner and isn't moored, it never leaves the shore. Never. It's always there, always white, rusted, pure, austere.

The rowboat isn't only the Source of All Mystery and the Vehicle of the Voyage. It's also an Icon of My Own Isolation. *C'est moi.* I never leave the shore. I don't know how to swim. Tears lift the waves to high water. The horizon is Hong Kong. I decide to cross the Pacific so I can stop speaking English, with which I am having considerable difficulty, and learn Chinese, which seems so much faster, so much more natural. No pauses, just jabbering. I decide to row across but have no oars. I decide to swim across but don't know how to swim. I can't even float. Though I haven't yet heard of Demosthenes, I speak to the Pacific, love how dark it looks as night nears. I want from the waves what he wanted: a little bit of cruel constancy. I orate to the ocean what I've heard about all day—that neither of the Rosenbergs and none of the Hollywood Ten were guilty—and, all alone in the night, I become witty, jocular. I explain to the Pacific how helplessly attracted I am to Ruth Greenglass's red hair, how erotic her betrayal of the Rosenbergs is for me. My voice picks up power, I'm drowning out high tide, I can't hear it any more. The Pacific is puny. China is mere chimera. I start to stand in the boat, bellowing at the waves, but as I rise I lose my balance and fall overboard. I learn how to swim: the water is not warm.

I hope it's clear this is no mere tale of a four-year-old finding his first flippers, even if swimming is finally only swimming: an undertow here, a red tide there, a scorpion in the sand. And a family is only a family. My family was only a family. It wasn't a nightmare. It wasn't a concentration camp. Each of us isn't the sum total of all the faults of his family. That's impossible. That can't be who we are. So I suppose I selectively remember that Mother was writing an article, Father was reading a book, and Beth was completing crossword puzzles, while I wandered the island, wondering whether I should cut off my tongue or simply put a pistol to my head. My family was living in language whereas I was dying in it, and I understand such a situation is classical, not in the sense of Demosthenes but *Herr Doktor:* the opposite of success is suicide.

Beth had done so well in a high school course called Psychoanalysis and Literature that when the teacher—a handsome man who wore loud blazers and said such things as, "Have any of you ever seen a picture of Kafka? He looks like a criminal. Do you know why he looks like a criminal? Because he was an artist. Do you know why the artist is a criminal? Because he steals our secrets"— got tired, he'd let Beth lead the discussion. So well dressed, so seraphically smart, she'd stand up and say, "Did it occur to any of you that Gertrude's last words—'O my dear Hamlet'—are not without meaning for us?" Years later, of course, I wanted to do even better than Beth had done, but when Loud Blazer called on me I'd shake my head No, or maybe nod Yes, then after class he'd come up to me and say: "Are you sure your last name is Zorn?"

Place-Names: The Name. Zorn, Germany: Zorn. Three hundred years ago: "Are you Zorns from Zorn?" "Why, yes, of course, all Zorns are from Zorn." German; Jew. So the secret has been stolen, and not by Kafka. So I am not Demosthenes. Which is why it's curious to me that Mother often said she never trusted German-Jews because their loyalty was divided between culture and country and, in some of the last articles she wrote, attacked Kissinger, really quite viciously attacked him, for that very reason. Didn't she trust Father? Is that what this means? Who knows? Maybe that's why Father always insisted we were Russian. He liked to see himself as one of those who would have contradicted the Cossacks if he had had the chance. I can't believe Mother had any reason to mistrust Father or that, on the other hand, Father would have listened to such a harangue against his lineage. If memory serves, though, that's precisely what happened. The discovery that I'm a descendant of the Zorns from Zorn was a recent product of my own research.

I've never been exactly sure what part of Europe Mother's people came from, but wasn't she always the Cossack and Father the cowering Jew? Wasn't this his chance to be tough and didn't he bow and scrape? It's fashionable these days to equate marriage and murder, and I don't mean to invoke such a simple formula, but it would be a lie to say Mother was ever anything less than a tyrant or Father anything more than a mole. Mother often gave dinner parties for the West Coast correspondents of other magazines—very lavish affairs at which they drank a lot, talked very loudly and learnedly about everything in the world, and told me Mother was a marvelous writer as well as a "great gal," but which were always being interrupted by a call from someone's copy editor "back East" who wanted the entire article on Governor Reagan rewritten by midnight. It was all very exciting.

It's one party in particular I remember. I don't remember what year it was or what season. Instead, I remember those terrible gingham curtains drawn back so the picture window presented rather spectacularly: the Bay and the Bridge, with a Moon. On one wall was a Klee print, and on the other wall was a black-and-white photograph, mounted and framed, of two children kissing, which, if you looked at it in the wrong light or without, say, love in your heart, you might take for nothing more than two water glasses touching. The first time Father saw it he thought it was waves, dark waves at dawn. Even now I cannot convince him those are lips. The party people were reading one another's articles in one another's magazines, as they spooned chocolate mousse, which Beth had been so good to make, and sipped coffee. They were praising one another extravagantly and meditating upon the power of the written word, the nature of attractive typography. Oh, I don't know, maybe a few candles flickered in the black wind.

Then Father found something offensive about one of the articles, and the moon dissolved. He read aloud the first paragraph of the story, which was written by an Englishman for Reuters:

At a $100-a-plate dinner last night sponsored by the San Francisco Jewish Welfare Fund, Israeli Prime Minister Golda Meir called for Jewish-American men and women to contribute one percent of their paychecks to the war effort, and all Jewish-American boys over the age of eighteen to enlist in the Israeli Army. She assured the affluent audience that visa applications would be waived for all potential soldiers. Alluding to Egyptian President Gamal Abdel Nasser's boast that "our aim is to drive Israel into the Red Sea," Prime Minister Meir said, "The people of Israel have never had, do not now have, and shall never have any intention of residing underwater," drawing a sustained, standing ovation from this charming city's ethnic elite.

" 'Affluent audience,' " Father said. " 'Potential soldiers.' 'Ethnic elite.' You call this objective reporting?"

Reuters, who was tapping the ashes of a sophisticated cigarette into his empty mousse dish, said, "For godsakes, chap, cheer up, will you? We call it 'in-depth analysis.' "

On the few occasions Father became furious, I always had the sense thirty years were receding before my eyes, and this time was no exception: the voice a vibrato; the face, quite literally, crimson; those thin legs very suddenly tight and mighty. Father stood, spilling his mousse.

"Teddy, sit down," Mother said.

Teddy—Father—sat down, then said, "In-depth analysis? What, are you kidding? This is slander."

"I found it—as a lead paragraph—wonderfully terse, wonderfully, really quite wonderfully, to the point," someone said.

"It's a nice mixture, Taylor, of reportage and local color," Mother said. "It really is."

"Annette, how can you say that?" Father pleaded, tugging on the tablecloth. "It's subtly, or not so subtly, anti-Semitic. I demand an apology."

And then, amid all the West Coast correspondents, Father put his napkin down on the table and just started weeping. Huge convulsive heaves of the shoulders and slobbering gasps for breath. While the discussion returned to more civilized concerns (international politics and pay raises and that kind of thing), Father got up and left, taking his mousse and a bent metal spoon with him into the bedroom. I'd like to say I went with him, helped him eat his mousse, held his hand, and told him I thought they were wrong, all wrong, but Mother stared at me to sit perfectly still, so I stayed. The control she had over people was really rather extraordinary. Maybe Father was bored silly with the conversation and just wanted an excuse to leave the table so he could sit up in bed, scoop pudding, and read some more about Sing Sing, but I imagine he squeezed a pillow tightly and cried the night away. He used to be such an emotional man.

And yet I don't see how he could have been expecting anything terribly much more from Mother, as it was just not her way to rush to Father's defense. She didn't do that sort of thing. Father was so helpless he would have needed the Russian Army as a defense and, although Mother was the Russian Army, she was never especially prone to eliminating the enemy for him. Or, rather, she *was* the enemy for him. Why was she always so sweet to strangers and so tough on Father? I wish I knew. The more helpless he became the more unhelpful she became and then, when she finally needed some attention, Father was nowhere to be found.

I don't mean to imply the sheer agony of watching Mother and Father argue was the sole cause of my curse. Sometimes, though, when I'm playing tennis I'll know I can't quite reach the ball if I hit it with a backhand, so I'll shift the racquet and return the ball lefty— a maneuver I didn't so much learn from Father as inherit from him—or when hurriedly filling out a form I'll realize my "Z," with its wicked horizontal slash, might just as well have been written by

Mother. It's times like these when I acknowledge that if my parents affected my tennis game and my penmanship they must have had some influence upon my mouth as well. I recently learned that Mother wasn't the first person ever to say: "The past is but prologue to the present," although probably no one ever said it as often as she did. It's a very nice if somewhat too alliterative axiom, and it might serve well as my emblem throughout these episodes. The past is but prologue. I suppose I should begin at the beginning.

2

CONTEMPORARY pathological theory—Sandra tells me—has it that "the stuttering problem begins in early childhood and develops as a negative reaction by the child to disfluencies while speaking." Right around age three, children find language for the first time. In their eagerness and anxiety to master the communicative process by morning, almost all little ones encounter considerable difficulty at one time or another with their diction. Every day they add dozens of new words to their vocabularies and, impatient for progress, they trip over this *t*, fumble with that *f*. If just about every child babbles occasionally from age three to age five, only a very select one half of one percent go on to make a nasty adult habit out of it.

Why do some "develop a negative reaction to disfluencies" while others do not? Why is every stutterer I have ever met a man? And why are his eyes always rimmed with fear? The reason ninety percent of all impeded speakers are male is, according to Sandra, that little boys feel more pressure than little girls to perform verbal magic. In some ways it's an attractive theory, but I have my doubts. Beth claims she was already reading second-rate mysteries when she was five, whereas I'd never pretend that at such an early age I was doing anything more ambitious than attempting to master the alphabet, that terrible catalogue of unspeakable sounds.

Still, I did always feel a certain subtle pressure to produce perfect speech, and for that I suppose I should blame Mother and Father, since Sandra is so convinced the origin of all stuttering is a scene in which one of the parents calls the child's attention to and scolds him for what is normal, everyday disfluency. The example Sandra uses is always the same: a boy and his mother lean out the second-floor window of a burning house, waiting for the boy's father to line up the ladder with the ledge of the window. The boy turns to his mother and says, "I-I-I'm afraid, Mommy." Sandra is certain that if the mother in such a situation says, "Don't worry, Melvin, Daddy will have us out of here in no time," Melvin will turn out all right, but if the mother says, "Don't say, 'I-I-I'm afraid,' Melvin, just 'I'm afraid,' " Melvin will try not to stutter on "I" the next time he says it. This, as we all know, is the beginning of the end. He will, as Sandra says, "develop a general orientation toward speech of 'what can I do not to stutter' instead of 'what can I do to talk.' " Poor little Melvin. I've always assumed his only hope was for the house to go up fast in flames.

There's no house on fire in my memory but, when Sandra insists that I must remember the origin of the disorder, I see a Pacific Palisades living room as the scene of the crime. Beth was away at a classical guitar lesson; Father, who had just returned from playing four sets of doubles at Rancho Park, was sprawled on the floor, bouncing a white tennis ball on the red Persian rug; Mother, who had to be in North Hollywood by noon to interview a screenwriter who'd been blacklisted and wanted to talk, was sitting in the Good Chair with her polished shoes on the stool and the puppy in her lap. The dog was named Bruin, in honor of Mother's alma mater, but it should have been called CIA, since it looked like nothing so much as the black-coated specter in *Mad*'s "Spy vs. Spy." And it would have been an appropriate appellation, too, as its only desires in the world were to claw your bare ruined legs, curl up in Mother's soul, and look at you lugubriously. It was wounded half a dozen years later when I got upset one afternoon about my inability to talk, even to a dog, and neglected to latch the back gate. Bruin ran right into the grillwork of a Mustang convertible.

At the origin of the disorder, in the living room on Saturday morning, Bruin was still healthy and dreaming in Mother's lap. Mother was sitting in the Good Chair, Father was bouncing a tennis ball on the Persian rug, and I was lying down on the couch. Yes, lying down on the couch, and I suspect the symbolism was intentional, since Mother said I should put a pillow behind my head and my arms at my side, just relax, close my eyes, and talk very slowly. I tried to do what Mother said, I honestly tried, but I was five years old, it was the month of May, and all that morning sun waxed the bay window with quasi-religious light, with reasons to live. It was obvious to me that outside the window was what is known as life, and inside the window was what is commonly referred to as death. I wanted very much to be outside and got up to go, but Father stood, guarding the front door, playing the patrolman for probably the first and last time in his life. Mother said if she could be a little late for her interview, "well, then, you can come right back here and lie down on the couch and listen to me for a few minutes, Buster." My name wasn't Buster. The dog's name was Bruin or, to free-associating friends of Beth's borrowing our house between marches throughout the sixties, Brewin'. The dog leapt off Mother's lap, pranced across the Persian rug, and Father opened the door to let her go outside. Beth was strumming Segovia transcriptions and eating fancy cookies in a nice Italian lady's house in Bel-Air.

"Are you comfortable over there on the couch?" Mother asked.

"Yes," I said.

"Are you happy?" she asked.

Surely she meant this as an inquiry into the general state of my spiritual life, what sort of reconciliation I'd arrived at between death and desire. Father sat upright and Mother raised her eyebrows when I said, "No, I'm not happy." She thought she was onto something. She thought I was going to tell her what she wanted to hear.

"Why not?" she asked.

"Because I'd rather be outside, playing," I said.

"Oh, right," she said, nodding. She slumped back in the Good Chair. Father returned to his prone position on the floor.

This wasn't working out the way she wanted. She wasn't establishing the empathy she was famous for establishing between herself and her subject. I guess I wasn't giving a very good interview. Mother went into the den to call the screenwriter and say she'd be a little late, while Father went to take a shower because in twenty minutes he was supposed to pick up Beth at the nice Italian lady's house in the hills. As he was walking out of the room he squeezed my shoulder and said, "Just relax, Jeremy. Don't worry about what Mom is saying." So then, of course, waiting for Mother to get off the phone, lying face down on the scratchy couch, I couldn't do anything except worry. Mother had just given me a new watch to teach me responsibility and make me acutely aware of my own mortality. Studying its blue face, its white dial, I admired the ease with which the silver second hand made its rounds, the way it couldn't stop moving if it wanted to.

When Mother returned from the den, she pulled the stool next to the couch, pushed the hair off my forehead, and blew smoke in my face. Then she brought out her rook for mopping up. She said this very softly and sympathetically, she said it while massaging my skull, but what she said was: "Do you realize, Jeremy, that sometimes you talk too fast? Sometimes you're in just such a hurry to say something the words trip you up. Have you ever noticed that, honey? Sometimes you'll want to say a word so fast you won't be able to say it at all or you'll say the first sound of the word over and over. I don't want this to become a habit for you. There's no need to be quite so anxious. People will wait to hear what you have to say."

"I don't do that," I said.

"Do what?"

"Talk too fast."

"Sometimes you do," Mother said. "Not a lot or even often, but now and then you try to rush your words and you'll stumble over one of them. Daddy has noticed it, I've noticed it, and Beth said she's noticed it."

Actually, studies show it's not stutterers who talk too fast but the mothers of stutterers; it's *their* fault.

"Beth said that?"

"Yes."

"When?"

"She said yesterday the two of you were looking at the map of the United States in the World Book and, when you were racing to see who could name all the capital cities first, you had some difficulty saying 'Philadelphia.' "

"I didn't," I said. "She's a liar." Beth was a liar, but she was also the winner of the map game when Harrisburg, of all places, rather than Philadelphia, proved to be the capital of Pennsylvania.

I listened to the shower running, to the expansion of the pipes. I watched Bruin press her black little nose to the window and beg to be let back in. I studied the threads in the couch. I computed the fantastic rate at which Mother was removing cigarettes from her pack. I did anything I could to miss what Mother was saying because the main theme of her monologue was: "I just want to show you how easily you can say 'Philadelphia' if you'll concentrate on saying it very slowly and carefully. Come on now, Jeremy, say it with me: Fill-a-dell-fee-a. You can do it. I know you can. Show me you can do it. Say 'Philadelphia' for me, honey."

I tried. God knows I tried. But "Philadelphia" lay like dead weight on my chest, like helium in my head, neither light nor heavy, and yet with definite gravity to it: with downward pull. Sandra says the only way to lose a fear of certain words is to treat them as utterly random and insignificant collocations of sounds; this has the added advantage of echoing a lot of fancy Frog philosophy about how everything, being language, is babble. I tried to visualize "Philadelphia" as "Fill-a-dell-fee-a," but all I could think was Philadelphia was too far away. It was clear across the country, the country was very wide, and I was too small, too weak, too afraid to make the trip. I was in the Palisades and Philadelphia was in Philadelphia. It was too far. It was definitely out of the question. It isn't even the capital of Pennsylvania, I kept telling myself, trying to weaken the enemy, but Philadelphia was Constitution City, Locus of Brotherly Love, Metropolis for men who had large yellow farms and long white wigs. Teeth on lips forever, and all I could come up with was an infinitely extended, infinitely painful *Ffffffff*. That's all. Only that. *Ffffffff*. Nothing more.

"I don't feel like saying that word right now," I said.

"What word?" Mother asked.

"That word."

"What word?"

"You know."

"Give it a try."

"No," I said. "Not now. Maybe later. Not right now."

Mother shook her head in sadness and disgust. She withdrew to the den to call the screenwriter, canceling the interview, and came back carrying six boxes of flash cards. She waited until Father left to pick up Beth, then kicked off her shoes, cozied up next to me on the couch, and told me to lay my head in her lap. I did what she advised. For what seemed like forever, she flipped flash cards in front of my face. I was supposed to say what each picture depicted, which was a sympathetic gesture on her part since it was a game we'd played before and I'd always enjoyed. She assumed it would restore confidence in my ability to communicate, but one by one the tangible things of the world vanished on me. I couldn't say a chair was a chair, or an umbrella was an umbrella, or a zebra was a zebra. As Sandra likes to point out, what you can't identify doesn't exist; no stutterer can say his own name. Mother must have flipped four hundred flash cards, and not one card could I call. I wanted to do what Mother called "caption the picture," but my mouth refused to open. The words weren't there.

Beth and Father returned sooner than I'd expected. When Beth walked in the back door humming the new notes she'd learned, the contrast—Beth the musician, Jeremy the mutation—was so striking I buried my head in Mother's lap and burst into tears. It was a wonderful feeling to produce such loud and continuous sound after I'd been silent for so long. A truly excellent cry redistributes the bones of the body; with the cessation of sobbing, I felt more completely cleaned out than I've ever felt before or since. It's a difficult emotion to explain, but it was as if the most complete emptiness had suddenly passed into purity. I thought the ugly language living in my soul had finally been killed. The future held in store only flashing phrases; perfect sentences; burning, noble words.

Father was so embarrassed by my behavior he changed back into his tennis clothes and left to go bang a white ball against a green backboard. He was never very good at the game but terribly devoted to it, and I can remember hardly a day when he didn't come back from the courts with a tin of balls in one hand, his Jack Kramer in the other, a sweaty smile on his face. Always attentive and eager to help, Beth stopped humming, marched straight into her room, closed the door, and played morose ballads for me on her guitar. She played well, though she always played well. She was a very gifted little girl. The dog had scooted inside when Father opened the back door on his way to Rancho Park; it was all over me now, scratching my neck and licking salt from the tears as they streamed down my face.

"You can go outside and play now," Mother said, sitting on the couch, handing me Kleenex, stroking my arm. "You still have some time to play before dinner, Jeremy. I'm sorry, I didn't mean to upset you. You know that, honey. I'm very sorry. Please don't let anything I said bother you, because you're going to be just fine. Most of the time you speak beautifully. Give me a smile, Jeremy. Don't you want to go outside and play?"

This was something of a first for me, to stay put rather than rush outdoors. When frolicking outside, it's fairly common for most children to experience what might be termed the opposite of the pathetic fallacy: to feel, after a few hours of fun, that the dirt, the grass, the trees, the sun, the sky are simply a part of them, are buried deep inside their bodies. But I'd never felt that way before about a living room. The scratchy couch, the Persian rug, the Good Chair, the unsteady chandelier, all these supposedly inanimate objects suddenly took on a life of their own and started playing house in my heart. For anyone to feel like a living room is a minor disaster, but for a boy-child it's the worst feeling in the world. The late afternoon sun dissolved into the artificial light of the overhead lamp. No, Mother, I didn't want to go outside and play. All I really wanted to do was close the curtains, turn off the lights, put my head on a pillow, and ascend. No such luck. "Come help me take out the garbage," Mother said, "and I'll make whatever you want for dinner."

• • •

MAYBE I'M deluding myself when I say this scene was the inception of the problem, since it's not as if from that time forward the only thing I've been aware of has been my disfluency. That's simply not the case. But, until Mother mentioned it to me, I'd never heard those hesitations that are now habit. Apparently, other people had. It offended them, they felt compelled to tell Mother, and she felt compelled to tell me. Mother didn't create the catch in my voice. She only heard that something was wrong and, like any good reporter, went straight to the source.

Sandra says I must have become aware of the impropriety of my speech earlier than age four but have chosen not to remember it. She says the "traumatic nexus surrounding disfluency is invariably established no later than three and a half." Maybe so. I couldn't say. The tableau in the living room is the earliest trauma I can come up with. Sandra's eyes light up and she gets giddy all over when I tell her, though, how solid middle class we Zorns were, because a disproportionate percentage of sputterers comes from the ambitious bourgeoisie, the rising gentry who, in the considered opinion of our finest historians, prompted the English Revolution. Mother would like to have covered the beheading of Charles I and Father would like to have fought at Philiphaugh, but I don't think either one of them realized how unrevolutionary they were, how upwardly mobile, how extremely middle class. The filthy rich are so rich they hire a private tutor to instruct little Theodore in the elusive art of elocution; the filthy poor are so poor they don't know where little Leroy is, let alone care how he communicates; but the filthy middle class are so middle class they call little Jeremy onto the couch and ask him why he talks so fast.

"Look at the graph," Sandra will say, pointing to some piece of paper on the wall. "Statistics don't lie." I suppose they don't. They show most stammerers coming from families on the move, families that don't have a fireplace but are seeking fame and fortune. The new chairs in the breakfast room, the well-swept patio, the maid on Friday, the stuttering son: these, apparently, are the true totems of the emerging capitalist. The rich will always be rich, the poor will always be poor, but the middle class is always in motion, is always in a state of suspended transformation, is not necessarily tomorrow what it is today. All that social sliding throws some children into a tizzy and their confusion comes out in strangled articulation.

The last thing I would want to do would be to ascribe this fascinating phenomenon to mere class conflict—titubation as the burden of the bourgeoisie—but I do want to acknowledge the cultural context of my disfluency. A voice from the burning bush commanded Moses to lead his people out of Egypt, but Moses was "slow of speech, and of a slow tongue." When the time came to inform the Israelites of God's command, Moses' brother, Aaron, "spake all the words which the Lord had spoken unto Moses." I always imagine Moses standing in the desert, trimming the bush, and pleading: "C-c-come on, Aaron, why d-d-don't *you* tell them?" From Moses on, Jews have worried about words.

"Don't you see?" Father would say. "Jews have always been in exile. We have had to be contemplative in order to survive."

"So they read books and looked for loopholes in the law," I'd say.

"Don't be silly. Kafka, Proust, Freud, Marx, Einstein: all Jews in one way or another. You should be proud they are a part of you."

"I am," I would say. "I really am."

But I'm not. I really am not. I'm tired of hearing that you can flee so many times before you start looking for more long-lasting shelter, that if you have been trampled by life you can triumph in language, that the only recourse to everything is to read and write yourself into existence. It's no longer romantic to me, this Hebraic hunger for words. I hear the ceaseless clickety-clack of Mother's typewriter at the beach; I see a photograph of Father hiking in the High Sierras with a biography of Alger Hiss sticking out of his hip pocket; I imagine Beth masturbating to the pictures in the middle of *Modern Drama Review*. I see, I hear, I imagine these things, and I'm depressed beyond despair.

3

SHORTLY AFTER Mother's death I happened upon her desultory journal, and perhaps the two most passionately wrought entries concerned her father, whom we called Puppa. The first one was about how he, unlike the rest of us poor fallen fools, had "style."

> Cleaning day—weekly battle with dust balls, cobwebs, grime. A day to be domestic. Wife and mother. Pick up laundry, gas car, replace bald tire, mail letter, deli for dinner, meet train. Maybe if I resist phone calls and errands of mercy, I can get it all done and not be crabby, put upon. Report on tire at dinner reminds me of car Puppa bought: four new first-line tires, filled up with gas, car wash. "Now it's yours." He had style. Bathed in the memory—soothing and delicious.

I've seen a photograph of this automobile at the moment of its debut, with its doors swung wide open like wings. It appears boxlike and beautiful. Still, was it our fault Mother couldn't maintain a stiff upper lip when it came to housework? Why, when she lost Puppa's gold watch to an alligator at the Steinhart Aquarium in Golden Gate Park, did she have to behave as if time's winged automobile had come to a screeching halt forever? Thanksgiving was her favorite holiday because it was Puppa's favorite holiday. The highest compliment she ever paid me was that my values reminded her of Puppa's values, whatever they were supposed to be.

He once owned a junk shop on Pico Boulevard. Mother liked to insist he had been a very great man and a model of moral integrity because he never sold anything that, with a little tinkering, wouldn't work reasonably well, and when the business was sinking he didn't hesitate to sell the shop to a colored man at a time when it was very unfashionable indeed to do business with a colored man. The only thing she kept in her safety box at the Bank of America, downtown branch, was a ring put together out of Puppa's tie pins. You would have thought it was sapphire plucked out of the sky by Adlai Stevenson in an excitation of wit.

In Puppa's presence, of course, I could hardly speak. For my failures of communication he had two principal cures: a cup of coffee with six spoonfuls of sugar because my body was deficient, he thought, in dextrose, and a tumbler of bourbon before dinner because I would stop "yammering," as he called it, once I acknowledged I was a man and not a little boy. To the coffee I thrilled, but to the bourbon I had headaches. I wasn't a man; I was a little boy. In the few years I knew Puppa he impressed me as having very unusual habits: when he shook hands he would extend an egregiously strong and prolonged grip, and when he walked down the street he'd stop and stoop over to examine a clod of dirt in a crack in the sidewalk, a discarded math assignment, a forty-five-dollar grocery bill, a trail of red ants, a very used postage stamp. When I heard that he'd died I ran downstairs to my basement bedroom and tried to cry, but all I thought, as Mother comforted me and told me Puppa had loved me most of all, was that I no longer had to shake his hand for half an hour, I no longer had to bend down with him and study candy wrappers, I no longer had to burn my tongue on his bourbon.

Mother's second journal entry went:

Late afternoon, walking Bruin through the eucalyptus trees. Thought maybe we would see Jeremy coming home. Would he stop and wait or pretend not to see us? Feeling of rejection crept over me—knew he would not want to walk home with us. Thought shifted to Puppa. I always ran to greet him, no matter where: baggy, dirty pants; sweat-stained shirt; battered old hat, but I wasn't ashamed of him, was I?

No, you weren't, Annette, and this qualifies you as an angel of light. I love the notion of "we"—Mother and the dog existing as the most closely knit couple in our family—and my banishment to hell based on feelings ascribed to me by her. It's unfair to overscrutinize someone's left-open logbook, but fairness was a doctrine that moved Mother only when she was ensconced in her office at the ACLU. And there it moved her to tears. At home she was always unfavorably comparing my father to her father. It ruined her relations with her husband, it ruined her relations with me, and I'm not so sure it did her any great favors in the workplace either.

When Puppa was still alive we used to have to visit him every Sunday and after brunch he'd always bring out a purple bowl with gold veneer, hold it aloft, hold it there for a moment, tilt it forward, spilling just a few coins at first, then turn it upside down until all the change clanged as it fell to the floor: rare old pennies, dimes with dirt in their rims, buffalo nickels, quarters smooth as table tops. I would take my mountain of money and buy cameras, watches, tape recorders, and he'd say: "Gadgets! You're buying gadgets, Jeremy. You should buy something you can use, such as a wrench." Hair had a way of blooming out his ears.

One afternoon, after Puppa had poured his purple bowl of accumulated change over my hands, I brought a white bank bag of the money to my friend, Charles, since he was two years older and could help enumerate nickels. Charles's parents owned and edited a pottery magazine at a time when pottery was nowhere near the apex of popularity it attained later on and pottery magazines were even less popular than they are now. Kitty-corner to a condemned church and up six flights of shaky stairs was the Ellenboegens' pottery magazine office. Cover the typewriter, clear the desk, put away the proof sheets, and you were in the Ellenboegens' living room; lift a curtain and you were in the kitchen. I used to dread visiting Charles because there were always earthenware vases lined up on the floor and ceramic necklaces hanging from the doorknobs. Invariably I'd trip over a vase or brush against a necklace. Mrs. Ellenboegen finally decided it was in her best interests to take a minute and escort me through the work space, past the kitchen, and into Charles's bedroom in back. She knocked on Charles's door and told him I was here.

Charles had plump stumps for limbs and wore black high-top Keds, striped shirts, tight tan shorts, and a Dodgers cap. When I entered, he was filling his room with smoke—he was seven years old and smoking half a pack of Salems a day—because there was so little else in it, only his unmade bed, a dusty bureau, and an immense bookcase filled shelf after shelf with past issues of *Fire Wheel*.

"How much this time?" he asked.

"I don't know," I said. "Thirty. Maybe forty."

"Forty?"

"Maybe forty," I said, holding the white bag of money above my head in obvious and poor imitation of Puppa, balancing the purple bowl aloft. I didn't have Puppa's patience. Instead of spilling the coins slowly, I tugged open the drawstring, spun around the room, and spangled the floor with silver. Charles could never show any enthusiasm for my money. He always had to finish his cigarette first, then rise slowly from his bed and say, "Well, I guess we had better gather up the coins and get them counted." He loved counting the change, then writing on the front of the bag how much it all came to. He loved telling me how much I was worth.

Charles took a broom from the closet and swept the coins into a spectacular pile in the middle of the room, where we sat down and started counting or, actually, he counted aloud and I listened because I couldn't keep up with him and made mistakes. He thought it would make more sense—just this once, since the booty was so big—if he handled the arithmetic. "Two thousand ducats," Charles said. No, of course Charles didn't say that, but he should have, sitting cross-legged on the floor, happy atop the pile of petty cash. He'd just separated the coins into homogeneous groups and counted a few dollars when his mother knocked on the door, entered the room upon receiving no response, and said, "Charles, dear, your father and I are correcting galleys in the living room. Will you and your friend be so kind as to keep it down?" Mrs. Ellenboegen always talked like that. She was very formal and dignified, even though she was only managing editor of *Fire Wheel*.

"Okay, Mom," he said. "We'll keep it down." As a parody of

cooperation, he started whispering each number while counting the pennies. I laughed at first, because that's what Charles wanted me to do, but also because there was something very funny about the sudden transition from loud broadcast to low hush. After just a few minutes, though, I was in rapture over that whisper. I lost all comprehension of sense—Charles could have been counting backwards from a thousand, for all I knew or cared—and listened only to sound: the incessant scrape of copper sliding across wood and clinking in his hands; the unnecessary and thus incantatory repetition of "Three dollars and sixty-three cents, three dollars and sixty-four cents, three dollars and sixty-five cents, three dollars and sixty-six cents, three dollars and sixty-seven cents"; but most especially the beginning of my best friend's baritone: the still small voice of a seven-year-old boy, the faint tone in which secrets are told.

It's difficult to describe a whisper. Sandra says it's "sibilant speech with little or no vibration of the vocal cords." I love the scientific way she has with words, but she doesn't do much to explain why a shiver shot across my back when Charles started whispering, or why I still get the chills whenever I hear a man lower his voice. It's the closest I come to inversion, this worship I have of soft masculine sounds, and it's probably why I spend so much time in Powell Library: in the fourth-floor stacks, the only acceptable mode of discourse is the dead hush. For other people it's the cadenza of a concerto, the longest line in a letter, the love scene from a sentimental movie, the final stanza of a perfect poem. It's not as if I'm incapable of responding to such stimuli, but for me the only sure-fire trigger of electric needles down the spine is a man's whisper.

Charles kept asking me to go into the kitchen and bring back a glass of water for his throat, which was parched from smoking so many cigarettes. I did what he said, but I knew what was going on. Every time I left the room and returned, the stack of quarters seemed slightly smaller until, at the end of the day, I could practically count the quarters at sight. I didn't care, though. That's the thing. I honestly didn't care. Charles could have deposited all the quarters and the silver dollars, too, in a long-term savings account, and I still would have brought him a tall glass of ice water—I would have brought him a bottle of *Château Margaux* '52, if that had been what he wanted—just to keep him talking in that soft voice that was tickling my ears and making my body tingle all over.

He finished counting the change, tying the drawstring, and writing on the bag how much it all came to, so I took my loot and said goodbye to my friend, who asked me to bring him one more glass of water, and to his parents, who didn't have time to glance up from their galleys. I walked through Los Angeles in the dark. Halfway home I caught my foot in a grate and spilled $47.21 down the sewer. I listened to a storm of money on a pool of mud. The sewer was a wishing well. I'd lost so much money I was entitled to at least one wish. I wished Charles would whisper to me forever.

4

A COUPLE of years ago I got talked into attending the premiere of a movie in which the lost daughter, leaving St. Louis for Hollywood to make her debut in dirty pictures, was named Flora del Presto. This kind of overt nominal symbolism we now find offensive since it fell out of fashion shortly after the publication of *The Faerie Queene*. But the first girl I ever knew and loved was named Faith. I didn't make that up. That was just her name.

Faith and I were preschool painters. Our parents drove us to studio openings, gallery shows, museum exhibits; bought us oversized, overpriced art books and triple overstock in paint supplies: chemically treated rice paper for work in watercolor, palettes round and rectangular, tubes of tempera, tiny brushes for oil touch-ups, high wooden easels, charcoal pencils, pure white smocks, sketch pads.

We took these sketch pads everywhere we went, painted what we saw, and immediately exchanged pages so we knew what we'd seen. We mailed purple finger paintings to each other. After school, at her house, we'd eat cookies her mother made for us and do still lifes of the bowl of fruit on the dining room table, the bottles of liquor in the den cabinet. She was much better than I was; it would have been impossible to be much worse. When she won a newspaper contest by drawing a likeness of Abraham Lincoln better than any six-year-old in Los Angeles County, she used part of the prize money to buy me a paint-by-numbers set, which I nevertheless accepted with appreciation because it came straight from her heart.

Father had been offered a job as public relations director for the Jewish Welfare Fund of San Francisco, and Mother had convinced *The Nation* she'd be able to carry out her duties as West Coast correspondent just as well, perhaps even better, in Northern California, so we were moving to the Bay Area. Faith knew I was leaving—she kept painting pictures of cable cars on the Golden Gate Bridge to help herself imagine what my new neighborhood would be like—but I had put off telling her goodbye until the actual day of departure. Father parked across the street from her house and told me to run in and out real quick with my rolled-up painting because he wanted to be well on the way north before the five o'clock rush.

Faith's mother told me she was at work in her studio and wasn't to be disturbed, but I banged on the garage door and told her who had come to visit. Her hands and lower arms were covered with various colors, her hair was pulled back, and she was wearing jeans and a white smock, so she didn't look her best, but I could have watched her forever as she glided around the garage, mixing paints. She'd thrown a sheet over the front of the easel. Brandishing my painting like a baton, intimating a trade, I asked if I could take a peek.

"No," she said.

"What are you working on?" I asked.

"Nothing. Just a little landscape."

I took a deep breath, concentrated on the cobwebs in the corner, and said, "I came to say goodbye."

"You're really going?"

"Yes," I said.

"Really, really going, forever and ever?"

"Yes."

She threw up her hands, splattering paint on my traveling pants, and said, "Well, goodbye."

I couldn't take much more of this without volunteering to be her life-long apprentice. I said goodbye and turned to go, but she wrapped her purple-green arms around my neck, kissed my cheek, and said, "I love you, Jeremy."

"I'll miss you so much."

"I really, truly love you with all my soul," she said.

"My Dad's waiting. I better go."

She took her arms off me and stepped back, straightened her smock. Then she said, "I've already told you I love you, Jeremy. Can't you say, 'I love you, Faith'?"

"I love you," I said.

" 'I love you, *Faith,*' " she insisted.

This little scene in the garage occurred only a few months after my futile attempt to say *Philadelphia* in the living room. Stutterers have a tendency to generalize their fear of one word that begins with a particular sound to a fear of all words that begin with the same sound. In the space of the summer I'd effectively eliminated every *F* from my vocabulary, with the exception of the preposition, "for," which for the time being was too small to incite terror. A few weeks later, my fear of *F* ended when another letter—I think it was *L*—suddenly loomed large. But at that moment, early October 1962, in Faith's garage, I was terrified of *F*s. I simply wasn't saying them. I hadn't called Faith by her first name for nearly a month and had, instead, taken to calling her Carlisle, as if her patronymic had become a term of jocular endearment.

"I can't," I said. "I can't say that."

And by way of explanation I took the rubber band off my painting and unfurled a Crayola crayon effort of a cowboy on a horse that looked more like a dog. This was figure. Ground was short green grass, pool-blue sky, burgundy mountains. Between the cowboy on his dog-horse and the short green grass, pool-blue sky, and burgundy mountains was a barbed wire fence because between me and life that can be touched there has always been a fence.

Talented as she was, Faith wasn't exactly Walter Pater when it came to other people's paintings. She didn't understand. She took my inability to say her name as an admission of insincerity. Maybe she thought I had some hot new watercolorist stashed away in Encino. She didn't even give me time to explain. She lifted the sheet over the easel, revealing a beautiful if unfinished self-portrait—it promised to be her best work yet—that she crumpled into a ball and shoved into my hands before running into the house with tears streaming down her face. I meant to run after her and explain everything, but I saw her mother lock the back door. Then I heard Father start honking the car. Like a dead man down a plank, I walked the driveway to our car, vowing to write Faith a full confession once we left Los Angeles.

The letter, of course, never got written. An hour out of L.A. I fell asleep and started dreaming about the girls up north. Frustrated artists, young lovers are like that: they have traitorous imaginations. We took the coastal route, the slower, prettier way, since Beth and I wanted to watch the waves and neither Mother nor Father was in any particular hurry to arrive in Northern California. They weren't sure they were doing the right thing, leaving behind good friends to take interesting jobs, and their uncertainty took the form of a sustained elegy to Los Angeles. Suddenly the Hollywood Bowl was "a lovely place to listen to piano," the *Los Angeles Times* was a "daily addiction," and Frank Tang's, where Father had once launched an entire dish of sweet and sour spare ribs into Mother's lap, was "the only Chinese restaurant anywhere that left you feeling full."

Their combined nostalgia grew so great, in fact, that halfway up the coast Father pulled the Rambler—a 1958 Rambler, one of the worst cars ever made—into a motel, where Beth and I swam in the heated pool and my parents tried to talk themselves out of heading back. Many years later Father, edging into another depression, wrote the Ellenboegens: "While I can't rewind the clock and there's little to be gained except anguish and soul-twisting remorse, I wish to Christ we'd never come up here in October of '62. Saddest move I ever made. Most regrettable. It's not in the stars but in us, said the man. There it is. I said how I feel and now we go from here.

Upward, I hope. Onward. We must." Why the Ellenboegens found it necessary to take time out from *Fire Wheel* to show me this letter when I moved back to L.A. I've never quite comprehended, but in October 1962 a house had already been bought, the furniture had already been moved: we would continue north. Out of such slight considerations, lives are made.

At noon the next day we stopped thirty miles south of San Francisco to eat lunch at San Gregorio Beach, which is now a nudist colony but then was only a long stretch of gray shore. Although the beach was packed with people, no one surfed or swam. No one constructed even a sand castle. For as far as I could see in either direction, they were huddled together on towels and blankets, listening to the third and final game of the National League playoff between the Los Angeles Dodgers and San Francisco Giants. The tinny reecho of a thousand transistor radios held in the hands of Giant fans: this was strange enough. Something else was wrong. The sky was ugly, the food was bad, the sea was green. Then I realized what was the matter. They were all tuned to the wrong station. They weren't listening to Vin Scully.

Vin Scully knows baseball about as well as it is possible or desirable to know any game. He is always fair, even complimentary, to the opposing team. And he has a voice that must have been a gift from the gods. I used to lie in bed with the radio beneath the pillow and earplugs on and listen to him talk until midnight. It was the clearest, most uncluttered sound I've ever heard, that man's voice, and it would enter my ears, absolve my body of all its burdens, massaging my troubled mind.

Russ Hodges, on the other hand, was shamelessly partisan in his approach and talked as if he were short, fat, and smoked smelly cigars, all of which he was or did. His one contribution to baseball was the absurd ejaculation, "Bye-Bye, Baby!" whenever the Giants hit a home run. In postgame interviews he'd always say, "Well, Willie, how did it feel to drop that pop fly with two out and the bases loaded in the twelfth inning?" Willie would always say, "That's right, Lon."

I asked Father to turn our radio to the right station, but he said,

"We're in San Francisco now. We can only get San Francisco stations."

I ran into the water and started swimming back to Malibu, back to Faith if she'd have me, but Father jumped in and pulled me out. A great roar went up from the crowd. I thought they were cheering Father's heroism. They weren't. The Giants, trailing 4–2 at the end of eight innings, had scored four runs in the top of the ninth to win.

5

I'VE ALWAYS been outside the general language. I've always insisted upon the one station that won't come in. The next day, I entered the first grade at a private grammar school that didn't look kindly upon a little boy who dared to enroll a month late, but Mother pulled some strings here and some arms there, then everything was fine. All the other children admired me because I received an uncorrupted box of crayons. I fell in love with a tiny Chinese girl who made me seem brash by comparison. But the real triumph and consequent tragedy came when Miss Kilner requested that we stop running around the room, sit down at our desks, and produce a short composition concerning the importance of Columbus Day.

This assignment was way over the heads of most first-graders. Some of them were still struggling with the alphabet. The class vetoed the task and went back to running around the room, but Beth had recently started collaborating with me on some shorter pieces, so I put pencil to big, blue-lined paper and started writing. Beth and I tended to write about not so much the importance of Columbus Day as the imminence of annihilation. I discarded "The Indians Were Here First" and pursued "The Death of Bozo the Clown."

Miss Kilner circled behind my desk, read "The Death of Bozo

the Clown" over my shoulder and, when she realized that until the penultimate line my little narrative wasn't in the least about Columbus Day, she was thrilled. I was glad she liked it, but then she had to call the class to order while her arms were wrapped around my neck, had to hold the essay over her head so everyone could see what the new boy wrote, had to read aloud the entire story, which all the children in the class laughed at because it was about a clown. If it was about a clown, they figured it must be funny. Miss Kilner told Mother, "Hubert Humphrey's appearance in a fictional work is an index of the lovely commingling of fact and fantasy in your child's rich imagination," and she told me it was "very, very good: ten gold stars next to your name, Jeremy." Miss Kilner was no slouch. She was teaching first grade for only a year, to help finance her fiancé through law school, then she herself was off to graduate studies in German at Stanford.

She demanded "The Death of Bozo the Clown" get the kind of audience she felt it deserved. For Open House, she framed it in red crêpe paper and tacked it up in the middle of the bulletin board, after taking everything else off. The children as well as the parents came to Open House. At the end of the evening I was standing next to my desk, watching Father eat the last few glazed doughnuts and Mother fend off a couple who'd come over to tell me they were really rather fond of Senator Humphrey. Miss Kilner clapped her hands and said, "May I have your attention for just a minute? Before you leave, please be sure to read the student composition on the bulletin board. I think it's outstanding. Thank you, parents and pupils, for coming. It's been a delightful evening."

It would have been a delightful evening and everyone would have trotted off happily into the night if a woman with a shiny white dress and red hair piled high—she was probably an enemy of Mother's who knew I couldn't talk and was getting revenge by humiliating me in public—hadn't said, "Very few of us have had a chance to read your paper, Jerry. Why don't you read it to us?"

My desk was way over by the windows. I contemplated standing on top of the desk and leaping to an early death, but there was a pack of people surrounding me, all of them sipping punch, nibbling glazed doughnuts, dabbing their mouths with party napkins, so I shrank behind Mother and pretended not to have heard the request.

The woman came over to me and said, "Why don't you read it to us?"

"No," I said. "I'm sure everyone has already read it."

The adults in the room shook their heads in unison and said, "No, we haven't."

"We'd like to hear it," the woman said, smiling and tugging on my sweater.

"It's right here on the bulletin board," I said, plucking down the controversial text and handing it to someone who looked like Bozo's right-hand man. "Why doesn't everyone just read it for themselves?"

Miss Kilner said, "Why don't you go ahead and read it to us, Jeremy?" and Mother said, "Yes, Jeremy. Go ahead. Don't be afraid." I took a gulp of Father's punch, ate half his glazed dough-nut, then walked to the front of the room and, before all my class-mates and their well-dressed parents, started to read "The Death of Bozo the Clown":

> B-B-Bozo was a clown. He walked around in b-b-baggy pants and b-b-big shoes and had yellow hair and a red nose and made people happy. Everyone loved him. The audience loved him. The b-b-balloon man loved him. The elephant loved him. The fat lady loved him, though not as much as Mrs. B-B-Bozo the Clown loved him b-b-because she loved him more than anyone else loved him and didn't even care if he came into the house with his b-b-baggy pants and b-b-big shoes still on.

Some of the parents thought I was giving an intentionally comic recitation and they tittered politely, but everyone else realized the rather sad paradox: the little boy couldn't read his own writing. What I found frustrating was that suddenly Bs were bothering me, and the story was studded with them, while Fs were for the moment as free and easy as vowels had always been. Of course. There was a grand total of two Fs in the entire fable. It was almost as if I craved the jolt of stuttering and went around every few months looking for new phonetics to encapsulate my pain. Miss Kilner had never heard me stutter before, but she seemed to have read enough monographs on the relationship between the wound and the bow to know she should act sanguine, while Mother gave me a look she'd lifted from watching Johnny Wooden too reverently at UCLA games: winners never quit, etc.

One day the elephant, not meaning to b-b-but not watching where he was going, either, hit B-B-Bozo the Clown in the head with his trunk and B-B-Bozo the Clown had a headache and got very sick and then he got sicker and then he died. Everyone was sad. The b-b-balloon man was sad. The elephant, who had hit him and was sorry, was sad. The fat lady was sad, though not as sad as Mrs. B-B-Bozo the Clown, who was so sad she asked Hubert Humphrey to change October twelfth from Columbus Day to National B-B-Bozo the Clown Day. Hubert Humphrey said no.

At the end the parents broke into a misguided if very emotional ovation. I didn't know what else to do, so I just sat down at my desk and ran my finger up and back the pencil trough.

Mother smooched me and said, "I'm proud of you for hanging in there."

"Another glazed doughnut, Jeremy?" Father asked.

My classmates were kind enough to file out the door and leave me alone with my eloquence.

CURRIER had an extremely effective public address system. Anyone could address anyone else in the entire school, but no one could address anyone else without everyone in the entire school listening in. There was no privacy, no discrimination to the public address system at Currier; I came to feel this lack every Friday afternoon, when the speech therapist called the same two boys into her office. We were both, as it happened, in the same class and we thought they'd put us together to keep the evil contained. She could have sent a note or tapped us on the shoulder at recess but, no, she had to let the whole school in on our problem. Bobby Rose and I would have to leave Miss Kilner's room with our heads down and mouths closed, pretending we didn't know why we were being requested to report once again to the Audio-Visual Center.

I didn't much care for Bobby Rose. I have always had too many anxieties of my own to have much patience with other people's problems. He had a dreadful lisp, and I could hardly stand the spastic way he spoke: the malformation of his mouth every time he said *S.* But I envied Bobby Rose because he seemed to have reconciled himself to the fact that he would never be rid of his disorder—he said a certain sound differently than everyone else and this seemed to him no great cause for alarm—whereas I was always searching for a solution. I would have good days on which I was able to do anything I wanted (read aloud, tell jokes, say my name) and there would be some real room for hope, then just as suddenly that hope would leave and not return for a month. My impediment was more unpredictable than his—more directly connected, I liked to think, to the riot of human emotions, so I struggled more with it.

The speech therapist at Currier Private Elementary School did very little to alleviate that struggle. She was a Romanian born in a tugboat on the Black Sea, and I think it ruined her for life. She had married an American—her name was Mrs. Fletcher—but she had only a rudimentary grasp of the English language. Bobby Rose and I spent as much time as we could correcting her grammar. She would tire of that and set us to absurd exercises. Whatever she had one of us doing she had the other one do as well, as if we were suffering from the same malady. Every week she came up with a new cure: talking while crawling around the room; while swinging our arms back and forth; while striking the table, lightly but rhythmically, with our knuckles; while nodding our heads vigorously up and down like marionettes; while pinching our forefingers and thumbs together; while producing a low drone in the bottom of our throats; while staring at a metronome; while listening to loud music in earphones; but the time I shall always remember and the time, I assume, Mrs. Fletcher shall always remember—for she was fired when the administration found out about it—was when she took her sewing box out of the closet.

I thought she was going to stitch my lips shut, which, I had read in a little manual for the inarticulate, Hippocrates suggested be done with hesitant speakers. This would have been a welcome if somewhat extreme relief for me, but all she wanted us to do was say the pledge of allegiance with a button on the tips of our tongues. There was nothing in the Audio-Visual Center, only three or four plastic chairs, a Formica table, Mrs. Fletcher's desk, and some taping equipment, but it did have a flag. Every room at Currier had a flag. It was a very patriotic school. After switching on the tape recorder, she gave us each a button. Bobby Rose and I placed them on our tongues and started saying the pledge of allegiance.

"Boys, please flag look at," Mrs. Fletcher said.

Although she was Romanian, Mrs. Fletcher was as patriotic as the next person at Currier, and we took her to mean we should be looking at the flag while we were saying the pledge of allegiance and balancing a button on the tips of our tongues. Which was all to the well and good, since Bobby Rose and I were as patriotic as Mrs. Fletcher. But the flagstaff in the Audio-Visual Center was way up high on the wall, and it was extremely difficult to look at the flag without swallowing the button. I coughed a couple of times, quickly decided I had had enough of this, and slipped the button into my pocket.

"I s-s-swallowed the button," I said.

Bobby Rose wasn't stupid. He coughed a couple of times and said, "I thwallowed the button, too."

"We're going to the nurse," I said.

"Yeth," Bobby Rose said, coughing up a storm. "We're going to the nurth."

"No, didn't you, couldn't you have," Mrs. Fletcher said. "Boys, come here back."

We were already out the room and sprinting down the corridor before she'd arisen from her seat. Bobby Rose and I were the only two people on the playground. We rode the merry-go-round and swung on the rings for a while before I asked him what he'd done with his button.

"I thwallowed it," he said.

"No, really."

"I thwallowed it," he said. "Didn't you?"

I shook my head and showed him the button. Then Bobby Rose started having trouble breathing. I rushed him to the nurse, who took him to the emergency room. They pumped his stomach and came up with a button, a staple, a postage stamp, and two buffalo nickels. I don't know whether the items in the bottom of his stomach had somehow been doing the damage, but he stopped lisping. From then on, he liked to come up to me while I was playing four-square, tap me on the shoulder, and say, "You should have swallowed the button."

I DON'T KNOW, maybe I should have. I just could never bring myself to swallow a button on purpose. Besides, by that time I was already engaged in what, very much later, Sandra was to call a "principal compensatory activity." I was only six but demonstrating the ability to pitch a softball faster than anyone at Currier could swing at it. Legend has it that when Father was in his mid-twenties he was offered a tryout with the Brooklyn Dodgers and someone named Van Lingle Mungo hit every pitch Father threw—into the left-field bleachers. Legend, I say, can keep it. But Father did have a strong right arm. I inherited my pitching strength from him.

Most softball pitchers swing their arm all the way back and around, windmill fashion, but I found this unnecessary. I simply threw the ball forward as fast as I could with a quick flick of the wrist. Most softball pitchers also have what they like to call a vast assortment of pitches—slider, dropball, palmball, spitball, knuckleball, curve, changeup—but I had only one pitch, a fastball, and no one could hit it. Girls would gather to watch me warm up against the wooden backstop. I always had trouble finding someone to agree to be my catcher, and whoever consented would demand that I provide foam pads for him to wear inside his glove. My team, the self-appointed First-Grade All-Stars, never lost. Not to the Second-Grade All-Stars, not to the Third-Grade All-Stars, not to the Fourth-Grade All-Stars. The Fifth-Grade All-Stars challenged us to a game at lunch time and the whole school shut down.

Currier must have been the only grammar school in San Francisco that had a grass field for a baseball diamond. A chain fence divided the playground between macadam and grass; that fence was right field. Left field was a stone wall that kept the upper playground separate from the lower playground—the children safe from the older boys—and here we were, the First-Grade All-Stars, parading about the lower playground, stomping on the grass as if we owned it. A high brick tower, with a library on the second floor and hour bells on the third, was to dead center field. On the day of the game, people sat on every window sill in the tower, stood on every step of the fire escape. There were people all along both foul lines, shoulder to shoulder behind the chain fence in right field, perched on top of the jungle gym on the other side of the left field wall.

I've never pitched so well or so hard as I pitched that game. We won, 2–0, when, with one out and one on in the sixth inning, I hit an off-speed pitch into the tower. The Fifth-Grade All-Stars were terribly poor sports about the whole thing. When the tower bell rang, signaling the end of lunch time and the conclusion of the game, they besieged me with bats in their hands. They went straight to the only weakness they knew I had. They pounded their bats on the grass and said, "Say 'Cincinnati,' say 'Chanukah,' say 'Golden Gate Park,' " but what they didn't realize, and what I hadn't realized until then, was that I often had no trouble saying a word if someone else had already said it, so I said *Cincinnati*, I said *Chanukah*, I said *Golden Gate Park*. They went away and let my teammates carry me on their shoulders back to class.

6

I HAD GOTTEN it into my head that, because my interlocutor never knew what I was going to say and once I said it he never understood exactly what I meant, it was incumbent upon me to underscore the impossibility of human communication by stuttering. I actually believed that. I thought it was my duty to insert into every conversation the image of its own absurdity. Worse than that, I came to think all fluent speech was "fascistic" (a word I had learned from Mother); was an assertion of authority in the one enterprise in which any assertion of authority struck me as ludicrous. Whatever I did, wherever I went, whatever I said, I assumed it had already been judged to be unwanted and unneeded. My apology was to tremble.

This way of thinking may have been nothing more than good old-fashioned Old Testament guilt, but I seemed to be suffering so, I seemed to be creating such a nasty cycle for myself: I felt sinful, so I stammered; I stammered, so I felt sinful. Kennedy was assassinated toward the end of the next year and, whereas most people can tell you that when the news came they were stepping out of the bathtub or buttering toast or watching "Hollywood Squares," I remember not where I was but what I thought: since Mother and Father had voted for Kennedy, and Mother, in fact, had been countywide media coordinator for the campaign, I, too, in the sense that whatever one's parents do one implicitly agrees with, had voted for him, so, no more but certainly no less than anyone else, I was responsible for electing him president. I had killed Kennedy. While Mother drove around the city getting interviews for her award-winning article, "A Shocked San Francisco: Too Numb to Respond," and Father and Beth sat in front of the television eating dinner, I scoured every room in the house for the best place to hide when the Dallas police came to get me.

Very shortly after the United States Treasury started producing Kennedy half-dollars, a girl brought to class a glass case of Kennedy halves, commemorative coins, and elegiac medallions. The glass case, of course, was shattered. All the money and memorabilia were stolen. Mrs. McCloskey asked us to put our heads down and shut our eyes. Whoever wished to speak with her concerning the burglary was to raise his hand and see her after school. I raised my hand, sat in a stall in the boys' bathroom until three-thirty, then walked up to Mrs. McCloskey's desk and said, "I just wanted to tell you I d-d-didn't do it."

Mrs. McCloskey was taken aback by this confession of innocence and said, "I'm sure you didn't, Jeremy. But then why did you raise your hand?"

"I just wanted y-y-you to know I didn't do it."

"But why would you think I thought you did?"

"I don't know," I said.

I didn't know. I still don't. Mrs. McCloskey got tired of posing Zen koans and dismissed me to the playground where, atop the stone wall that was left field, I attempted to explain to myself that I was not the perpetrator of every foul deed in the land, gave up after a while, and went home. I think this whole dreadful circle of pain and purgation would still be inexplicable if a month later, while dusting the mantelpiece, I hadn't broken Mother's sculpture. Without this event, I'd now be at a complete loss.

MOTHER WAS BORN in Steubenville, Ohio, a town whose only fame rests on the fact that it was a punchline to a joke in an episode of "Get Smart," a television show I used to watch as a child and from which I would derive exquisite pleasure because whenever the Wise Chief and Foolish Spy had something secret to discuss they'd go into a glass bubble. They'd never be able to understand each other before the bubble would rise. Steubenville sits on the shore of the Ohio River, and I suppose adorable little Annette swung over the rim of the river on a tire tied to a rope tied to a tree and ran barefoot in the woods in summer and skipped stones across the creek at night, but it would be preposterous to assert that Mother was ever anything resembling a river rat. I see her instead writing only one word—"Uneventful"—in her diary at the end of each day and reading mysteries under the covers with a flashlight until morning. I see her doing these things because Mother was never the storyteller Father was; she never liked to talk about her distant past.

Girlhood strikes me as one of life's more unfathomable mysteries, and I haven't the faintest idea what Mother did when her family moved to Los Angeles in 1940. She wasn't sitting in a malt shop wearing a tight pink sweater, waiting to make it big with Paramount, because she always had tiny breasts like wings. And she wasn't falling in love with the star linebacker because, until her too-late twenties, until she met and married Father, she had a terrible time with pimples. I suppose she was busy hating her father, whom she thought she loved, and envying her brother, whom she thought she admired.

Uncle Gilbert is now chief science counselor to the American ambassador to Japan, and when he was working for the Atomic Energy Commission he discovered something about the nature of entropy that won a Nobel Prize in physics for the chairman of the AEC, but when he was just a kid in L.A. he was content to wander around the junk shop, fixing whatever his father thought was irreparable. Gilbert transformed a dark corner of the garage into a lab, where he had an impressively low number of nuclear near-explosions, and every science class he took at Dorsey High he ended up teaching until, in his senior year, Puppa decided that Berty deserved to study at the very best college in the country, within a reasonable distance. On a full fellowship in physics, he went to the California Institute of Technology.

Annette did not go the California Institute of Technology. She went to UCLA. Any girl, if she is able to secure a parking space, can attend UCLA. And Annette wasn't even plagued by this problem, since she was living at home and hitchhiking to school, something which very few other "Uclan co-eds" were doing. Something which even fewer of them were doing but which Annette was doing, with deep, unapproved pleasure, was smoking two packs of Kents a day through a filter, if indeed Kents were in circulation in

1942 and, if not, two packs a day of another equally strong brand through a filter. Something which no one, absolutely no one else in all of Westwood except Annette, was doing was being the managing editor of the *Daily Bruin*. She did very little all day other than call up the police station and correct proof sheets, then hitchhike home in the dark.

Whenever she had a couple of hours to kill, she'd walk across campus to her studio in the basement of the Art Department, where a certain professor of Post-Impressionism would invariably stop by to speak very favorably of the work she was producing in clay. Nearly all professors of Post-Impressionism are sexual in the extreme; this nice man probably just wanted Mother to put down her piece of clay and kiss him unconscious. Mother avoided such implications, if she was even aware of them, and concentrated, instead, on her statue, which she took very seriously. Spending a couple of hours when the spirit moves you does very little to enhance the quality of a work of art. Upon graduation, Mother had created only one small sculpture, and even it wasn't quite finished. The left foot had only four toes.

Mother was proud of that piece of clay, despite its flaws. I think it was the only thing she ever made with her hands and she wanted other people to see it. When she married Father, she thought it should appear over the fireplace. Father agreed, though he thought it more properly displayed in the attic. When we moved north, she paid the Bekins moving man twenty dollars to wrap it carefully and hold it in his lap while he drove. Mother was disappointed, however, in how he handled a few plates and felt she had to file a protest with his employer: "Despite my repeated requests for the use of extreme care in handling and packing our fine set of imported china, these dishes were stacked together and wrapped only in coarse paper, unprotected by any kind of separating cushion. I was shocked to find this gross negligence, especially when such items as a plastic measuring cup were packed with more care than that accorded Limoges china." She could certainly take the high road.

She placed the sculpture in the middle of the mantel, the first thing guests saw upon entering. I've avoided describing the figure because it's so difficult to describe without making it sound grotesque. It was sort of a tragic self-portrait in red clay: an adobe woman with eyes of lead and hair of rock, her head bent sadly and impossibly between her legs. Her left foot was still missing a toe, her *mons Veneris* was curiously box-shaped, her breasts had the appearance and texture of acorns. I don't know whether this was the artist's intended effect, or whether it's in extremely bad taste to comment upon the private parts of your mother's sculpture, but I was touching those acorn breasts, thrilling to their strange roughness, when Adobe Woman fell from the shelf.

It was Sunday afternoon. Father, Beth, and I were trying to clean house before Mother returned from a weekend of interviewing state senators in Sacramento. Father was vacuuming the hall rug, Beth was mopping the kitchen floor, I was dusting the den furniture. We were all listening to Vivaldi's *Four Seasons* turned up loud and playing over and over again on the hi-fi. We were all hard at work and happy and eager for Mother to return and compliment us on our cleaning. Then I picked up Mother's sculpture in order to dust the mantelpiece. Above the sound of the *Four Seasons,* above the sound of the whining vacuum cleaner, Father and Beth could hear the crash.

After turning off the music, Beth stood at the edge of the kitchen floor and her only comment was: "You're dead, Jeremy. Now you've really had it."

Father shut off the vacuum cleaner and tried to piece the sculpture together, but it was hopeless. Adobe Woman had a crack down her spine, her right arm stopped at the shoulder, her feet were missing.

"If I glue it together and put it back where it was, maybe Mom won't notice the difference when she returns," Father said. "I don't want to upset her after a long weekend of hard work."

"Don't even think of trying that," Beth called from the kitchen.

"Why not?" he asked.

"You know how disdainful Mom is of duplicity."

"Yeah, Dad, d-d-don't piece it together. I'll just tell her what I did when she gets home."

Mother was, above all else, a woman of moods. If she'd been escorted out of the San Francisco Press Club for wearing slacks or her editor in New York had tampered with her lead, dinner would be a long silent affair, the rest of the evening she'd try to find fault with us, and we'd stay out of her way. But when things broke right for her, when *The Nation* played her story on the inside front cover, or an important politician invited her to ask the first question at a press conference, she was capable, I think, of divine love. She would give back to us the blessings the world had bestowed upon her, and in her glory we could do no wrong. She'd gone to Sacramento with the intention of talking to a few senators, some assemblymen, and maybe a couple of lobbyists, but Arnie Logan, Mother's former sports editor on the *Daily Bruin* and now Pat Brown's press secretary, had arranged an exclusive interview for her with the governor, and on the way home she'd sold it as a free-lance feature to the Sunday supplement of the *San Francisco Examiner*.

She wanted so much to share her triumph with us that she bought Father another book to add to his The Rosenbergs Were Not Guilty Library, she bought Beth a marionette, she bought me a box of cinnamon gingerbread men, and she bought herself a bottle of champagne. When she handed me my box of cinnamon gingerbread men, I handed her the broken pieces of Adobe Woman and said, "I'm sorry, M-M-Mom, I dropped your c-c-clay lady."

On that Sunday afternoon, I don't think the death of her father would have seriously dampened her spirits. She was so giddy with success, so drunk with champagne, that she just looked at the pieces and laughed and tousled my hair and said, "That's okay, Jeremy. Don't worry about it. It was an ugly old thing, anyhow, don't you think? I didn't care much for it any more. Cheer up, hon, it was only a statue. All is forgiven if you'll promise to be as honest with me about everything as you've been about this. Will you do that? From now on, if you do something I should know about, will you come tell me rather than make me find out for myself? Good. Now, may I have one of your gingerbread men? I've always liked best the kind with icing on the nose."

This was certainly a side of Mother I had seen little of until then. I wanted to show my gratitude by giving her the whole box of gingerbread men, but she said, "No, I'd rather get a dozen kisses from you later tonight." When she came downstairs to tuck me in and kiss me sweet dreams, she still had on her perfume, her triangular earrings, her lipstick, her purple dress, her gold bracelet, her gold watch, her black high heels—all that evidence of having competed in the world and won—and looked so pretty I decided I must never lose her love.

In order to make certain I hadn't forgotten to tell her something she should know about, I took to telling her anything that could possibly be construed as bad behavior. For a while, this was a charming enough ritual—every night after dinner, Jeremy sitting on Mother's lap and recounting all the little misdemeanors he'd committed—but very quickly I became fixated upon filling her with negative information. No offense was too trivial, no confession was too exhaustive. If while playing with friends I indulged them by speaking of Willie Mays as a "nigger," or while walking the dog I pulled the leash so hard I made little Bruin choke, I couldn't wait to rush home and tell Mother how dreadful I'd been. My after-dinner apology grew so lengthy Mother would lie down on the living room couch where, while she kept one ear on what I was saying, she'd watch Chet Huntley, dip oatmeal cookies in lemon tea, and read the *Examiner*. Before I finished my disclosures, she'd be sound asleep with oatmeal crumbs across her lips, and the paper—open to the Op-Ed page—at her feet.

The only way to attenuate the atonement was to do no wrong. I set out to be perfect. I treated Bruin with respect. I called people only by their Christian names. I crossed the street at the stoplight, a mile away, on top of a hill. I gave blood. I didn't listen to baseball games in bed. I emptied the trash twice a day and went out at night to hose it down. I burned comic books whose binding staples I determined to be inexactly aligned. I gave all my money to skinny girls in Africa. These devotions lasted for months, but they amounted to nothing because goodness gave way to spotlessness. I showered and showered and showered. I washed my hands so often a rash formed on my palms and when the rash cleared I washed my hands so often a rash formed on my palms and when the rash cleared. . . . What money I didn't spend on African girls I used to buy a small-scale vacuum cleaner. I dusted on top, in between, underneath, inside. After dusting, I'd vacuum. After vacuuming, I'd dust. I changed bed sheets every night. I changed clothes every hour. I wiped the towel rack until it broke. I scrubbed the sink until the splash of tap water felt like iron filth upon my marble white sculpture. My nightmare image was a *National Geographic* photograph of a parched lake bed cracked into an infinity of caked chaos. Last week, while we were packing up my parents' ex-house, Gretchen called me "the boy in love with bare rooms."

Mother's cover article for the National Federation of Nurses monthly magazine was called "From Tears to Triumph," and its opening bars I could practically hum:

> The reactions of parents to the birth of a malformed infant involve a form of grief closely associated with the mourning process. Some mothers quickly see the birth defect as a realistic problem; others may continue to look at the child as proof of their own inadequacy, visible evidence of their own imperfection. Mothers usually react with strong feelings of hurt, guilt, and helpless resentment to a congenitally deformed child.

"From Tears to Triumph" ended up winning for Mother the coveted Nightingale Award from the National Federation of Nurses and, if there is power here to the prose, it seemed to me to owe itself to the fact that it sounded as if she were writing about her son. For all I know, she just might have been, because this insane epistemological touching, this hypochondriacal perfectionism in which life appeared primarily as a problem, this sickness got sicker.

The two impulses—the desire, on the one hand, to be morally impeccable and the need, on the other, to be squeaky clean—came into dramatic and rather ludicrous conflict one evening when I was taking a bath and a beetle crawled onto the hot water valve. I lived in the basement, beetles were always barging in, but I'd never before answered the question: was it more important to be virtuous (let the bug live) or keep the bathroom clean (squash the silly insect)? Suddenly it seemed like the only serious problem I'd ever contemplated. I got out of the bathtub and paced up and back on the blue tile, cleaning up after myself as I dripped, pondering whether I should kill the beetle or let it live. For half an hour that dichotomy was the one idea in my head. I sat down on the stool to get a different perspective on the situation. Then the beetle fell off the faucet and drowned.

It's difficult to be impeccable in the damaged universe. As hard as I tried to be moral and immaculate, I would have certain lapses and my environment would have others. Mother simply refused to listen to any more *mea culpas*—she said if I pestered her any more she was going to refer me to a child psychiatrist, who was paid to listen to such lunacy—so every night I sat up and wrote a list of all the infinitely important, infinitely unimportant things I'd done wrong during the day. The last item on the list would always be that I'd wasted electricity by staying up late to write the list, which sounds like one of Father's jokes left behind on the borscht belt but was, nevertheless, the degree to which my mind had wrapped in on itself. In the morning I'd leave the list in Mother's purse or on the front seat of her Fiat before she left. After a while she wouldn't even glance at it before throwing it out and we got so we didn't have to talk about it. She knew I'd leave her a list, I knew she'd throw it away, and we both were happy. This went on for years and now it seems too close to psychosis to endure for more than a few minutes, but at the time Mother seemed to have arrived at a puzzled acceptance of it and I did, too. I thought I'd be observing beetles from the bathtub and writing notes at midnight forever. I forget how or when all this madness ended; God knows I can still get trapped in the interstices of the OED or the marginalia of some torn, blackened page I've rescued from the refuse. But before the initial disorder ceased, the lists—in the way that everything language touches it focuses and refines—made things worse.

I became imbued with the notion that to carry dirt from one spot to another was to spread germs and endanger people's lives. In the house, this was easy enough to avoid. If I removed my shoes on the back porch, then showered six or seven times and washed my hands every time I came in contact with something, I was in no danger of distributing any mud. Outdoors, especially on the playground at Currier, the mania got magnified. I'd be running merrily across the yard, step in a puddle, realize what I'd done, then run back and soak my feet until I felt the dirt had returned to its point of origin. I used to spend entire recesses digging my heel into a grease spot I suspected of being the repository of the black spot on my shoe.

The climax of this campaign came when Charles flew up from Los Angeles for my ninth birthday, and Father took us to see *Citizen Kane*, which I didn't understand, but Charles explained, "It's about money. All great art is about money." Charles is now employed by an association in Sacramento that has no address or phone because, as Charles explains, the government monitors all union organization of service workers. Although this was the sixth time he'd seen the movie, Father said some of the visual effects were stunning. I couldn't distinguish a visual effect from a subplot, but I thoroughly enjoyed the buttered popcorn, the icy Coke, the pink box of Bon Bons. As we left the theater and walked toward the car, everyone was content until I intuited a certain stickiness on the sole of my shoe. It was July, I hadn't brought a sweater, but when I said, "I think I left my sweater on the s-s-seat, I'll meet you back at the car," they nodded and kept walking because Charles was never any more observant than Father was.

Another showing of *Citizen Kane* was already on. I walked up and down the aisle in the dark till I found my little sled, I mean till I found my seat, which was occupied by a man with a monocle. He whispered to the girl next to him, young William Hearst looked at page proofs, and I rubbed my foot on the candy-coated floor until I felt I'd returned all the sweet viscidity to where it belonged.

This was definitely a low point. But the dementia had its rewards. Racing around as much as I did to return soil to its source, I turned into a runner. My legs were tan, hairless, and beautiful. My legs were legacy. Classmates would boast about my legs to their friends at other schools, and Mother said a lot of girls would give their right arm to have legs like mine, which was a messy accumulation of anatomy, but I got the point, and Beth, with fat white thighs at thirteen, agreed. Once, in my bare feet, on grass, at Currier, I ran fifty yards in six seconds, which is unheard of for a nine-year-old white boy. Black boys would cross town to challenge me and return to Hunters Point saying they got a bad start, man. It wasn't the races, though, or the timed sprints that mattered. What mattered was running alone when no one was watching, running up and down the hills of San Francisco into a sun that was setting the golden bridge on fire and that I wanted to burn me alive, running until there were no distinctions to be made any more between feet and legs and arms and hands, and my entire body was all only fluid movement forward, running until I felt I could run forever and let out my kick and never look back and no one could catch me.

7

FATHER WOULD GO to sleep at nine o'clock and awake to darkness in order to lace up his sneakers and tug on his jogging suit— navy blue pants with zippers up and down both sides, his smelly sweatshirt, and on top of that his sweat jacket with *Speed of Sound* stitched across the back. Birds would be just starting to call, black would still streak the colored pencil soft blue of the sky, Father would be jogging. In an hour he'd run twenty times around a track which was without bleachers or lighting or lanes, which had weeds in the center and a dry water fountain at the end of the far straight-away and a running path littered with glass and rocks. It wasn't what would be called a fast track. He didn't care. He pounded his feet through the dirt and pumped his arms and kept his rubbery legs moving until, by the very stomping of his feet, night withdrew and morning came. He jogged because he preferred to go to sleep before Mother did and awake before she'd even begun to dream. What did she dream about? I suppose she dreamed about justice.

Father once wrote me, apropos of nothing: "I am, no surprise, that same skinny kid who ran with the speed of Pegasus through Brownsville's streets in quest of a baseball." He doesn't really run anymore, so what did he mean other than to turn himself into a figure in a frieze? We share that trait, we Zorns, all the way down the nondistaff side. A little too often for my taste Father likes to say,

Backward, turn backward, O Time, in your flight,
Make me a child again just for tonight!

Father's mother, after whom Beth is named, died when he was eight, and it's fashionable in certain psychiatric circles to see this as the formative event of Father's life. It was not. The formative event of Father's life was this: he and his friends were crossing train tracks when little Teddy, last in line, stepped directly on the third rail, which transformed him from a happy vertical child into a horizontal conductor of electric current. It's difficult to think of Father as young once, since he's so old now, so very old. In 1919 he didn't have six pairs of eyeglasses, a bald head, or false teeth, though maybe he already had the Dumbo ears, the empty blue eyes. The train, a slow-moving local but nevertheless a train, with wheels and gears and steel, rattled down the tracks toward Teddy, who was lying flat on his back, powerless to prevent his own, unfortunate, self-induced electrocution.

I wouldn't be here today if Big Abe, a seventeen-year-old block of massive triangular stone, a wrestler who wore black shirts and a purple hat, hadn't slid a long piece of dry wood between galvanized Theodore and the third rail, flipping him high into the atmosphere only seconds before the train passed. Teddy was bruised about the elbows and knees and, later in summer, was a near-corpse as flesh turned red, turned pink, turned black, and peeled away to lean white bone. Toenails and fingernails crumbled and what little hair he had on his body was shed until Teddy himself had nearly vanished. His father, named Nate, sued Long Island Railroad for one hundred dollars, which paid—no more, no less—for the doctor's visits once a week to check for infection.

I never met Father's father. This past Christmas, from a straight-backed bed at Montbel, Teddy tried in all seriousness to pin Nate to the page for me: "You can tell, Jeremy, can't you, how his life touched me? There was the sense of doing things for his fellow men; there was the kindly, mediating approach. *Ess vett soch oy spressen,* he liked to say. It will press itself out. It will take care of itself. This, when told about a problem. He couldn't cope with problems. He let them drift, grow, fester, or fly away. Recognize some of your dad's penchants and peccadilloes in that?" My favorite thing Nate did was fall asleep on the subway every morning after reading one paragraph each from the *Jewish Daily Forward,* the conservative paper, and *Freiheit,* the Communist gazette, as if he knew even then how communication can cancel itself out, how "penchants and peccadilloes" alliterates a little too easily. In the summer of '56 Mother and Father had gone to Balboa to give Mother a shady haven in which to edit copy for a special double issue of *Open Forum,* the ACLU "in-house organ." Mother was pregnant and Beth was three, with a blood blister on her left foot. When Father's sister called from the nursing home in Floral Park to say Nate was dead, Father somehow found this cause for confessing his fear that I was going to be too much of a burden for him because he had a history of depression.

"What do you mean?" Mother said, who was a young thirty-one. "Like you get down in the dumps every now and again?"

"I think I'm on the road to having it licked," he said, "but after the war, then again during a brief period of unemployment before we met, I needed a little electroshock to get me through some bad patches."

Mother literally dropped Beth, blood blister or no blood blister, onto a rocky part of the sand, then fainted face-forward into that parked rowboat which soon figured so prominently in the iconography of my childhood. Who knows what damage that did to my diction? I don't think their marriage ever really recovered its equilibrium after that.

LIVING WITH a manic-depressive wasn't like living with a drug addict. It wasn't like living with a funeral. I got a twentieth birthday card from Gretchen that shows the word "HAPPY" being manufactured by a bunch of goofy little guys who look like Santa's sugar battalion. It was more like that: just knowing every lake is man-made and sooner or later needs to be emptied. Mother virtually carried in her wallet an article written by some psychiatrist friend of hers that said "manic-depressive illness is not simply a series of manic or depressive episodes but rather a continuing personality disorder punctuated by these dramatic episodes." She wanted to be able to track an atom in a centrifuge and she couldn't and, if she hadn't died first, she might have driven herself mad as well. For four years he'd be fine and funny and athletically buoyant, then one day he'd come back with an entire roll of negatives of the freeway. His qualifiers would slide downward: "whole, worth-while"; "modest, feeble." "If a shirt comes to you from Macy's, it's from me, Dad," he might keep saying. "The shirt is from Dad." Then you'd be looking for some leftovers in the fridge and come across a note Scotch-taped together, sticky with blood stains, like advertisements for a sympathetic reader. Mother would pack his suitcase and he'd wave shy goodbyes like a boy leaving for camp.

Which fairly took the wind out of my sails because, with a pause here, an inflection there, he used to be able to convert the most unpromising material into such high tragedy, such low comedy, such an enjoyable narrative. In the forties and fifties he supposedly got invited to the most exclusive Industry parties in Beverly Hills for the solitary purpose of telling Yiddish jokes. He told many, many stories very, very well, but the only one I want to remember is the only one that was true. Father would writhe on the rug, waiting for the train, and leap on top of the hi-fi console when Big Abe lifted him into the trees. When I was ten years old, Father was making noises that intimated another stay at Montbel—he flew to Sacra-mento on behalf of the poverty program of the county of San Francisco and airmailed me an epistle consisting entirely of blank pages for no real reason I could make out—so Mother lent me her tape recorder and told me to tell him I'd forgotten some of the finer points of the third-rail story. Father and I had some problems fig-uring out how to work the recorder, but once we realized the stupid thing had to be plugged in we were all set. He lay back on my bed with pillows under his neck while I sat in a chair, holding the microphone, sitting over him, listening to him talk with his eyes closed and the bed lamp focused on his face. I felt like his shrink. I wanted him to sit up or open his eyes or ask me to turn the lamp away, but he entered immediately into the prologue: "I want to tell you, Jeremy, about the world I have lost. It seems like it existed a thousand years ago, if indeed it ever existed. One sweltering Indian summer day. . . ."

I didn't know what was the matter. I expected him to be pinning his arms to the mattress and bouncing up and down on the bed to indicate the thrill of the third rail; flipping the lamp on and off and whistling through his teeth in imitation of the oncoming local; arcing across the room to show how he'd been saved; stripping off his clothes to show how his skin had peeled; doing all the things I'd seen him do so perfectly at parties, but he was doing none of that. He was telling the tale as if he didn't know what came next and, worse, as if he didn't care. I turned off the microphone and asked, "What's the matter? You're not telling it like you usually do."

"I think that microphone throws me off," he said, opening his eyes for the first time. "I feel self-conscious with just you and me and Mom's tape recorder. I need more people around me, a party atmosphere, a couple of drinks."

I got up and brought back a cup of cold water from the bathroom, but that didn't seem to do the trick and Father returned to worlds we have lost, to sweltering Indian summer days. Every scene was slowly set, every amusing little digression was relentlessly pursued, every character was described down to the contents of his lunch pail. When I go back and listen to the tape, what's even more noticeable than the relative banality of Father's recital is his endlessly sibilant S, his fluttering F. He seems to be on the verge of stuttering. Sandra says S and F are voiceless sounds that arise from air flowing from the lungs to the tongue; if Father was having trouble with S and F, his stomach must have been in knots, his chest must have been constricted, his throat must have been thick with pressure: he must have been very nervous. And I'm the one who created such an awkward situation. I'm the one who moved the microphone down his mouth and urged in a stage whisper every five minutes: "Relax, Dad, just relax. Tell it like you usually do. Just pretend I'm not here." I'm on the tape, actually saying that, barely audible in the background: "R-r-relax, Dad, just relax."

Sandra has heard the third-rail tape and says Father is definitely not a stutterer. "No more than six percent disfluencies," as she would put it. I would put it that the third rail didn't produce in Father a speech impediment, but that it's probably the origin of his preoccupation with the Rosenbergs. He nearly wrestled once with Uncle Gilbert over Gil's lackadaisical pace proving the Rosenbergs' innocence through special-access AEC documents. It's himself Father sees at Sing Sing: electrified at last, purged of all pain. Sometimes I think I've inherited all of that from him: the relentless misdirection, the oblivious wandering, the fatal footfall, the helpless passivity, the catch in the voice. He used to tell me about the time when, waiting for a subway back from Coney Island, he watched the impatient crowd push a pretty girl onto the tracks just as the Brooklyn train was arriving; on certain late summer afternoons he can still smell the pretty girl's body burning. That's sort of the way I think about the third rail. In certain situations I can still feel Father's body vibrating from the voltage because that's what has been passed down to me: nervous energy running nowhere. Sometimes I could swear those third-rail currents are coursing through my veins; sometimes when my jaw jitters I could swear all the circuits have been disconnected.

I don't mean to suggest that, ordinarily, Father was anything other than fluent. It was only when he was shy or unsure that he faltered. I hear him hesitate as he introduces himself over the phone to Mr. Somerby before he asks Mr. Somerby if he would like a free estimate of the market value of his house from the real estate company Father has so recently and temporarily joined. Then I hear him hesitate when he calls me cross-California: "J-J-Jeremy?" he'll ask and I'll say, "Yes, Father," because with Father I'm always articulate, because of Father I'm not afraid. Beth says when she visits him occasionally he'll babble a bit, but that's more the result of old age than the manifestation of any neurosis. And yet I hear him at dinner one night a decade ago.

Mother worked part-time as editor of *Eureka,* the monthly magazine of the San Francisco Historical Society. She came home around five some Friday with the news that we should eat and run since in just a few hours the society was unveiling the exhibition the public had been panting for: Charcoal Drawings of the Damage Done by the 1906 Earthquake. None of us had the heart to tell her we were less interested in perusing fuzzy re-creations of the wreckage than staying right where we were—drinking lemonade, scouting hummingbirds, barbecuing steaks. Mother appeared at the steps of the patio and said, "Okay, you guys, time to get ready. Gulp it down and get changed and let's go. We don't want to be tardy."

We didn't want to be tardy. We didn't even want to be present. We wanted to lie back in our lounge chairs and let the night fall. Mother returned ten minutes later, looking very sharp in an Indian-style hoop skirt. Still quite cheerful, she said, "What's the matter with you lazy bums? I'm offering you an education in art and a night on the town, and you're guzzling lemonade. Come on. They'll be waiting for us."

Father took the easy way out. He stirred the coals in the barbecue and said, "I don't think the kids want to go, Annette."

The kids were age ten and fourteen, and could speak for themselves, but had chosen not to. Mother's face turned the color of one of our medium-rare steaks. She rustled her skirt and stomped about a bit in her boots, nearly crushing Bruin, who was begging for a scrap of meat. I suppose if I had to say what it was I despised about that sterile dog it was how it was always either scratching at you for something or stretched out on all fours for you to scratch it, like human desire reduced to the lowest common denominator.

"What do you mean the kids don't want to go?" she said.

"I mean I think the kids don't want to go."

"You mean you think you don't want to go, but just don't want to say so, is that right, Teddy?"

"Yes, that's right," he said, squirting more lighter fluid onto the coals.

She asked Beth and me if we wanted to go.

"No, thank you."

"N-n-no."

Father, suddenly very brave, said, "I'll go if you need a hand to hold."

"Oh, no, you won't, if you're doing me a great big favor. I work on *Eureka* so my family can take advantage of some of the social affairs, and when the biggest event of the year comes along—Mayor Alioto will be there, champagne, the press—you want to stay home and wipe grease off your mouths."

We wiped grease off our mouths. Then, in the wonderful way in which only Mother's mind could work, and which we were accustomed to accept as sane, she suddenly decided she didn't want to look at earthquake etchings, either. She wanted to go to *La Guerre est finie,* some sort of political thriller that was getting good reviews. She slumped down in a chair that had a bad front leg, drank the last of Beth's lemonade, and asked—told—Father to call the cinema. We had an extension cord on the telephone that probably would have allowed Mother to make a call from the Embarcadero Freeway if she ever really needed to; Father dragged that cord out to the patio. While putting on some more steaks, he dialed the theater. He listened to a man on a machine. I don't know whether he was trying to do too many things at once, or trying to please all the people all the time, or whether he knew, or thought he knew, Mother had no intention of missing the Society bash and was sending him through a farcical task. But he did have trouble telling Mother what time the movie started. He had his problems.

He said: "I-i-it starts at seven th-th-thirty."

Mock-sincere, stirring her lemonade, Mother said, "Do you mean to say a movie actually starts at seven-thirty-three?"

She had to say that. She had to wreck Father's barbecue. He went inside to change clothes so he could escort Mother to the exhibit, or the theater, or wherever it was she finally decided to go. The steaks caught fire and a great flame went up until Beth had the presence of mind to pitch some dirt onto the pit.

SO FATHER WASN'T the high sovereign on the home front. We all find some place we are powerful, though; we all go somewhere to be strong. Where Father went, Sundays in summer, was to Golden Gate Park. In the early 1930s, Father had worked as a minor league umpire on the East Coast, teaming up occasionally with Emmett Ashford, who was something of a showman and thirty years later became the first black umpire in the major leagues. Some people thought all of Father's behind-the-plate antics amounted to nothing more than "white Ashford." We'd go to Giants games not when Koufax was the competition or bats were being given away, but when Ashford was calling balls and strikes. All game long, Father would keep the binoculars on Ashford and say to me, "Emmett's calling a low strike," "Emmett was out of position on that one," "If that guy gives Emmett any more guff, Emmett's going to give him the old heave-ho." Then I'd look up and Emmett would be giving the guy the old heave-ho.

It wasn't the major leagues that played at Golden Gate Park. It wasn't even the minor leagues. It was something called the industrial leagues. The Machinists would play the Accountants, Pacific Gas and Electric would play Western Airlines. But they played with a hardball, they played for blood, their wives cheered like enraged schoolgirls, and Father was the referee. He'd leave for Golden Gate Park early on Sunday morning with his spikes and metal mask already on, his chest protector underneath his blue uniform, and a little whisk broom, with which to dust off home plate, sticking out his pocket. I'll never forget the first time I saw him umpire.

We lived a short bus ride from the park, so Father went ahead and I was to follow after him. I watched alligators yawn on cracked rocks in the Steinhart Aquarium; bought a fortune cookie, whose message was that I should spend less time on business and more on love, at the Japanese Tea Garden; found the Botanical Garden, on the other hand, a little too pretty to appreciate; and finally worked my way toward the baseball stadium, which wasn't really a stadium at all but an immense field without fences. There was a diamond, though. There were dugouts and a half-circle of stands. I stood behind the screen, watching Denny's Restaurant play Safeway Market. Neither team meant a thing to me and after a few innings I looked around for Father, who I figured must be working the next game.

Then I realized the big man in blue, squatting behind the catcher with every pitch, was Father. In certain sections of the country, in certain leagues and stadiums, the spectators are expected to focus all their economic and sexual frustrations upon the lonely figure of the umpire, but in San Francisco, in Golden Gate Park, on at least one Sunday in the summer of 1966, they didn't do that.

Denny's Restaurant and Safeway Market weren't playing up to par. Father soon emerged as the main attraction. When a batter took a called third strike, Father would parody the victim's indignation. When a batter drew a walk, Father would run halfway to first base with him to speed things along. He was the only umpire working the game, so on balls hit to the outfield he'd run down the foul line to make sure the ball had been caught, and on balls hit to the infield he'd run to first base to be in position to decide. He signaled *safe* by spreading his arms and flapping them, as if readying for flight. He signaled *out* by jerking his thumb, and the entire right side of his body, down: an expression of disgust for all this drossy dirt. Between innings he juggled three baseballs in the air.

At one point he walked back to the screen and, not realizing who it was, told me to take my fingers off the wire because a foul tip might crush them. I said, "You're doing great, Dad." Later, while a new pitcher was warming up, he told me to run and get him a lime Sno-Cone. I was still quite mortified by *L*s and said: "How about cherry, Dad? Cherry's better."

He said, "No, Jeremy, lime."

I told the lady at the snack bar: lime. It took a while. All the colors of the lady's face; all the colors of the people in line, the advertisements, the glass window, and the wooden counter; all the colors of the plastic wrappers, red and black licorice, pink, plain, and hot buttered popcorn; all the colors of the machines, the soft drink cups and the money melted into one sticky, greenish liquid in my mind as I struggled to say the word, all one smeared, acid mess, but I brought back a lime Sno-Cone and Father munched it down first chance he got.

He worked all day, four long games, ten in the morning until six at night, and at the last out of the last game the fans applauded. It was only light, polite, scattered applause and maybe they were only clapping for the winning team, but to me it was a thunderous ovation and they were thanking the umpire. I stood up behind the screen and joined them. I cheered for Father.

One of Father's favorite baseball players was the old Brooklyn Dodger outfielder Pete Reiser, who had a nasty habit of crashing into cement trying to make the putout. Later that summer I was devising a complicated miniature golf course throughout the house to entertain my friend, Charles, who was flying up to spend the weekend. I took a break from landscaping the front nine to find Father dashing back and forth between the two freshly painted white walls of the living room. From one to the other he bounced, sullying the varnish, cursing his head, wailing, mutilating himself like Pete Reiser revved up to cartoon speed, and all I wondered, selfish soul, was whether this prisoner who was my father would get carted away before Charles arrived to attempt birdie putts from the rear hallway into Bruin's water bowl. One of the few musical refrains I ever heard Father sing, and he sang it all the time, was a little ditty that went: "Don't mess with Mr. In Between." That mess looked to be just about complete. Mother drove him to Montbel in time for a late lunch.

8

SO FATHER'S ONLY arena of glory was the ballfield. Where was mine, then? That was what I wanted to know: where was mine? One of the more interesting phenomena of mumbling is that most stammerers can read aloud to themselves for hours without the slightest hint of hesitation, which suggests that the perplexity is neither biological nor chemical but preeminently social: one person's failure to imagine himself in pleasant relation to another. I would sit on my bed in the early evening with the door closed, the blinds drawn, the lights off, and read aloud what I thought was the most beautiful passage in all literature—the last paragraph of *The Quality of Courage*, by Mickey Mantle. I would read it over and over again into the recorder, then play it back, and my voice would return high, soft, shy, girlish, but fluent: absolutely unbroken. Almost lyrical. And yet this was no triumph. It was only further isolation.

Mother especially felt this to be so. She snuck into my sound system and recorded a message that contained a few garbled words but could be transcribed without difficulty.

J, hi, it's Mom. It seems to me that you're a singularly walled-off little boy. I've had the experience of observing a young person crash through his protective wall and have only the most banal inner core to disclose.

Whom she was censuring here I haven't a clue. Maybe some disinterested suitor from high school.

Not so in your case, J, I am convinced. Since I was at least twenty before I conceded the need for intimacy, you are ahead in the game.

I hadn't conceded a thing and the act of communication has never struck me as a game.

But you will learn, as I did, that being available for intimacy means taking risks. Also, there are many facades that present themselves as intimacy, only that isn't what they really are. But being really close to another person—open and trusting and caring—is an indispensable part of life. Don't deny yourself that dimension in human relationships. As time moves along it turns out that closeness to others adds up to one's number one treasure.

Mother didn't seem to hear how hilarious it was to be lecturing about the crushing need for human warmth on a reel-to-reel Sony. Until I was twelve I was, in a certain limited way and only in full profile, pretty and did a little modeling for a toy company that advertised in the Jewish Welfare Fund *Community Bulletin*, which Father edited. Rather than pay me, which the toy magnate said would be vulgar, he'd let me choose a toy from the display shelves. By far my most cherished possession was a space mask that was a white helmet holding outsize green goggles and a red speaker that fit over the mouth. When you talked, your words had the quality of transmitted authority. Charles recently sent me a postcard with photographs of snakes on the front, and on the back the happy information that "four principal kinds of snakes need to be avoided: rattlesnake, cottonmouth, copperhead, and coral snake. A few rear-fanged snakes are poisonous, too, but less so than these. Of the harmless kinds many are of great benefit to mankind. Studying the complicated interdependence of animals and plants (ecology), we learn that the plant or animal that needs nothing does not exist." The last ten words were underlined by Charles, who is now a Marxist transcendental meditator. As time moves along it turns out that closeness to others adds up to one's number one buried treasure. *All phonemes denote nothing but mere otherness.*

In person, Mother suggested I might shed some of my neurasthenic self-consciousness if I pursued a selfless discipline such as politics. Integration of the schools was quite the rage at the time and Mother was researching a three-part series for *The Nation* on bussing in the Bay Area. This was my last year at Currier, which was opposed, on principle, to impurity. It was one of the only and certainly one of the oldest private grammar schools in the city. Although the board of directors was perfectly willing to accept, as they were known then, Negroes, it flatly refused to start offering full scholarships to promising six-year-olds just because they came from the wrong part of town. This effectively reduced the nonwhite population at Currier to none.

Mother not only promised to smear Currier in the first part of her article but also threatened to send me to a public school if I didn't campaign, on a strict desegregation platform, for student body president. I didn't want to run for student body president, I didn't care if Currier didn't enjoy Negroes, but I liked the school's playing fields, its insular walls, and I wanted to stay for my final year, so I consented to become a candidate.

I think Mother was the first person ever to take a school election seriously. At Currier, elective office was pretty much the exclusive province of thoughtful, unattractive girls who wanted to earn a Block C and had nothing better to do with their afternoons than bang gavels on Formica tables or read aloud the extremely tedious minutes from last month's extremely tedious meeting. This election was no exception. There were three presidential candidates, and Currier's stand on desegregation hadn't touched two of them. California didn't have a state flower. One of the pet projects at Currier was to get everyone to write letters to our congressman, urging him to lobby for the Shasta daisy as the state flower. Quite what stake Currier had in the Shasta daisy I never discovered, but Tracy Gordon campaigned on the solemn promise that by the end of her term the Shasta daisy would be flying on the flagpole or at least potted spectacularly on the governor's front lawn. Patricia Hewitt was a little more circumspect. She was very fat and ran—but *ran* is the wrong word—on one issue: mandatory physical education was an infringement of her rights, one of which was to be obese. Alphabetically speaking, Zorn was last on the list.

In trouble caused, in attention received, in anger aroused, I was the only one in the campaign who counted. Misses Gordon and Hewitt found the actual act of electioneering beneath their contempt and refused to come down into the courtyard to solicit votes. The election was on Friday; speeches were on Thursday; we were encouraged to canvass on Monday, Tuesday, and Wednesday; I campaigned so hard I forgot I didn't care. I distributed buttons that said on one side LET 'EM IN and on the other GIVE 'EM GOLD. I unfurled long banners that announced in orange HELP THEM HELP THEMSELVES: EDUCATE THE UNDERPRIVILEGED, which was meant as a reference to the poor tykes in the Mission District but which may have been misinterpreted as a confession of my own inadequacies. During recess I walked the halls with a cardboard sign—I'M A FREEDOM FIGHTER, ARE YOU?—hanging from my neck, and bought third-graders, who seemed old enough to enjoy the gesture but not old enough to judge it, cartons of milk and sugar cookies. Most of my posters were removed. Most of my buttons were edited to read LET 'EM SIN and GIVE 'EM MOLD, placed on my seat, with the pin up. I responded to the antagonism, though. I appreciated the hatred. No one had ever liked me at that school, I'd never fit in, and it was nice to see the antipathy out in the open. At night, Mother called every Currier parent in the phone book and excoriated racism.

All of this was only prologue to the speech. It was that I worried about, that which was giving me bad dreams. Mother suggested I write a speech that omitted all the sounds which were then so ominous to me (*B, D, P, R,* and *L*) and when I said that was impossible—"bussing," for instance, "desegregation," "president," "race," "love"—Mother said, "Love?" then said she could do it, she'd write it for me. No, I told her, I was writing my own speech and leaving in all the letters of the alphabet. I had no particular desire to stutter excessively before six hundred people, but I also had certain things I wanted to say and thought paraphrastic constructions would only occlude communication.

At breakfast on Thursday, Mother sang:

> Today, oh, today's the day
> They're giving the presidency away.

I don't know what she thought she was doing. Maybe she thought her little carol was making light of the whole election or filling me with confidence. She kept repeating the rhyme, I wanted her to stop, and all I could say in response was: "No, Mom. The speeches are today. The election is tomorrow. The teachers like to have a day to warn the students against voting purely on the b-b-basis of who told the funniest jokes."

My idea of breakfast was to hide behind a semicircle of cereal boxes, wrapping myself in a cocoon of sugar shock and upbeat promotional promises. Mother reached over a particularly tall box of Alpha-Bits to hand me a vitamin and sing:

> Today, oh, today's the day
> They're giving the presidency away.

She finally arrested her aria to ask if I'd give my speech while she finished her coffee, and Beth also wanted to hear it, but I insisted the substance of my address remain secret until the general assembly and Mother was curiously acquiescent, so I marched off to school with my bag lunch and books in my satchel and, in my hands, in one of Mother's glossy white folders, the text of my talk.

The upper playground at Currier was a steep cement hill and, when third-period classes were dismissed, the entire slope was filled with unfriendly faces. At the bottom of the bank was a row of chairs in which the candidates sat, and a microphone mounted on a podium at which they suffered. The presidency was not the only thing being given away that day. There were all the candidates for all the class offices; for boys' athletic manager, who distributed the kickballs at recess; for girls' athletic manager, who didn't; for vice president, who had nothing whatsoever to do with the president; for secretary, who had to have nice handwriting; for secretary-at-arms, who had to have a nice left hook. All these aspirants came to the podium and spoke, and all their speeches were soporific. The speeches for president were last. Miss Hewitt delivered a lecture in favor of fatness. Miss Gordon tossed a bouquet of Shasta daisies to the audience. Mr. Kirby called me to the mike.

I don't especially revere the poetry of Robert Frost, but I've always loved the way he stood in the snow in 1961 and tried to read a poem that the wind kept shaking out of his hands. He was so old, the glare was so strong, the poem was so corny. He kept trying to read "For John F. Kennedy His Inauguration" until he realized he didn't need that piece of paper. He knew another poem. He let the page fly away and mumbled from memory. There was no snow the day I gave my speech, no wind, no senility, but there were boos when Zorn was introduced, suggestions that Zorn be sent to Zambia, shouts (which could hardly be contradicted) that Jeremy was a Jew. Although I didn't toss away my address and speak from memory, I persevered. Amid catcalls and paper airplanes, I began.

Principal Kirby, Vice Principal Brinkley, Assistant Principal Wilkerson, Dean McCafferty, teachers, students, classmates, friends: good morning.

So far, so good. This was the standard opening. The audience liked nothing so much as the standard opening and the initial hostility dissipated into a more passive skepticism.

And it is a good morning, isn't it? The sun's shining, the sky's blue, the fog's far away. We're happy. We—all of us gathered here today—are happy. We come from good homes, we have good parents, we wear good clothes, we read good books, we eat good food. We're good. We're happy. But on the other side of this city, ladies and gentlemen, in the Mission, in Hunters Point, in the Fillmore, the sun isn't shining and the fog's thick. The boys and girls in those areas don't wear good clothes. They don't read good books. They don't eat good food. They're not happy. I urge us to do all we possibly can to make these poor people happy.

There are only a few times in my life I've been so excited that I lost my awareness of language, but this was one of them. It wasn't just adrenaline or the articulation that is anger. It was some beautiful form of fear, an ethereal realm of complete panic in which the mind shut off, the mouth popped open, and words came of their own accord. I heard someone shout, "Yeah, they eat shit, but they drive Cadillacs," and someone else project the same syllogism into what I took to be a rhetorical question—"If they're so poor, why do they dress so fancy?"—but I couldn't have stopped talking if I'd wanted to. Good words emerged from my mouth and were amplified for miles. A microphone is said to be very sexual. Maybe it is, maybe it isn't. Who cares? All I know is I squeezed that thick, throbbing object in my fist and did what all of Mrs. Fletcher's pamphlets on public speaking had so strongly encouraged me to do because it's such incontrovertible evidence of the orator's mastery over his situation. I walked away from the podium. *Away.* I picked the microphone off the podium, walked toward the audience, stood at the base of that huge hill, and finished my speech.

I urge us to accept little Negro boys and girls from the Mission, from Hunters Point, from the Fillmore, and I urge us to give them scholarships if they can't afford to come to Currier, which they can't. I think they can learn from us, but I think we can learn even more from them.

I hope you'll let me tell a little story that points a moral in this direction. Most of you know I'm a very fast runner. This past summer, I ran every Saturday in the invitational track meet at CCSF. All my opponents were Negroes and, although I ran in the twelve-and-under, some of them weren't twelve and some of them weren't under. Some of them were more like sixteen. Every Saturday I ran only one race, the seventy-five-yard dash, and every Saturday I won. I won by six, eight, ten yards. I forget my times.

At first there was what in the track-and-field world is called "bad blood" between me and my competition. They didn't like the fact that I won so consistently and easily. They didn't like the fact that I wasn't a Negro. They told me to go back to Snob Hill, they claimed I was wearing illegal spikes, they told me my nose was an unfair advantage in the wind. But on the last Saturday of summer they finally admitted that they weren't going to beat me and, after the race, they gathered around and asked me my name and bought me soft drinks and pinched my thighs in play. One boy showed me how to shake hands. Another boy asked me over to his house. I say: Let's gather around them and ask them their names and pinch their thighs in play. Let's show them how to shake hands. Let's ask them over to our house. Accept Negroes at Currier. Support them with scholarships. Let 'em in, give 'em gold! Jeremy Zorn for President.

I thought I hit just the right grace note at the finish and began to bow when Mr. Kirby rushed up and grabbed me by the arm. At first I thought he was trying to congratulate me, then I thought he was trying to arrest me, then I realized what was going on. Third period immediately preceded lunch time, and when dozens of upperclassmen brought their bag lunches to the assembly no one had suspected any foul play, but now a good percentage of the male population of the fourth, fifth, and sixth grades were throwing a good percentage of their bag lunches at me. I think even some of the third-graders were throwing the sugar cookies that, in all good faith, I'd bought for them. The girls weren't throwing things. They were calling me names I really don't need to repeat. The microphone, which I'd left on the ground, screeched. Some students whistled, others popped bags, a lot of people were booing. But it was the older boys, my peers, who pelted me with apples, eggs, peanut butter sandwiches, bags of Fritos, animal crackers, carrots, cartons of milk. After a bullfight in Barcelona, this would have been an expression of admiration, even love, but, epilogue to a speech at Currier, it was something less than laudatory.

Mr. Kirby got hit by as much as I did, and as he walked me back to my seat he said, "Someday you're going to learn, Mr. Zorn, that if you ask for trouble, goddamnit, you're going to get trouble." I hadn't asked for trouble. I'd only asked for a chance to say what I wanted to say, and when I said it I was ecstatic and the rank and file were agitated. I crawled underneath the chair and, watching food fall at my feet, listened to Mr. Kirby announce: "Assembly, dismissed; conduct, disgusting." The teachers took their sweet time suppressing the riot. I don't think they much liked my speech, either. Out of the crowd, ostensibly on business, with a camera around her neck, a note pad in her hands, and tears in her eyes, came Mother, shouting: "I got it. It's all on film. You were beautiful, Jeremy. My little Demosthenes—you're going to be famous!"

9

MOTHER'S ARTICLE was rejected. I didn't become famous. I lost by a landslide. Miss Hewitt got so fat she had to enter a hospital. Miss Gordon received four out of every five votes but was unable to establish the Shasta daisy as the state flower and was defeated in her bid for reelection by a girl from Sausalito who thought Currier should install soft-ice-cream machines in the cafeteria. . . .

Fame? Virgil stuttered. He wrote and rewrote the *Aeneid* the entirety of his adult life, averaging one hexameter a day. In his will he told Tibullus to burn the poem because the last eleven lines of Book XII didn't scan properly. One can't help but want to go back to the *Aeneid* with greater patience after hearing that. In his first speech as prime minister, Winston Churchill sometimes paused as long as five seconds before crucial phrases. The House of Commons thought he was employing silence as a rhetorical device. He was trying not to hyperventilate. Later he said, "I have nothing to offer but blood, toil, tears, and sweat." He adored alliteration. There's hardly a sentence he wrote that doesn't swoon in sound. Handsome Loud Blazer, instructor of Psychoanalysis and Literature at London Prep, once said, "In every staccato rhythm, every pinched phrase, every aborted clause, the alert reader can hear echoes of Mr. Maugham's speech defect." Which strikes me less as literary interpretation than pedagogical sadism. Demosthenes, of course. Moses, of course, whose Ten Commandments tablet God rived in half to remind him he couldn't control language. Aristotle. Aesop. Charles I. George VI. Erasmus. Marilyn. All tellers of tales really, in one medium or another, and all people known by only one name, as if they'd contrived a way to contract their tongues' Tower of Babel to a manageable logo.

The pressure that underlies stuttering also generates the ambition to succeed—to succeed hysterically and on the same field as the original failure: somewhere within the world of words. Very few stutterers I've ever met yearn to become glassblowers. Promptly after losing the presidential nomination, I joined the chorus. Mother didn't think this was a very good idea, since singing was very low in her cultural hierarchy—vocalization being one of the performing rather than creative arts—while Father, bouncing back nicely from Montbel, thought it was an even worse idea: all the rehearsals were pointing toward a Christmas concert in Ghirardelli Square. I didn't care that we sang hymns in praise of someone else's savior. The material didn't matter. What mattered was coming to school an hour before classes started, donning my red robe, standing on the stage with a hundred other red robes, and being unable to hear my own voice: being part of a long song outside myself.

What mattered even more was a soprano named Cindy Du Pont de Nemours, who prompted the first real romantic passion in my life since I fled Faith five years before. Cindy Du Pont de Nemours was driven to school in a black limousine, was the only girl at Currier to wear either nylon stockings or high-heeled shoes (which nearly got her expelled but ended up causing a furious new trend in fifth- and sixth-grade fashion), and would get people Gauloises if they asked very nicely, but what I loved about her was that during rehearsal she wore the collar of her robe up. The white collar on her red robe: she wore it up. I never asked if she knew the white collar on her red robe was up. I thought maybe that was the style in Montparnasse or maybe she just liked it that way. With her collar pressed to her cheek, French pastry stuffed during quick breaks into her mouth, and her hair tied in an auburn bun, she looked like a saint.

She would say, "I like zuh azelete." She actually talked like that. She added a *Z* to every word she possibly could, so I took to calling her *Z*, as in "You looking forward to the Christmas concert, Z?" or "Hey, Z, g-g-got any *croissants* left?" Her English was nah zo good, but she sang beautifully, without the trace of an accent, and she was our only soloist. Whenever we rehearsed one particular song, whose title I forget but whose theme was quite clearly the beauty of the Christian night, Z would step onto her very own carpeted platform and descant on the beauty of Christian night, then sashay back into the soprano section while the conductor held her hand and said, *"Merci, mademoiselle, très bien!"*

The conductor was a voice coach at the San Francisco Conservatory of Music. I suspected him of spending the first hour of his morning at Currier for the exclusive purpose of escorting Z back into the soprano section after she sang her solo on the beauty of the Christian night. Everyone else he treated with a contempt bordering on repulsion. He had a wooden leg and would limp up and down the stage, tapping people on the head with his cane when he thought they weren't giving it their all, clapping his free hand on his good leg to some distant rhythm that only he heard. He also had a gold front tooth; he liked to stand next to one of the floodlights and let that tooth glint into your eyes and say, "I'm sorry, but under no circumstances can I call that singing."

He never said that to me. He never told me he didn't like my singing. I was in a special section of the chorus, way in back. It wasn't exactly alto, wasn't exactly tenor. It wasn't bass. It was a special section for boys whose voices cracked on every eighth note, boys who had no real business being in chorus. To us he'd say, "You're doing fine. Not so loud, though. A little softer, okay, guys? You're our muted harmony section, our low melodists in the background. I want you to be singing that close"—he'd hook his cane on his left arm, holding his right thumb and forefinger an inch apart—"to a whisper." Then he'd hobble up to the front and ask Z what song she wanted to sing next.

On the night of the Christmas concert Father said he felt like he had his sea legs all the way back but also said he wouldn't be caught dead listening to the children of the rich sing Christmas carols to white-shoed tourists in Ghirardelli Square, and Mother's opinion was that the whole ball of wax was too vulgar for words. They both ended up going, of course. Only Beth didn't come. She was typecast as a frustrated little fat girl in *The Prime of Miss Jean Brodie* and couldn't skip dress rehearsal. What was this aspiration of hers to become an actress? It would have been about as likely as me winning a slot on the six o'clock news. Once she even tried out for cheerleader and came home crying; I served her dinner in her room and tried to come up with reasons to live.

While Beth was spreading malicious rumors concerning the art teacher and Miss Brodie, I was singing ballads about a virgin birth. Christmas in San Francisco never has anything to do with snow or sleigh bells. The moon hung above us soft and full, the stars were white light on a warm black sky. We sang atop a three-tiered platform to the patrons of a shopping plaza in the Square. The conductor had his own little stand. Some people, when they got a look at his limp, figured us for a needy group and rang quarters at his feet. I'm sure he would have kicked the money back to them if he could have. He seemed a little distracted, but everyone else was happy. All the parents, shoppers, and visitors applauded our performance, taking pictures, requesting numbers they used to sing when they were kids. Right below us, a water fountain rose pink and fell blue. Above us, on the terrace, sounds of crystal and silver came from an outdoor café. The boys and I in the muted harmony–low melody section must have gotten carried away by the festive atmosphere because we forgot about our instructions to remain musically anonymous and sang so loud that, even though we were standing in the last row of the last tier, the conductor came up to me during intermission to say: "I could hear you."

I thought the chorus in general and my little coterie in particular was having its best night ever. I assumed he was complimenting me on knowing when to let out all the stops, so I said, "Oh, thanks. You could actually hear us all the way in back, out of all those voices? Great."

He was propped against a lamp. With one hand he was twirling his cane, and with the other he was trying to get his gold tooth to refract the light of the lamp and blind me in the left eye. "You don't understand," he said. "I don't want to hear you. I thought I told you to be that close"—he let go of his gold tooth, pressed his thumb and forefinger together—"to a whisper."

"You did," I said. "B-b-but I thought, what with all the water f-f-fountains and people and all the applause—"

"A TV crew is supposed to be here shortly and there's a chance we'll get on the eleven o'clock news. On the rest of our songs, I want the five of you to mouth it."

"Mouth it?"

"Yes. Just move your lips. Don't sing any of the songs, don't say any of the words. Just mouth it, okay? I don't want to hear any of you coming through on the news."

I looked up. Mother was waving. Father was snapping pictures with his Nikon. They both seemed so much a part of the Christmas spirit that I didn't want to ruin their night. Somehow I'd been appointed spokesman for the Last Tier Quintet. I said, "Okay, we'll mouth it."

I think the idea of hearing themselves on the eleven o'clock news threw dread fear into the hearts of the other four fellows. They didn't seem to mind mouthing it and, as a show of solidarity, I went along with them. We opened our mouths wide, gestured meaningfully with our eyes, and shook our arms with baritonic temerity while singing in silence. The finale was Z's solo on the beauty of the Christian night. She stood in the center of a floodlight, caroling into the camera. The boys and I in the back row, covered in darkness, mouthed the words right along with her. There's something about overheard harmonies, songs sung over *there,* that lends them more weight than music played on your own headphones; the rapture of the soul in anguish, etc. Afterward, Z rushed up to me and said Channel 7 promised the concert, or at least part of her solo, would appear, if not tonight, sometime later this week. Then she introduced her parents, who made Mother and Father look like provincial street peddlers by comparison.

Z said, "Zuh conzert: it wuz—how zoo you zay—a zukzess! Wazn't it, Jeremy? What iz zuh matter? Why iz zuh azelete zo zilent?"

I've never easily accepted my sweethearts' successes—surely this is little more than an aversion to Mother's lofty accomplishment in periodicals—and after that night I never felt the same about Christianity, either. I blamed my humiliating silence upon Christendom in general and Ghirardelli Square Christmas shoppers in particular. Chanukah was in its fifth night. Suddenly I was devout.

I'D PERENNIALLY LOVED the candled incantation—*Baruch atoh Adonai Elohaynu melech ha'olom, asher kid'shawnu b'mitzvosawv v'tzivawnu l'hahdleek nair shel Chanukah* —because I didn't know what it meant and it was pure, tribal sound. Now I wanted to know what it meant, what Chanukah, Rosh Hashanah, and Yom Kippur meant, what was contained in the Talmud and the Torah. Now I had something like patience for Father's explanation of how this night was different from all other nights; something other than contempt for Beth's Hebrew Youth Group; something other than cynicism for Mother's assertion that an aunt of hers on her mother's side was related to Louis Brandeis. The dripping wax on the menorah, the spinning dreydl on the kitchen floor—these things that I had hated with all my heart I wanted to love. As dinner concluded, I announced that as a demonstration of my faith I was going to fast until the end of Chanukah.

Father was opening a present. He put down the package and said, "But you don't fast on Chanukah. Chanukah is a celebration. You fast on Yom Kippur, Jeremy. That was in October."

"And *you* never fast past noon," Mother said.

"Yeah, Jeremy, by ten-thirty you're already filching cookies from the cabinet," Beth said. Beth would often use words like "filching."

"I'm going to fast until the end of Chanukah," I reiterated.

Father had opened his present and didn't know what it was. It looked like a miniature guillotine.

"Don't you know what it is?" Mother said, opening her own present and blowing smoke into the sacred air. "It's a little device I got at Dubon's that pumps up your balls when they go soft."

Beth looked at Mother. Mother looked at Beth. Together they broke into a terrific fit of the giggles. Father held up the guillotine for closer inspection and looked like he was going to cry.

"Oh, don't look so put upon, Teddy. Your *tennis* balls. It'll pump up your Tretorns for you."

Father brightened.

"Oh, how nice," Mother said, gripping a little black gadget. "A battery charger for my tape recorder. Beth, did you think of this?"

Yes, she had. Beth had thought of this. Beth thought of everything. I'd thought of fasting. Friday night until Tuesday morning: it was a long time. I thought I could do it. While my family ripped gift paper and ate halvah, I'd swallow air.

The impulse of starvation is barely distinguishable from a yearning for death; I understand that now. I see my eleven-year-old self standing before a burning, bright mirror in the bathroom, my absurdly small hands pressed together around my absurdly small waist, my head aching with hunger, my feet stuck with sweat to the blue tile floor, my white crotch impatient for the production of pubic hair. I step into the shower, opening my mouth, letting the cold water gush until I gag, then climb into bed, lying on top of the sheets, shivering, reading and rereading a book called *Rabbit, Run* because it was about basketball, tearing off the top and bottom of each page and chewing gray paper until morning. Not until I started researching senior thesis possibilities did I realize the author of that book built such ornate syntax to retaliate against his own stutter.

For three consecutive nights I performed the same ceremony, but famine's no fun, dying's too arduous. Monday, on my way home from school, I bought a bag of groceries, snuck in the back entrance to my bedroom, and feasted on Muenster cheese, lean pastrami, pumpernickel bagels, Beer Nuts, no beer but a half-gallon of grapefruit juice, mint chip ice cream, Nilla-Vanilla Wafers, apples, oranges, bananas. A fraction of the food I left in the bag and deposited in a drawer underneath some sweaters, but the large majority of it I inhaled, then I collapsed and slept until Mother came downstairs and asked if I wouldn't like to break bread with my family on this, the last night of Chanukah.

The room was dark. Mother stood behind me like some shadowy Eurydice. I rolled away from her and pretended still to sleep, but she turned on a light, pressed a damp rag to my forehead, again invited me upstairs to the banquet. "No," I said, pushing the rag away from my face. "I'm not breaking my fast until tomorrow morning."

"It's not healthy. You'll starve yourself to death. You're skinny enough as it is. Besides, this is the last night of Chanukah and your father got you quite a nice present. Please come up and join us," Mother said. She stomped one of her feet on the floorboards.

"No. Tomorrow night I'll eat with you, but not tonight."

"Please, Jeremy. For your father's sake if not mine. He can't wait to see the look on your face when you open your present."

"He can keep the present. I j-j-just want to stay down here and read *Rabbit, Run.*"

"Parts of that book are pure pornography. You shouldn't be reading it, anyway. You should be upstairs with your family, opening presents, feeding your face, having a good time: being normal."

Then something quite abnormal occurred. Mother was a reporter. She was trained to be on the lookout for abnormal occurrences. When a trail of red ants started to make its way up her leg, she noticed it instantaneously. She let out a shriek. Brushing the ants off her skirt and felling them on the floor with the heel of her boot, she asked me what in the world ants were doing not only in my room but up and down her hose.

"Oh, you know, the cold. Ants like to come inside when it gets cold."

"But *red* ants and so many of them?" Mother asked, following the ants from her foot to the floor, the floor to the door, the door back to the bureau, and the bureau to the bottom right drawer, in which green ice cream was dripping on gold sweaters, half-eaten apples were turning brown, and the red ants of San Francisco appeared to be holding their semiannual convention.

Mother was delighted. I swore I'd broken my fast only a few hours earlier, but she refused to believe I hadn't been gorging myself the entire weekend: her little martyr wasn't so stoical, after all. She hugged and kissed me, laughed a good deal, and cleaned the drawer. We walked hand-in-hand upstairs to the dining room, where Father sat atop a purple bicycle, pedaling in place. "Happy Chanukah," he said. "A brand-new Schwinn, just for you. Look, Jeremy: it has three speeds, a bell, a basket in back, two reflectors, an air pump, and a chain lock."

SOMETIMES my childhood seems to me nothing more than an endless series of obsessions, overwrought attempts to get beyond a voice that bothered me and, like any saint in the grip of a metaphor, I desired either to vanish forever or to emerge triumphant. I never emerged triumphant. The nearest I got to vanishing forever was watching Robert Shields perform mime on Montgomery Street the day after I'd asked Z, at the Currier graduation dance, to let me have the last slow one for old times' sake. Not meaning to be nasty or vindictive but only mocking my speech in the way I'd always mocked hers, she answered affirmatively in such absurd, abrupt, repetitive, broken rhythms that I told her she could go find someone else to dance with and ducked back into the dark crowd. This concomitance—falling in love with significant gestures twelve hours

after listening to an immigrant make fun of my disfluency—bred my
newest devotion. I decided to become mute. That was all there was
to it. I would end the exchange. All summer I practiced sign language and, although no one in my family knew the first letter of
the manual alphabet, I thought a perfect time to cease oral communication would be when we went on our annual hike in the High
Sierras the first two weeks of August.

The High Sierras: mountains of such magic importance to my
childhood as to be commensurate with aboriginal promises of beauty
and peace; jagged pinnacles far, far away, but oh so close, so om-
nipresently in the mind; background to a poster of Beth's that said
IN WILDERNESS IS THE PRESERVATION OF THE WORLD, which is not
exactly a novel idea but which in its balanced incantation had a
certain charm for me; subject of innumerable slide shows when
Beth and I were too young to hike, and Mother and Father would
return with color pictures of melting snow, rushing water, tents,
cabins, silver drinking cups; site of Mother and Father's tenth an-
niversary, on the last day of which Mother threw out her shoulder
and pleaded with Father to pop it back in place for her, but he
could not—he was simply incapable, he said, of causing her pain—
so they had to walk all the way back to the ranger station, where
a very nice and quite good-looking young forester was eager to
oblige.

The summer I turned twelve, while they were shutting their suitcases and locking the windows of the house, I handed the members
of my family three-by-five typewritten notes that said:

Dear——: Hi! I just wanted to tell you I'll be conducting a
little experiment during our stay in the Sierras. For the next
two weeks—beginning right now—I'm not going to talk. I have,
as you know, been studying sign language. I'll bring along the
manual alphabet guide, so you can ask me a question, then
follow my answer in the guide book. If that's too much trouble, I'm going to tie a notepad and pencil to my wrist, so I can
write down and hand to you my opinion on important matters
of discussion. You can talk to me. I just won't be able to talk

to you. Thanks for your cooperation. Here's (nevertheless?) to a happy vacation.

Jeremy

Beth thought I was kidding, Father said let's get on the road before nightfall, and Mother asked whose permission I'd obtained to use her typewriter. On the drive north I was unable to entertain my family in the way I usually did, conflating billboard phrases into a mad rush of meaningless sound, and was forced to forfeit my turn when Beth decided all the punch of Twenty Questions was lost when it was played in pen. Other than that, though, I didn't have any special problems during the journey. In restaurants I'd tap Beth on the shoulder, point to what I wanted, and she'd tell the waitress. At gas stations I let Father ask the attendant where the men's room was, then followed him. In the car I stayed silent, concentrating on pastoral scenery.

Once we got on the trails, I just watched white water without identifying my feelings. I didn't have to say the waterfall was strong or loud or blue or beautiful, the deer was fast or afraid or dangerous or female. I didn't have to say the sun was hot, the trail was steep, the mountains were gorgeous, my backpack was heavy. In wilderness was the preservation of the word. When we stopped and spoke to other people on the trail, Mother would explain that I had a very hoarse voice from singing for six hours around a camp fire. At night I'd lie awake in my sleeping bag, look up at the moon and stars— enormous white ink blot on black paper, hundreds of sparkling asterisks—and think I'd at last arrived at the proper relation of man to his environment, probably solving my speaking problem as well.

But on the last day of this high-camp paradise—why is there always a *but* and why is it always on the last day?—I got it into my mind that I had to run the entire distance to the way station where our car was parked. I ran uphill, downhill, through streams, over rocks, faster than deer. I'd run until I was out of earshot, then jog in place until my family caught up, and listen to Mother say: "Don't run, Jeremy. If you run, you won't notice the trees or the animals or the falls. That's what we're here for: to feel one with the beauty of nature, not to set sprinting records." I already felt one with the beauty of nature. I wanted to set sprinting records. I'd hold up a sign—*See you at the next bend*—then turn my back and be off.

Father finally had enough of this silence game and, in a cool glade right at the timberline, caught up with me. Bounding over the rocks, snorting and puffing, he looked like nothing so much as a mad goat. I sat in the dirt, carving *JJZ* into a boulder with my pocket knife. What a wordsmith. He took off his pack, sat down next to me, and patted my leg.

"Don't you think you've done quite enough to make your mother and me miserable without running away from us on the last afternoon of our vacation?" Father asked.

I nodded.

"We've let you hand us notes for two weeks. Won't you walk these last few miles with us?"

I shook my head.

"Won't you please, Jeremy? It would make your mother so happy."

I shook my head.

"Please walk with us the rest of the way."

I stood, picked up my pack, and started to run back onto the trail, but Father caught my foot and gave a little flip, which he really shouldn't have done because I had an open knife in my hand. The knife, the pack fell out of my grasp. I landed in the dirt, Father pounced on me, and then—in a clearing at the timberline of the most beautiful mountains I know—we commenced to wrestle. It was the worst melodrama, the most absurd tableau: clutching each other's clothes and rolling around on a bed of pine needles. He kept shouting, "Why won't you walk with us? Why won't you talk to us?"

Perfectly legitimate questions, but I didn't have the answers and, besides, I was more interested in what had happened to the knife. Though it may have been only the sun setting his fingers on fire, I thought I saw the red handle of my pocket knife sticking out of his hand. I didn't stop to contemplate whether I was encountering pure hallucination or potential homicide; I pushed him off me, grabbed my pack, and didn't stop running until I was at the bottom of the mountain, a hundred yards from our car, sitting on a rock and skipping stones across a placid lake.

It seemed like it took forever, but they finally came trudging down the trail. Mother shook her hat at me. It was an extremely ugly hat. It had purple polka dots scattered across the brim like a disease. I've never seen her quite so angry as she was the moment she saw me sitting on a rock, skipping stones. She said she'd thought I was lost and now here I was, skipping stones. She said I had no right to run ahead of the pack, no right to make her worry like that, no right to ruin everyone's vacation by playing dumb. I nodded, and in sign language said I was sorry. She thought I'd made an obscene gesture and, explaining that twelve years old wasn't too old to be spanked, struck me across the back and legs with her steel-tipped walking stick until words came out of my mouth: not very pretty words: rather ugly words, in fact: so ugly as to be dishonest: but words, nonetheless: "I hate you. I hate all of you."

10

DID YOU KNOW *that corporal punishment is often used for petty and trivial offenses such as throwing gum or not stripping for gym? Did you know that it is sometimes administered with split baseball bats and with slotted paddles? Did you know that it has been done in front of other children, as well as by students? Did you know that it has been done to disturbed children who need to be helped rather than hurt, that in the name of discipline grown men will hold a resisting child down on the floor and hit him many times?*

Did you know that, when Mother got worked up about an issue, she could crank out a purple pamphlet with the best of them? Well, I suppose you did. . . . It wasn't so much that I hated the members of my family as that I couldn't communicate my love. That is always a problem, I've found, being unable to communicate one's love. It gets one into the least attractive type of trouble. And I did love them. I loved them as ferociously as it's possible to love one's field artillery. My family was committed to the ideal of social justice but addicted to the tension of internecine warfare. It seemed to me Mother thought the only reason to exist was to perform an endless number of good works. Where in the world would she get such an idea? No wonder Beth's doctoral defense was going to be a revisionist view of the Levellers.

The primary beneficiary of Mother's largesse was the Negro People. There were far fewer honeymoon pictures of Mother and Father kissing each other than of both of them kissing some black-faced, white-robed statues in Palm Springs. And that seemed to set the tone for the remainder of the millennium. Father rooted for the Dodgers because they were originally from Brooklyn, but we as a clan stayed loyal to them because they hired the first black baseball player (Jackie Robinson), retained the first crippled black baseball player (Roy Campanella), and started the highest number of black players with Stepin Fetchit faces (Johnny Roseboro, Jim Gilliam, Tommy Davis, *et al.*). There was something slumming in all this, something that was wrong, and I knew what it was when I was nine years old: we would love someone only when he was helpless. Gretchen thinks most of my problems pretty much stop and start on that sentence. One Easter weekend at Watts Towers Mother looked smogward through some latticed wine bottles with a positively religious sparkle in her dark eyes. When cousin Sarah married a black man from Philadelphia, Sarah's mother couldn't come, so Mother substituted and brought the temple down with an a cappella finale of "Bridge Over Troubled Water." Never in my life have I met anyone who meant so well.

She began working full-time as the public information officer for the first integrated junior high school district in California and proceeded to make the Levellers look like a gang of Georgia Democrats. Mother sat on the side at the Tuesday night school board sessions, attacking her antique typewriter as if she were H. L.

Mencken in *Inherit the Wind.* Whenever she grouped school children for posed pictures she insisted there be black faces in the crowd, but she was such a poor photographer that the black kids always came out as smudgy studies in ebony. She wrote the bimonthly newsletter that was distributed to the teachers, *my* teachers, and nearly every issue offered a signed editorial polemically in support of desegregation of the schools.

"We were all babies," she wrote, explaining the origins of human sympathy. "We all have parents who love us. We all live in some kind of house. We all have families. We all have friends. We all need food. We all have feelings." She got giddy about people she'd never met in a way she never could about people with whom she lived in some kind of house. Mother needed a scrim between herself and love, in the same way Father has relied upon the periodic cancellation of his memory; Beth, the space of time; and me—at twenty-one I already seem to suspect I'll never marry.

One day Mother came home and stood on our tiny plot of front lawn, pounding a FOR SALE sign into the grass, shouting at us to come outside.

We followed orders.

"What's for sale?" Beth said, wise guy, as she was deep in some homework assignment. "The lawn?"

"The whole blessed house," Mother said. She pirouetted ecstatically in the windy twilight.

"The whole house?" I said.

"We're moving," she explained, waving her hammer at me.

"Back to L.A.?" Father hoped. It was the only true paradise he ever experienced, way in the past.

"No, into the Fillmore district."

"She's lost it," Beth whispered to me. "She's finally joined Daddums in the burn ward."

"Honey?" Father said. "The Fillmore?"

"At today's Human Relations meeting, Ike said, 'Revolution comes the day white families give up their houses in Pacific Heights to move into the ghetto.'" It was 1968. Mother took what Ike said as a personal challenge. Ike pronounced the word, "ghetto," with exaggerated emphasis on the first syllable to make it sound like he still lived somewhere near there.

"Honey?" Father tried again. "Don't you think Ike meant it just sort of rhetorically?"

Mother refused to entertain the notion that words were ever meant as anything less than a direct call to arms and, while we paraded up and down the sidewalk with flashlights, accosting inquisitive pedestrians, Mother got on the horn with a hundred realtors, trying to get one, just one, to have enough imagination to foresee what a publicity coup it would be for them to work out a swap with a black family from the Fillmore. It's a pity Father hadn't earned his real estate license yet. Maybe he could have figured out a way to get us waking up every morning in the projects.

That wouldn't have been his style, though. He was more circumspect about his role in the revolution. That fall, Father was fired from his post at the Jewish Welfare Fund—he wasn't getting enough one-liners about last night's charity dance into Herb Caen's gossip column—and accepted a much lower-paying job as director of the poverty program in the Mission. He sat in a one-room office without central heating and called grocery stores, wanting to know why they didn't honor food stamps; called restaurants, asking if, as the sign in the window proclaimed, they were indeed equal opportunity employers. Sometimes, on weekends, he flew to Sacramento or Washington to request more money for his program. In the Mission district, they worshipped him. They called him the Great White Hope. Watts rioted, Detroit burned. Father said, "Please, I'm just doing my job." They invited him to barbecues, weddings, softball games. At the softball games he outplayed everybody. The salary was seventy-five hundred dollars a year, but he was happy. The ghetto was his.

Father called a landlord to ask whether the apartment listed was still available and received assurances there was a vacancy, but when he returned that evening with a skinny black man who'd just arrived from West Texas the landlord said the room had been rented. The poverty program filed a complaint with the city housing department, but when weeks passed and Nicky was still without a place to live Mother told Father to move Nicky's luggage into the guest room.

Nicky didn't have any luggage but he stayed until spring. He showed me how to shake hands, how to play pool, play cards, how to dance, how to dress. He bought me liquor and dirty magazines. He played basketball, baseball, football, tennis, and track with me and let me win. He didn't leave until he met and married a pretty white girl, but what I remember is this: the morning after he moved in I walked into the bathroom while he was showering, smelled his body as burnt butter, hot heated jelly, damp sweet sweat, and vomited into the sink.

With Father working to improve the ghetto and Mother working to get children sent out of the ghetto, they couldn't very well, in all good conscience, keep me going to a lily-white private school. Besides, neither of them was making anywhere near as much money as before and they couldn't afford such exclusive education for me any longer, especially since Beth still had another year to go at Jack London Preparatory Academy. Also, Mother thought it would be good for me to mingle with unpampered people; I might get off my high horse and loosen up a little. Instead of going, as most Currier graduates did, to Borough Hills Middle School, which was neither in a borough nor on a hill but in the middle in the sense that it was an intermediate step between private grammar school and prep school, I went to Bayshore Junior High in the heart of the city.

BAYSHORE was different from Currier. No grass fields, no left field walls, no right field fences, no tower with hour bells. But no speech therapist, either, no farcical student elections, no red-robed Christmas chorus catering to tourists and appearing on the eleven o'clock news, no all-night Open Houses. Just gunmetal gray lockers, gunmetal gray corridors, gunmetal gray classrooms, and little black boys carrying gray metal guns. They left me alone; they knew who my parents were. My reputation as a runner had also preceded me, and they weren't going to harm someone who, come track season, promised to be so valuable.

After school I'd walk into the Mission, leave my books in Father's office, then go to the court in the ghetto, which, after the murder in Memphis later that year, was renamed King Memorial Recreation Center. A hoop, a swing, a clay tortoise. At first I just watched. Black basketball is to white basketball as hockey is to, say, hopscotch: they're not the same sport. I'd played white basketball in well-lit gymnasia, on glassy surfaces, against glass backboards, dribbled a leather basketball, passed it politely to my teammates, allowed my opponent to score a reasonable number of points, acknowledged the fact when I committed a foul. I'd played that game. Even when I played with Nicky, we'd play with people from the Heights and, if he had any jazzier gestures, he never revealed them. Maybe he just wasn't a very talented athlete. The Mission version—wearing purple socks and black boots with a steel comb in your hair, never passing the ball to your teammates or shooting from beyond five feet, refusing to confess your most flagrant infractions, and kicking your heels and leaping off cement into rarefied ether—I'd never encountered before and was awed.

From the library I checked out *Rattling the Rim,* which concerned the heroes of street basketball in New York City. I'd memorize the myths, then appear at the Mission playground and, during water breaks, in halting tones, tell sad stories about Bedford-Stuyvesant drug addicts who could jump through the moon. The San Francisco stars didn't want to hear about the New York stars. They didn't care if Earl Manigault could touch the top of the backboard with his elbows, if Connie Hawkins could spin the ball on his nose while coming down off cocaine. They didn't care. They weren't interested. They wanted to be left alone and not be compared to anyone else and dunk until dark.

I shut up and just watched, but I kept reading about basketball until I found an even better book, *A Sense of Where You Are,* which was about Bill Bradley, who attended Princeton, won a Rhodes Scholarship, then played competent if unspectacular professional basketball for several years. During half time of the Harvard game, while Coach Van Breda Kolff was explaining how to handle the Crimson's full-court press, the future Rhodes Scholar was off in a corner with a towel draped around his neck and his Converse high-tops unlaced, reading Donne's *Holy Sonnets.* At half time of the Harvard game, in Cambridge, trailing by six, he was slouched against an open locker, scanning "Batter my heart, three person'd God; for, you/As yet but knocke, breathe, shine, and seeke to mend;/That I may rise, and stand, o'erthrow mee, and bend/Your force, to breake, blowe, burn, and make me new." He put the book away, laced up his shoes, and scored thirty-six points in the second half, including a left-handed hook from behind the basket to win the game in double overtime.

A sense of where you are. I wanted an unalterable compass of my position, not this other, disgusting feeling, this childish apprehension that wherever I was I was hopelessly lost, wherever I stood was quicksand. I stopped going into the Mission district, had Father nail a hoop to the garage door, and started practicing—with Nicky when he was around, by myself when he wasn't.

Although I was the fastest twelve-year-old boy in San Francisco, I had what in basketball circles is known as white man's disease: as a vertical leaper, I had feet of lead. I couldn't do tricks around the basket, hang on the rim, hold the ball in one hand, dribble it through my legs, pass it behind my back, spin it on my finger counterclockwise, but Father said all of that was only fancy-dan foppery. He said, "Let me show you how Joe Lapchick used to shoot them at the Garden in the thirties."

I didn't especially care how Joe Lapchick used to shoot them at the Garden in the thirties, but Father parked the car, slammed the garage door, and trotted onto the court, clapping his hands and calling, "Pass the old apple over here, Jeremy." Maybe Joe Lapchick used to call the basketball the old apple, but I didn't want to be seen playing with someone who did and who was standing at the edge of the driveway wearing suede Hush Puppies, mismatched socks, checked pants, a striped shirt, a navy blue blazer, and tinted sunglasses; clapping his hands; requesting that I pass him the old apple.

Our house was at the top of a hill. If your shot was short, it would hit the handle of the carport door, take a crazy bounce, and roll all the way down the hill into a crowded cable car. I thought most of

Father's shots would fall short, and I'd spend the hour before dinner chasing the ball down the hill into various crowded cable cars, so I didn't pass him the old apple. I just stood there, dribbling it idiotically against one particular crack in the pavement. Father rushed at me, putting on the press, so I handed him the ball and took a seat on a little wooden fence that divided the driveway from the front porch.

He dribbled around the driveway, slapping at the ball with his right hand while holding his left arm straight out to the side. He threw the ball against the carport door a few times, using the old-fashioned two-handed chest pass. It looked ludicrous. Then he ran to the top of the slope, cradled the ball in both hands as if it were a baby or pumpkin—something immense, heavy, and round in only a general sense—knocked his knees together, rotated his wrists, and let fly from the waist a flatfooted, two-handed, arching set shot very much in the style of Joe Lapchick. It looked even more comical than his chest pass against the garage door. The net danced. I clapped, more out of surprise than admiration, but Father barely managed a smile. He retrieved the ball, jogged to the top of the driveway, and threw up another set shot. The old apple barely rippled the cords. For a solid hour he ran around the court in his Hush Puppies, wiping sweat off his bald brow, taking his belt off at one point, putting it back on at another, always adjusting his sunglasses, sinking Lapchickian set shots from every angle. Occasionally he missed. The wind probably came up on those attempts or maybe he was just trying to show he was human. When Mother rang the dinner bell, he finally stopped.

"You've got to forget about the fancy-dan tricks," he reiterated. "Just get the two-hand set shot down and they won't be able to touch you. Joe Lapchick used to shoot them like that in the Garden during the thirties and was unstoppable. Put a little English on it, a little backspin, follow through, and listen to the crowd roar. Knees together, wrists cocked, right over the top. That's all there is to it. Get that shot down, Jeremy, and you'll be dynamite."

Then he went inside and listened to Mother ask why he'd forgotten to post her letter on his way home. In this important epistle, addressed to the superintendent of schools, Mother had outlined her plan for receiving the right kind of publicity on the multimillion-dollar bond issue. At that moment, I think I felt for Father something like love. Immediately after dinner, I went outside and, by the light of the street lamp, worked on the rudiments of the two-handed set shot. For two months I did nothing else. I played an hour before school, usually with Nicky; all afternoon; all evening when Father installed a floodlight on the balcony above the court. I'd play until Mother waltzed outside in her nightgown and said, "Okay, hon. That's enough. The bounce of that damn ball is driving me crazy. I have to get up early tomorrow." I'd go inside and squeeze a hard rubber ball until my fingers itched and my palms turned red, run up and down the stairs with sand bags tied to my legs, do sixty sit-ups a minute on the hard floor of my bedroom.

Not surprisingly, I became extremely adept at the two-handed set shot. Father was still a little more accurate than I was, but I could shoot from farther distances. Sometimes, exhausted and all alone in the floodlight, I'd make a basket and look up; there would be Father, standing on the terrace, thrusting his fist triumphantly into the night sky, and yelling, "Listen to the crowd roar." I listened. The crowd wasn't roaring. Other times, I'd be dribbling in the driveway at four o'clock in the afternoon, Beth would bring a few of her theatrical friends home with her, and by way of introduction and dismissal she'd say, "This is my brother. He plays basketball." I had a fine, tight, little body. That summer, when we visited Father's Relatives and Historical Landmarks Back East, the prettiest actress at Jack London Preparatory Academy asked Beth to snap a photograph of me in shorts, standing next to the Lincoln Memorial, and Beth had to oblige.

One Saturday morning, after having been away for quite a while, I ventured back into the Mission. I was hoping they'd remember who I was, but when I arrived at the court no one was there. The fog was in, the wind was up. I figured they'd all decided to stay home or had jimmied the lock on some gym. I'd grown accustomed to a straight basket, a mesh net, and a half-moon backboard with an orange square in the middle. At first all my shots were falling short and to the left. *A sense of where you are,* I kept telling myself, *a sense of where you are,* and soon enough my touch returned. I moved all over the court, farther away from the hoop, and became more accurate as the morning lengthened. It wasn't unlike playing in the driveway, only without the sound of the net swishing and, instead, the rusty clang of loose metal as the ball wriggled through the rim.

Around noon, someone came to keep me company—a little guy wearing a wool cap and black tennis shoes laced every other eyelet with a kind of light rope. He was no older than I was, but he had a goatee. His name was Jupiter. I never knew his real name. I think it was something like Howard Morrison. His nickname was derived from the fact that, although he was very short, he could jump to Jupiter. The only other thing he was known for was setting Siamese cats on fire. I felt a little self-conscious shooting two-handed set shots while a leaping pyromaniac leaned against the pole, chomping on a toothpick, combing his goatee, and drinking chocolate milk. I stopped shooting and said, "Hey, Jupiter, where's everybody else?"

"Don't know, man. They's probably at home watchin' the Saturday morning comics."

Jupiter held out his carton of chocolate milk and asked, "Want the rest, man?"

I was thirsty from playing all morning and went over to take a sip. Jupiter threw the empty carton onto the cement. I went back to shooting baskets.

Jupiter asked: "What's this girlish-lookin' gunk you throwin' up, man?"

I heard him but didn't know how to reply, so I said, "I'm sorry, Jupiter. I didn't catch that. What did you say?"

He hit the ball out of my hands, did an extremely poor imitation of the shot Joe Lapchick did so much toward making legend at Madison Square Garden in the 1930s, and said, "I says, Mr. Zorn, what's this two-handed, knee-knockin', flat-footed, fairy-wristed, double-backspin booshit?"

Jupiter had a way with words and I didn't. I banked a few shots from the right side, then said, "My father showed me how to shoot." "I'm sure he did, man. But that shit don't wash here. I mean, you shoot that shit: it get knocked back. In your face, man, down your drawers."

I had to reply or go home early. I said: "You want to go a l-l-little one-on-one, Jupiter, just until everyone else shows?"

At first, Jupiter thought my challenge was too funny for words and leaned against the pole, laughing like one of the crueler dogs on the Saturday morning cartoon shows. Then he said, "Shit, man, I ain't got nothin' else to do. I'll play you to twenty-one and spot you five, man." I refused the advantage, thanking him graciously. That got him mad. "Okay, Zorn, I'm playing for real now," he said, sticking his steel comb in his hair, removing his jacket to reveal a purple tank shirt that said in silver *Cunning Linguist,* stepping out of his black dancing pants into cutoffs slit to the waist. "Take it out, man," he said.

In the Mission they played Make It–Take It; if you scored a basket you remained on the offensive. I must have made four or five shots from twenty feet before Jupiter even got his hands on the ball. When he did, he dribbled through his legs for the longest time, executed eye fakes, shook his shoulders, wiggled his hips, stopped, started, twisted, turned, spun, jumped high, but he couldn't shoot to save his life. I'd grab the rebound, dribble to the top of the circle or into either of the far corners, and arch my antiquated set shot cleanly through the rim.

"Come inside on me, man, and you'll eat a leather sandwich," Jupiter kept saying.

I stayed outside. I didn't go inside. I didn't do what's called penetrate the key, and the sexual analogy is apposite because it's always been my philosophy, as the inauguration poet observed in another context, to back out of all this now too much for us, to stay away from the center and perform some archaic, immaculate feat where no one can touch you. That, such as it is, has always been my philosophy. Jupiter, whatever else he had, did not have a philosophy. He had springs in his legs, and philosophy wins out every time over springs in the legs. Or, if that isn't quite true, it was true this time. I won going away.

"Let's play again and this time I'll give you a little lead," I suggested.

Jupiter threw his box of toothpicks at me—little cinnamon spears—and said word better not get out what the score and who the victor was of our little encounter, or he'd murder my mother. Word didn't get out, but it didn't have to. I was the surprise sensation of the Bayshore tryouts. I was the only white player on what had traditionally been an all-black team, the only virgin in the lineup, the only starter under five feet tall. The coach was white and thought white people should be coaches and captains, so he made me captain, which meant I shook hands with the other team's captain before the game and called our plays during the game. I panicked when I had to shout in a packed gym. We worked out a system by which I simply held up a certain number of fingers to indicate what play we were supposed to run. Play number four entailed everyone else standing shoulder-to-shoulder on the left baseline, me dribbling behind them, and taking my shot. I signaled number four a disproportionate percentage of the time. The coach didn't mind since I never missed. He'd approach me in the locker room—the marching band's storage space—put his arm around me, and say, "My job depends upon your performance." I didn't know what he meant and wasn't sure I wanted to; I took him to mean he liked my Lapchickian style of play.

Each starter had his own specialty. One rebounded mightily. Another dribbled well. Someone else passed beautifully. The fourth played extraordinary defense. So when we needed a rebound we looked to Michael. When we needed to prevent the opposition's hero from scoring we looked to Kenny. When we needed a basket, though, when we needed two points in a hurry, they looked to me and stood back and watched.

"Listen to the crowd roar," Father would yell as I ran up and down the court, tossing in set shots. He never missed a game—home or away—and sat in the front row, taking home movies so I could study minor problems in form. Mother showed up once with

Nicky and said she thought it quite beautiful the way blacks and whites worked in harmony on the basketball court. He gave her a look, stepped away, and said, "Black and white can't work together off the court?" Mother, mortified, said she only meant she felt there was a feature story here, some good publicity for the junior high school district. Another time, Beth came and said the arena reminded her of the Oregon Shakespeare Festival's stage set for *Troilus and Cressida*. I was the basketball correspondent for the *Bayshore Recorder*. While playing, I would hear in my head phrases to describe the momentum of the game, the shot I just made, the pattern of the other team's jersey. This seemed to me pretty much the culmination of existence: living and triumphing, then going home and writing about it in detail.

We won the city championship by such a wide margin that our substitutes played the entire fourth quarter. After receiving congratulations and various cheap trophies and having dinner at an A&W Root Beer stand with the rest of the team, I went home, sat down at my desk, and began my narrative. The *Recorder* was planning to play it in the top right-hand corner of page one as the March issue's lead story, but it had to be in the following morning, so I stayed up late finishing it, then brought it upstairs to get Mother's corrections. She was sitting at her desk in the den, tape-recording the eleven o'clock news because there was supposed to be a report on an interracial rock-throwing incident in San Jose. The house was asleep. Bruin was snoring on the sofa like the shadow of Mother's psyche. The room was dark. The only lights I had to guide me were coming from Mother's white nightgown, the blue radiation of the television screen, the slice of moon and ball of street lamp glowing through green-tinted windows. I sat on the floor and watched the news with Mother. The rock throwers never made their appearance. Mother sighed, shut off her tape recorder, and was drifting off to bed when I held her hand and requested that she read quickly through my account and mark any mistakes.

"Tomorrow," she said.

I insisted.

She returned to her desk, switched on a lamp, took out her glasses, and examined the story:

BOBCATS CLOBBER REDWOOD IN CITY FINAL

—

Zorn Scores 36 Points on 18–18 from Field;
Redwood's Highly Touted Center a Washout;
Baxtrom Snatches 22 Rebounds;
1200 in Attendance

—

The Bayshore Bobcats bombarded the Redwood Forest, 71–45, for the 7th grade public school championship of San Francisco Wednesday, March 12, at the Cow Palace.

It really was no contest. The Bobcats (your Fighting Lynx!) outhustled, outshot, outplayed, outeverythinged Redwood from opening tip to final buzzer. Jeremy Zorn scored the first two points of the game on a set shot from straightaway, Michael Carr scored the next two on a left-handed drive down the lane, and from there on the Bobcats were not to be stopped.

The score at the end of the first quarter was 19–8. In the second quarter the Bobcats put on their full-court press, which left Ward Riley, Redwood's highly touted center, a fumbling fool. The second half was just silly. . . .

The story continued—with summary, then analysis, then quotation, then poetic outpour—for twenty-seven triple-spaced pages, but Mother quit halfway through the third paragraph and broke into laughter, which sounded eerie so close to midnight.

I was standing over her as she read. I stepped back into the lamplight and asked, "What's so funny?"

"Well, for one, honey, the clichés," Mother said. "Every sentence is a tissue of sportswriting platitudes."

I'd thought sportswriting was a wonderful convention and the best you could do was follow its formulae. I made a mental note to exploit the convention next time I wrote a sports story. I sat in a chair across the table from her and asked, "What else?"

"Well, the immodesty is not very becoming. Will your by-line appear on this article?"

"Yes."

"Won't people object to such self-publicizing?"

"No. Everybody already knows how good I am."

This last remark struck her—this last remark struck me—as a little too proud. She handed back the article, saying the rest of it seemed fine. She put Bruin in her basket and I was a good boy: I didn't kick her in the rib cage. Mother turned off the lamp and walked with me down the dark hallway, carrying the rough draft of a book she was writing called *Every Generation Must Win for Itself the Right to Be Free: Civil Liberties for Young People.* It was Mother's hope that "some of the readers of this book will be the lawyers and judges and legislators who will help make the Bill of Rights stronger for the next generation in the continuing battle to be free." Nicky was just pulling into the carport. At the end of the hallway the stairs to my bedroom began and a white door gave onto the bedroom. Father was snoring. Beth was reading, oh, I don't know, *The Tibetan Book of the Dead.* Mother whispered: "Sometimes when people ask me if all you do is play basketball I want to tell them, 'At least he's devoted to *something,* at least he has an activity which he loves and at which he excels,' but other times I wish you were obsessed with something a little more permanent, that you had a devotion which was a little more dignified."

I whispered: "Yes, I know."

"Sometimes I just want to tell those people: 'Leave me alone. Leave him alone. He's like a dancer on that damn court. That's where he's king,' but what I usually tell them, what I really feel, and I guess what I'm trying to tell you now is that I wish you'd dedicate yourself with the same passion to a slightly more refined endeavor."

"Yes, I know," I whispered again, turning and trotting off to sleep.

11

THE SLIGHTLY more refined endeavor I decided to dedicate my-self to was trumpet. This didn't meet with Mother's approval, either, for not only was music, as she'd said before, one of the performing and hence one of the lesser arts, but the trumpet wasn't even a stringed instrument. Furthermore, most of the band members were black. Although Mother was doing all she could to desegre-gate the school and loved the way I mingled so well with minority students, she believed each race finally had, as she also said, a discrete realm, had something it did better than any other race did. Band music, even more than basketball, was *theirs*.

I proved to be worse as trumpeter than I'd been as back-bench Christmas choir boy. I was always ready to slave away at transcen-dent sound and spent long spring nights alone in my room, sitting before sheet music, blowing my golden horn, but the mouthpiece would yield nothing, the keys would collapse, the spit valve would spit back at me, and I remained eleventh chair in a ten-chair trum-pet section. At the one concert I was allowed to participate in—a flu epidemic had taken the first four chairs—I got so excited I played right through a seven-measure rest. The conductor, a tall, ex-tremely beautiful black woman who wore short skirts and drove a pink Corvette, told me where to put my instrument.

I informed Mother I was quitting the band—not a dignified enough discipline to devote my time to—and she was thrilled with this news, but not so thrilled that I continued to associate almost exclusively with black boys, especially after Nicky's withdrawal. I liked their addiction to addictions, their disruption of ordinary syntax, their desire to seize idiom and make it speak for itself. I would hear them use a certain expression, then six months later hear the boys I walked home with use the same phrase as tentative white slang.

The boys I walked home with hated my nigger friends, they hated me, and I never knew why. Father said they hated me because I was a Jew. Mother said it was because I let them know I thought I was better than they were. Was that woman never wrong?

As I walked home with these boys, one of them would slip my wallet out of my pocket and at the end of the block he'd say, "Oh, hey, Jerry, isn't that your wallet back there?" I'd have to go back and pick it up while they'd keep walking. Or they'd discuss in depth Jack's thirteenth birthday party, which all of them had quite obviously attended and thoroughly enjoyed, but to which I hadn't been invited. Occasionally we'd play tag on the way home and I, of course, was always nominated to be It first. They'd try to lure me into running in front of cars, but I knew their tricks and was much faster than any of them, although whomever I tagged would turn around and chase only after me, so I'd have to run all the way home, patting my pocket to make sure they hadn't taken my wallet again.

Other times they'd play what was known as the silence game, talking among themselves, refusing to address one word to me or answer a single question during the entire walk to or from school. On Halloween, they made a habit of hurling eggs and flaming pumpkins at our front door. I wanted to believe Mother and Father when they assured me our house was so heavily pelted because it was across the street from the high school, but I knew the Halloween ghouls were my little friends who didn't like the fact that I both played basketball and quoted Steinbeck. Once, I received an anonymous letter which, mock-homosexual, complimented me on how smooth and brown and strong my legs were; wouldn't I like to meet in the boys' bathroom on Saturday?

They liked to do that sort of thing. They liked to turn the communication process into low farce. One of their principal entertainments was to gather at someone's house and make witty telephone calls to unsuspecting parties. One Friday night they asked me to join them. I didn't want to. I wanted to stay home and play Scrabble with Beth. I made various excuses, apologies, requests for a rain check, but they insisted, and I feared reprisal if I didn't participate in their pranks, so I went.

They were all sitting in flame red chairs in the garage of a boy named Bill. They all had names such as Jack or Bill, Jim, Art, Steve, Mark, Ron, Lee, Hank. Sometimes I think they selected me as their scapegoat because my first name had more than one syllable. The chairs were arranged in a neat circle, and the telephone sat in the center of the circle like some immense insect they were trying to tame. They were all drinking cans of Coors and smoking Camels. I visualized Beth and Mother sitting in the den, eating popcorn, drinking pink lemonade, creating word combinations, and I yearned to be with them, but Jack handed me a beer, Art placed a cigarette in my mouth, Jim pulled up a chair for me, and I had to stay. I didn't like the taste of beer and I was incapable of either lighting a match or inhaling smoke, so I put down the aluminum can and the cigarette and ate M&M's, which were consumed in great quantity by the gang so that Bill's parents—who couldn't have cared less or known more—would smell sweet chocolate rather than bitter malt or black tobacco.

These abstentions, of course, did little to endear me to the denizens of Bill's garage, but I sat back in my flame red chair and watched them dial. They'd request that a large pizza be delivered to the house across the street, then half an hour later rush to the garage window and laugh at the next-door neighbor's rebuff of the poor pizza man. They'd ask beautiful little girls: if your Uncle Jack was on the roof, would you help your Uncle Jack off? They'd tell lonely old women: I'm from the Electric Light Company—would you please look outside and tell me if your street lamp is on? It is? Well, would you please turn it off? You're wasting electricity.

This was a droll enough way to spend a Friday evening and I was starting to enjoy a little the blind dialing, the passing of the phone, the random cruelty of the calls, but then it was my turn. The telephone was placed in my lap and I said, "No, I just came to watch. I told Bill that when he called. I'm not calling."

I stood up to depart, but they blocked the door.

"Oh, yes you are," Jack said.

"Come on, Jerry, be a sport," Art said.

"Yeah, Jer, don't puss-out on us," Jim said.

"You can't watch and then not call," Hank said.

Perhaps Hank was right. It was unfair to watch the wickedness without doing the deed—in that way, not unlike a night I spent recently on Santa Monica Boulevard watching naked girls dance on dimly lit stages, but running in terror when approached by a coolly attractive and surprisingly inexpensive prostitute—so I returned to my chair, held the phone in my hands, and asked, "Who do I call? What do I say?"

"You call who you want," Steve said. "And you say what you want, but it's got to be nasty."

I tried to think of something nasty. At the time, there was a television program in San Francisco called "Dialing for Dollars," whose master of ceremonies interrupted a very old movie every five minutes to call one of our lucky viewers out there and ask (for progressively larger amounts of money until some spinster finally knew the answer): who won the Academy Award for Best Supporting Actress in 1956? Who is the only person to have been nominated five times for Best Actor and never won? Where was Gig Young born, and who was his leading lady in *Last Train to New Orleans*? What movie are we showing tonight? Is anyone, is there a single blessed soul, out there watching and, if so, why? To call someone, tell him it was Pat McCormick from "Dialing for Dollars," ask a perfectly simple question, and—no matter what our lucky viewer said—say I was sorry but that was not the answer we were looking for: wouldn't this be nasty enough? I thought it would, dialing.

"Yullo," an old man answered after a number of rings and burped. Immediately, I saw him: recumbent, in gray socks and white whiskers, on a prickly couch; overhead, dirty red drapes; at his feet, trustworthy schnauzer and trusted Scotch.

I was thirteen years old, my voice was very high and hesitant—obviously not that of the exceedingly smooth Pat McCormick—but all the boys were looking at me and listening. I said, "Good evening, sir, this is P-P-Pat McCormick on 'Dialing for Dollars,' Channel 2 Weekend Movie. We've just stopped at the climactic scene of *Snowbirds in the Sahara* to call and ask you a question worth twelve h-h-hundred dollars. That's right, twelve h-h-hundred d-d-dollars. We're looking for the name of a movie that's currently very popular and stars K-K-Katherine Ross, Paul Newman, and Robert Redford. It's called *Butch Cassidy and the Blank Blank.* We're looking for the blank blank, sir. Can you hazard a guess? It's worth twelve h-h-hundred d-d-dollars. The clock is ticking. . . . "

I couldn't tell whether the boys were laughing at the brilliance of my hoax or the obvious schism between who I claimed to be and who I was.

The old man said: "I don't know the name of any goddamn *Birch Calliope and the Blank Blank,* but I damn well know you ain't Pat McCormick. I know the sound of that man's voice and you ain't it. You're a kid who's got a speech problem, isn't that right, kid? Well, whadja callin' here for?"

"N-n-not even a w-w-wild guess, sir? Ten seconds and counting. . . . "

"Whadja doin', kid? Your speech counselor toldja to make telephone calls, impersonatin' public personalities or somethin'? Whadja doin'? You ain't 'Dialin' for Dollars' any more than I'm the 'Flyin' Nun.' But I can tell ya somethin', kid, you've got a mouthful of marbles. I never heard a kid talk so bad as that before. Callin' here like that, you otter be ashamed."

"F-f-five seconds. F-f-five, f-f-four. . . . "

"I got a solution, though, for you, kid. Read about it in *Reader's Digest.* Last month, I think, maybe the month before. Listen good, now, here's what you do: stick a coupla wads of cotton in both your ears. That's right, just stick some cotton in your ears. You won't be able to hear yourself when you talk and it'll do wonders for you, kid. Really, you gotta try it."

Actually, I did try it several years later in the form of an electronic gizmo called the Edinburgh Masker, which was approximately as effective as the cotton cure.

"No, I'm sorry, *Butch Cassidy and the Sundance Kid* is not the answer we were l-l-looking for. Heh-heh. No, I'm s-s-sorry, that's wrong, sir. We'll just have to call another one of our lucky viewers. B-b-but as a consolation prize we're sending you a forty-five of Nancy S-S-Sinatra s-s-singing, on one s-s-side, 'These Boots Are Made for Walkin' ' and, on the other, 'Love Is a Velvet Horn.' That's right, absolutely free. Bye, now. Yes, bye. Goodbye."

I returned the receiver to its cradle and tried to laugh a little with the guys—took a sip of Coors, a long drag on a Camel—but I was sweating profusely, my hands were shaking, and the boys understood what had happened. They were oddly commiserative, too. They clapped me on the back, told me it was a good prank, and Mark even picked up the phone to try the same stunt on someone else, but the old man was still on the line. That happens sometimes: one person hangs up, the other stays on, and the connection remains unbroken. All night long the old man reclined on his prickly couch, sipped his Scotch, and said, "Let me talk to the kid with marbles in his mouth. Yeah, Pat McCormick; put him back on." I had to listen until midnight to the details of the cotton cure.

12

THIS DIALOGUE was rather discouraging, but human intercourse is often one person's obstinate attempt to dominate another person, and one of the unfortunate facts about disfluency is that you never get to dominate. It's all very well and good to assert that communication comes down to a mad dogfight, but it's something else altogether to confess you're always the poor pup who loses. Another unfortunate fact about disfluency is that it prevents you from ever entirely losing self-consciousness when expressing such traditional and truly important emotions as love, hate, joy, and deep pain. Always first aware not of the naked feeling itself but of the best way to phrase the feeling so as to avoid verbal repetition, you come to think of emotions as belonging to other people, being the world's happy property but not yours—not really yours except by way of disingenuous circumlocution. It was precisely this failing, what might quite properly be termed the inability to love anything other than language, that preordained the irretrievable divorce between me and the first girl ever—at the bottom of a heated, heart-shaped swimming pool—to kiss me flush on the lips with feeling.

Audrey Robbins lived alone in the Haight at a time, 1969, when it was still very stylish for eighth-graders to be living alone in the Haight. She was thirteen, a waif, immensely sophisticated, beautiful beyond belief; had tortured ballet toes, Russian ancestors, and a leather purse; but the telling detail about her was that she liked nothing better than blowing Double Bubble at the same time she was inhaling Tareyton 100's. She was an amazing mixture of pink innocence and smoky extinction: one day, she was all light and dance and Communist bloc folklore; the next, she was all gloom and doom and standing with me on the Golden Gate Bridge, looking down.

It was she, of course, who made the first overture. I've never had the courage to want the world. I've always let it come to me, which is a rather negative approach to existence, but the funny thing is: inevitably, it comes. Sooner or later, whether you want it or not, the world comes to you, it comes at you, and in this case it came in the form of someone with a taste for the simultaneity of Tareytons and Double Bubble. She was head cheerleader of the Bayshore Bobbettes and, though she didn't know a jump shot from a running pick, she accepted the post—she told me later—not for the enormous prestige it heaped upon her person but because she was obsessed with the color and shape of my legs in the artificial light of the gymnasium in the afternoon.

All during basketball season, she'd cheer loudly when my name was announced, bring me sticks of grape licorice at half time, and jump up and down whenever I was shooting a free throw, which caused my free throw percentage to drop a few points, but I didn't care: she looked so happy, jumping up and down and screaming like that. Week after week of buying gum and cigarettes for her at Safeway, walking her to the bus station, talking on the telephone until midnight, but nothing was ever said, nothing was ever done. Then, two weeks after the eighth grade basketball season was over, in the extraordinary manner in which junior high school romance is carried out, I was handed a letter by Elaine, the assistant head cheerleader of the Bayshore Bobbettes and Audrey's nearest and dearest friend, which said:

Sweet Jeremy: March 27th (Tomorrow!) as I hope u already know is my birthday! I'm gunna be 14! You (of course!) are cordally invited. Pleez! Pleez! don't bring any presents. All I want u to bring is your ID (that's identificashun, dummy!) bracelet and if u don't have one you're rich enough to go get a nice new one! I hope u don't have to ask what the ID brace-let is for, but if u do you'll just have to wait until the party to find out! (Surly u can guess, you're so smart!) Also: I got a big! big! check from welfare tuesday, so I'm renting a motel room in the mountains of Marin that I heard about (special heart-shaped swimming pool) where we're all gunna swim and smoke and drink and lie out in the sun celibrating my 14th! Oh, also: Elaine's brother volluntiered to drive us all out there (he gets a free dip in the pool as pay-mint) so meet tomorrow at Elaine's house (u know where it is, doncha?) at 10 am, sharp. All u gotta bring is your ID bracelet, a beach towel, and some snazzy swim trunks!

XXXXX OOOOO
XXXXX OOOOO
Audrey

March twenty-seventh wasn't her fourteenth birthday, and she probably hadn't received a big! big! check from welfare so much as gotten hold of some very high-grade acid and sold it at triple profit. I honestly didn't know why she wanted me to bring an identification bracelet to the party, but I purchased a silver chain bracelet with my initials etched on the underside, a couple cartons of cigarettes, an entire bag of chewing gum, and a pair of red swimming trunks with a blue anchor at the crotch. I arrived bright and early the next morning at Elaine's house.

Other than Charles, whom I hadn't seen for a while, I didn't really have any friends, so I couldn't say Audrey ran with a different crowd than I did. They were certainly a switch, though, from the kind of people who showed up at Mother's coffee klatsches. Audrey's friends all seemed to have parents who were dead, diseased, or sadistic. They all seemed to have spent a night in jail or a month with Synanon. They all loved, absolutely loved, The Dead. There was a story called "The Dead," which at the time was completely incomprehensible to me but about which in my later, more discursive years I concluded: "When all of Gabriel's attempts to communicate at a nonverbal level—holiday ritual, music, sex—fail, he returns to overblown rhetoric: sheer language overwhelms, sound drowns out sense, and pathos lapses into bathos." Have I always had only words to play with? I thought The Dead were maybe an occult group that scavenged shallow graves, looking for dybbuks, since Audrey's friends liked to say that, at thirteen, they had lived and loved and now were ready to die. They'd gone out in the world and found it a waste, whereas I was still trying to build up the nerve to walk alone through North Beach.

This discrepancy between my innocence and their decadence made me a little uneasy, but they'd say, "That's what Audrey digs about you, man. You're one of the few uncorrupted cats left." I disliked being called a cat—I saw myself, instead, as an infinitely poignant cocker spaniel—and thought Audrey had selected me because she was obsessed with the color of my legs in the artificial light of the gymnasium in the afternoon. Lately I've been attempting to project an image of brooding, masculine depravity, but Gretchen always ends up saying, "Who are you trying to kid? You're so innocent. You're such a baby." I suppose Audrey was unusual only in being the first to perceive this fact.

None of these hesitations seemed to matter any more when I was sitting with twelve other people in the back of Elaine's brother's red pickup truck, smelling spilled beer, feeling Audrey's fingers crawl across the floor toward mine.

"I hope you brought the bracelet," Audrey said, rubbing her wrist.

I patted my shirt pocket and nodded.

The motel was something of a disappointment. It wasn't on the edge of a cliff overlooking the bay, as its brochure said it was, but on a dirt road with an unobstructed view of an abandoned filling station. The swimming pool was indeed heart-shaped, but was enclosed by a barbed-wire fence—no obscurity to this motel's symbolism—the gate to which had to be opened for you. The room Audrey had rented was a dusty, dark affair, with gold bedspreads, sliding doors that wouldn't slide, and Venetian blinds that blinded. A color TV hung from the ceiling like a dead turtle. Quite a few of Audrey's pals wanted to watch late morning cartoons as desperately as my Mission district playmates had, but, as the station announcer insisted on informing us every thirty seconds, we were experiencing difficulty with the audio portion of our program. "Cartoons without sound ain't shit," one of the partygoers observed and everyone agreed, so the television set was turned off.

Apparently, Audrey had told everyone not to bring presents but, if they really wanted to bring something, a carton of Tareytons and a six-pack of Double Bubble would be great! because everyone handed her exactly the same thing. Some people had brought bottles of liquor or water pipes for themselves. While they drank and sucked, Audrey blew smoke rings and popped gum bubbles. I sat at her side on the gold bedspread, reading Double Bubble comics. Someone asked the manager of the motel to unlock the gate to the heart-shaped pool. None of them wanted to swim. They just sat along the edge and watched me tread water. They were extremely impressed with how long I could keep bobbing up and down, but it's nothing, really. I've always been able to stay barely afloat forever. After a while, Audrey grew bored sitting in the sun and watching me swim. It was her party, so when she asked me to bring her the bracelet I jumped out of the pool and ran across the rocky parking lot to the room. When I returned, Audrey was leaning back in the lounge chair, and they were all gathered festively around her.

"Here it is," I said, handing it to her.

"Well?" she said.

" 'Well?' " I said.

"Well?" she said.

"Well, here," I said, taking the bracelet out of her hands and giving it to her again. "Happy Birthday."

"Won't you be so kind as to wrap it around my wrist, sweet Jeremy? For as of this moment you and me are goin' steady."

Most laughed. I thought maybe I'd been brought here as a comic example of pubescent sincerity or that Audrey was sexually slumming—going through initiation rites she'd outgrown when she was nine. But she, if not the rest of them, also seemed deadly serious. Her perfect blue eyes were aching with emotion, with a thirteen-year-old's thirst for romance. Maybe her mock-epic tone was for the amusement of her friends. I knelt down and clasped the chain around her wrist. I didn't know what it meant to be going steady, but I supposed it meant I couldn't see other girls, and I wasn't, so going steady seemed fine.

"It's beautiful. It's so silvery. I've never owned silver before. Never owned J.J.Z. before, either," Audrey said, digging her fingers into the carved initials, tugging on my trunks. "To celebrate, I'm gonna go slippin' down the slide, but I don't know how to swim real well, so you catch me when I hit water, okay?"

Everyone else stood off at a distance. I dove in, Audrey climbed the ladder. At the top, she stopped and spat the chewing gum out of her mouth, as if she were doing away with whatever was silly juvenilia. Her legs were spread, her arms were flapping, the straps to her suit were slipping off. She was lying when she said she couldn't swim. She could swim as well as or better than I could. She grabbed my hair, wrapped her legs around me, and pulled me under. The deep end was only six feet, so we went all the way to the bottom. Through air bubbles and chlorinated water, she kissed me. One always wonders what the first kiss will be like; suddenly one is in the midst of it and it doesn't seem to matter any more what it should or would or might be like. It is. What it is is something entirely different from familial good night and good morning kisses. It's a different thing altogether. The shaking of heads, the rubbing of bodies, the touching of tongues—all this seemed excellent enough. But what I really thought was too wonderful for words was that someone finally liked my mouth, someone finally liked me and was concentrating all her admiration on my mouth: on my trepidant lips. I came up for air first. Then, a second later, Audrey rose, looking for all the world like a mermaid in love.

13

IN THE WAY that all people in any deep passion attempt to separate themselves from their society, Audrey said goodbye to her group and, while I didn't bid farewell to my family, I temporarily stopped seeing them as the center of my universe. Audrey sent me ungrammatical love letters in geography class. I wrote poems (very free verse) to her during math. It was eighth-grade romance, spring passion, a flush feeling in the face.

Although Audrey was still smoking too much to be in very good athletic shape, she joined the girls' track team, principally, I think, to look at the color of my legs in the natural light of the playground in the afternoon. Soon enough she'd turned herself into a tough little sprinter and was running anchor leg for the girls' quarter-mile relay team. I ran the last hundred and ten yards for the boys' team. Sometimes the boys would race against the girls. I'd receive the baton a second or two before Audrey did, wait for her, run shoulder-to-shoulder for ninety yards, then let out a little kick at the end. It's always seemed to me that, if you're really fast and know in your own mind how fast you are, from time to time you'll let the other person win. I've never been that fast in anything. I've always had to prove how superior I was.

Once track practice was over, we'd run together around the playground until the last school bus came to take her home. The Bayshore track consisted of nothing more than a painted white circle describing the width of the asphalt field. We'd run round and round the circle, holding hands, me in baggy gray sweats and *de rigueur* Adidas, and Audrey in absurdly brief briefs, white tennis shoes with pink laces, a San Francisco Giants baseball cap, and sunglasses ("shades, man, to obstruct reality"). There is a particular feeling, when you are young and sweaty and exhausted, that gathers around dusk and macadam and has much to do with a delusion of immortality—with the pervasive sense that the world is dying but you are indestructible. There's no feeling the physical world produces which is quite so fine, but you're only supposed to get it when you're alone and, even then, only once or twice a year. I was getting the feeling every day: every afternoon, at dusk, on the paved track with Audrey.

She didn't say anything about cement or everlasting life, and at the time I wasn't one to ruin paradise by conversing about it. "Running like this, with you, sweet Jeremy, it almost makes me want to quit smoking," Audrey said. The pavement was starting to give her shin splints, though. One Saturday morning she called and said we were going running in Muir Woods. Muir Woods was like the High Sierras in that just its name sent shivers down my spine: it was formally framed and therefore, to me beautiful. We took a bus across the bay, then hitchhiked through the mountains to the forest. While other people were taking guided tours of the trees, looking at labels in Latin, feeding chocolate bars to chipmunks, counting year-rings and exclaiming, Audrey and I ran deeper and deeper, higher and higher into the woods, back where the trail narrowed, vegetation rioted, and big trees were kings.

Audrey had brought a backpack of snacks. When we'd run far enough that we could no longer hear the troops below, we stopped and she spread a table cloth across a patch of pebbles and crabgrass, offering apples, processed cheese, Ritz crackers, and a bottle of Ripple. The entire gesture—the white tablecloth, the prepared lunch, the Saturday morning excursion to a local landmark—was so uncharacteristically and hopefully domestic of her that I passed into a state of such profound happiness nothing could perturb me. I lay back, looking at timber, tiny bugs, and bluebirds, with cheese and crackers in my mouth and Audrey's head in my lap.

That head, into which so few thoughts entered, was, in such an idyllic setting, receiving more data than it knew what to do with, and Audrey finally blurted out: "Damn! Sometimes, you know, I wish I had parents. Some people seem like they have parents. Other people seem like they don't. You do."

"Do what?" I said. I was studying a tree twig and didn't want to talk.

"You heard me. Have parents. You seem like you have parents."

"Yes," I said. "I have parents."

"Don't play dumb, Jeremy. I'm talking seriously for once. Sometimes I wish I hadn't grown up—if that's what you want to call it—in an orphanage. Sometimes I get tired of filling out forms and telling people I live with my aunt. Sometimes I wish I had a home to, you know, go home to."

I couldn't believe anyone was so innocent she actually believed that houses were great hearths of banked fires, that families were healthy groups offering comfort and reassurance. I pulled her hair back, kissed her somewhat awkwardly on the nape of the neck, and said, "You can always come home to me."

It was a sentimental thing to say. It was meant as nothing more than metaphorical consolation. But maybe she never had anyone tell her that before. Tears came to her eyes and she fairly attacked me with kisses. She kept saying she loved me and banging my head against the ground. I couldn't tell whether she was hysterical or just very happy. I thought it best, in either case, to let her do what she wanted to do and not interfere. She seemed to have been through all the motions before, while I had no idea exactly what my responsibilities were. She licked my ears, unbuttoned my shirt, tugged at my trousers, and I just lay there. I wasn't only afraid of serious arousal. I was incapable of it. I don't know about other boys at twelve-and-a-half, but I was still prepubescent. I was perfectly content to run and clasp hands and kiss on the lips.

Audrey, bored, rolled off me, took solace in a Ritz cracker, and said, "What's the problem?"

"Nothing."

"Then why did you stop?"

"Stop?"

"Don't you want to go all the way, man?"

"No," I said. "No, Audrey, not here, not yet. Maybe soon. Indoors, somewhere, at night, in a week or two. Do you mind?"

She waited three long weeks for me to grow up, during which

time I consulted numerous anatomy texts and even visited an East
Bay medicine man who, in a *Berkeley Barb* classified advertisement, promised Organ Increase. At the end of three weeks was the
eighth-grade graduation dance. It was tradition for couples who had
yet to sacramentalize their unity to do so on mattresses along the
side of a hill that overlooked the gymnasium. Audrey wasn't waiting
any longer.

She came dressed in a black evening gown she'd borrowed from
Elaine; stockings, which I'd never seen her wear before; and high
heels, in which she was slightly taller than I was. With my hair
combed across my forehead and my shirttail flapping, I must have
looked like her younger brother or eldest son. Everyone, absolutely
everyone including my basketball coach, invited Audrey to dance,
but that night she had eyes only for me and said no to every last
one of them. We danced every dance—the fast ones, at which she
said I looked like a skittering jackrabbit, as well as the slow ones,
during which I smelled the miscegenation of the sweat on her back
with the perfume behind her ears. Whenever the jukebox broke
down, I'd buy plastic cups of orangeade and we'd go kiss in dark
corners.

As the dance progressed, there were fewer and fewer people in
the gym and almost no couples. Audrey's hints that we ought to
take a walk in the dark or get a breath of fresh air became increasingly persistent and obvious. I finally agreed to leave. Walking along
the base of that hill was like coming into a war zone: hearing bodies
collide, great screams of pain and expectation. It terrified me. When
Audrey took my hand and suggested we—as it was called—climb
the mountain, I panicked and ran. At night it always seems like
you're running faster than you ever have in the daytime, and I felt
like I was flying. I ran all the way home. I didn't look back once.

I dreamed about international hand-to-hand combat and the next
morning got what was coming to me—a letter from Audrey, delivered by Elaine with knowing condescension.

Jeremy: I am writing this lettter at three oc'lock in the morning in my dingey little apartmint the lectricity the gas the heat

none of them paid for and none of them probably ever will. Goddam you, anyways! I have given you 4 hole months of my life, and what do I get out of it, a lousy crushed Dixie cup of orangeaid! Why did you run away from the hill like a scittering jackrabbit? Scared, huh? Afraid? Mama told you not to? Well, I've had enough of Little Boy Blue and his goody-goodiness all the time. I just can't take it any more. Inclose pleez find your ID bracelet (slitely scrached a bit on the back— sorry!—twenny minutes ago got mad and took my penknife to it!) Maybe we can still be friends kinda like Elaine and Rob, and I know I'll always value your advice on things, and your buying me all that gum and cigarettes (musta cost you a fortune!) and the nice way you talk and all the running we did together waiting for my bus to come and my birthday party at the motel (First kiss is always best!) and, most especilly, sweet Jeremy, your legs in the gym's flooresent lights right around quarter a four in the afternoon. But I'm sorry! All the lovey-dovey handholding and kissing is fine for awhile, but finilly I want someone who's willing to climb the mountain with me at least once in awhile, doncha know? I'm sorry, Jeremy, you just aren't giving me enough action. I need someone a little older or at least a little more experienced. It was just too embearassing to be alone at midnight at the bottom of the hill at the graduation dance. Maybe like I say we can still be friends, and I do still love you but only like friends.

Luv:

Audrey

P.S. Maybe we can do some running together this summer!

Yes, maybe we could still be friends. Maybe we could do some running together this summer. Maybe the Golden Gate Bridge would collapse. It was eleven o'clock ("oc'lock": I loved that) on a Saturday morning in May. I sat in a chair in the living room and read the letter six or seven more times, to savor all the misspellings but also to make sure I hadn't misinterpreted its overall message, then staggered down the stairs to my bedroom, where I drew the curtains, killed the lights, took out a black-and-white photograph of Audrey, crawled under the covers, and made my first prolonged attempt at self-abuse. It took nearly forever. Twenty minutes later I was still squirming on the sheets, holding the snapshot in one hand and my barely increased organ in the other, shaking the latter like a pen that wouldn't work. I created blood blisters around the rim, producing fluid that was neither as yellow as urine nor as white as semen, and I finally quit when I'd reached not so much orgasm as utter anguish.

We've all heard that the essence of eros is its incommunicability. The terror that lives at the heart of love is silence, etc. We've all heard that a hundred times and I daresay we've all heard wrong. What's valuable about love is that you at last get to talk to someone. You at last get to be heard and the words hardly matter any more, only the reassurance of their sound—unless, of course, you've run away from the mountain of mattresses or talk with a catch.

''HERE'S THE CHURCH that will wake me up Sunday morning at eight,'' Audrey wrote in her minute script on a postcard she sent last summer from Port Townsend,

and, if I linger, at ten. The only time I ever hear the bells is while I'm in bed, trying to sleep. I've probably seen half a dozen weddings. Somehow, maybe because everyone looks so small, these scenes (caught from the upstairs window) seem like movies. I'm always imagining ex-husbands, kids from previous marriages. No one is young, no one wears white that I remember. My favorite groom was a fat man in his fifties. The young ones must marry in a bigger church, not this tiny one on a side street. They must look bigger, even from a distance. I don't think I'd be as impressed. I have also become a fan of the ferries across the sound to Victoria and San Juan Island. It doesn't matter much where so long as I can sit on the deck reading my latest detective novel. It's very late at night and I bet the ten o'clock bells will ring for me tomorrow.

In seven years she'd moved seven hundred miles north and learned how to spell "o'clock."

Nothing ever changes for anybody.

The love that lasts the longest is the love that is never returned.

14

MOTHER WAS HAPPY my junior high school education had come to an inglorious end. She thought my two years at Bayshore had been a disaster: playing basketball with drug addicts, going steady with an orphan girl. Mother was quite disappointed in the public school system for which she was working and decided to give me another go at private education. Beth entered her first year at Stanford—she contemplated the first double major ever in set design and the English revolution—and the hope was that with four years of rigorous secondary school instruction I might still be permitted to migrate south to Palo Alto.

The joke one heard about the Jack London Memorial Preparatory Academy in the Arts and Sciences was that if the Chinese New Year and Jewish New Year were ever on the same day the school would shut down. Most of the students in the sciences division were Asian and punched the buttons on their calculators during recess. Most of the students in the arts division were Jewish and disliked the Asians for not being political enough. I drifted toward the arts division and Father thought that, surrounded by "my people," I might stop mumbling. Guess again, Father. London was fanatical about sending its students to the best colleges in the country, which meant London was the only high school in the city that had an art gallery, an air-conditioned theater, or an aquarium of tropical fish, but which also meant, if you weren't producing, they pounced on you. I wasn't in school three weeks before Loud Blazer, instructor of Psychoanalysis and Literature, came up to me in the hallway and said, "You're Jeremy Zorn, aren't you, Beth's brother?"

"Yes."

"Has there been some trauma in your family recently?"

"No. Why?"

"Are you upset about the onslaught of adolescence?"

"Excuse me?"

"Are you uncomfortable, coming from the poverty of Bayshore to the luxury of London?"

"Not really, no. Why are you asking me all these questions, sir?"

"Not one, not two, but three of your teachers, Mr. Zorn, have recommended that you receive speech therapy or, at the very least, undergo comprehensive diagnostic verbal examination. Mrs. Sherfey is one of the very best adolescent speech therapists in San Francisco. That is, she herself isn't an adolescent—she must be in her early thirties by now—but she's a top-notch expert at ridding adolescents of their speech problems. Why don't you go see her? I wouldn't mind spending an hour a week with her, myself. Heh-heh. She's one of the prettiest little things to occupy a counselor's office in years."

I hadn't seen a speech therapist since I fled Mrs. Fletcher eight years before and wasn't all that eager to start up again with metronomes on the table and buttons on the tongue. I'd temporarily resigned myself to the fact of stuttering and was more interested in casting about for all-encompassing compensations than trying one more remedy, but Loud Blazer insisted I see her at least this once, to the point of dragging me into her office by the collar when I attempted to postpone the appointment. Heh-heh, indeed. She was a pretty little thing, though not especially my type: high cheekbones, long blond hair bound in a bonnet, glassy eyes, alabaster skin, silver earrings, much makeup, a lot of fall colors in her wardrobe. A little too cherubic to be truly inspiring. Most speech therapists must order their rooms from the same catalogue because, just like Mrs. Fletcher, she had a flag on the wall, a tape recorder and metronome on a Formica table, a desk for her, and a chair for me. The idea, I learned later, was to create a "verbal surround," as if language might be disassociated from existence.

The only difference between Mrs. Fletcher's room and Mrs. Sherfey's room was that Mrs. Sherfey had tacked up a number of optimistic posters on the walls, and this made perfect sense, for not only were these extremely popular at London—thought to be high motivational forces—but Mrs. Sherfey was an insufferable optimist herself. There was a poster of a seagull in the sky, with a quotation from Langston Hughes to the effect that a dreamless life was a wingless bird; a gaudy color one of a peacock fanning Emily Dickinson's observation, 'Hope' is the thing with feathers; Beth's poster of the Sierras, with the same inscription; an unillustrated one consisting of Camus's request that humanity walk neither ahead of nor behind but, rather, beside him and be his friend; and a picture of a burning sun, underneath which was written, Each day comes another dawn—E. K. Lorrenson, whom I'd never heard of but whom I assumed had it on excellent testimony that tomorrow the sun, having no alternative, would rise with a handful of fire. Going into that room was less like reporting to a counselor's office than entering an estuary. My first impulse was to shield my face from the meridian sun and descending seagull, but I simply shut the door and shook her hand.

"I didn't think you'd be quite so short," she said.

I thought maybe studies had shown that all stutterers were short—no palliation for the little people—but that Mrs. Sherfey hadn't thought I'd be quite so short. I was fourteen years old, five foot four, and I had a mad moment's hope that was what she meant, since Mother was five foot eight and Father was five foot eleven. Sooner or later I'd simply outgrow this midgets' disease. Attempting to enunciate every word clearly and cleanly, I asked, "What . . . exactly . . . do . . . you . . . mean . . . by . . . that . . . Mrs. . . . Sherfey?"

She swiveled around in her chair for a while, then said, "My husband is Brad Sherfey. You know, the Brad Sherfey, All-Pac-Eight forward for the University of Washington Huskies, 'fifty-nine and 'sixty. He still follows all the games in the 'Sporting Green,' even the junior high school leagues. Rick's something of a fan of yours. He told me that, whatever I do, I'm not to tamper with your set shot. I'm surprised a star basketball player is so short, that's all."

I recognized this as the most ancient of all therapeutic ploys—

give the poor kid *something* to take pride in—but it still worked. I blushed and smiled and shook my head and tried to act like an athlete. She proved to be surprisingly knowledgeable about the game, and for the next half hour we talked about how it doesn't matter if a guard is short if he knows how to protect the ball; what a shame it was her husband, after being a third-round draft pick of the Los Angeles Lakers, broke his back the first week of the season; how embarrassing and absurd it was that London had a girls' field hockey team but no boys' basketball squad; how *A Sense of Where You Are* was good but *The Last Loud Roar* was probably even better.

Then she had to turn on the tape recorder, hand me a mimeographed interoffice memorandum, and say, "You've been speaking really well, Jeremy, only a few minor disfluencies here and there. Let me hear you read for a while."

"Oh, I read fine," I said and wasn't being intentionally insincere. I remembered giving the integration speech at Currier and reading aloud in my bedroom. The Bozo the Clown fiasco was too long ago to recollect. I saw myself as a relatively articulate reader.

"That's funny," she said and started rummaging around in her desk drawer for some study or other. "Almost all stutterers have at least a little trouble when it comes to oral reading." She couldn't find the monograph that proved it.

I, on the other hand, disliked the label. It sounded like *atheist* or *heretic* or *cat burglar*. Stutterer, life sentence, with no chance for parole. Nor was I pleased with her sudden and complete redefinition of me from admired, if short, basketball star to terminal titubant.

"I don't see myself exactly as a stutterer," I said. "It's more just a case of getting nervous in certain situations. When I feel comfortable, I never have any trouble talking."

This wasn't true, but I felt pressed.

"Well, you feel comfortable with me, I hope. Why don't you read aloud that memo? We'll record it, play it back, and you tell me what you think."

Her remarks had a prophecy of doom about them, but I sat back in the chair, attempted to derive some omnipotent peace from the white seagull against an empty blue sky, and began to read. The memo was from all the principals, deans, vice principals, and assistant principals to all the guidance counselors, psychologists, nurses, and therapists. The gist of it was that students should be urged to transcend (via arduous scholarship) rather than dwell morosely upon (via paralytic self-absorption) their emotional problems. The finer points of the communiqué I really didn't follow, since I was paying more attention to form than content.

At the time, my particular plague spot happened to be words beginning with vowels. This text, for one reason or another, was riddled with them. I kept opening my mouth and uttering air bubbles, half-human pops of empty repetition. She didn't have to play it back for me to know it had been the very embodiment of babble, but she did, and then, raising her right eyebrow, asked, "Well?"

I explained that the whirring of the tape recorder and her ostentatious tallying of my errata had made me nervous. The proof I wasn't just one more stutterer was that I could whisper.

"But, Jeremy," she said, opening her drawer to find another study to support her new point. "That's one of the hallmarks of stutterers: exaggerated enjoyment of whispering." She couldn't find the folder in which there was a graph affirming this fact.

I seized upon her inability to come up with any conclusive evidence and, pounding my hand on her desk, said, "That's not true. You're lying. I know you are. You're just saying that. Stutterers cannot whisper. I know they can't."

"Please take your hands off the papers on my desk, Jeremy, and, yes, they can. Virtually all stutterers can whisper and take enormous pride in their whispering. You're a stutterer. I want you to admit that fact. It's an important step on the road to recovery. Once you acknowledge the abnormality, we can get to work on correcting it. I want to help you. When you're a professional basketball player, I don't want to see you giving hesitant interviews at half time."

The flattery tactic didn't work this time, not least because she was wrong: the athletic aesthetic is always to assert that the ecstasies experienced by the body are beyond the reach of words. Interviewed warriors answer every question with the proper platitude, like Zulu tribesmen retaining possession of their souls by refusing to be photographed. I'd regularly distinguished myself from the common run of repeaters by the fact that I could whisper and now, informed I was one among ten million, I was enraged—at what or whom I didn't quite know, but enraged.

I stood and said, "I don't want your happy posters or your happy smiles or your happy basketball chitchat. I don't want to be happy. I want to be u-u-unusual." Then I did something I thought was very unusual. I tore down a poster—I think it was the one with the colorful peacock—and ran out of the room.

IT RAINED a lot that fall in San Francisco and I spent most of my time sitting on one particular bench in the courtyard, wondering about the effect of rainwater on metal railing, since all my classes consisted of Socratic dialogue and I disliked playing Plato's part. When I did attend class I'd sit in back, pretending not to hear when called upon and, when pressed to respond, would produce an answer that I knew was incorrect but was the only word I could say. I studied with extreme devotion the dictionary and thesaurus in the hope I could possess a vocabulary of such immense range that, for every word, I'd know half a dozen synonyms and thus always be able to substitute an easy word for an unspeakable one. My sentences became so saturated with approximate verbal equivalents that what I thought often bore almost no relation to what I actually said.

One day I was asked whether the origin of the American Revolution was essentially economic or philosophical. I wanted to say, as Mother and Father always said, that revolution arises from an unfair distribution of wealth, but instead I replied: "The Whigs had a multiplicity of fomentations, ultimate or at least penultimate of which would have to be their predilection to be utterly discrete from colonial intervention, especially on numismatical pabulae." The teacher roared; the class shrieked; within hours I was begging

Mrs. Sherfey to take me back, which she did, with open arms and the promise of eloquence.

Still, I hated walking across the London campus with Mrs. Sherfey. Everyone knew who she was; they, unlike I, thought she was sexy, and it defined me ineradicably as a boy castrated by his own tongue. Although they'd heard me falter in class, I hated them seeing my attempted recovery. I hated having to listen to Mrs. Sherfey's earnest benevolence with a hundred eyes on us as we circled the swimming pool. She, of course, knew this and as often as possible escorted me the long way round the courtyard on some fool's errand to the science wing. It was, she felt, for reasons that have remained obscure to me, integral to even the possibility of improvement. En route to the science wing she'd curl her arm inside mine as if we were lollygagging through Lincoln Park.

She changed all my courses, enrolling me in Public Speaking, Spanish Conversation in place of Mexican Folktales, and a special section of English Literature in which the *modus operandi* was for students to stand in front of the room, recite poems, and explicate them. I was a poor public speaker, but when I did an imitation of Mayor Alioto I finally relaxed and the class applauded its approval. I dreaded Spanish conversation because I didn't have the resources of an extended vocabulary I had in English. "Cerca" was "c-c-cerca." It couldn't be "quite proximate to where I'm now standing." When I adopted a mock-elegant Castilian accent, however, I spoke perfectly. Modern poetry seemed a little too laconic, but I recited iambic pentameter as if I were Sir Philip Sidney at a court masque. A principle of linguistic redemption emerged: distance converted to clarity.

Mrs. Sherfey was determined to press this phenomenon into habitual glibness. The drama department was doing *Othello* for its winter performance—a torrid play for a cold season—and Mrs. Sherfey thought I'd derive such confidence from speaking a few poetical lines to a packed house that I'd stop stuttering forever. When I didn't meet her at the first night of tryouts, as I was supposed to do, she drove to my house, knocked on the door, and said, "Let's go, Iago." Mother was so sympathetic to other women who were completely wrapped up in their work that she nearly hugged Mrs. Sherfey into submission and Father joked—like Loud Blazer—heh, heh, wasn't I a little too young to be going out with someone so beautiful?

Mrs. Sherfey was right. I did want to play Iago. It seemed to me his play moor than it was Othello's. His rhetoric created every event of the play, he stood alone at the end of each of the first two acts and thought about turning people into pawns. I loved his innate sense of transverse alliteration: his "prattle, without practice"; his "night and negligence," a truly gorgeous phrase; his "How poor are they that have not patience! What wound did ever heal but by degrees?" I gave what I thought was a fairly good reading of Iago's "Put money in thy purse" speech, but the general consensus was that Iago should exude a little more malicious energy than I appeared to possess, so I was given the role of the Sailor.

Nearly everyone who reads the play, or sees it performed, fails to find the least significance in the Sailor. It's true he appears in only one scene and is in and out in a flash; true, too, he has only one line, but what a line he delivers! What meaning he compresses into so few words! First, "within"—offstage—he says, "What ho! What ho! What ho!" At first glance, these lines look simple enough. They appear to be nothing more than the Sailor's rather rude way of entering. But in his triple reiteration of "ho!" is he not in fact preparing the audience for Othello's much later, and more universally appreciated only because so much more transparent, treble repetition of "Oh!" in "O Desdemona! Desdemona! Dead!/Oh! Oh! Oh!"? I think he is.

The Officer acknowledges the clear importance of the Sailor by saying, "A messenger from the galleys." Perhaps a pun is intended here on "galleys" in the sense of "printers' proofs"; the Sailor is a messenger of language itself, a nautical representative of poetry. The Duke further surrounds the Sailor in mystery by asking, "Now, what's the business?" and then the Sailor comes straight out with it: "The Turkish preparation makes for Rhodes./So was I bid report here to the state/By Signior Angelo." One hardly knows where to begin the elucidation of this line. Doesn't "The Turkish preparation makes for Rhodes" hint at the entire movement of the play, the descent from Venetian city streets to Cyprus goats and monkeys, and isn't the leitmotif of *Othello*—the schism between the desires of the individual and the demands of civilization—caught in the Sailor's winning phrase, "So was I bid report here to the state by Signior Angelo"? Doesn't "report" register the impossibility of marrying spoken words to perceived realities that is so fundamental to the drama? Isn't that impossibility further underscored by the Messenger's immediate contradiction of the Sailor's dispatch, with the news that the Turks are sailing for Cyprus and only gathering guns at Rhodes? Why give a man only one line in a play and make that line a lie? Why give that part to someone who was a little weary of speaking only a few words and all of them wrong? Why?

For a good month I lived with these lines. I knew everything there was to know about them. I knew that my offstage line took two and one-quarter seconds to say, and my onstage line exactly twice that long. I knew that "What ho!" rhymed with "Signior Angelo," as if all twenty-four words I spoke were meant to form a neat little poem. "What ho!" became my all-purpose exclamation to express surprise, perplexity, encouragement, happiness, grief, and to the lit mirror in the bathroom, to Bruin in her basket, to the metal railing at London, I bellowed: "The Turkish preparation makes for Rhodes./So was I bid report here to the state/By Signior Angelo."

I practiced my lines so much on my own because I hardly ever got to say them at rehearsal. Whenever we worked on my scene—I.iii—Desdemona always got to gasp that she wasn't about to spend her wedding night away from her black hulk, and Othello always got to run through his tedious explanation of how he seduced Desdemona by telling her war stories. The director's only concern was that I not foul up the blocking: that I come to center stage for a second, then quickly retreat into a corner and pretend to chat with the attendants.

She was very severe and capable of being cruel to her actors but such an outstanding director that Berkeley kept inviting her to join its theater arts department. She never left London, at least while I was there, since she had total freedom and an unlimited budget, and her name was certainly still on the stage door when I went wandering around my alma mater just recently over Christmas break. Her sole responsibility was to produce three spectacular performances a year, and she had two favorite sayings. "Shakespeare occupied a wholly verbal universe." My kinda guy. And "D is L." Drama is Life, which didn't mean life was an extremely theatrical affair, but the obverse, really; the only thing which mattered was whatever play she was doing at the time. I didn't believe that and I didn't like the people in the cast who did. In fact, I didn't like any of the people in the cast. They were older than I was, more sophisticated, and prettier. They seemed to me some nightmare union of Audrey's and Beth's friends: very intelligent, but disdainful of anything even vaguely sincere and quite fond of saying reality was for people who couldn't handle LSD.

I hadn't tried LSD, but at the time I was still determined to embrace the physical world on its own limited terms and resented anyone who had already rejected it. Opening night, they were all terribly relaxed. I suppose they'd been through the crucible before and it no longer fazed them. Charles and his parents had come up from Los Angeles to see the performance; Beth was home on Christmas vacation from Palo Alto, where she'd pretty much turned the history department upside down with her monograph on the eschatology of the Puritan radicals during the English revolution; Mrs. Sherfey and Mr. Basketball were going to be there; and I was trembling like a boy riveted to the third rail.

Although the show didn't start until eight-fifteen, I arrived at the theater at quarter of six and started putting on my makeup and sailor suit, which consisted of a white hat, a blue and white shirt, white bell-bottoms, and a gold sword at the waist. No one else had arrived yet, so I marched around the dressing room, repeating my lines to the cold mirrors and empty costumes. By seven everyone was ready. At eight the director stood on the top step of a ladder and gave a more inspiring pep talk than I'd ever heard from an athletic coach. It ended with everyone gathering at the bottom of the ladder and chanting, "D is L! D is L! D is L!"

I watched the first two scenes from the wings. Desdemona was standing next to me and kept saying, "This fucking dress is too tight." I tried to ignore her and do nothing but say my lines over and over, softly to myself. Iago tricked Roderigo, Iago tricked Othello, then the stage was set for I.iii. The Duke, Venetian Senators and Officers, and their attendants entered stage right and sat down at a table in their council chamber, which was on a special platform to suggest, when Othello and Desdemona came panting in, the difference between law and love, and lit by torches because it was the middle of the night and the Senators wanted to talk about Turks. I wouldn't have missed my cue for the world, but when she heard the Duke say, "The main article I do approve/In fearful sense," Desdemona gave me a little shove and, still offstage, I yelled, "What ho! What ho! What ho!" This ejaculation went off without a hitch, very loud and seafaring; I was thrilled that I was already halfway through.

Then I came to center stage. The only experience I can compare it to was seeing the inside of Dodger Stadium for the first time when I was four and crying with joy at how green the grass was, how silver the fences, how enormous the arena. It wasn't exactly joy I felt upon entering the stage and I certainly didn't cry, but I was overwhelmed by the beauty of the balcony. Although I couldn't spot the ten people whose orchestra seats I'd reserved, I knew they were out there and I wanted to win their approval, their admiration.

"A messenger from the galleys," the Officer said.

"Now," the Duke asked, "what's the business?"

I stepped into the spotlight and spoke my line perfectly, until the last word. The "A" of "Angelo" suddenly stood like a capitalized mountain barring entrance to the rest of the word, so I replaced "Angelo" with "Gratiano," a Venetian bureaucrat who appears later on. A minor alteration, and who'd notice? I wasn't proud of myself for evading the sound, but at least I'd survived.

"How say you by this change?" the Duke asked.

Which was his proper line and meant to convey nothing more than his surprise that the Turks were heading for Rhodes instead of Cyprus, but, in my agitated state, I thought he was asking why I'd substituted Signior Gratiano for Signior Angelo. I was so angry at him for pointing out my error to a thousand people that I drew my sword.

"This cannot be,/By no assay of reason," the First Senator said, and then I was sure we were outside the drama. I pointed my sword at him, too, and told all the attendants to stand back. The lights went out. The curtain came down. Iago, who wasn't supposed to be in this scene until three hundred lines later, ran onstage and, with all the malicious energy he was supposed to possess, disarmed me and carried me into the dressing room.

Ten seconds later the lights returned, the curtain rose, and the Messenger was already launched on his windy speech that contradicted and supplanted mine. Opening night survived my little blunder. The rest of the play went smooth as silk. Everyone except Cassio—and who really cares about Cassio?—died. Afterward, Othello and Desdemona went off to swallow LSD. Mother tried to cheer me up by saying she took my scuffle with the Duke as a new and valid interpretation of the Senate scene and, anyway, it was important always to experiment with classical drama. They got the Clown to say my lines at the rest of the performances.

15

COULD MY ONE bright night under the hot lights have altered the genetic structure of my sebaceous glands? I thought the first impression the benevolent and beautiful girl who had yet to discover my charms would have was that I had ugly abscesses on my face and the second impression she would have was that my tongue was tied in a knot. As we exist in appearance by our face and in reality by our voice and on both counts I was a little too conspicuously marred, there wouldn't be a third impression. Father predicted the pustules would disappear if I stopped eating so much chocolate and worrying so much about getting good grades, and

Mother tended to favor the more general plague-of-growing-up theory, whereas the origin of the problem lay, as with all real problems and all real origins, in family history.

Mother still had pockmarks on her cheeks as evidence of a diseased childhood, with patches of pink skin on her nose acquired in more than one surgery to remove the skin cancer that was her reward for believing, as a teenager, too many doctors' X-ray radiation cures. In a faded photograph of her brother wearing khaki in Okinawa, his face appeared to be on fire. A doctor at Stanford Hospital told Beth he was the most decorated dermatologist in the Bay Area and there wasn't a thing he could do to improve the quality of her skin until she was at least twenty-six. Only Father's face was beautifully clear, though whenever he cut himself shaving or the impress of his glasses left a red mark at the eyebrows Mother would claim that he, too, had a horrible background. They used to have perfectly absurd arguments over who was responsible for the cluster forming on my chin.

It wasn't only in the cleft of my chin that the rash erupted. It flourished on my forehead and scalp and behind my ears. It made a mockery of my cheeks and troughs of my temples. It burned my neck, appeared sporadically on my foreskin—no neonatal rite performed on this half-Jew—visited my stomach and all up and down my back and buttocks. It was like an unwilling monotonous tattoo, plus variety of type. There were whiteheads on the nose, blackheads on toes, dense purple collections that finally burst with blood, white circles that vanished in a squeeze, dilating welts that never went away, infected wounds that cut to the bone, surface scars that looked hideous, wartlike protuberances at the side of the head. In just the last year I've endured collagen injections, punch grafts, and chemical peels. This is what living in L.A. does to one, or such is the depth of my endless, hateful redefinition.

Millions of times Father, exasperated, said, "Jeremy, will you please stop picking at yourself?" Sometimes he'd get impatient and slap my face—as if he were both reprimanding me for squeezing scabs at the dinner table and expressing compassion by striking the source of all the distress—but he was certainly justified in whatever frustration he felt. My hands were always crawling across my skin, always probing and plucking, then flicking away the root canker. The inflammatory disease bred a weird narcissism in which I craved the mirror but averted any accurate reflection. Isn't that what narcissism is, vanity skewed by huge self-doubt? I retired to the boys' bathroom at London every chance I got but I'd retreat from the mirror until my face looked fine: just a little red and slightly swollen. I'd gaze at myself in night-lit windows, brood upon the image coming up out of the coffee at breakfast. I became expert at predicting which kinds of mirrors, both in the house and in the oppressive world outside, would soften the effect, and which—it hardly seemed possible—would make things worse.

I started washing with oval brown bars and transparent green squares, soft baby soaps that sudsed, and rough soaps that burned. I applied special gels, clear white liquids, mud creams. I took tablets once, twice, thrice a day; before, after, and during meals. I went on milk diets and no-milk diets, absorbed no sun and too much sun. I believed in erythromycin, tretinoin, Cleocin, Panoxyl, Dioxyl, Benoxyl, isopropyl myristrate, polyoxyl stearate, silicate, collodial magnesium, polyoxythylene, butylated hydroxytotuluence, hydroxpropyl-methylcellulose. I saw doctors and doctors and doctors.

A doctor in Chinatown who had been recommended by a friend of Mother's promised three acupuncture treatments would purify me of all imperfections but resigned himself to using more conventional methods when Mother said no, absolutely not, no acupuncture. The first time I visited him he bowed and said, "So sorry. Face is full of uglies."

He bowed and said, "Mrs. Mandel, a most beautiful lady! A lump on her lip: one puncture; no more lump. But on phone your Ma say no punctures for you. Therefore, I provide scientific American method. Please come in."

He wore a Mao cap, a gray waistcoat, and slippers. The waiting room had bamboo mats on the floor and black-and-white photographs of Peking, circa 1947, on the wall, but his office was thoroughly modern. He had me lie down on a steel table and immediately started squirting liquid nitrogen into my open wounds.

"Freezes face until handsome," he said with one of the deepest and most reassuring laughs I'd heard in my life. I loved the feeling of dry ice on my skin, the sensation of being only cold. Then he locked me in a closet that had a glass window, placed black goggles over my eyes, and shot ultraviolet rays at my head.

"Your Ma much afraid of radiation. She say not to use. She have bad experience with quack Americans. They not know how to moderate. I have know-how," he explained.

He dipped my face in a solution of hot water and curious chemicals, pressed a pimple popper to what he called "the spot troubles," and wiped away the blood with rubbing alcohol. While I was leaving, he handed me an immense plastic bag of sample panaceas and said, "Try all of these. Come back next week and please to tell me which works. Also, go to beach a lot to get sun on face and chase tan girls."

All winter of my sophomore year I went to Dr. Huang to absorb his liquid nitrogen and radiation and hear his words of encouragement. He said I was showing remarkable progress, but I didn't see any improvement. He said my advance would be more dramatic if, as he had instructed, I rubbed salt water into my skin and received the reflection of the sun off the ocean. He probably hadn't been to the beach in ten years; the bay was always overcast and the ocean was replete not so much with restorative salt water as repulsive kelp.

May fourteenth—Mother's Day, 1972—broke clear without early morning fog. Since Beth was still immersed in reading period in Palo Alto, Father was competing in a Class C tennis tournament for men sixty years old and over at the Pool and Racquet Club, and I'd forgotten to get her a gift, I offered Mother the pleasure of my company during a day on the coast. I gathered all my unguents into one bag like a vacationing egoist committed to the perfect tan, the difference being that the sun god is bent on elaborating beauty until it becomes bronze, whereas I wanted only to look acceptable, to appear normal. Two years later I airbrushed my yearbook picture into virtual unrecognizability, and four years after that my second idea for this project—a family album with photographs—dissolved in my inability to use any pictures that didn't flatter myself and my subsequent realization that the flattering pictures ended shortly after catastrophic consciousness began—say, when I was twelve. Mother suggested we make a real excursion of it and drive to San Gregorio, the beach where, via a rough voice on the radio, I received the first intimation that San Francisco was going to be a sympathetic paradise no more than Los Angeles had been. For some strange reason I've always rather enjoyed returning to places of crisis, so we went. It was the weekend and warm: the freeway leading out of the city was as clogged as I'd ever seen it, but when Mother was in a good mood the world disappeared and all was well.

She opened the sun roof. She kept rewinding and whistling to an extremely happy tape of Prokofiev which, although she found the Russian composers in general a trifle florid, was her favorite piece of symphonic music. In the back seat she had a picnic basket and a binder containing the rough draft of a book on mental illness she was ghostwriting for an illiterate Beverly Hills psychiatrist. Mother couldn't wait to bury her toes in the sand and start getting all scientific about the dark night of the soul.

San Gregorio was even worse than I'd remembered. It was difficult to get from the cliffs to the beach; I had to carry the picnic basket, the rough draft on mental illness, and my bag of lotions, then catch Mother when she slid down on her butt. And once you got there you didn't necessarily want to be there. Sand dunes stood at one end of the shore like extremely obvious emblems of human destiny and despair and, beyond them, caught on the rocks, loomed a blank lighthouse. Packs of seagulls pounced upon every scrap of food, every minuscule fish that dared to surface. The sea, the sand, the sky, everything was gray.

Four men banged plastic golf balls against the crags and another dug dirt with a metal detector. A woman sold wilting roses and postcards of the Pacific Ocean. Babies in cribs, boxes of Kentucky Fried Chicken on woolen blankets, adolescent lovers searching for each other in the surf, the smells of beer and pop and pot—Mother and I walked through and away from all this to the empty end of the beach, where the tide came up a little higher and the shore was somewhat rockier, but we had our own cove and that was what we wanted.

Mother was starting to get a feel for the errata of the rough draft, every so often waving her blue pencil in the air and shouting, "The syntax! This guy's syntax is all wrong!" and I was applying coat after stinging coat of creams to my face when a band of naked colonists descended the trail and appeared before us. No clothes, no towels, only tubes of fat around their waists and, in their hands, AM/FM radios, bags of potato chips, cans of Schlitz. Six men and six women, most of whom seemed to be exactly thirty-eight years old—nearly middle-aged and yearning for youth—standing in front of me and Mother like precursors of a new race.

One of them, a woman with heavy hips and a red bandana across her brow, said, "This section of San Gregorio is nudist. You'll either have to strip or, like, depart."

I took her to be sort of the governor of the colony—maybe the bandana was like an official badge—and her warning drew a number of rude observations from the rest of the crowd.

"The old lady's got a good bod for an old lady," said a bald man who was at most five years younger than Mother.

"The kid isn't bad, either," said a woman with tiny breasts. "Good legs. Real good legs. The face, though: 'tis a pity, the pimples."

"Kinky couple, don't you think?" said someone I couldn't see because he was standing in back. "What would you say? Fifteen and forty?"

This last insult made their fat bounce with laughter, and yet it wasn't far from wrong. I was fifteen, Mother was forty-seven, and the trend of married women taking teenage lovers was accelerating at such an alarming rate in San Francisco that I couldn't tell whether the colonists were kidding or whether they actually thought Mother and I were a close-knit couple. Mother was wearing the only swimsuit she ever owned, a one-piece black monstrosity, and I was wearing the red trunks, with blue anchor at the crotch, which I'd bought for Audrey's birthday party. Mother had seen me naked until I was nine but, except for one purely accidental glimpse of her running from the shower to the bedroom the early evening of February 11, 1964, I'd never seen her. I really didn't want to because I'd heard severe psychological maladjustments were the inevitable result and I really don't think she wanted me to, either, because she was a good guardian and a moral woman. There seemed only two alternatives, though—returning three miles to the crowded beach or undressing at the command of our captors like victims in a vulgar film—and neither plan struck me as wholly desirable.

Mother asked them questions: why do you want us to disrobe? Do you ask everyone you meet on this side of the beach to disrobe? How long have you been living here? Do you find the term "beach bum" pejorative? Would you define yourselves as beach bums? As nudists? Does a bare body have, for you, any political significance? Do you have little huts along the coast?

At first I thought Mother was just trying to stall them by posing diversionary issues, but then I realized she was perfectly sincere and genuinely interested in their replies. She was working now as a feature reporter for the *San Francisco Chronicle* and, if this wasn't the lead story in next week's Sunday supplement, thirty years' experience had taught her nothing. She only regretted she hadn't thrown a camera into the trunk of the Fiat so she could shoot carefully shaded pictures of the subjects in their birthday suits. Mother had a talent tantamount to genius for transforming whatever absurdity she saw around her into just more stuff of her own fame: taking away its terror or ennui by exploiting it.

They seemed to have heard of her when she told them who she was. When she told them why she was asking so many questions, they gathered at her feet. She sat with her back to a boulder and recorded, in shorthand on the reverse side of the rough draft on mental illness, their inane answers. No one was paying any attention to me any more, not to my real good legs, not even to my pitiful pimples, so I slipped away with a blanket and my bag of gels. I settled on a spot in the middle distance between Mother's colonists and baggy men playing plastic golf.

Every half hour I sprinted to the shoreline and rubbed saltwater into my welts. Other than that I did nothing more strenuous than apply patented cures to my face. I spent the entire day asleep on the sand, with my hair combed back so the sun wouldn't forget my forehead, that most flawed of all facial areas. The sun, creams, and saltwater seemed to be working together very nicely to reduce the blisters. My skin felt softer and smoother than it had in years. The bumps burned away. Even my forehead felt fine. There was a public cabana standing, in all its indignity, on the edge of the hill that dropped down to the beach, and I felt compelled to confirm— through study of the image in the mirror—my inkling that I had at last found salvation, in Mother Nature herself.

I climbed the little cliff, then pushed open the door to the outhouse, which was a typical beach bathroom in that the smell of urine was overwhelmed only by the fumes of defecation. Centipedes crawled across the cement, flies had a field day around the toilet, broken water pipes dripped, and I had an acute sense of pervasive darkness. There was a bare little bulb above the mirror to illuminate the reflection. I looked, I looked again, and was appalled.

The white of the ointments, the red of the sun, the green of the sea had formed a melting blue of the body. My whole face seemed to be falling off. I looked like a clown—like Bozo—caught between the acts. All the boils were raised to the highest degree and glistening in a terrible blue hue. Suddenly I was seized with the perception that I had a multitude of debilitating personal problems and there was no cure for any of them: not nature, not nurture, not love. When one thing goes, the rest usually follow right behind and, in that stinking dark cabana, all alone at three o'clock in the afternoon, a mile and a half from a nudist colony, I could find no reason to continue. I decided to dive thirty feet off the cliff to the sand. I turned the switch on and off for twenty seconds until a shadow of gray filled the room: wet skin on cold glass. I closed the door. Shutting my eyes and turning off the light, I tried to imagine what broken glass would sound like in the dark.

I bolted out of the bathroom, ran barefoot over pebbles and tough grass to the edge of the cliff, and leapt. Right around the middle of good Aristotelian books, there's supposed to be an action that reveals the protagonist's hamartia—in this case, for instance, excessive self-absorption as a function of disfluency—and also transforms the rising action into falling action. But the cause of the falling action isn't supposed to be quite so literally A FALL. It's supposed to be a little more metaphorical than that. Still, I can't alter the story of my life to conform to some archaic theory of dramatic structure. There's a book to think about, but there's also the pressure of the past.

The light went out of the sun and the sand came up to greet me. I did one entire flip, so I landed on my feet, but my left leg was bent across my body at an extremely awkward angle and, when I touched beach, the thigh bone of that leg cracked. I couldn't get my left leg back on the left side of my body. My left foot twitched in the sand like a crab. The femur had broken skin and looked ghastly. The pain was so exquisite I started screaming the worst words I knew, as if incapacitation of the body were the death of language. The ocean kept lapping closer and seagulls circled above to determine whether I were more coastal litter for a late lunch.

Oddly enough, the first person who responded to my cries was one of the plastic golfers, although maybe he'd wandered over my way just looking for a lost chip shot. "Upsy daisy," he said and tried to yank me out of my misery, but I couldn't have moved if a whale had come floating ashore on the next wave. While the golfer went and got Mother, a hundred people who otherwise would have been bored on Sunday afternoon formed an extremely tight three-ring circle around me. The colonists stayed away since they weren't allowed at this end of the beach, which was a good thing because the clothed population was fatuous enough. They talked among themselves, and most of them thought I was probably permanently paralyzed. Others thought I would never have been bit if I hadn't been swimming so far out at high tide.

Mother burst through the throng, clutching her interview notes and saying, "You shouldn't have wandered away in the first place." Those were actually her first words. She was very sympathetic later on, but her first reaction was barely concealed indignation.

The men in white coats returned to the ambulance to get a scoop stretcher to dig me out of the sand since my left leg couldn't fit on a flat stretcher. Mother climbed into the back of the ambulance with me and held my hand. I couldn't tell whether she was so calm because she knew that was what observers were supposed to do in emergencies, or because she'd already arrived in that beautiful realm she occupied when she knew she had a first-rate story in the bag and nothing else really penetrated.

"You know, Jeremy, Mother's Day, 1947, my mother threw out her hip on Lido Isle. Isn't that quite a coincidence?" she asked.

Yes, I said, I thought that was quite a coincidence. I'd never met her mother. The siren started, Klaxon twirled in the sunset, and then I lost consciousness.

16

THE REASON WHY it was not just one more broken leg, why I imbue it with significance, is that, to Mother's relief, I was never again able to play competitive sports. Two months in traction and nine more in a metal leg brace nullified whatever dreams I still had of becoming an athlete and forced me into finding another way of ordering my world. Phrasemaker that she was, Mother called this the silver lining of a very black cloud. I still believed in love at first sight, the ultimate triumph of political justice, and the consolation of beautiful language.

Conventional wisdom has it that poetry begins when the pain or at least the boredom gets intolerable. Conventional wisdom has it right for once, since immediately after dispensing with the last of sophomore year course work I commenced to write the first and last series of poems I've ever written, a satirical sonnet sequence too pathetic to look at again, even here. I took as the subjects of the Hospital Cycle the standard themes of convalescent life—the cold doctor, the cheerful nurses, the bland food, the tedious visitor—whereas what I wanted to write about was the sound of the little Korean woman's voice when she entered the room at sunrise, selling papers, screeching *"Chron-eee-cle, Chron-eee-cle,"* as if she were consciously attempting to reproduce in her intonation the undesirability of morning and irritability of the world.

In July I began purchasing the newspaper from her because I could no longer abide the sound of her voice and wanted to dismiss her, with a ten-cent tip, as quickly as I possibly could, but also because I was becoming increasingly interested in the adventures of Thomas Eagleton. There I was, flat on my back in a body cast from chest to tocs, and there he was: Poor Tom, wearing checkered sportcoats, running around getting assurances, sweating on national television, crying, hugging his wife, having that dead metaphor "skeletons in his closet" applied to him so often that I came to think of him carrying, quite literally, a little closet wherever he went, with a plastic skeleton dangling from a coat hanger. My curiosity about Poor Tom derived, I suppose, from Father, to whom he represented the Right of the Electrically Shocked to Live without Shame.

Father would come visit me on his lunch hour, shaking his head, licking his lips, complaining of a muscle he'd pulled when he tried to sprint the final 440 of a five-mile jog. Upon entering the room he'd rattle the bed frame, which was meant as a gesture of paternal jocularity. He would sit in a metal chair with his arms folded and sunglasses on, as if he were blind, criminally suspect, or excruciatingly shy: looking straight ahead, saying nothing. But then the noon news would come on, Poor Tom would appear, and we'd start exchanging information from magazine articles and reports we'd heard on the radio. In that there was nothing in the least heroic about him, Poor Tom was an unlikely hero, but via the vice-presidential candidate Father was attempting to prevent another visit to Montbel, so we waxed eloquent.

"I'm a thousand percent behind him," Father would say.

"I'm two thousand," I would say.

"I think he has Woodcock's support."

"I don't know about Woodcock. I don't know if he's a thousand percent behind him."

"Nine hundred," Father would say, laughing.

"Eight hundred," I'd say. "Maybe eight-fifty."

"Well, at least they aren't going to find any more skeletons in Tom's closet."

"Just little things now, like second-degree m-m-murder or sodomy."

"Right you are who say you are," Father would say, using one of his favorite if somewhat opaque phrases. "Nothing's worse in the eyes of the democracy than a man sensitive enough to have been depressed once or twice in his life and sought help."

"Exactly."

"How's the leg, Jeremy?"

The leg was all right until the doctor misread, on the X-rays, a knot of still broken bone as healing scar tissue. Mother and Father were called to Kaiser Hospital. I was rushed from physical therapy into surgery, and a metal pin was inserted near the bone to lend support. The pin is still there. When the weather shifts suddenly to rain, I can feel it rubbing against my bones. In airport inspections, it invariably triggers an electronic beep; I take from my wallet and pass to the police a letter from my doctor explaining that I have not a revolver in my hip pocket but a hollow rod in my left leg. After strenuous exercise of any sort—rock-climbing, full-court basketball, difficult-angled desire—I get a twinge where the pin was inserted, I drag my leg a little, limp walking uphill, and must shower soon after the exertion or my nerves will pinch and the next day I'll have to lean on the cane I've kept in the closet all these years.

Six years later, such minor handicaps are the only after-effects of the accident, but when I was sixteen it seemed like a near-mortal wound. Over the summer I'd grown several inches and lost twenty pounds, so when I walked across the parking lot and appeared in the courtyard a few minutes before the first bell of a new year no one recognized me. They all took me for some crippled kid who'd transferred. It was a nice enough feeling at first—having doors opened for me and held—but I soon wearied of it. I appreciated people's condescension no more than my own passivity. I missed athletics so much that for a while I consented to serve as scorekeeper and assistant manager for the girls' field hockey team, but there's no experience quite so degrading as being bossed around by a phalanx of stocky, padded girls waving sticks; I turned in my key to the towel room.

Both Mother and Father urged me to escape from immobility into the wonderful world of literature, and Mother even went so far as to set up a kind of course for me in the *Bildungsroman*. Every afternoon, upon coming home from school, I would unbuckle my brace, lie on my bed doing leg exercises with the rope pulleys and ankle weights I still had from my basketball days, then read variations on the theme of my own childhood from Jean-Jacques Rousseau to Henry Roth. It was a little late to begin reading seriously—I think Beth had read all the comedies by the time she was twelve; "All what comedies?" I once asked, and she said, "Tell me you're kidding"—but at least I was finally reading with, to Mother's elation, a certain compulsiveness and insatiability.

When I mumbled something about trying my own hand at this stuff, a brand-new electric typewriter magically materialized on the top step of the stairs to my room. My first story was about a boy who "puts toe to gleaming metal and leaps off the most beautiful bridge in the world." My second story focused upon a boy—the same boy, I think, resurrected—who, while waiting for the traffic light to change, imagines the inner lives of the drivers in front, behind, and to either side of him, comes to comprehend the latent sexuality of automobiles, the vulnerability of pedestrians, and the symbolic force of the color red. My third effort was based upon the tragic misfortunes of a man Father had known when he was director of the Mission district poverty program. There was present in all three stories an opposition between the Individual and Society, as well as a kind of Gothic despair that I thought was probably pretty important to good writing, but you can't write a *Bildungsroman* when you're in the middle of your *Bildung*, and I wasn't enthusiastic enough about other people to write well about them, so I gave up my first go at fabrication.

I remember one very long night I spent doing leg exercises on the rope pulley while Father—who not only had never become the Jerusalem correspondent for United Press International but also had to watch and make as if to cheer while Mother rose higher and higher in the field of feature journalism—explained that I. F. Stone was doing more practical good for the world than *Twelfth Night* ever did. Perhaps because *Twelfth Night* was Beth's favorite comedy, I set out to prove Father right: I would navigate the nonfiction section.

Although newspapers are meant to be read very quickly and then thrown out, or used to start fires or line trash bins or wrap fish for the freezer, Mother had had the *Daily Bruin* for her tenure as editor, 1942 to 1945, bound in green leather. I don't know where those volumes are now—Beth is so very much the archivist she probably has them locked away in Puppa's trunk slid beneath her four-poster bed in the Berkeley hills—but when I was a child I used to read back issues of the *Bruin* all the time. I have no idea what I was looking for, since it wasn't like a yearbook in which there would have been black-and-white photographs of Mother at her more immature. It seemed to me like any other newspaper, only a little yellow around the edges, a little more directly irrelevant. Apparently, it was one of the very best college dailies in the country and, in any case, beyond comparison with the crosstown competition, which printed lead editorials in praise of the USC football team.

When FDR died, Mother put on the front page a picture of him puffing a cigarette through a nicotine filter. This wasn't an appropriately glum photo for the president's funeral, and she caught so much flak from the chancellor that she threatened to resign until the entire editorial staff delivered an eloquent letter of support. Every Thursday evening Arnie Logan (who later became Pat Brown's, then Bobby Kennedy's press secretary, but who at the time was nothing more than sports editor of the *Daily Bruin*) conspired with the rest of the boys in Sports to write an article which, if you read it linearly, made almost no sense at all but which, if you read it backwards and skipped every other line, produced a rather risqué narrative. Every Thursday evening they'd try to sneak these naughty tales past Mother into the Friday edition. I think it would be unfair to say Mother ever had a particularly dirty mind. She was an amazingly precise proofreader, though, and she never let their lewd little stories get by her. I feel for Arnie and the boys. Growing up, I used to feel *like* Arnie and the boys, speaking backwards to rebel against Mother but never making it into her Friday edition, her heart of hearts. Mother was always the editor, I was always her little cub reporter turning in rough drafts, and she was always sending me back for one more rewrite.

I became, by default, editor-in-chief of the *London Journal,* which the principal thought was ghostwritten by Mother because I was so meek in person and so mean in print. Every other week I wrote what was called "A Satire," but which was really an all-out assault upon myself, a sort of suicide note in the guise of covering student government. One night, while I was staying late to work on what I thought was a particularly wicked essay, Mother knocked on the door of the newspaper office, ostensibly to bring dinner but actually to determine whether I was doing justice to the name that meant so much in mass media. When I was a junior in high school, I hated everything but the sound of the door being closed from the inside, and there she was—on the other side of that door, peering through the glass window, tapping with her key ring, wanting in.

She was wearing her black leather boots (what Beth called "boots not made for walkin' "), her Pacific Ocean blue business dress, and a weird string of wooden beads. Perfume was apparent, as were lipstick, eye shadow, and rouge: Mother as Mature Model. In one hand she held her reporter's notebook in which stenography recorded every word uttered at a press conference whose highlight was Mayor Alioto's denial that he'd ever met his brother-in-law, and the other had a sack of food that she'd bought for me at an A&W Root Beer stand on her way home after Father told her I was still at school. While I inhaled hamburgers and french fries, Mother walked around the *Journal* office, studying the assignment sheet on the bulletin board; trying out the typewriter, which was missing plastic caps to vowel keys and had a jammed margin release; flipping through the photo file, dead black negatives of all twenty-seven candidates for student body president.

In the way that anyone human would have asked how you are doing, Mother asked, "What are you working on?"

"My column," I said. Mother was not the most loyal fan of my column, but she did think every fifth or sixth effort scored some marvelous sociological points.

"How's it going?" she asked, still flipping through the photo file.

"Fine. I just finished."

"Are you happy with it?" For Mother this wasn't a question so much as a direct challenge, since she was never happy, at least publicly, with her own work and assumed no one else would admit he derived any pleasure from his own expressions either.

"Very happy," I said. I couldn't help it. I liked the column a lot.

"It can't stand any improvement?" she asked, tilting her head to the left. She leaned against my desk, watching me sweep crumbs onto the floor with a ruler.

"No, Mother."

"That's great. It must be very good. I'm eager to read it." *And woe to you if I am at all disappointed.*

"It'll be out on Friday," I said, pushing back my chair and locking my leg brace. I was still supposed to be using a cane, but I'd left it in my locker, so I limped across the room to throw my A&W garbage into the wastebasket. Mother followed. When I leaned against the wall to gather strength before making the return trip to my seat, she cornered me.

"Jeremy honey, can't I take a little peek at it now?" she asked.

"No."

"Why not?"

The fluorescent lights flickered like melodramatic special effects for a storm scene.

"It'll be out on Friday," I said, resting against her to get my balance, then limping back to my seat. "You'll see it then."

"Why won't you let me see it now?" she asked, shoving some papers aside, sitting on the side of my desk, tapping her toes on a plastic chair.

I wouldn't let her see it now because I remembered how thoroughly she took the fun out of the city championship by calling my article a "tissue of sportswriting platitudes." I said: "Because I don't want to hear your criticism until it's too late to do anything about it."

"How silly. What kind of newspaperman are you?"

"I'm not a newspaperman. I'm a s-s-satirist."

"I won't criticize it, I promise. I'm just curious to see what you've been working on. I wrote three thousand words today on Joseph Alioto's ancestry. You can look at that and laugh. Let me just look at your lead," Mother said, descending to her most transparent strategy.

"It's not a lead. It's more of an overture," I said. I'd just read *Swann's Way* and really liked the word "overture."

"Lead. Overture. Whatever. Let me take a look at it, for Chrissake."

"No."

"Please?"

"No," I said, squirming in my seat, banging the brace against the leg of the desk.

"Pretty please?"

"No."

"Pretty pretty please, Jeremy honey?"

This could have gone on forever. Mother's sweet sincerity was starting to get on my nerves, so I opened my desk drawer, took out my satire, and handed it to her. I figured the least I could do was let her look at my lead, if that was what she really wanted to do, although of course she read the lead, then the paragraph after the lead, then the paragraph after the paragraph after the lead, all the way to the column's sad conclusion:

A SATIRE

Reflection in a One-Way Mirror
By Jeremy Zorn

I'd like to applaud, with unabashed pleasure and amid great revelry and excitement, the replacement of windows with mirrors in the principal's offices. Silver, one-way mirrors.

I've been told the windows were replaced because in the

sun they caused glare. The reflection of the sun off the windows was disturbing, was discomforting to passersby, and comfort should be our first consideration.

There were, though, other disadvantages to the windows. They were, first of all, windows, clear glass panes: people could see in and out. We could stare at one another. If safety should be our first consideration, then privacy should be our second consideration.

Also, the windows revealed ugliness. I often found evidence of fingerprints and dust and dirt and rain and mud on the glass. If safety should be our first consideration; and privacy, our second; then cleanliness should be our third consideration.

The silver, one-way mirrors, on the other hand, appear spotless and reveal no smudges. They are easier to clean, too.

As to privacy, there's now a sense of security, even peace, for students needn't know whether there's anything recognizably human behind the mirror. All we can see is our own reflection in black shadows of silver. This is how it should be.

Lastly, as to comfort, the silver mirrors dull the sun's glare, so what's seen isn't the reflection of the sun but the glossy image of ourselves. I'm pleased that I no longer have to avert my eyes as I walk by the windows. I cheer for the new mirrors.

I hobbled around the office, pretending to clean up, putting away scissors that didn't cut and staplers that didn't have staples, while she brandished her blue pencil—she actually carried an editor's blue pencil at all times—and interrupted her reading of the article only twice: at the end of the third paragraph to ask if I wanted a ride home ("y-y-yes") and at the end of the fifth paragraph to ask if there was an ashtray around anywhere ("n-n-no"). She commenced her attack upon my little column immediately after she finished reading it.

I guess now I can admit the irony is heavy-handed, the last few paragraphs are dominated by overwrought figures, the prose is repetitious in a coy, anachronistic sort of way, the basic idea is needlessly Manichaean, but at the time I thought it was killingly good, and when Mother lit into it I wanted to scream. She said one of these days I really must begin to take into account the objective world of reality.

She said I had better learn how to write a "straight news story" that "tumbled down cleanly," if I ever wanted to amount to anything as a journalist.

She said there was editorializing and there was editorializing, but this was psychosis.

She said there might be a "decent four-inch filler of a factual story" buried somewhere in the satire and, if I wanted, she'd stay late "digging it out."

I imagined a night of Mother and me sitting next to each other at a wobbly desk and giving the thing a much closer reading than it deserved. I asked her to stop smoking and told her I didn't need a ride home: it was nice out, I wasn't tired, I'd walk. She said if I couldn't take constructive criticism I was a baby. With that, somehow, I fell apart. I clumped around the room in a crazy circle, yelling, "Get out, Mother, please get out," and tearing up the satire, only to spend the rest of the night on the floor piecing it, then taping it together, although the next morning I decided not to print it, anyway. Not enough space.

That was the way Mother ran a newspaper. That was the kind of chaos she could create so quickly. It's a wonder to me Arnie and the boys didn't lock her up in the ladies' lav until she promised to be less imperial, but she served her reign without a whisper of insurrection. On the Monday after commencement, which Puppa did not deem a signal enough event to attend, she started working as the editor of the "house organ" for the ACLU, which have always been interesting initials to me in that *ACLU* is an anagram of *UCLA*, as if wherever she went Mother, in contradistinction to her disfluent son, changed the language to suit her own needs.

17

I DIDN'T WITHDRAW again into autism, but I was certainly down in the dumps when I trudged home for dessert. Mother's attempt at encouragement was to say that, despite her serious reservations as to the *content* of "Reflection in a One-Way Mirror," she thought I'd at least learned how to write a correct sentence. There was no reason I couldn't speak one, as well—a neat inversion of the usual idea that only after mastering speech do we graduate to reading and writing. All I had to do was know what I was going to say before I said it, write it down, memorize it, and then, speaking only in perfect sentences, just . . . say it. In the abstract, the principle, like most abstract principles, functioned fine. Invariably, though, I'd pause halfway through the perfect sentence to consult the crumpled piece of paper in my pants pocket or, worse, encounter the sympathetic eyes of my listener, who hadn't a clue why I'd been speaking in such stilted syntax and was now talking in such halting tones. I figured maybe only Mother was capable of kneading language.

She reiterated that, if I could only force myself to speak within certain formal conventions, my verbal violence would vanish. I doubted this, but she pleaded with me to give her plan at least one more shot, so I enlisted in the London Forensic Society. Forensic societies everywhere are collections of outcasts. The forensic society at London was a positive House of Bedlam. The London disputants were the strangest of the strange, the most eccentric at a school insistent upon eccentricity. They were all little guys, prematurely serious with their locked briefcases and navy blue ties. They knew and cared passionately about the raw data of the world in the same way I once knew and cared passionately about the pitching and batting averages of the Los Angeles Dodgers.

We convened twice a week in the social sciences department,

where the debate coach, an anthropology teacher, had his office—
a desk never not cluttered with spears, masks, Indian arrowheads.
He was a very nice, very old man who, regardless of the weather,
wore a sun visor, and he spoke to us, although we sat three feet
away from him in a semi-circle, through a megaphone. His favorite
expression was: "Your affirmative rebuttal, Mr. Zorn, is a ladder
without rungs." Whenever he said that, I'd have to get up, go to
the library, and conduct research until my affirmative rebuttal had,
in Dr. Hoblock's opinion, rungs. Every Tuesday and Thursday afternoon in the social sciences department, all six of us would sit in
soft chairs, pretending we liked the taste of his black coffee, feeling
the four o'clock sun on our backs, and arguing, passionately though
precisely, whether: *Resolved,* the United States should convert to
the metric system; *Resolved,* the electoral college should be abol-
ished; *Resolved,* the Federal Communications Commission should
enforce stricter standards concerning prime-time violence on
television.

The topics were innocuous, but to a stutterer content cannot
easily represent anything more than yet another opportunity to figure out form. *On the contrary, contents are formal and forms are
contents. If modern art is appreciated as an experience in psychosis,
working with forms is the most radical way to seize the moments of
crisis.* Dr. Hoblock wanted the "loud eloquence of London boys
bellowing." What he really wanted was a minimum of two hundred
and fifty words per minute out of every one of us, for he had a
theory, based on his debating days at Boston College in the late
thirties, that rapid speech rate was the only way to judges' hearts,
and toward that end he drilled us in speedy diction.

"Faster," he'd cough into his megaphone. "Faster. Get rid of those
words. Keep your mouth moving. Turn those tongues into silver-
tipped trumpets. Faster."

I spoke weirdly well when forced to speak fast. There wasn't
time to choke, and I started talking the way I'd once imagined the
Chinese conversed on the horizon: no gaps, just unintermittent jabbering. I talked so fast I became our first negative. In San Francisco
any discipline with a noble or vaguely classical tradition is outlawed

before it gets out of hand and there were very few forensic foes we could find to face, so we spent most of our time with Dr. Hoblock, drinking his bitter coffee, answering his arcane questions, debating on Tuesdays and Thursdays until the sun went down.

Toward the end of spring—it must have been April of my junior year because I remember limping onto the platform; no cane, no crutches, just the metal brace belted tight to my leg—Doerner Country Day, a girls' school in Marin, challenged the London Forensic Society to a two-school, four-person debate upon whether: *Resolved,* the California State Assembly should reinstate the death penalty with reference to mass murder, kidnapping, and the homicide of public officials. Doerner Country Day would argue the affirmative.

For the next ten days, we met every afternoon and sometimes during lunch to increase our speech rate, share our research, and consolidate our argument. Only two of us were actually going to be in the debate, so the other four did nothing but look for statistical evidence that murders-per-capita were directly correlated to death-penalties-imposed, then report back to Leo Gogol and me. Leo was second negative, first rebuttal. I was first negative, second rebuttal. I didn't like how dispassionate he was about the idea of the death penalty. He had a side to support, he'd support it, he wasn't going to lapse into, as he said, "asinine emotionalism," whereas Mother and Father had always taught me that capital punishment was positively medieval, and I was eager to lapse into asinine emotionalism when the time was right.

At seven o'clock on some Friday night in late April the time was right. Only the place was wrong, the amazingly large auditorium at Doerner Country Day, solid with the pert expressions of bright, rich, attractive girls come to hasten the collapse of the London legacy in forensics. Dr. Hoblock was backstage, computing the median cost of a life sentence in North Dakota in 1961, while our assistants sat in the front row with stopwatches around their necks and flashcard reminders—"Quote your mom's *Nation* article (9/22/69) as evidence of prison rehab," "Dismiss as naive syllogism all deterrent theory"—in their laps. Leo and I sat onstage in this cold building, waiting for the debate to begin, pouring each other entirely too much ice water from the plastic pitcher, looking past the podium and microphone to our opponents at the other end of the table, who were serious beyond belief: not talking to each other, not drinking any water let alone slurping any ice, not adjusting their skirts but, instead, labeling the monographs in their briefcases, sifting through stack after stack of meaningless material; scribbling in shorthand the crucial points they wanted to make in their case for more death.

The judge took her seat on stage. Dr. Hoblock shook hands with Miss Keil, the coach of Doerner Country Day. Leo and I shook hands with Alicia Stephens and Josephine Nordlinger. The moderator marched to the podium, adjusted the microphone, and said, "Welcome. Contestants, coaches, spectators, Doerner girls, London boys—welcome. Welcome to the first and, I should say, we very much hope, the first *annual* debate between Jack London Preparatory Academy [whole huge chorus of boos from the predictable crowd] and Doerner Country Day School [long pause for screaming ovation]. I should hope, and I do assume, the disputants already know the rules, which we shall be observing strictly tonight, of the Revised Illinois Formal Debate but, for the benefit of newcomers to forensics, I shall outline the format. First affirmative and first negative, ten minutes apiece; second affirmative and second negative, five minutes apiece; first affirmative and first negative cross-examination rebuttal, eight minutes apiece; second affirmative and second negative cross-examination rebuttal, four minutes apiece. Total time: fifty-four minutes. No final summaries for either side. No sarcasm tolerated from the debaters. No heckling tolerated from the audience. Good luck, boys. Go get 'em, girls."

If Mother had been there, she would have loved the moderator's last line. Even with Mother absent, the crowd howled its approval of this parting exhortation, then quieted to a hush when Alicia Stephens blew into the mike and commenced advocating not mercy but justice. She trotted out the usual statistics concerning the rising homicide rate in California; the percentage of criminals who, within six months of their release, commit the same crime for which they were initially incarcerated; the exorbitant cost to the taxpayer of keeping people alive and happy in prison. She gave detail after lurid detail supposedly related to Juan Corona's recent murder of his twenty-six farm workers in the San Joaquin Valley, and mused aloud, with lavish irony, whether in a decade or two Juan would be free to hire a few more farm workers. She finished her affirmation by claiming to have asked "literally hundreds" of potential criminals in the Fillmore district whether the "black specter" of the death penalty would deter them from committing murder, and pretty near all of them said it would deter them from even carrying a gun.

All four of our assistants raised and waved their signs: "Dismiss as naive syllogism all deterrent theory."

Alicia thanked the audience. She thanked the moderator. She thanked the judge. She thanked the visiting "challengers." She thanked her coach. She thanked her teammates. She thanked her mother. The crowd, including her mother, howled its approval. Alicia sat down. Confronting five hundred unfriendly and five friendly faces, standing on the stage of an immense cement building on the wrong side of the Bay, feeling the floodlights melt down my fingernails, I was not a little nervous. My tongue bore no relation to—Hoblock's favorite image—a silver-tipped trumpet. I thanked Alicia for her provocative presentation, complimented her on the passion of her approach and, following these bows to proper form, I felt glib.

I mused aloud, with train-wreck irony, whether the proper function of the state was to embody the highest ideals of humanity or the lowest common denominator of the animal kingdom. I cited case after case of men proven innocent only after they'd been given a guided tour of the gas chamber. I dismissed as naive syllogism all deterrent theory. I displayed a graph that showed, sort of, that in 1971 North Dakota didn't impose the death penalty and had the lowest murder rate in the country, .2 per 100,000 people, whereas Alabama did impose the death penalty and had the highest murder rate, 13.7 per 100,000. I wasn't sterling. I was adequate and, besides the beginning, I didn't stutter, so I was satisfied.

I hardly listened at all to Josephine who, when I did tune her in, seemed extraordinarily shrill and rhetorical without saying much of anything: Hoblock's ladder without rungs. Leo, especially by way of comparison, was the very voice of rational persuasion, using all the right debaters' transitions ("If, on the other hand, we consider the issue from the perspective of the murder victim's mother-in-law . . ."), leaping to pun here and self-deprecation there, pulling graphs out of his hip pocket, quoting from memory the important portion of Mother's 9/22/69 article on prison rehabilitation, never pausing, never taking a breath, talking a mile a minute until the moderator said, "Time!" and then again "Mr. Gogol, your time is up. Time! Mr. Gogol, you will conclude that sentence and be seated."

Mr. Gogol concluded that sentence and was seated, but a minute later he was back on his feet as first negative cross-examination rebutter, wondering with a wry smile just how reliable some of Josephine's sources were, then, eight minutes later, turning around to receive her counter-attack, to defend his own data. Alicia and I sat on the sidelines, not so much listening to our teammates as attempting to stare each other down as we went into the final bout. In romantic comedy, two pairs of lovers disagree about something or other and exchange partners and finally get reunited with their true loves. This was like that except none of us had a true love with whom to get reunited, so we were forced, according to the rules of the Revised Illinois Formal Debate, to argue the night away.

I figured Leo and I had a fairly large lead entering the final round. If I kept Alicia on her toes with an endless series of incredibly niggling questions, then dodged every doubt she threw my way, we'd win. I asked: "Isn't the rising homicide rate in California a function not of any especially new or terrible trend toward violence but of dramatic state-wide growth in population? You claim, Miss Stephens, that within six months of their release thirty-four percent of all criminals commit the same crime for which they were initially incarcerated, but after serving extended sentences how many murderers ever kill again? You speak of the 'exorbitant cost to the taxpayer of keeping people alive and happy in prison,' but exactly how happy are they there? Have you conducted a cost/benefit analysis of a jail cell compared to the price of a decent apartment down-town? If not, why not? If so, do you actually believe it's possible to place a monetary value on human life? We all sympathize with the farm workers Juan Corona plowed under during harvest season in the Valley, but surely the man is insane, surely you don't mean to argue for the execution of the criminally insane, or do you? Do you have with you tape recordings of the conversations you had with the so-called potential criminals in the Fillmore district concerning the alleged deterrent value you claim the death penalty would have upon them? Did it ever occur to you that they assumed you were a plainclothes parole officer, and therefore were lying through their teeth?"

My metal brace was belted so tight it had begun to cut off the circulation in my left leg. I wanted to sit down and rest and cele-brate the victory, but Alicia sidestepped all the questions surpris-ingly well and came clawing back. There's a particular rebuttal technique which, when successful, brings the other person out from behind his barrier of formal language. Through feigned belief and outright accusation, you attempt to force your opponent into asi-nine emotionalism, into some eleventh-hour plea for compassion and love—the death knell for any debater. Alicia appeared to have heard of this technique.

"Do I understand you correctly," she asked, "to be saying that, *re* capital punishment, the state should be not just but merciful? Would that be a fair assessment of your position?"

"No, it wouldn't," I said.

"Then I *am* confused. What exactly is your position?"

"That, *re* capital punishment, the state should be not retributive but just."

"A fine distinction indeed."

She meant "fine" in the sense of "minute," but I decided to re-ceive it in the sense of "excellent" and said, "Thank you, Miss Ste-phens."

That was the beginning of the end. That got her mad. She paced up and back on the stage, flipping through her index cards, looking for a loophole somewhere, while I gripped the podium, trying to stay on my feet the final four minutes.

"You claim," she said, "that in 1971 North Dakota had the lowest murder rate in the country, .2 per hundred thousand, whereas that rate was actually 1.2 per hundred thousand, and the year must have been 1970, since 1971 figures have, to my knowledge, not yet been released."

Only much later did I discover she was making all of this up. At the time I thought she just wanted to set the record straight.

"Is that right," I said, "1.2 rather than .2? I'm sorry, I didn't realize. And 'seventy rather than 'seventy-one? I don't know how I could have made such errors. Thank you, Miss Stephens, for pointing them out. My argument, however, remains essentially the same: North Dakota, which didn't and doesn't enforce the death penalty, had and has the lowest murder rate in the country, whereas Alabama, which did and does enforce the death penalty, had and has the highest murder rate in the nation. QED: capital punishment, so far from functioning as a deterrent of death, creates a climate of blood."

We had been passing the microphone politely back and forth, but this time she fairly yanked it out of my hands, attempting to arouse the audience as she entered the last two minutes of her cross-examination tirade.

" 'Deterrent of death,' Mr. Zorn, 'climate of blood'? Aren't you regressing now to sheer rhetoric? And yet I do sympathize with your strategy, since all you have left is language." She actually said that, Sandra. Somewhere in her dark heart she knew. "Alabama didn't have 13.7 murders per hundred thousand but, rather, 13.45 and it didn't lead the nation in murders-per-capita in 1970; Mississippi did. Furthermore, you earlier cited a case in which a Portland man was proven innocent in 1965 after he'd been executed in 1964 whereas, if you'd read the October 11, 1966 issue of the *Portland Gazette*, you'd have discovered he was found guilty again."

General, heartfelt applause from the Doerner girls. Hoblock waving an anthropological spear at me.

"It doesn't matter," I said. My left leg was swollen. I wanted to sit down.

"It doesn't matter?" she said, slapping her hand to her head like a cartoon character and eliciting shrill whistles from the crowd.

"Are you attempting to derive valid principles from invalid premises? This is certainly a novel interpretation of the rules of the Revised Illinois Formal Debate."

Loud laughs from the balcony section.

I don't know why at this point, with a minute left, I descended to asinine emotionalism. I don't know why I grabbed the mike back from her, limped to center stage, and started shouting. I suppose there was something in Alicia's tone that, like a chemical, converted pain to anger. I forgot all about debaters' decorum and hollered into the floodlights: "No, of course it doesn't matter. It doesn't matter at all. The Portland man was guilty. The man he killed, the judge who sentenced him, the foreman of the jury, they were all guilty. We, all of us here, are guilty. We're all murdering ourselves and each other. We're all going to die. Instead of tossing more bodies onto the bonfire, we might try treating one another with a little pity. That's not a very original idea, but then neither is the notion of revenge. I've never been a great fan of Portia's, I've always tended to side with Shylock in that particular confrontation, but we could do worse than respond to her benediction: "The quality of mercy is not strained,/It droppeth as the gentle rain from heaven/ Upon the place beneath."

I've never been sure just what happened next. According to most accounts, I droppethed upon the place beneath—slipping from the stage into a front row seat. Apparently my left leg gave out and I lost my balance. Dr. Hoblock stabbed himself in the heart with his spear. Leo never spoke to me again. Our assistants tossed their cards at some giggly girls. I attempted to get the clasps on my brace locked so I could stand up. The crowd clapped compassionately. And Alicia cartwheeled across the stage, for she knew she had won.

18

I FIND IT DIFFICULT but necessary to admit that no matter what we do, whether we stutter, stay silent, or break into declamation, we inevitably embarrass ourselves. The point never quite gets across, the communication is never completed, we fall off the stage and attempt to stand up again. . . . But perhaps I'm generalizing too grandiosely from personal experience. I can, after all, speak—or not speak—only for myself. Perhaps it would be better to stick to personal experience: I fell off the stage, I attempted to stand up again, I stood up again, the metal brace came off later that spring, from early May until the end of August I walked without the aid of anything except a cane, the cane served more than one purpose and was misperceived in more than one way at a midsummer rally in Golden Gate Park to stop the Cambodian bombings.

There were rallies all across the country that afternoon—in San Francisco and Los Angeles, in Eugene, in Chicago, in Ann Arbor and Madison, in Chapel Hill, in Washington, Boston, and New York—and by far the largest demonstration, the one that attracted the most attention to itself and caused the most damage to people and public property, was in San Francisco. Initially, I had preferred not to attend. I was pleased with the progress my left leg was making and didn't especially want someone to poke the wooden point of a placard into my still-healing wound. Mother, though, explained how it was part of my duty, as a burgeoning citizen, to protest the policies of the state; and Father chanted "Helen Gahagan Douglas," an ex-congresswoman who was scheduled to speak and whom I adored because Nixon red-baited her out of office, until I agreed to go.

It used to be possible to gather five thousand people in Union Square to protest a dramatic increase in perceptible fog, so I was expecting a large accumulation but was completely unprepared to come upon people occupying hill after hill of cordoned city blocks for as far as I could see in any direction, carrying placards and posters, pressing bullhorns to their mouths, yelling at the red-eyed helicopters that buzzed overhead. Before the march began, posters and banners were distributed and now we were instructed to hold the signs above our heads until our arms ached. A man drove by in a painted truck, shouting at us to stand in a straight line. Mother told me to tuck in my shirt. Beth wrapped a banner around her waist, aping beauty. A woman carried a baby in a backpack, pushing a quadriplegic veteran in a colorfully festooned wheelchair. She took my left hand (the one not carrying a cane) and, without saying a word, ushered me into the veterans' camp. She must have thought I'd been injured in combat, though to anyone who wasn't Lucy in the Sky with Diamonds it was obvious I was closer to sixteen than twenty-two. Mother and Father came running after me. Never quite sure whether she was participating in life or covering it, Mother alternately chanted slogans and took notes, while Father, intent upon producing a fine photo essay for, if not the *Chronicle*, at least the family photo album, was trying to get a good light reading. Both of them were proud I had become—had been dragged by my heels into becoming—an integral part of the parade. Beth straggled, chatting up a graduate student in military history from Berkeley.

I didn't like being mistaken for a maimed ex-marine. I didn't like having to overemphasize my limp to keep pace with the men in electric wheelchairs. Although they were all wearing khaki, none of their uniforms fit quite right, since they all had a leg missing, or no hands, or a steel left arm. I couldn't stomach so many cripples in such a small space. I walked backwards for a while, painfully, and shouted at Mother, who was taking notes, and Father, who was taking pictures: "Let's get out of here. Let's go home. Can't we at least take a rest?"

A man dressed to look like Lt. Calley carried a sign that said: WE ARE ALL LT. CALLEY. This was a theme with which I had next to no trouble aligning myself: universal human guilt. I paused to share a power shake with the lieutenant and wound up with slivers from a

sort of wooden sword he held in his right hand. *Ho Ho Ho Chi Minh,*
the rally kept repeating, *NLF is gonna win.*

"I feel twinges all up and down my leg," I told Mother when she
caught up with me. "It hurts."

"Look around you, Jeremy, and you'll see some hurts," Mother
said, twirling a poster that urged, in syntax a little too complicated
to untangle at first glance, the immediate end of all U.S. combat
missions and the retroactive repeal of the Nobel Peace Prize
awarded to Henry Kissinger. One or the other or both. I looked
around and saw men so attenuated, so incomplete they seemed to
be wheeling along in some country almost beyond pain.

"I know," I said. "I know what you mean. I just don't want to
hurt my leg again."

Mother returned a raised-right-eyebrow-head-tilted-left-eyed-
wide-mouth-pursed-supremely-ironical look that could be best translated: "There are war veterans standing or, rather, sitting next to
you who don't even have legs any more. Don't you dare speak of
the little wound to your left leg in the same breath."

This was part of what always seemed to me an exceedingly del-
icate strategy. On the one hand, we were Against the War. Even
after "victory in Vietnam" two years later, I applied for conscien-
tious objector status on the basis of the fact that my parents had
brought me up to be incapable of immorality. Physically incapable,
I explained. On the other hand, when I complained once too often
about the lunch Mother had packed for us on some hike in the High
Sierras, she insisted nothing would improve my personality quicker
and cleaner than a two-year hitch in the navy. Why the navy I
haven't a clue. I suppose it had something to do with her attach-
ment to the Maritime Museum. At Stanford Beth was revising and
revising a little too lovingly a term paper on Revolutionary War
pensioners. Approximately what it amounted to was that war was
bad but warriors were good.

From the Golden Gate Park entrance to the immense field where
we finally sat down and listened to purple prose (where, six years
before, I'd watched Father call balls and strikes for the industrial
leagues), I limped along with the veterans, leaning on my cane, and

silent: in honor of all the men around me who had been hurt so bad. Every now and then I looked back at the woman carrying her baby in a rucksack and pushing her husband in a wheelchair. Though she had every right to, she was the only person in the peace march who didn't seem to regard herself as a martyr. Her husband and her husband's friends were actually wounded, but it was everyone else who had the same permanently pained expression on their faces, as if the burden of being right about everything had subtly bleached their blood. Everyone except her. Everyone except Lucy in the Sky. Despite the heat, she wore a long leather glove on her left hand, slacks rather than a skirt, and hard shoes. She was short and compact. And she wasn't smiling. She was alone with her difficult family and didn't pretend to belong to Humanity at Large. For what felt like and what may have been the first time in my life, I experienced unpremeditated desire.

I didn't meet up again with Mother and Father until the parade emptied out onto the field. There, beneath the dead heat of a late July sun, Mother translated her notes from shorthand into English, while Father wound another roll of film onto the spool. I ate the bag lunch Father had bought for me, then lay back on the grass, looking for Lucy, happy just to be prone for a while, trying not to listen to the Oakland assemblyman who told all of us to raise our clenched fists in defiance of the leek-green helicopters flying overhead. His sound system was turned all the way to the top. A woman behind me asked to sit rather than squat. I could tell from her voice it wasn't Lucy.

"Have you seen Beth?" Mother asked me. "The last I saw of her she was talking a mile a minute with that grim-looking man from Berkeley. Military history? How could she?"

A pregnant woman stood at Father's side until he agreed to buy three *Arrest the War Criminals* buttons from her. Mother pinned one on her pants pocket. Father stuck one on his camera strap and tried to hand me the third one, saying, "Here, Jeremy, wear this button."

We were too far away from the speakers' platform for me to pretend Father had been drowned out by the assemblyman, so I just simply ignored the offer, rubbing my leg to eradicate the stinging tingles.

"Look, Jeremy. I bought you this handsome button. Here, take it. Stick it on your shirt pocket."

I pushed his hand away, attempted to focus all my attention upon the Oakland assemblyman's eloquence, and said, "I don't want to wear a button."

"Here, take it. I'm giving you a gift."

"Yeah, Jeremy, wear the button," Mother said.

"No, thank you."

We were sitting near the back, so he yanked me out of the crowd and dragged me under a bush at the edge of the park, sticking the button on my shirt pocket. It pierced my skin. This was, without a doubt, one of the most impressive demonstrations of Father's physical prowess I'd ever witnessed.

"Why do you want me to wear this button?" I asked.

"Because," he said.

"But why?"

"Get back in the crowd."

INDIVIDUALLY, we aren't so bad (or, if that's not true, at least we're bad only in isolation) but, why, collectively, are we quite so noxious? What happens to us all when we form a mass? Stuttering struck me as a failure of communal spirit that, nevertheless, needed to be exorcised away from the community. Way away. I never diverged very greatly from my parents' political agenda, but I always found the enactment of their program fraught with too many contradictions to resolve. Mother said in her entire life she'd met only one person more self-involved than I was.

"Who was that?" I said, thinking maybe she meant Dalton Trumbo.

"Your father."

Labor Day weekend Mother, Father, and I drove to Eugene, Oregon, to meet Barry Subotnik, who was the Peace & Freedom candidate for governor. He was related to someone Mother had been fond of in the secretarial pool at the junior high school district. The goal was for Mother and Father to map out his publicity campaign for him in less than seventy-two hours and, the way they worked, closeted in his motel room until midnight each night, I assume they accomplished nothing less. I hugged a kickboard in the indoor pool, and on the last day of the colloquium all four of us played tennis at the university: Mother and Father against me and Barry. I was still dragging my left leg and Barry waddled around the court like a pregnant walrus. He was a great big guy with a beer keg belly. Mother and Father clobbered us, of course, on the strength of some pretty dubious drop shots, and they chortled a lot over their straight-sets victory. I'm not sure it wasn't the happiest I ever saw them together.

We were all famished and Barry treated us to Sunday brunch or, rather, tried to treat us to Sunday brunch, since we drove up and back the strip, trying to work our consciences free to eat at a restaurant called Sambo's or a café that once fired a Chicano busboy. It is perhaps the most emblematic event of my childhood: Father mute behind the wheel, me nursing my left leg, and beside us Mother and Barry playing Top This Arcane Indignation. It would be difficult to overestimate either the length of the main drag of Eugene, Oregon, or the number of times we traversed it. It was five miles long and we stopped once for gas.

You could taste the first drip of honey on your hotcakes. Or surely Father could, gripping the wheel so tightly I knew he was going to halve it. Barry was what Gretchen would have called a "beefer," and my guess was that politics took a distant second place in his stomach to a stack of French toast, but he wouldn't give Mother that satisfaction.

"We can't eat here," he said. "See that sign in the window for the NRA?"

This was as nothing to Mother.

"The architects who build Denny's have notorious links to the mob in the Midwest."

"Annette, come on," Barry said, "why even worry about the builders? It's a chain."

By now which restaurant served the best brunch seemed the most trifling irrelevance. Mother and Barry were in an apoplexy of denial, and I doubt they would have ever come out of it if Father hadn't lurched into the wrong lane and got shunted onto a road that led out to Barry's treehouse in the country, where we nibbled nuts and berries along with the watching chipmunks. What did Barry do to get so fat? Did he think no one noticed? I guess the idea was that Mother was impressing him with how serious she was and Barry was impressing Mother with how serious he was and Father and I were impressing them with how we were just a couple of charter members of the *hoi polloi* who liked to eat food.

Mother's heroes were always political people, and she took real pride in the fact that Barry copped one quarter of one percent of the primary vote. She worshipped the director of the ACLU, the superintendent of schools, her editor at *The Nation,* all of whom I'm sure were the leaders of the free world Mother conceived them to be. What got my goat was the way she constantly presented these men to me and Father as exhibit cases of our own inadequacy. I never wanted to be congressman of the United States. I just wish Father had spoken up for us once in a while, but the best he could manage was to memorize a sentence from a biography of the Rosenbergs: *On June 19, 1953 two people charged with having transmitted the secrets of the split atom to a foreign power were executed after judgment by a jury of their peers.* Particularly just before entering or just after leaving Montbel, Father clung to this line as the embodiment of subjective pseudo-objectivity or something like that. He could sound beautifully rational, explaining all this to you.

19

THE ONLY GAME SHOW I enjoyed as a child was called "Jeopardy." The host of the show and his contestants spoke a pixilated, interrogatory syntax, as if they were aphasiacs trying to reconstruct which word went where. *As long as the aphasiac does not regard another's speech as a message addressed to him in his own verbal patterns, he feels, as a patient of Hemphil and Stengel expressed it: "I can hear you dead plain but I cannot get what you say. . . . I hear your voice but not the words. . . . It does not pronounce itself."* This, I suppose, is the appeal of any translation. As a London sophomore and junior I studied Latin, and by my senior year I'd come to love that dead language.

"But why Latin?" Mother would say. "No one speaks Latin any more except homosexual classics teachers and Vatican Catholics. It's a shame to be living in California and not know Spanish."

"You don't even know the history of your race," Father would say, "but you've memorized the language of a people that collapsed in two centuries."

They didn't appreciate that Latin could never again be articulated. It existed only on the page, on stone tablets in Rome, on metal plaques outside the cages at the zoo, over the archways of marble buildings. It was always capitalized, vertical seeming and squared off, militaristic, masculine, untouchable. It was always silent. I read Cicero, Horace, Livy, Martial, Propertius, Tibullus, Pliny, Quintillian, Ovid, Seneca, Terence, Plautus, Juvenal, but then I read Catullus' fifth poem to Lesbia:

> Vivamus, mea Lesbia, atque amemus,
> rumoresque senum severiorum
> omnes unius aesteimemus assis!

soles occidere et redire possunt:
nobis cum semel occidit brevis lux.
nox est perpetua una dormienda.
da mi basia mille, deinde centum
dein mille altera, dein secunda centum
dein, cum milia multa fecerimus,
conturbabimus illa, ne sciamus,
aut ne quis malus invidere possit,
cum tantum sciat esse basiorum.

Oh yes, Lesbia, oh Christ yes, let's live and love and kiss a thousand kisses, then a hundred, then another thousand, then another hundred, then one more thousand, then one more hundred until neither I nor you nor dirty old men can keep count! An extraordinarily loose and attenuated translation, to be sure, but who cares? This wasn't just third-year Latin: The Alexandrians. It wasn't just *Catulli Carmina* Number Five. These were thirteen lines I took absolutely seriously and, against the imminence of Catullus night of perpetual sleep, I resolved to love, if not Lesbia or Lucy, who weren't available, at least a harlot in the Tenderloin, who was.

THE BACK PAGE of the *Chronicle*'s art section was solid every morning with commercials for onanism. When she noticed me going first thing all the time now to "Daily Punch," Mother praised me for finally taking a lively interest in cultural affairs. I was partial to The Question Man, from whom I won ten or twenty-five dollars at age eleven for submitting the question: "How do you impress a woman?" It was a legitimate concern of mine in the sixth grade, what with Mother seeming to be pretty much unwinnable, and I remember going to school the day The Question Man used my question, seeing Z on the other side of the big ballfield, and feeling intuitively that the way to impress women was to appear oblivious to them while performing a difficult feat intently and well, so I slid down the banister on my hip. I'm not sure I'd answer the question so very differently even now. By the fall of 1973 The Question Man was losing his allure for me, the theater reviews and editorial cartoons had misplaced their pungency, and movies about sado-masochism alone retained my interest. Or, precisely, advertisements for movies about sado-masochism, since I had yet to see one, and less the blurry images in the ads than the words, whose inevitable alliteration ("Debasement, debauchery, and defilement—beyond human dignity!") sounded like the tintinnabulation of desire.

The *San Francisco Chronicle* is perhaps the only newspaper in the world that would have seen a new wrinkle in the technological development of pornography as meriting a full-length review. I remember the review was by someone named John Wasserman, and the beautiful dreamers were the Winchell Brothers, who also brought us Flasher Gordon in *Lust in Space*. I wish to hell John Wasserman hadn't written that review. I wish to hell the Winchell Brothers hadn't pursued the project. I wish to hell they hadn't, because the Impossibility of Relief from Loneliness presented itself to me like a tabloid headline the night I ventured into the Tenderloin district.

One Saturday night when Mother and Father were attending a party with Beth in Palo Alto in honor of an English professor who felt he'd been denied tenure for telling a senior seminar that in *Typee* Herman Melville had produced a Marxist analysis of Jacksonian democracy, I walked toward Market Street. I still walked with a little limp. This was the first time I'd ever been alone in the Tenderloin and I was struck, first, by how *turista* the crowd was—so many white shoes and colorful shirts with collars folded over sport jacket lapels—and, second, by how self-contradictory the promenade was: on the outside, Denver businessmen trembling to enter movie theaters, equipment stores, whorehouses; on the inside, bored teenage girls committed to methadone. The opposing camps had nothing to say to each other, I didn't want to align myself with the Denver businessmen, so I looked for the Winchell Brothers, who were situated between a kind of bookstore and dance hall.

"Let us live," I said for the last time to the back page of "Daily Punch" I kept in my back pocket, "and love and kiss a thousand kisses."

Now, of course, in 1978, phone fantasy booths are a staple of every self-respecting red light district, but John Wasserman seemed to feel the first black box was born right here. *Mr. Zorn, come here, I want you.* The fact that I didn't look eighteen didn't seem to deter me at all once I paid the ten-dollar admission. When one cannot talk, it is advisable for one always to have a piece of paper to point to. I took the ad out of my pocket again and pointed to the booths. The receptionist, an old woman with broken nails, made a broad gesture in the general direction of infinity. Her weary nonchalance was the first surprise among many. A lot of married couples were walking around together, well-dressed Asians, hippies high on life. Saturday night at the sex emporium had less the quality of saturnalia than a Webelos meeting.

I put in appearances at the bachelor party in a back room and the floor show, but I seemed to know on some obscure level that the test I'd come to take was the phone fantasy booth. There were several women squeaking themselves against the glass of their booths: what I'm afraid I've come to recognize as the usual Pam Greer lookalikes and geisha girls and dirty blonde morphine addicts. I'm so obvious, I'm as predictable as pain: a snaky-haired, smoky-eyed vixen froze me with an emptying glance. I purchased tokens from a man behind a podium.

"One dollar—one token," he explained, like he was talking to a two-year-old. "One token—one minute. Tipping not required."

My initial impulse was not to hurt the other girls' feelings by going directly to the dominatrix holding up the far wall, so I walked around the phone fantasy area as if the decision were an agonizingly difficult one, clinking my tokens, which were the size and heft of old Kennedy halves. Ridiculously, I imagined myself pursuing some important, transformative purpose.

The booth was divided in half with glass. When I put my first token in the slot a screen creaked upwards to reveal my bitch-goddess mock-masturbating in an orange bikini and white high heels. She had little purple marks around her lips like poorly applied makeup. When I picked up my receiver she picked up her receiver, and when she picked up her receiver my side of the booth dimmed to darkness. I can't emphasize that enough. I can't imagine a more concise statement of what's gone so riotously wrong with my life: *when she picked up her receiver my side dimmed to darkness.* So far as I can see, that sums up the situation.

"Gimme another dollar," she said.

"I thought tipping wasn't required," I said.

"That's only for the black girls."

"Oh," I said and started to slide another token into the slot.

"No, dummy," she said. "Cash."

All this was on the phone. She wasn't supposed to be able to see me, but apparently she could spy through the shadows. Maybe she just heard the sound of the tokens.

"How?" I asked.

She rapped on the edge of the glass, pointing to a slit in the plastic that joined the mirror. I gave her a five to get things going. I'd borrowed the money from the *London Journal* emergency fund, of which I was treasurer, bookkeeper, and primary recipient. I planned to reimburse the money sooner or later. I thought the adventure might make an interesting feature article some day and, if this wasn't an emergency, what was? When you're sixteen nothing seems quite so serious as sex.

And yet this was sex and not sex. The purpose of the glass was to insure that you wouldn't actually have to touch the other person. The process was all pretty self-explanatory as it went along, but it was unclear to me whether the lady on the other line might not break down the glass or come up out of a trap door if I paid her enough money. I even had hopes that, like Clark Kent, I'd swap my pimples and repetitions for a capital red *S*.

The screen creaked down, so I spent another token to witness her orange ass rubbing now against the mirror, causing the pane to wobble a bit. She was sticking her finger in and out of her mouth like a little girl with languorous eyes, but she had the receiver hanging down around her waist and I wanted to talk to her, so I spoke up.

"Hi, my name's Jeremy."

"Hi. What would you like?"

"I don't know," I said, "just for you to talk to me, I guess."

Still facing away from me, she adjusted and readjusted her bikini bottom in apparent discomfort and swayed to one side to show me the shelf of sex toys and hair- and skin-care products behind her. I frequented Mother's bathroom and self-help magazines enough to know what they were: all her eye shadow and black arts. She had an unusual way of moving her mouth as she spoke, almost squinting to emphasize her misplaced purple lipstick.

"What do you like?" she said.

I was about to answer when the screen rose again. She insisted on another tip for not turning my "underage ass" in to the management. What did I care? It was the London Journal emergency fund, but her certainty that I was going to pay her aggravated me. She was very sexy, like a witch at the beach. She knew she possessed my penis in her little pinkie and she seemed to need to remind me of this debt every half-minute or so. This aggravated me, but she also seemed to understand that I was the type of boy who didn't know what he liked other than to be further aggravated.

"So: talk? That's what you like?"

"Yes," I said.

"Like what kind of talk?" she said.

"I don't know," I said.

"Like maybe real dirty talk?" she said, squinting.

"Yes," I said. "I guess."

And then, immediately, she began. She spoke with all the pent-up passion of the lady you get on tape when you call time and hear a perfect replication of human speech only without the pauses between numbers for breath. Which, of course, was the excitement of the exchange: her disinterested control. She scratched the glass with her long nails and, moaning into the mike, repeated degradations through her China-doll smile like she was suffering from Tourette's syndrome. I'm not sure the thesis committee needs to dwell overly long on the details: all kinds of analogies between me and most barnyard animals, my identification with my own waste products, my desire to curl up in a ball at her feet. As I dribbled into my denims she faced me directly, though the idea was that she still couldn't see my eyes in black light.

She was supposed to have stayed in her booth until I was visiting valet parking, but she peeked out her door—for one last bonus, I guess. So far I'd spent twenty dollars for the opportunity of hugging myself. I gave her five more dollars and she seemed to take pity on me because I was so easy. She scraped her weird purple lips against mine in a lunge.

"Come back soon, sugar," she said. "You're unusual."

The cabby had some trouble finding what he called my "hotsy-totsy address." After a few wrong turns onto one-way streets, he arrived at the destination and kept the meter running while I went inside to get more money for his tip. I had to hope Mother and Father hadn't returned yet from the Melville party in Palo Alto. They hadn't. I tipped the cabby one hundred percent, as if to palliate what I assumed was his acute sense of my eccentricity. For reasons I can't say I understand, I thought he thought I was homosexual. I watched him drive down the hill, then I just stood in the street for a while, shivering on the sidewalk, watching the blinking lights of the city burn, trying to recall the story Father told about the censor who was so adamant in his deletion of the navel from movies that his austerity stunned even the studios. After he died, police found in his desk an immense album of photographs featuring women's navels. They were his only hobby.

HERE'S WHAT HAPPENED at the *Typee* party in Palo Alto: Michael, the Berkeley military historian Beth met on the march, came to the protest party with his star student, Charles Ellenboegen, my friend from childhood. Beth attended the event partly to support her least favorite professor but more to see Mother and Father for the first time in a month and even more to see Michael, whom everyone let finish introducing Charles to Beth and Mother and Father before the coincidence inaugurated laughter. The entire party wound up on President Lyman's lawn around midnight, carrying candles and placards of instructive passages from *Typee*. President Lyman said he was sympathetic but, at quarter of one, kind of tired. Sunday morning, of course, I was subtly insulted by Mother and Father for not having driven an hour and a half south through date-night traffic, and I was raked over the coals even more thoroughly by a letter apparently written in candlelight by Charles, hand delivered by Father. Charles was two years older than I was, an eighteen-year-old sophomore, and he had a lot to share.

"I have come to grips with the fact that violence will have to be used at one time against the powers that control this country," went the salutation. "This is materialism—looking at the objective conditions of a situation and drawing a conclusion. I plan to be very disciplined in my studies with few distractions. I'm learning to look at people not in such a linear fashion but in process. I've realized that most of my criticism of others was a result of this oversight and my own egotism. Things are neither good nor bad. They just are. This is the materialistic conception of the world: no matter if we would like a pie in the sky or whatever, we gotta deal with what is there. I am also a student of dialectics, which is the science of transformation where change takes place in a material sense. The act of liberating oneself is a fine and splendid idea, Jeremy, but how is it to happen?" I don't know, Charles. "Many make a practice of standing above society and expressing themselves in some form or another, doing things they were not taught to do, and by doing so they feel they are in fact liberating themselves. However, liberation is a political act."

At the *Typee* party Mother and Father found Michael grim to the point of being gruff, stiff to the point of being stuffed, etc.

20

INHERENTLY UNFULFILLABLE fantasies were one thing and first love, I wanted to believe, was another. Only in California could she have entered my life wearing a tennis dress in January: Barbie Levine, a mid-year transfer student from a public school down the Peninsula, a junior so Jewish as to be Father's long lost sister who died at sixteen, standing in the doorway of the *Journal* office. It was late Thursday afternoon, the paper was being printed on Friday, and I was furiously correcting galley sheets when I heard the words: "Is this the office of the *London Journal?*"

Which wasn't a very intriguing question, so I continued correcting galleys without looking up.

"Well," she said, "I hate to bother you, you look real busy, but my name is Barbie Levine and I'd like very much to join the staff of the *Journal.*"

I just kept making notes in the margins. "Uh-huh," I said. "What experience do you have?"

"Features editor for two years at the *Aragon Aristocrat.* Teacher profiles, student hobbies, music reviews, Q and A columns. You know, that kind of thing."

We received high school newspapers from all over the Bay Area and the *Aragon Aristocrat* was always the one I threw out first. She was the former features editor of the worst high school newspaper in northern California. She used "real" as an adverb. Her voice was polite. She didn't seem terribly promising. I still hadn't looked up.

"As you can see, I'm actually rather busy right now, Barbara. If you'll sign up for Advanced Journalism, check the assignment sheet next Tuesday, then write me a two-page double-spaced story I'll—"

"Look, you," she said, "I don't know who you are. You're probably just some lowly assistant sports editor or something, but for ten days I've been trying to build up the courage to come into this office and you're not making it any easier. I transferred here just to work on the *Journal.* I love your layouts, your editorials, your twenty-one-point headlines. No one at this stupid school has yet to say a kind word to me. I heard people at London were real cold, but I didn't expect them to be this bad. Are you all like that? Don't any of you ever stop for a second to catch your breath? The course load is criminal, the teachers are frightening, the students are insanely intelligent and they know it, the modular schedule is confusing, the courtyard is too clean, the swimming pool is too long. I was hitting a tennis ball against the backboard, the girls' tennis team came and kicked me off, I stayed for a while to watch them, and even they were imposing. Aren't there any normal people around here?"

I refused to define myself as normal chiefly to make her feel better, but she had expressed her admiration for the *Journal* and I thought the least I could do was look up. She was crying. Her hair was in her eyes. Her tennis dress was, as Father would have said, "oishkispieldt"—in disarray. Her socks were down around her ankles. Her left shoe was untied. She was crying. Her aluminum racquet was in one hand, her satchel of books was in the other; I took the racquet and books out of her hands, pulled up a chair for her, poured her some coffee from my thermos, presented her with a box of tissues, and brushed the bangs off her face.

"You're real nice," she said.

"You're real upset," I said.

"Do you have any more coffee?" she asked.

"So," I said, pouring another cup, "you play tennis?"

"No." She knew my question was a straight line and thought her answer was the quintessence of wit. "I carry this thing around to swat mosquitoes."

I laughed loud to make her feel good and said, "We'll have to get together sometime to play."

That Sunday overweight husbands and white-socks-with-pink-puffballs wives were playing doubles to either side of us and arguing about proper application of the territorial imperative, while we were content with the pleasure of new balls bouncing from my racquet to hers, tight strings, the song of a good rally. We lay down on the grass and used opposite ends of a bath towel Barbie had brought and drank Cokes charged to her father's account.

Suddenly, out of nowhere, when language was unnecessary, while stirring her ice, she said, "You limp a little on balls hit to your left."

I wanted to kiss her for uttering a line with such perfect sonic balance, but instead I told her the story of the day at the beach, the summer in traction, the brace on my thigh. Complications. She touched where the stitches had been, the scar tissue around the bone.

"Does it still hurt?" she said.

"No," I said. "Not really. Only when it rains."

"When it rains?"

"Yes," I said, wiping my face with my part of the towel. "When it rains I get a twinge in my left leg. When it rains"—I exaggerated to make myself appear brave—"I can feel the pin rubbing against the femur."

"When it rains it pours," she said.

"Yes," I said, smiling, though I had no idea what she meant by this, which didn't matter, because language doesn't represent life: it prophesies it. Within thirty seconds of Barbie's curious remark clouds collided, precipitating precipitation.

Although Father vociferously urged us not to see it because he felt both the book and the play romanticized and thus exploited mental illness, we saw a production of One Flew Over the Cuckoo's Nest off-Geary. Brandenburg Concerto Number Four, the happiest moment in human history, played over and over while Barbie drove us there in her fast-back Mustang. Her window was down. Cold, clear air blew through the air like promises. High school seems like it happened such a long time ago. Barbie sipped diet soda. Traffic was thick. The play was just well lit, overacted insanity—maybe Father was right for once—but Billy Bibbitt, the guy who played Billy Bibbitt, I explained to Barbie, who was so sympathetic she nearly cried with compassion, the guy who played Billy Bibbitt was God.

The fluorescent lights still flickered and the typewriters still had jammed margin releases, but soon the Journal walls were bright with posters of Mrs. Levine's from various shows at the DeYoung Museum and "funky" tapestries (Barbie's word). We took ourselves too seriously and had an office in which to work—all those long tables and folded proof sheets, reams of faded mimeo paper, grade-school scissors. I was the editor and Barbie was the assistant editor. I scribbled the story assignments in pencil, so no one could read them and Barbie and I could write all the articles. The newspaper was, to me, the unwilling child, the final truth-teller of the school, not that the students or teachers read it. The more unpopular the Journal, and Barbie and I, became, the more vengeful my satires and the more allusive the paper as a whole tended. With deepening desperation and frequency, we retreated to the white walls of the little office, where we hated everything except each other and the sound of the door being closed from the inside—a sound I believe I may have mentioned before. By the end of the year it would have been difficult to argue that what we edited was anything other than a five-column, four-page biweekly private correspondence.

Barbie was chief photographer as well as assistant editor, clicking pictures wherever she went, the Instamatic camera strapped over her shoulder like a purse and the pink gloss applied like a kind of lipstick. She was such a demure and polite interviewer that most people, especially less good-looking vice principals, felt compelled to fill the silence with sensational revelations. She also had the ability, which never ceased to wow Mother, to write a headline that not only precisely fit the line's word count but also contained some semi-obscure pun. And she cultivated a smooth writing style, although sometimes her coy confessions and subtle self-mockery dominated a story to such an extent that the casual reader was soon more interested in the dark recesses of Barbie's soul than the pressing need to recycle aluminum cans.

The first time we drove together to the printer in South San Francisco the bay hadn't been visible from 101, but as we exited the off-ramp, spiraling onto a gravel road, we suddenly saw the sun backlighting the water. Suddenly we were looking at not license plates and guard rails but the benediction of white beams on a circle of blue lead. Like Charles's whisper when we counted change or the Last Tier Quintet's song in dark silence, the refracting shimmer made conversation sound absurd, so we drove the rest of the way to the printer and most of the way back without a word spoken between us.

MOTHER GAVE ME all sorts of advice as to proper etiquette—napkin placement, knife position, witty repartee, that kind of thing—and Father said, "Whatever you do, be true to yourself," four words of which rhyme but which I accepted, nevertheless, as sound counsel. Difficult to follow, however, when I was greeted on the front porch by a Venezuelan maid in white hat and apron, offering what must have been a dozen choices of cheese, while the three of them— Dr. and Mrs. Levine and Barbie—came forward in excellent attire.

Dr. Levine was wearing a suit and vest and those special brown shoes with air holes in the toes that seem less than ludicrous only when worn by the medical profession. With a yellow corsage pinned to her pink dress, Mrs. Levine looked like spring, though clouds swirled from the west. Barbie was wearing white buckled shoes, a white lace dress, her hair in a pony tail, and a watch on her wrist that gleamed. The only suit I owned was too short in the sleeves and it was this too-short, quite faded outfit in which I was sweating when Dr. Levine said, "Barbie tells me you're a perfect genius at running the newspaper."

"Barbie said that?" I said. "Well, that's very nice, but it's not really true. After a while, the paper practically runs itself."

"Oh, now, I know that's not true," Mrs. Levine said. "At least with *creative* writing that's never true. I mean, my Harlequin Romances never write themselves. Down to the last line of dialogue, I'm inventing and cogitating and analyzing mood and character."

The dining room was dark except for candles on a white tablecloth with white roses. I assumed the maid had prepared the delicious dinner—brown rice and fruit salad, beef stroganoff, asparagus, honeydew—because Mrs. Levine looked like she hadn't lifted a finger, except to type up mood and character, since she was in college.

"So, Jeremy," Dr. Levine kept at me, "so what do you see yourself becoming?"

"Becoming, sir?"

Barbie kicked me with her buckled white shoes.

Dr. Levine dabbed more butter on his rice and said, "Yes, Jeremy. Becoming. Don't young men want to become anything any more? Your mother is a fine journalist. Your father is—still? Am I right?—director of the poverty program. I'm an ear-nose-and-throat man, as is Barbie's older brother. What profession do you want to enter, Jeremy?"

"I see what you mean," I said, stalling, pouring myself and Barbie more milk. "I think—I think I w-w-want to become a writer, sir."

"Call me Lew."

"I think I w-w-want to become a writer, Lew."

"Really? What kind of writer?"

"A real writer."

"What does that mean?"

"Honey, you know what Jeremy means," Mrs. Levine teased her husband. "There's no more noble calling than good work with words."

"Fill me in, Jeremy," Dr. Levine said. "Explain it to the cultural ignoramus. What's a real writer? And why do you want to become one?"

I wanted to become a writer because it struck me as my last opportunity to cease being the victim of language. However, I didn't think such an unhappy insight was appropriate dinner table discussion—it was the very kind of *faux pas* Mother had coached me against committing—so I said, "Well, my mother is, as you know, a journalist and my father used to be a reporter and he reads a lot of books and tells funny stories and writes good letters. I want to be like them but different."

"Good," Mrs. Levine said, clapping her well-preserved if highly lotioned hands over her head. "More power to you. Very good."

"Different?" Dr. Levine said.

"Not be a journalist. Make stuff up, I guess. I don't know yet."

Dr. Levine didn't much like either of my ideas—that children could surpass their parents or that words might be used in an unusual way—and he shifted the topic to his strong impression that Barbie was going to follow his footsteps into medicine.

"Maybe, Dad," Barbie said. "I said that last year. But that was before I met Jeremy."

"What?" Dr. Levine said with such violence that he blew out the candle at his end, and we sat in semidarkness until Mrs. Levine—the very embodiment of the creative principle—relit the wick.

"I've so enjoyed working with Jeremy on the *Journal* that I think maybe—I'm just thinking about it, so don't get mad, Dad—I'd like to become a writer as well, maybe a magazine writer like Jeremy's mom. You should read some of her articles in *The Nation*, Dad. They're really good."

Dr. Levine did not want to read Mother's articles in *The Nation*. He didn't care if they were really good. He swirled his finger in his coffee cup saucer and refused to touch his eclair, which Mrs. Levine offered me and which I, never sated, saw no reason to reject. That upset him even more and he said, "Come on, Helen, we're going to a movie," which Dr. and Mrs. Levine always did whenever Dr. Levine was irate. Apologizing to Barbie and me for her husband's behavior and telling us to let the maid clear and wash the dishes, Mrs. Levine followed Dr. Levine out the back door, the sharp slam of which caused Barbie to exclaim: "Do you realize they won't be back for at least two hours?"

Well, yes, I said: the drive to the theater, the feature film, the drive back. Two hours. Easily.

"In most things you are, as Dad said I said, a 'perfect genius,' but in some things"—she started tickling—"you're so *stupid*."

Barbie's room was what her mother called "classic anal-retentive." For all my impulses in this direction, by the time I was seventeen my room had receded from view as the repository of any portion of my selfhood. Shirts and shoes fell like maps and mice all over my carpet while Barbie's room was a series of right angles, everything tucked and fitted in girls' colors. Every book was shelved the same way, nothing floated on the thick red sea of the rug, her electric typewriter was shrouded. There wasn't anywhere to relax. Her mother was always urging her to throw a slumber party. This, I suppose, was it.

We lay on her bed with all its pillows and panda bears, brushing the hair out of each other's eyes and slowly removing each other's clothes. When you get older you undress yourself, but the first time and for a while thereafter you undress each other. It takes a lot longer, but it's really much nicer.

"Ear-nose-and-throat?" I said, taking off her watch. "You were really once going to—"

"Damn straight," she said, employing the vernacular to suggest this wasn't her house on Nob Hill—she had lived. She kissed my ears, my belly button, the soles of my feet.

. . . with the lights off because we were still only seventeen, with the air conditioner on so the maid couldn't hear, with blankets and pillows on the floor and pretzels and soda in bed, with both male and female contraceptives to correspond to our feeling that the future didn't exist. My bad leg tightened up and she misinterpreted my scream. She herself did not scream. She patted my head. It was over much too soon. The sensation was unsensational. The experience was disappointing. We repeated the disappointing experience and—if memory serves—repeated it again, looking, I would imagine, for increasingly profound revelations about ourselves and each other and finding, instead, only the regressive frustration that exists at the core of any act of communication. I thought her parents would be returning soon. I told her I loved her, gathered my clothes, and tiptoed out the room, looking for light.

The maid was partial to police dramas or shows, at any rate, that featured flashy gun play. Whenever a criminal tiptoed into view, she'd rub the Levines' butterscotch candies like rosary beads and imprecate: "Bad man, bad man, bad man." Never one to sidestep a chance to crucify myself mercilessly, I scooted through the dark living room around midnight and heard her address an assailant peeking in a patio door, which I took as the simple truth from someone who knew.

21

FATHER WAS—STILL? am I right?—the director of the poverty program and hired me as a teacher's aide in a Hunters Point summer school for black children who'd been bussed uptown during the school year, failed their courses, and now had to attend this remedial session in their own neighborhood. The second-grade teacher I was assigned to assist called in sick the first day; boys stood on top of desks, pushing one another off, and girls gathered in a circle, flashing pocket mirrors and combing their hair. One little boy was hanging out the window, another was climbing in: they collided. Kids were eating crayons, spitting water, wrestling. I removed my coat and said, "I'm in charge here." Louder I said, "My name is Mr. Zorn. Jeremy Zorn. I'm teaching this class."

"You what?"

"I'm teaching this class."

"The fuck you are."

"Shut you mouth, white boy."

"Big nosed motherfucker."

"I-I-I'm teaching this class and would appreciate your undivided—"

"You what?"

"I'd—"

"Get out of my face, jewboy."

"Faggot."

I called roll and nobody answered except a little girl with crooked teeth and her coat still on named Lorraine Warren, who raised her hand, said she was here, walked to the front of the room, picked up a yardstick from the chalkboard tray, and smashed it against the desk in front of her.

"The man said he was in charge here," she said.

Silence obtained.

The second Monday of the six-week session the teacher called in sick again and I said, "Close the windows. Stop running. Stop wrestling. Stop drinking. Stop eating. Stop talking. Shut your dirty little mouths and sit down in your seats. Give me your attention because I'm in charge of this classroom." I unrolled a map of the world. "Do all of you know what this is?"

"Atlas."

A little boy who squinted and needed glasses but couldn't afford them explained that it was an encyclopedia. Lorraine said it was a map.

I said, "Yes."

They said, "Shut your face, girl."

They said, "Kissass."

They said, "Niggergirl."

They *sang* words.

Lorraine wriggled in her seat and zipped up her coat. It was the middle of summer and she was cold.

"What does the blue mean?" I asked.

"Blue means crayon."

"Blue means paint."

"No, sucker, means air. Blue means blue sky."

I asked Lorraine what the blue meant.

"Don't know."

I asked her again.

"Don't know."

"The blue means water," I said. "Ocean. The Pacific Ocean. The Atlantic Ocean. The Arctic Ocean. The Indian Ocean. Is the world flat or round?"

"Flat."

"Flat as J.J.'s sister."

"The world is round," I said.

"Get off."

"White man's crazy."

"Do you know where your ancestors came from? Can you point on the map to where they came from?"

"They come from uptown."

"They dead."

"Have you heard of A-A-Africa? Do you know where it is? Can someone come up and point to A-A-Africa?"

A girl with ankle bracelets walked to the map and pointed to Paris.

"Do you know what country you live in? What state? Do you know what city? Do you know where you are?" The bell rang and I said, "Nobody's leaving until someone comes to the map and points to what city we're living in."

Lorraine got up, walked to the map, stood on a chair, stretched, pointed, and the class loved her.

Friday of the next-to-last week we took them on a field trip to Water World, a zoo for fish. Parents' permission slips had been sent home and returned with signatures that resembled children's penmanship. The kids came dressed to kill: boys with pressed pants, white shirts, black button-down sweaters, and girls with lipstick— seven-year-old girls with lipstick—and skirts and bouncy blouses. Lorraine wore earrings, eye shadow, glossy white lipstick, and a taffeta dress to her ankles. All this for Water World; imagine if we had taken them to the theater. They stood in single file according to home room, pinned name tags to their clothes, and boarded the buses. The principal loaded his camera. Lorraine sat next to me and asked questions: "Will you open the window? Would you like some gum? Can you please push the seat back? How old are you? Do you have a girlfriend? Do you like me?"

Her hip rested against my leg. Everyone on the bus was singing "Then Came You" and Lorraine sang softly, out of key, in my ear. She held my hand and squeezed tight as we walked across the parking lot to the turnstiles. We walked arm in arm, Lorraine and I, through an underground tunnel that was lined on both sides with tanks of dogfish, hammerhead sharks, skates, sawfish, deep-water spiny eels, flute mouths, sea horses, and at every tank Lorraine pressed her nose to the glass, said she was scared, asked me to hold her, asked me to read aloud the little blurb about each fish. I did my best. She purchased a Water World pennant for me. She gave me her lunch and stole extra milks for me. We went to the whale show and when that blue monster flopped onto its belly, splashing waves into the balcony, Lorraine buried her head in my chest to keep dry. At the end of the day, when we were counting heads, she hid so I'd find her. On the bus home she fell asleep with her head on my lap. She was seven and in heaven.

Wednesday of the last week we held Open House. I stayed late after school, rearranging the room and tacking up student papers and drawings. I told the parents how well their children were progressing, how much I enjoyed working with them, how confident I was they wouldn't have to stay back when school rolled around in the fall. I encouraged the parents to read to their children, to have their children read to them. We drank punch and coffee, ate stale sugar cookies. In the auditorium a slide show of the field trip was presented, at the conclusion of which the audience stood, applauding, some so happy they cried. An elegant black woman with hair high as the ceiling walked toward me and said, "Lorraine told me about you."

"You must be—"

"I don't like that color slide of Lorraine whispering in your ear. I don't like that one bit, mister."

"I was sleeping."

"You keep your itchy paws away from her, you understand? You so much as touch her and your ass is glass."

"She's seven years old."

"Glass, mister, do you hear me?"

The principal's final evaluation of me consisted of one sentence: "Should try to be more relaxed around students (has bad speech impediment)."

22

"HAVING ONE'S WAY isn't always possible," Beth explained last weekend while we were puttering around the family hearth, gathering goods. "Neither is it always preferable. You do have a tendency toward absolution. I mean absolutism. Whatever." Until she became a disciple of Meher Baba—"Don't worry, be happy"—the closest she ever came to religious conversion was when she was reading Cotton Mather sermons. The fondest memory I have is the two of us sitting together against her headboard reading the comics in early light. When we were little, if either of us was sick, we'd both stay home and take double baths; I'd splash her ponytail from behind, mercilessly. She was always seeking my hand and my hands were always deep in my pockets. I always seemed to be running away, away from Beth, who'd be playing her zither in an uncomfortable chair.

She must have held out her chewably chubby little hand, and I must have blanched once too often because, following a Halloween on which I was Lucifer and she was a princess, our masks were permanently in place. I can only see her flat-footed in the back row of ballet class, overdressed at Renaissance Faires, trailing even Mother on Yosemite expeditions. We all stopped to feed a deer in Tuolumme Meadows and Bambi came this close to ripping open Beth's stomach when the Oreos were gone. I often felt sorry for her; I at least had symptoms. Her sorrow swooned in her body, swelling it. We were forever arguing about something superficial—me wanting to read *Parsley, Sage, Rosemary and Thyme* liner notes the minute she started reading them, me saying she looked gargantuan perched in a miniature dollhouse (with tiny Tide and scaled-to-size Kleenex) Uncle Gil had given her. When I was a baby she set up camp outside my crib, offering her arm through the slats whenever I chanced to look up. I have pictures. This is exhibit AA. Examine the tangle of thorns.

I've never understood my sister very well. She's always been four years older and far away and fabulously intelligent. I wish I knew her. I'm not pretty any more, but I'm afraid she's even less pretty. She has a large nose and long chin and apple cheeks and eyebrows that almost touch and she wears overalls and black high-tops. I don't know if that's much of a description. I suppose it isn't. What did Michael see in her and she in him? He was the first man she'd ever kissed and, for all I know, maybe the last. Now her eternal suitor is Meher Baba. She has postcards of Meher Baba pasted up all over her place in Berkeley. "Mayor of what?" Father likes to say. Michael was just a shy guy recovering from divorce who needed someone with whom to discuss the plight of Revolutionary War pensioners.

I thought a lot about Beth when I left for UCLA, since I came here precisely to escape the influence of such seminal thinkers as Beth and Mother. L.A.: city not of words but pretty pictures I could walk around in. From Father I'd inherited my definition of Los Angeles as a good place for forgetting the difficulty of the interior life up north, and why wouldn't it be romantic arcadia for him? Here, in the first few years of their marriage, Mother used to call Father *The Man*. Although it's difficult for me to imagine Mother ever having called him anything other than Your Father, I've always acknowledged that such an epithet must have been earned, for this was no mere nickname. It was a title of almost absolute authority: Mother tucked mash notes, red ink on creamy white stationery, into his suitcase whenever he traveled.

Maybe the problem later on was that he just didn't travel often enough or far enough. They frequently drove together to Sacramento and got lost, with Father bearing the brunt of blame for not being an expert cartographer or not remembering to ask for a funnel as well as a can of fuel. . . . A piece was missing from a frozen cake. Mother went around the table in that inimitable way of hers. We all denied doing it. "Well, I don't care if you believe me because I know I didn't do it," Father said. "Well you *should* care because it means I don't trust you," Mother said. . . . After a gruesome argument, whose subject matter escapes me, Father had a dozen roses delivered to Mother, who garbage-disposaled them and dismissed the gesture as "schoolboy." I was at the time a schoolboy, as I suppose I still am, and I yearned to understand what she meant. What she may have meant was that she always wore hats in photographs to cover her face while Father removed his glasses and really mugged, hungry for something on the other side of the flash. She was bitter that he was so handsome and helpless, so decidedly not a dream guy for a girl in distress. . . .

And yet, before I was born, Mother and Father and Beth had lived quite happily on Carnation Street in the Silver Lake district. I didn't at all remember Carnation Street, since shortly afterward we moved to what was then still very much the middle-class outpost of the Palisades; while my fellow freshmen were attending orientation sessions, I drove around Silver Lake, imagining Carnation Street as a narrow one-way at the top of a hill, on which horses drew carriages and crushed petals of pink carnations, and Chinese lanterns swung boxed light. The house would be made of carnations, too, a wood frame packed solid with pink flowers. I got lost in an interesting Latino neighborhood in the middle of the night and there were no petals anywhere. I drove up and back the streets in the dark, looking for a porch light that ran burglar alarms in my heart.

Beth, three years old and arms around Raggedy Ann, probably

slept under a blanket of carnations while in the next room, on a sofa mattress of pink petals, The Man and, as Mother did not to my knowledge have a nickname, The Woman went at it for my sake. I've never been very good with numbers but I can figure out that it must have been the fall of '55: Annette stepping out of the shower with her hair wrapped in a towel and Teddy smoking a pipe, which he puffed for a few years at the beginning of their marriage because Annette told him it made him look like Adlai Stevenson. (The resemblance was infinitesimal.) I can hear Annette turning out the lights and the bed of carnations bouncing up against the wall that separated their room from Beth's. I can hear Mother thinking, at the most climactic moments, about work the next morning—what to wear, what to write—and attempting to coo in the manner Teddy told her his first wife had done, but her heart wasn't in it. Their technique in 1955 couldn't have been too sophisticated: a few quick kisses, the placing of pillows, a twitch in the thighs. Annette must have been unaware there was any possibility of pleasure in this for her, either. I see Father as too selfish, too much the athlete on the attack. Tall, thin, and bald, Teddy must have looked to Annette like the very instrument of his masculinity. Mother probably thought she heard Beth crying and got up to check while Father lit his pipe, a happy man. Did the sky open wide? Did the smog lift or freezing rain fall across Los Angeles? I doubt the house was even covered with carnations.

Probably apocryphal but endlessly reiterated: Mother was in such pain that she didn't stop to think what she was doing when Father, unable to find the emergency entrance to L.A. County Hospital, parked on the sidewalk, pulled her out of the back seat, and told her to hold the handrail. She slowly ascended the stairs, crying, until, at the top of the steps, as an extremely nice nurse was opening the door, she collapsed. Mother awoke and screamed for the next twelve hours, at the end of which she had a breech birth. The danger of a breech birth is that the head—in this case, my head—comes out last, which dramatically increases the possibility that the umbilical cord will get wrapped around the neck—in this case, my neck. Choking myself by clinging too long to Mother. I entered the world feet first, then remained in the hospital an extra week to get a little R&R in a warm incubator that Father guarded like a goalie whenever anyone came within striking distance. If I lay still for more than a few minutes, Father apparently pounded on the glass dome. I wasn't dead, Father. I was only sleeping.

Of course I mentioned Mother's name five minutes into the first conversation I had with the *Daily Bruin* editorial board. Of course I scoured the archives, seeking the palest shadow of Mother's legacy to us all. Of course the bound volumes didn't go back beyond 1950. Of course the *Front Page*–like sweatshop in which Mother labored found no analogue in our new cold-type headquarters. Of course I was the only freshman ever allowed to write a cover story for the *Daily Bruin*'s weekly magazine before Thanksgiving vacation. Of course. Of course. Something called New Journalism—the idea was to show up at shipwrecks and free-associate from the sand on the shore—was still quite the rage at the time and I thought this might be an easy way to be imaginative without actually having to work up any extended empathy for anyone else. Since the Second World War the Southland Department of Oxygen Masks has pretended to be interested in building a monorail from San Diego to Bakersfield, so I evoked ticket-takers falling asleep in the caboose, teenage girls moving their lips as they read Mrs. Levine's *Sweet Savage Surrender,* beach towns passed in the night, whereas the editor wanted the article to focus upon projections of passenger use, turbo engine theories, electrified track analyses, catalogues of delayed beginnings. I wrote the story the way he wanted it, which he splashed across page one with pictures and maps and which Mother said was "nothing less than a first-rate piece of investigative if slightly speculative journalism," but it wasn't what I wanted to be doing. I wanted somewhere in the world I was writing about for my own mind to dominate.

My next assignment also concerned the future of an illusion: Southern California Edison's desire to build a nuclear power plant in the Mojave Desert. In a longish, if to me very lovely, opening paragraph, I attempted to evoke the exact color of goldenrod in the natural light of the falling, February sun at quarter of four on an ex–Air Force base, and in the final, perhaps somewhat too apoc-alyptic paragraph I imagined all that gorgeous goldenrod melting down. When the magazine editor edited out these two—and only these two—paragraphs from what was otherwise a soporifically dull account of the debate, I called Mother around noon.

"Where are you calling from?" Mother asked. As a little kid I so loved listening to Mother interrogate people on the phone that I purchased my own extension, and my only problem was remem-bering not to mention some tidbit I'd learned eavesdropping. I loved her voice: how *interested* it could sound. I knew she was at her desk in the den, cradling her phone between her ear and left shoulder while tamping a cigarette and flipping pages of the paper. She was working now for a think tank that studied governmental abuse of computer data banks and paid Mother an amazing amount of money to translate their sheets of statistics into cautionary articles.

"My apartment," I said. "Why?"

"Don't say anything controversial, Jeremy. I think my phone is tapped."

"You're joking, right?"

"I wish I were. Ever since I started working for the institute, I hear a distant beeping noise every time I talk long distance."

"Have you talked to the phone company about it?"

"Oh, honey, you are a freshman, aren't you? The phone com-pany is the government. The government is the phone company. Aren't you aware yet of the interpenetration between bureaucracy and big business?"

I held the original version of my article in one hand and sneered at the published copy on my kitchen table, waiting for an oppor-tunity to read them aloud for Mother to compare. Finally I said, "Politics and tapped telephones aside, Mother, how are you?"

"I'm fine. Your father and I miss you, but we're doing fine. We've been playing a lot of tennis. How are you, honey?"

"Oh, I'm okay, I guess."

The article fell out of my hand. I had to crouch down to pick it up and didn't hear what Mother had said, so I just said, "Right."

"Jeremy?" Mother said.

"Yes?"

"Is there any particular reason you're calling in the middle of the day?"

"The magazine came out today with my article about Southern Cal Edison and . . ."

"Jeremy, remember: nothing politically controversial over the phone," Mother whispered.

". . . they got rid of the only two paragraphs I cared about in the whole story. Can I read them to you and get your reaction?"

"Sure, but make it quick because this is an expensive call and nothing political because I know this phone is bugged."

Her only comments were that I seemed to stutter so much worse when reading aloud—why was that?—and that she wouldn't have had a moment's hesitation taking a blue pencil to either paragraph.

"Then, quite frankly, I wonder whether I want to do j-j-journalism any more if all it is is an anonymous arrangement of trivial facts. I want my writing to be a r-r-register of my—"

"You're still using too many big words, sweetheart, and you're still stuttering miserably. If you don't want to write journalism, don't. If you want to r-r-register your sensational uniqueness, go ahead and register."

I slammed down the phone, rushed to my bedroom, and quickly composed an epic poem, solving my speech problem by turning the harsh habit of repeated sound into the pleasing strategy of transverse alliteration and retaliating against Mother by using language to rearrange the world. It wasn't quite that simple, but I did say, "Then I w-w-will. I might just do that. Toodle-oo to the telephone tappers."

I WAS ENROLLED in a 100-level Latin course in which math majors and pre-med students, boys with photographic memories but no interest in literature, nevertheless translated Plautus so perfectly that for the first time comedy actually seemed somewhat funny; read Latin aloud with such anapestic precision and grace that Terence—even Terence, that pedestrian pederast—sounded less like a grammar exercise and more like a Gregorian chant; and were appalled when they saw me carrying around, let alone consulting "trots" of the early Roman comedies. I could read Latin, but I couldn't read Latin. I didn't get the stresses right.

My Latin sounded—in comparison to these mostly Catholic boys who'd been pronouncing things right since the third grade—like muttering Spanish, and in my mouth supposedly hilarious stichomythia inevitably had the word "lest" pinned to the middle of it. I thought I must be able to do better than this, come a little closer to staying even with the Aquinas contingent, and toward that end I entered Powell Library one early fall morning of my sophomore year and have no memory of leaving until the end of the quarter.

I checked out every edition of Plautus and Terence, every translation of Plautus and Terence, every available issue of *Arion* and *Studies in Latin and Greek.* I checked out every Latin-English, English-Latin dictionary, including the monstrously outsized Oxford University Press version, which I robbed from the reference room. With these books I filled the shelves of a carrel in the stacks, on the west side, on the third floor. I placed sweaters and stuff on the neighboring carrels so no one could disturb me. I listed and studied declensions and vocabulary words on index cards, which I filed in a metal box; translated Terence word-by-word onto the blue lines of a binder; consulted dictionaries; whispered Plautus to myself.

Sometimes I'd arrive at eight in the morning, leave at midnight, then arrive again at eight in the morning, then leave at midnight. Sometimes I'd do this for weeks. Sometimes I'd bring my toothbrush. Usually I'd fall asleep at six o'clock with my head on the desk and twilight on my back. Sometimes I'd masturbate in the men's bathroom to picture books of Roman goddesses. Sometimes I'd attempt to masturbate in the men's bathroom to picture books of Roman goddesses but for one reason or another—intellectual preoccupation to the point of bodily disinterest, the distracting smell of dope—fail. I became a fan of the angry graffiti in every stall, its admirable attempt to turn words to shit. I wouldn't shower for days, weeks, and my hands would be so dirty that I blackened the books I read. I'd journey round and round the library in blue socks, buying coffee and Butterfingers bars at the canteen, falling in love with every painted hand holding every yellow Hi-Liter over every open page, parading up and down the back stairs of Powell, talking to no one in particular and myself only in Plautine Latin, yearning every night for the thump of all the lights going off as a warning that the library would be closing in fifteen minutes and then savoring for a second or two the isolated blindness, the thin window, the cool cement. *Imagine what broken glass would sound like in the dark.*

The thing about the translation of Latin is that you can't force the translation: you mustn't make one language into another prior to prolonged contemplation, you must—as every good stutterer, who has a set of synonyms for every conceivable situation, knows—exist within the dizzying ambiguity of a dozen words, not committing yourself in one syntactical direction or another but, instead, letting the language itself take you where it wants to go and where it has taken so many other sorry souls for millennia. . . . Well, I forced the translation. When called upon in class to read aloud I'd do even worse than before because, after such elaborate preparation, I felt such self-imposed pressure that I couldn't perform. There appeared to be an inverse relationship between how much I knew and how little I could communicate and this dichotomy was deepened in my, as well as the professor's, mind by the excellence of my term paper, "The Pun on 'Gemina' in Terence and Plautus: Twin as Pardox," on the last page of which Dr. Dreissen wrote: *"Optimum opus,* only slightly vitiated by occasional vagueness. Please come see me." "Please come see me" was a passionate plea for a student-teacher, Roman-style love affair, which I ignored despite the fact that I was lugging around an erection as imperishable as Aristophanes' phallus.

IT'S AN ANCIENT STORY, beginning before Demosthenes, and it has a simple moral: we try to but cannot construct reality out of words. Catullus has nothing to say to the cab driver. A poem isn't a person. Latin's only a language. Stuttering's only wasted sound. It can't become communication.

Sandra strongly disagrees concerning the next point. She says personality disorders arise from stuttering whereas I seem to want to feel only the stutterer is faithful to human tension every time he talks, only in broken speech is the form of disfluency consonant with the chaos of the world's content. Stutterers are truth-tellers; everyone else is lying. I know it's insane but I believe that.

I was having such extreme difficulty conducting conversations anywhere other than the shower that in March, out of semi-suicidal desperation, I walked down Westwood Boulevard to the UCLA Speech and Hearing Clinic. My hearing was fine. I could hear high whistles and low whispers. The structure of my cochlea was impeccable. The clinic is—"is," for two years later I still see Sandra twice a week—a four-story marble building with brightly colored carpeting inside, long echoing corridors, stone staircases, and room after room of one-way observation mirrors, black cameras in the corner, cassette recorders on wooden desks, and anxiety attacks in plastic chairs.

I'd called a few days earlier—depressing dialogue in which my voice betrayed my purpose before my message did—to schedule an appointment, so I gave my name to the receptionist, then sat in the waiting room until Sandra approached with a clipboard and, briskly shaking my hand, said, "Jeremy? Jeremy Zorn? Hi, I'm Sandra. I've been assigned to be your clinician."

I didn't like "assigned." It suggested reluctance. I didn't like "clinician." It suggested Buchenwald. I went with her into a private room that was apparently meant for three-year-old possessors of cleft palates and six-year-old lispers, as all the chairs were tiny wooden structures and there were coloring books stacked on the undersized table, plastic toys to play with on the multicolored carpet. Sandra and I sat at the absurdly small desk in our absurdly small chairs, like double Gullivers among Lilliputian furniture. She turned on the tape recorder, signaled to the camera, then asked me to tell the abbreviated tale of my titubancy. I said, "I see Mother hovering above me like a hawk on some spring day in the living room. I see Father, barefoot, sweaty, bored, bouncing a tennis ball on the Persian rug. I see Beth—no, I don't see Beth, since she's always absent—away at a classical guitar lesson. I see myself lying on the couch, watching Mother flip flash cards in front of my face, and not being able to say what each picture depicted. That's the beginning of all this business, Sandra. I see myself alone at Lido Isle, determined either to cut out my tongue or abandon English for Chinese. I see myself, at six, being unable to read 'The Death of Bozo the Clown' to my Open House audience; at seven, on the playground at Currier, surrounded by the Fifth-Grade All-Stars, with bats in their hands, being told to say *Golden Gate Park. . . .*"

I thought it was going okay. I wasn't stuttering. I was using language as well as I could to communicate the difficulty of using language, but Sandra punched off her tape recorder and said, "You realize what you're doing, don't you?"

"No."

"You're afraid you won't be able to start up again once you stop, so you just keep talking."

In what little space there was on the minuscule chair, I realigned myself slightly. I thought Sandra would be impressed with my rhetoric, but she was closer to being embarrassed for me. The chair creaked and I was afraid the legs would collapse, so I stood up.

She continued: "I hope you also realize that in a phrase like 'the beginning of all this business' you're getting back at all those years of bouncing *Bs*."

I didn't think anyone else was aware of the secret pattern of my speech. I assumed no one else understood that, for instance, "the beginning of all this business" was meant as mock commentary upon and partial triumph over being eight years old, wearing warm-feet pajamas, and saying, "Mommy, what's our b-b-b . . . what's the name, Mommy, of our b-b-babysitter?"

Sandra knew the answer to that question and she had large, technical words like "two-to-three unit repetition of initial phoneme" and "reinitiated voicing" with which to describe the circumlocution (her word) of the question itself. If I laughed, I guess it was nervous laughter, but I was also sincerely grateful that she instinctively knew what I could never have explained.

I should have realized but somehow I forgot that while I was discussing Mother's domination of dinner table discussion and Father's faint second fiddle; Beth's sad brilliance (in high school she painted a picture of a strawberry and mailed it to James Kunen, the author of *The Strawberry Statement,* who flew out to meet her but feigned a connecting flight immediately after lunch); my extreme dislike of the label *stutterer* (Sandra: " 'Stutterer' has, for you, negative connotations?" Me: "No k-k-kidding"); my particular fears of addressing an audience, reading aloud, talking on the telephone, confronting a stranger; my current dread of *F* and *S* (emblematic, Handsome Loud Blazer might have asked, of *fuck* and *shit?* "Good god, no," Sandra would answer, *F* and *S* are fricatives, that's all"); my previous dances-of-death with *M, N, B,* and *D;* my allegiance to long, and anxiety about short, sentences; my consistent substitution of any approximate synonym for a feared word; my reliance upon stutter steps, saying sentences at a certain pace so I would be able to leap through the dreaded word—while I was talking about all this and while Sandra was outlining the philosophy of the clinic (behaviorism, patient responsibility, bimonthly fee payments), I forgot that the miniature black camera in the corner was rolling. Toward the end of the hour Sandra and I marched downstairs, down the rainbow hallway, past people with monogrammed coffee cups, down the terrible stone steps to the Audio-Visual Center to study my speech.

Joined by the taping equipment technician, who sucked Lifesavers that were Platonic models of the discs he rotated, Sandra and I watched and listened to the last ten minutes of our talk together. The Audio-Visual Center was nothing more than one square room bound by glass walls and populated by a dystopian number of closed-circuit television screens. The picture on screen nine kept flipping vertically until the graduate student technician stepped forward and touched a switch. The image popped into place: Sandra, composed but a little pallid with her chalky skin, closely cropped hair, boyish chest, white blouse, dark jeans; me, my hippie hair tousled as always, my pimples glistening in the fluorescent light, my shirt sleeves so poorly rolled up as to resemble Elizabethan armlets, my head bent so low it was almost touching the top of the tiny table.

Not on the tape but in reality, Sandra turned to me and said, "You really can't stand to look at your listener, can you?"

"I'm sorry."

"Jeremy, will you please try to stop being sorry?"

"Sorry," I said. "I mean okay." The most amazing postcard ever written was written by Mother and mailed to me from Stanford Hospital exactly a year later: "Beth says I'm always making you feel guilty. About what I don't know. That certainly isn't my intent because you have nothing to feel guilty about so far as I'm concerned. But I have a strong need to let people know where I stand and, if in their judgment I'm wrong, then it's their responsibility to argue it out with me."

On the screen I encountered considerable difficulty with the word "sister." Sandra put her finger on my screen neck and said, "Do you see how tense your thorax, glottal, and mandibular areas are?"

"Yes," I said. "Yes, I do."

"Now watch as you raise your eyebrows and blink your eyes before releasing the air flow in your blocked vocal folds."

I watched. My eyebrows raised. My eyes blinked. My vocal folds, whatever they were, released the blocked air flow, whatever that was. After a few seconds, I said, "sister." Unblamable Beth, cause of so much confusion. Sandra turned the sound down, but not off, in order to discuss the types and patterns of my disfluencies while she had the audio portion of our program in the background as quiet collaboration. I wasn't paying much attention to her, though, since I was owned by the image on the screen, horrified at how high-pitched I sounded, how consistently spasmodic my speech was—how many pauses, interjections, and restatements there were.

Sandra realized I wasn't listening to her, so she turned up the sound and the two of us sat there, silently watching TV with our hands in our laps. On the screen I was reading an article from the sports page of the *San Francisco Chronicle*. I was doing fine until I came to the final word of the following sentence: "The record was previously held by Whitey Ford." Note well, sweet Sandra, the variables: the oral recitation, the short sentence, the dreadful F at the end of the phrase to arouse my suspicion and apprehension all along. I simply couldn't say it. I blinked my eyes, raised my eyebrows, wrinkled my nose, threw my neck to the left, said the first seven words of the sentence over and over again, but I couldn't complete the final sound.

Ford. Ford. It's so easy to write. Why was it so difficult to say? Name of the spastic President, brand of a bad automobile, reefy part of a river: what was so imposing about it? Almost cruelly, it seemed to me—or, if not cruelly, then for what ostensible purpose?—Sandra played this portion of the tape perhaps ten times rapidly in succession. At the end of the last showing I still hadn't said the word.

"Turn it off," I said. "Please turn it off."

Sandra didn't turn it off. She told the grad student technician to freeze the final frame of that sequence, then leave. He left. There was a sickness about my lips that threatened to bleed the black and white of the picture into lurid purple and so much fear in my eyes I thought I might faint. Off-camera, for the first time in years, I cried. So maternal, Sandra handed me a box of Kleenex and killed the lights. The only lucidity in the room was the bleak image of myself babbling.

As I was crying, sniffling, and coughing into my Kleenex, Sandra said, "I just wanted to demonstrate how severe your speech problem is, Jeremy, how unhappy it has made you."

23

SHE DIDN'T HAVE to demonstrate that. She really didn't. I already knew how unhappy the problem had made me. Still, until Sandra's telecast I hadn't experienced the depth of my distortion. I'd sounded the shallows. The last six weeks of the school year I gave more attention to my clinic sessions than I did to all my academic courses combined. Critical Theory—Longinus to Barthes—was all right, as classes go, but in speech therapy a late entrance into the human equation was being studied. Sandra said, for instance, that all locution could be divided into five "parameters": airflow, voicing, tension, movement, timing. Some scientist somewhere had separated utterance into a pentathlon of interrelated aspects and everyone had agreed with him, so now Sandra waxed eloquent about these divisions and sometimes spent as much as half a session saying, "Raise your thoracic tension, now lower it, lower it still further, now say 'feather.' Increase the air flow at your articulators, increase it even more, now decrease it, decrease it even more, still more, now say 'sincere.' " Lightly I said *feather*. Sincerely I said *sincere*. These abstract conceptualizations continued to carry very little meaning for me, even after I'd completed over and over the assignment of walking up to a stranger at the bus stop on Wilshire and asking what time it was, saying each word at a slightly different level of tension or slightly different volume of voicing.

A woman with a digital watch said, "Four fifty-six and fifty seconds."

I said: "I'm sorry, I didn't quite catch that."

She waited a moment, then said: "Four fifty-seven."

There were also five levels of tension: abdomen, thorax, neck, glottis, articulators. Anywhere from your lungs to your lips your language could get lost. Sandra would have me tighten up, then relax my stomach muscles, tighten up, then relax my glottal folds, tighten up . . . et cetera. This was all very educational, but I didn't see what good it was doing me since I was still ruining Plautus every time I read him aloud and, in Critical Theory, still too self-conscious about communication to correct the teaching assistant when he got his Schiller wrong.

Somewhat more interesting, or at least a little more personally relevant, was Sandra's chart of my struggle sequence: fixate articulators while stopping airflow at the level of the larynx; tense thorax, glottal, and mandibular areas; increase subglottal air pressure until the glottis is forced open; reduce tension in the glottal and mandibular areas; reinitiate voicing and movement of the articulators toward the next phoneme. Toward the exposure, I thought, of some larger precept underlying the pain, I was instructed to compose a hierarchy of situations, beginning with the least and finishing with the most traumatic. Although I was fascinated by the numerous dichotomies that emerged here—darkness and light, distance and intimacy, vertical and horizontal, me and everybody else, disruption and silence, affection and function, men and women, authority and weakness, fear and admiration, anticipation and regret—Sandra, wisely, wasn't. The whole purpose of the assignment, she explained, was to show me how unnecessary my overreactions were. I nodded. I knew. I'd heard it all before.

We argued for the first time when, during exam week, I did what passed with me for exploding. "Sandra, please. Language is more than just a lot of lists. Speech isn't just a mechanical behavior, some neutral physical activity. It's suffused with emotion."

Which is obvious and yet I had to say it. We'd been transferred to a clinic room designed for normal human beings rather than midgets. The blackboard, presently untouched and never to my knowledge touched, was glistening in the corner like the reminder of a headache. Someone—Dr. Hemley, the director? Neil, the technician?—was peering through the black-edged, silver, one-way mirror. I was sitting with my legs stretched out and my hands tapping on the table. Sandra was sitting with her legs crossed and her hands held politely together in her lap. When I said what I had to say, her hands fairly flew out of her lap, landed on my happily tapping hands, and squeezed them.

"Don't you see?" she said, lifting my hands in the air, rubbing them, dropping them back to the table. I didn't understand this business with my hands. Maybe it was an imitation of Shaking Sudden Sense into me. "If you're ever going to make any progress, you've got to distinguish between, on the one hand, the emotions surrounding speech and, on the other, the mechanics of communication. Sure, stuttering has psychological, though not necessarily pathological, origins; sure, speech is a highly emotional activity, but if you want the romance of psychoanalysis you'd be wise to take a good hard look at what Freud said about disfluency. His only hypothesis was the half-baked notion that the quivering of the stutterer's lips was a rather futile attempt to return to infantile nipple-sucking. Is that what you want?"

No, Sandra, that wasn't what I wanted, and you knew that wasn't what I wanted, and you knew if you phrased the question that way you'd succeed in persuading me to take back to San Francisco in June, and pursue, the UCLA Speech and Hearing Clinic summer home program—reading aloud to myself, making deliberate changes in the five parameters when talking on the telephone, not avoiding feared words, noting stressful situations, observing and analyzing speakers I admired—but, Sandra, let's face it: the summer home program was a colossal flop, my speech went to hell because I was too busy writing my first short story, and I was too busy writing my first short story because Mother contracted cancer right through her heart.

24

MOTHER WAS WORKING now for two oddly complementary organizations: the California Council on Health Plan Alternatives, which lobbied for nationalized medicine, and the Stanford Medical Center, where she publicized the radiation lab. It might seem as if I've rearranged Mother's résumé to underline the symbolism of something or other, but I haven't. There was just some cell inside her that was screaming about sickness and survival.

Hyperthermia—abnormally high body temperature—when used with radiation or chemotherapy is a promising new avenue for treatment of tumors.

Kidney cancer may be killed by a new nonsurgical technique that shuts off its blood supply and starves it to death.

The nursing profession continues to develop passive, conforming, neutral people at a point in its history when there is an urgent need for nurses who can think imaginatively and develop new solutions to increasingly complex problems.

This was the order of sentence Mother was composing on her classic black Remington as July turned surprisingly warm in San Francisco, so when she cried, "Announcement! Announcement! Everyone around the hearth for a heart-to-heart," who among us could have expected it would be anything more than another chance for her to discuss the Women's Liberation movement in the context of a realignment of the family chores? She had a remarkable manner of entering rooms. I've never met anyone who so completely determined the mood of a particular space the way she affected every feeling that emerged from the floorboards, and I remember her walking into the living room four months before her fiftieth birthday. Whereas anybody else would have been carrying a handkerchief in one hand and a bottle of sleeping pills in the other, Mother was carrying gift-wrapped packages. Ten years before, she'd entered the hospital for a minor operation (nodule, nose) and upon her return brought me a transistor radio. I had loved that radio's white earplug, black dial, black leather case beneath my pillow at night, and now here she was again—home from the doctor with three presents in her hands. She read her mail and mixed a large gin-and-tonic without any tonic while we unwrapped our presents: a jogging suit for Father; *The Riverside Shakespeare* for Beth, who, in her second year of graduate studies at Berkeley in British history and first year of residing with Michael, missed the dramaturgy of her recent past; and for me a text entitled *Disfluency Dissolved,* which belonged to the genre of self-help quackery—swing your left arm when talking to someone on your right side, swing your right arm when talking to someone on your left side—that Sandra despised.

Father looked up from his sweat pants and said, "Honey, I assume these wonderful gifts are in celebration of a perfect report card from Doctor Braun."

Father, Beth, and I were sitting, quite literally, at Mother's feet. Mother's feet were resting on, of all things, the foot rest of the Good Chair. She fiddled with the FM dial of the hi-fi, pouring herself more

Beefeater Gin and petting Bruin's ancient, fat, but still glossy back. That dumb dog's sole desire in life was to eliminate all itches. When, in her youth, we tried to get her to debauch a beagle from around the block, Bruin pranced away like a poodle with dancer's attitude.

"I suppose," Father said, "these wonderful gifts are in celebration of a perfect report card from Doctor Braun."

"Do you like the book, Beth?" Mother asked. "Is that the right edition, the one you wanted, with the color pictures in front?"

Beth was a grad student at Berkeley at a time when being a grad student at Berkeley made you answer: "Certainly there are going to be those who prefer the Signets, Mother, the individual paperback editions with those gorgeous Milton Glaser covers."

Beth didn't mean to hurt Mother. Nor did I when I said Sandra wouldn't let me even look at *Disfluency Dissolved*. Nor did Father when he said the jogging suit would fit fine after a couple of washings. The living room was almost totally dark now and for some reason Mother prohibited anyone from turning on the lights. She tilted the foot rest, threatening, or so it seemed, to kick it over but managing quite nicely to keep it on *pointe*. Drinking entirely too much gin, she petted Bruin so vigorously the animal finally flopped off her lap. At 1490 FM, KKHI, as if by thematic prearrangement with Mother, was playing Schubert's "Unfinished Symphony."

"I guess these gifts are in celebration of a perfect report card from Doctor Braun," Father said.

"Yes," Mother said, "yes, I mean: no, nothing like that at all, no." The Unfinished Symphony finished. Bruin tried to establish sympathetic eye contact with the other members of the family. Mother gulped a full glass of gin. "Actually," Mother said (for the first time ever she had trouble talking, her voice cracked, she couldn't enunciate), "I found a little lump in my breast, and the day after tomorrow we're having it biopsied." Here she found it necessary to lie. "It's not going to be malignant. I'm going to be all right. None of you is to worry." She laughed unconvincingly, too high, too abruptly aborted, to herself.

I wasn't there with Mother in the examination room when she made Doctor Braun feel one lump in her left breast and another along her lymph nodes, when she told him about the blood dripping from her nipple, when he kept saying, "I hope you're wrong, I really do," in response to her saying, "I'm sorry, I know, I just do, I know my body, so let's go after this with everything you've got." Still, I see the harsh white light of the overhead lamp, the crinkly paper stretched across the narrow table, the doctor's little desk in the corner, the icy steel chairs, the silvery-glassy reflection off scissors and bottles, the tardy antiseptic of rubbing alcohol, Mother's toes almost touching the cold floor—and I wonder why she didn't tell us when she found out for certain that she had a year and a half to live. Me and Beth, at least, if not Father, since shortly after this he was back at Montbel. It was an extraordinarily misguided decision, to leave us guessing all along. She pretended to be so public and transparent, but she was surely as secretive as the rest of us. The only person she told was Elaine Ellenboegen, who shared this information when she showed me Father's letters.

In the living room, when Mother said she was sure the tumor wasn't malignant, I recalled stopping in Salt Lake City on the way home from Jackson Hole. We were admitted to an overpopulated auditorium when Father told the doorman we'd come "all the way from San Francisco to see the senator." The rally was for Eugene McCarthy; it must have been 1967, I must have been eleven. Afterward we swam in or, actually, on Salt Lake. Mother, stretching out seductively in her ubiquitous black one-piece, called to Father: "What else is like this? What in all of life, Teddy, is such an uninterrupted lull?" We had dinner near the state capitol at a restaurant that featured a waterfall and served twelve courses including as many Italian ices as you could eat. Father ate more than he could eat and fell asleep the moment he lay down back at the motel room. Beth and I swam in the indoor pool while Mother sat in a wet chaise longue, somehow both reading the *Congressional Quarterly* and admiring us. Mother said it was time to towel off but first bought us bottles of orange Fanta and lit a cigarette. As we crossed the parking lot to the motel room, Beth warned Mother about the likely lethal effects of inhaling nicotine and tar. "It's not the quantity of life," Mother said, "it's the quality of life." Surely this was the most meaningless platitude she knew. She only wanted Beth to give back her matches. Somehow, though, there we were, the three of us walking across the parking lot, waiting for Mother to finish her cigarette. Clinging like gossamer to Mother's banality was the sensation of something seized: the sun disappearing into the bottom of the soda bottle, the Great Salt Lake rushing into the indoor pool, Father dreaming he was a soldier in boot camp.

Immediately upon absorbing the significance of Mother's upcoming operation, Father yielded conscious control over the left side of his brain. By comparison, Beth said afterward, Lucky's monologue toward the end of *Godot* was practically a model of decorum. Father kneeled like a begging Bruin, wailing and crying into Mother's lap: "No no 'Nette please no O love dearheart No I life so O no love 'Nette I O please dearheart no no." Beth and I stared at each other with the worthless weight of our books in our hands, not knowing where to go till we surrounded Mother and started hugging either shoulder, calling her "Mom" for the first time in I don't know how long. The one thing she couldn't accept was sympathy for herself. Nothing if not a martyr, she didn't want to be anybody's burden but her own. Later, when she was really ill, she photocopied a statement that said: "I ask that drugs be mercifully administered to me for terminal suffering even if they hasten the moment of death. I do not fear death as much as I fear the indignity of deterioration, dependence, and hopeless pain." All those *d*s. She stood, kicked over the foot rest, and said, "You'll excuse me. I'm going to bed. Nighty night." She was sloshed.

Pressing his jogging suit in a bundle to his chest, Father followed after her, crawling across the carpet. Like so many of his other gestures—the way he kissed people or shook your hand, how he made a toast at a fundraiser—this struck me as an act. It was as if he were always portraying what he imagined might be laudatory. Even away from all the electrodes, he never impressed me as having a genuine core upon which to draw. He could get very flustered if anyone else in the room said they were seriously sick. That was his province.

Mother dissuaded Beth and me from visiting her at the hospital, but Father virtually lived there. He was working now for the city as a housing inspector of slum dwellings and accountable to no one. When Mother came home, she looked basically the same as she had before. She never had much of a bust, so I could hardly tell the difference when she returned or when, a little later, a prosthesis was strapped to her shoulder.

I don't understand what chemotherapy does and I'm not sure I want to, but it seems to cause mothers to fall asleep, lose their balance, and vomit into the soap catch of the shower. Chemotherapy doesn't strike me as an overly marvelous therapy.

She missed little more than a month at the California Council on Health Plan Alternatives, where a big bill with Senator Kennedy's backing awaited Mother's hand to hammer it into final form. They took what amounts to a team picture the day she went back to work; looking recently at the photograph in the family album, I couldn't distinguish her from all the other overworked health planners. I found and focused my little loupe. She might as well as have been me trying to say *Ford*. The veins in her neck were like two long fingers in the claw of a canary.

MOTHER STOOD in the doorway between the kitchen and the den, pulling a white rope over and back a chin-up bar in order to regain strength in her left shoulder. I sat down in a chair and talked to her about stuttering: how much it had bothered me while growing up, how hard I was trying to improve my speech this summer, how much it defined who I was. If I had known she was dying, I wouldn't have talked about stuttering with such solemnity, since it would have seemed so inconsequential. But I didn't know she was dying and I wanted us to be like two injured veterans trading war stories. *I can comprehend pain, Mom—tell me where it hurts.*

Five o'clock light came into the kitchen, making the yellow linoleum look liquid and the top of the round Formica table like a floating saucer. Mother was only a few feet away, but she might as well have been on the other side of the San Andreas Fault: on the den side of the door, a step down from the kitchen, in semidarkness, wearing bathrobe and slippers, grunting as she raised her shoulder a little higher with each effort.

Between rope pulls, in response to my speech about speech, Mother said, "Do you know something, Jeremy?"

"No, what, Mother?"

"I hate to say it, but I think two years of college have turned you into a terrible bore," she said, then started pulling on her rope again.

"Oh, no," I said. "I've always been a terrible bore."

I'm not dead, Mother, I'm only sleeping.

She laughed a little, or maybe it was just a huff of exertion. She said, "You've lost your sense of humor, honey, and this family is known for its ability to laugh, its *joie de vivre*, if you will."

"Certainly I will," I said, attempting to show her I hadn't lost my sense of humor. There's a difference, though, between a sense of humor and pointless word play. Mother kept pulling on her rope while I squirmed in the kitchen chair.

"Your father used to be invited to the most exclusive parties in Beverly Hills to do his borscht belt routines. I've been known to turn out a witty column or two in my day. Even Beth, who used to be such a sourpuss, made a very funny card for my birthday, which you, incidentally, completely ignored. What's happened to you, honey? You used to have such a great laugh."

"Ha-ha."

"You used to write those wonderful satires about mirrors and parking lots and crowded lecture rooms for the high school paper. You used to rush home to tell me the latest joke you had heard. You used to love your father's stories. Now you're all dark and depressed, all sense and sensibility."

You can see what a leg up on the rest of us it gave Mother to be the only one who knew she was dying, since under the gaze of eternity all our little mishaps must have looked pretty comical. I stood and said, "That's just not true."

Mother pedaled her feet in the air while yanking the rope around.

"All s-s-summer," I said and thought to myself *abdominal tension, excessive air flow, forward moving speech,* "all summer I've been writing a play about a clown. It promises to be very funny."

This was a total fabrication. I'd seen an off-Geary production of a one-act play of Chekhov's called *Swan-Song,* which wasn't funny but did concern a clown.

Mother never lost a chance to demonstrate how little she knew about literature and said, "That doesn't show a sense of humor. It doesn't even show any originality. The Frown Behind the Clown is one of the most well-worn themes we have."

"Yes, I know, Mother, but this play of mine is actually very f-f-funny."

Why is this a stressful situation? I wondered. Don't avoid feared words. Make changes in the five parameters, especially tension and timing.

"What's it about?" she asked. Mother always liked to know what something was about. She didn't like poetry because it was rarely about anything.

I said it was about a clown who was calling it quits. On his last night under the big top, unable to decide whether he loves the fat lady more than the thin man, he shoots them both, gives a very wise and witty monologue concerning the relationship between imagination and reality, then leaps from the trapeze to his own death.

"Yes," Mother said, back on her feet, rotating her left shoulder counterclockwise, "but what's it about?"

I wanted to say, "Good Christ, Mother, it's about me!" but I could hear in my head a mechanical click that told me I'd stammer on "Mother"—virtually every stutterer I've met mentions something similar: a vague shadow blotting the view—so, instead of arguing, I pulled down the aluminum bar from which her rope dangled and threw the bar into the far corner of the den, where Bruin, thinking it was a bone, gnawed on it.

"That," I said, "that is fuh . . . fuh . . . fuh. . . ." I couldn't finish the word. I was trying to say "hilarious."

Sandra says I then experienced guilt, self-revulsion, communication-hate, people-hate, and melancholia. I suppose that about covers it. Every night for a week I sat alone in my room, reading *Billy Budd* aloud to myself and writing letters to Mother I neither mailed nor delivered. Finally I wrote a short story, as an apology, as an early elegy, and in one night.

NOTES ON SUICIDE

Prompted by no more compelling motive than having nowhere else to reside, I moved here three months ago and soon became aware that below me lived a woman who was quite as alone and secretive, as inaccessible, perhaps even (and my heart cheered at the possibility) as near to death as I have been all my life. And yet I never saw her.

It was, I confess, the most inadmissible of all evidence upon which I spectacularly misjudged the woman downstairs. Her voice, echoing in the pipes and elevator shaft and settling in the attic in which I live, demanded my attention because she spoke, as a child or an old person does, to no one but herself. She talked back to the radio and television and extrapolated from the Bible, altering the tone and theme of her discourse as easily as she changed channels or turned pages. There seemed to be, nevertheless, a hidden order, some obscure coherence to her monologues.

Her mailbox did not have her name on it and its emptiness was never invaded by even the most insignificant piece of junk mail. Not that I received fierce love letters from exotic points, either, but at least my name was scrawled across the slip of paper taped to my mailbox. Occasionally I took the elevator, when it was empty, down to the first floor mailboxes, adhering to a strange and unfounded belief that communication—some unexpected epistle—would arise from nowhere, from nothing, from no one.

In the early morning she often stomped around her apartment and banged her hands against the walls, sending slight vibrations upstairs, where I lay awake, listening to the sounds of her insomnia. She cursed and placed herself in the throes of what I took to be an elaborate ritual, laden with gestures and movement and meaning.

Even more curious were her eating and cooking habits, which were disturbingly irregular. At noon I smelled meat cooking and at midnight eggs frying. And she was a pathetically ineffectual chef, burning most of what she cooked. The smell of heat and smoke crawled into my apartment. She broke glasses and plates.

I flattered myself, of course, to think that I, with my over-sensitive antennae, was well suited to the task of decoding her bizarre behavior. It is true that at first I only sporadically jotted down my impressions of her and was not even especially aware that I was doing so. But in less than three weeks I was enthralled with the prospect of collecting all the details of her apparent disorder and listing them, cataloguing them, categorizing them and ordering them until I solved her puzzling existence.

I realized—what a nervous moment that was!—that my character was of no use to me here, was in fact a hindrance. Perhaps, then, this was what so attracted me to the challenge: the healthy egotism on which I have survived all these years had to be discarded if I were to succeed in comprehending, not to mention getting acquainted with, this elusive woman. I did nothing else but keep lists of what she was doing or, rather, what I thought she was doing. With thin, sharpened, charcoal pencils, in my minute and uniform if illegible handwriting, I wrote endless columns of numbers and words. And still I did not understand her.

I paid such strict attention to her habits that I was able to discern the room to which she was going and from which she was coming by counting the number of taps and scrapes she made with her cane. Occasionally she tapped her cane frightenedly—perhaps twenty times consecutively on the same spot on the floor—and I heard no concurrent footsteps, while other times I could tell she was walking but I heard no sign of the cane. Moreover, she did not limp. I am quite sure of it. She did not limp.

There was a slight crack in the metal heat vent on the floor of my apartment, through which I was able to see just the darkness of her room. For hours at a time I lay face down alongside the vent and put my eye to the slit. The only light ever present in her room radiated from, I think, the television screen. She never turned on a lamp or an overhead light. Every night I wrote that her room was dark the moment the sun went down.

At night, usually, or in the very early morning (how she read without a light I had no idea; I supposed she simply knew the quotation) she repeated the same Biblical passage, from Isaiah, until the words slurred in her mouth. Each time she began the passage as if she were a demure schoolgirl methodically, knowingly reciting the correct answer.

> *On that day deaf men shall hear*
> *when a book is read.*

Then she would bang her cane against the low ceiling, taunting the author of the passage to come down and answer for it.

> *And the eyes of the blind shall*
> *see out of impenetrable darkness.*

When she got excited, she dropped her book; the thud sounded more like a heavy suitcase than even the most lavish and carefully annotated and footnoted edition of the Bible.

> *The lowly shall once again*
> *rejoice in the Lord, and the*
> *poorest of men exalt in the*
> *Holy One of Israel.*

But if she had memorized the passage why did she need the book? On the other hand, how could she have read it without light? Each evening I wrote down when she began, how long she read, how many times she repeated the passage, over which words she stumbled, the last word she uttered.

Nights I pulled out the desk drawer and, sitting in my

wooden chair, circled the aberrations on that day's list—the screams I did not expect, the elongated silences, the sudden noise from her television—although after a while nothing could have surprised me except the emergence of a predictable pattern to her life. When the words and numbers squeezed together and vanished, when I saw but a pool of light at the tip of my nose, I went to bed.

I slept in two hour intervals—asleep two hours, awake two hours—until I was rested enough to stay awake. While awake in bed I wrote down in the yellow margins of the Bible what she was doing. There was something terrible about being awake that late at night, with the clock ticking and the lamp glowing, as I plotted the movements of a woman I never saw.

And yet what I have been trying to say, which I am having obvious (if understandable) difficulty relating, and which I now feel compelled to present because I am afraid that I am all too characteristically dwelling on the complexity of my own consciousness, rather than addressing the matter at hand, is precisely this: a week ago I detected an appreciable reduction in her actions. That day I made fewer entries than I had on any previous day. Maybe, I thought, I was not listening as well as I had before. Perhaps she was making the same noises and I was just not hearing them.

Her movements were still unpredictable and random but, in fact, much less frequent. In four hours she tapped her cane and turned the television on and off. Nothing else. I reviewed the lists and calculated a slight, if steady, decrease in the number of entries I had made, starting two weeks ago, though she had not been anywhere near as inactive as she started to be last week. Which left me with little to do except wait.

The lists grew shorter, dwindling to almost nothing, like a candle burning out. She broke fewer glasses, no longer tapped her cane, and rarely turned on the television or burnt the coffee. Instead of compiling a list of what she was doing, I maintained a log of the length of intervals between entries. The intervals grew longer. I listed what was not happening, what was not there. Every other day she read from Isaiah in a dull, somnambulistic monotone. Occasionally she stumbled into a chair or flushed the toilet. She slept for days.

Two days ago I stopped keeping lists because I no longer heard anything from downstairs. Not wanting to waste all those charcoal pencils and sheets of paper, I listed, upon waking, the side of my body on which I was lying, where my hands were, how many times the clock ticked in a minute.

I slept with the windows open, the water running, and the lights on. I slept naked with my head under the pillow. The air was warm and I wrapped only a sheet, like ropes, around my legs. In the day I napped to recover from oversleeping. I gobbled aspirin to relieve my headache and slept even more. This past week I never went to sleep after midnight nor awoke before noon.

Until this morning. Asleep in dreamless, soundless empty spaces of time, I was awakened by her loud recitation of the Isaiah passage.

On that day deaf men shall hear
when a book is read.

In the dark, stumbling over furniture, I ran into the living room, turned on the desk lamp, and sat down in my chair. I wrote down what time it was, as well as what she was saying. She banged her cane against the wall and her voice rose to a pitch approaching a scream, her Bible reading uncontrolled for the first time, blurted out rather than chanted.

And the eyes of the blind shall
see out of impenetrable darkness.

All of a sudden she dropped the book, and I heard her gasp. Her breathing sounded like a child sucking on a straw. I opened the heat vent and put my ear to the grate.

No, she said. It is dark. It is too dark. Give me light. I am in black clothes.

I heard her cane, followed by her body, fall to the floor.

She coughed uncontrollably. I wanted to pour water down her mouth. The seat of the chair felt cold, like a bed pan, under my naked buttocks. She turned on the television, from which came a toneless beep.

There was silence for a while (perhaps as long as thirty seconds, I really don't remember; I had, quite understandably, lost all track of time to the point of forgetting that I was wearing a watch). Then, wheezing, she took deep, heavy breaths until she had to exhale. She yelled an obscene word and gasped as she blew air out of her mouth for the last time.

I walked down the stairs, slowly, shaking the handrail, carrying a flashlight, trying to calm myself down. I banged on the door and rang the doorbell. I beat on the door with my flashlight and kicked it with my foot. I knelt down, without any clothes on, and looked into the keyhole, holding the flashlight next to the keyhole so that I could see into the room. I did not see her body. Instead, right below me, near enough to touch, in a shaft of dim light which darted through the keyhole, surrounded by darkness, the handle of her white cane reflected light.

And now, before the other apartment-dwellers awake (and before, as it is so easy for me to do, I forget and simply go on), I will step into the elevator on the sixth floor and close the doors tight behind me. I will turn off the fan. Above me there will be a panel of descending floor numbers. Everything will be silent except for the rattling of the pipes and bars in the elevator shaft. And I will take this black box down into the basement where the noise stops and the light ends.

25

THERE ARE DEFINITE difficulties here: the swollen syntax; the compulsive subsets; the near-absence, and refusal to place quotation marks around what little there is, of dialogue; the repetition in the extreme to the point of echolalia; the abstraction of the monologue, its essayistic airiness, its woodenness. The nameless narrator's attic prison, in addition to being a bohemian bromide, is a reflection of the way I've always felt, what I've always hated about my basement bedroom. Most of his obligatory pessimism is mine, too, I suppose. But why is he so much more impoverished than I am and why is Helen Keller so much closer to death than Mother was at the time? (Suddenly I know why: to win your pity.) I had no inkling Mother was mortal, I believed her when she said she'd be fine in a few years. Written words work in an unfathomable way; I can't explain it.

Gretchen Noyes could explain it. She said, " 'Notes on Suicide' revivifies David Hume's terrible apprehension that his body was literally made of words. The endless convolution going nowhere except deeper down into this fastidious fop's incapacity to *see* the old woman dying in her blindness—that's perfect, Jeremy, it really is. These pages are his notes; he kills himself, right? It's an incredibly moving evocation of the very details of loneliness, an ode on the impossibility of love, a textbook example of purposeful withholding of narrative info, a compressed though not reductive remaking of—"

"No, it isn't," I said. "It's about my mother."

I'd returned to Los Angeles shortly after writing the story and hadn't shown it to my family, so Gretchen was the first person to read "Notes on Suicide." She was twenty-four, a third-year graduate student in American literature, and the editor of the UCLA literary magazine. I'd never heard anyone who wasn't lecturing talk quite like that. It was a very nice office, the long room in which *West-words* was put together: lots of old lamps and comfortable chairs and a beautiful round window that overlooked Pauley Pavilion. Gretchen was sitting in the most comfortable chair, scrutinizing the window and tapping her pencil on the editor's desk while she spoke to me.

"Well, yes," she said, "perhaps the text does have a certain, inevitable autobiographical origin—the signal of apprentice fabulation—but the teller isn't the tale, the dancer is distinct from the dance. I mean, you don't reject the notion of negative capability, do you? This story isn't a private exorcism, though, granted, it might be that, too, among other things. It's private pain gone to public catharsis, don't you agree?"

"Yes," I said. "Yes, I do." Her hair shone in the late light like gold, pure gold. She had her little brown-socked feet up on the desk. This was the editor I'd always been looking for: one who praised, praised, praised, even if I couldn't understand exactly what she meant.

"Obviously I want to publish it. Obviously. It'll be the lead story in the winter issue. It's the best undergraduate writing I've seen here or in Palo Alto."

"When were you in Palo Alto?"

"Two years ago. I got my B.A. there."

"Did you know my sister, Beth?"

"Jesus, you're kidding. Miss historian? You have such a talented family."

I blushed, changed my position in the chair, tapped my foot on the floor.

"You're only a junior? We have to celebrate your future. Come on, I'll buy you a drink at Someplace Else," she said and, standing, took my arm.

Gretchen always talked like that: very arch, very stylized. Most of the amusement of being with her was wondering whether her formality would ever fade, whether just once she'd live inside an event and not worry about expressing its essence. After a year and a half of close inspection I can confidently report that she never has.

Someplace Else is a homosexual bar in West Hollywood. Gretchen seemed so at home there it occurred to me to ask: "You aren't gay, Gretchen, are you?"

Either she didn't hear me or chose to change the topic of conversation. Stirring her Scotch and soda, she answered, "No, I'll be writing my thesis *next* semester. Nathanael West. This is research: I'm soaking up atmosphere."

She was soaking up a lot of Scotch while entertaining skinny men wearing white shirts and blue hankies, telling her barfly friends about me—from what little I heard, how earnest I was—but I tried not to pay attention and listened, instead, to tinkling glasses, flushing toilets, spinning nickels, and a one-armed man playing remarkable jazz drum.

When her audience had wandered away, Gretchen patted my hand and said, "The only good bar in Palo Alto was the gay bar and I'm beginning to think the same thing's true even in L.A." I was worried again about the channel of her love life. "Only in gay bars is there that elusive *ambiance,* that unnameable *milieu"*—she pronounced both words with an exaggerated French accent—"which is both sexual and asexual, intimate and wonderfully detached. Only here is there the dimmest comprehension that personality is fluid, identity is constantly being forged, the self is not some dull static thing but baroque mask upon baroque mask."

I'd never heard Someplace Else talked about in quite these terms, but I listened because I always listen to whatever Gretchen says. I love the way she has with words.

In the failing light of some fall evening in the *Westwords* office, she leaned over and gently licked the inside of my ear. I've always been fascinated by this phenomenon, as if there's a direct line between our ears and our loins. It's final evidence that whatever we listen to constitutes life itself.

"What?" I said.

"What do you mean 'what?' " she said.

"You s-s-said you wanted to tell me s-s-something."

She laughed, whispered ocean sounds into my ear, and said, "G-g-got it?" Then, very softly, "What do you like? Tell me what you like."

"Well, you."

"What?"

"You," I said. "I like *you* very much."

"That's sweet."

"I mean, I like you more than very much. I—"

"Please don't say that, Jeremy. Really. You don't even know me."

I once telephoned her at home and when she answered I tried to say, "Hi, Gretchen." I could only say, "Hi, Grr. . . . Hi, Grrr . . . Grrr . . . Grrr . . . Grrr . . . Grrr. . . ." like an ineffectual bear growling about a thorn in his foot. Gretchen kept saying, "Hello? Jeremy? Is that you? Is this Jeremy? Honey, talk to me." Although I knew she knew it was me, I returned the receiver to its cradle.

Out of eagerness, out of anxiety, out of an excessive need to please, out of a considerably less strong but nevertheless quite real desire to be pleased, out of a sheer sense of relief, I think, just to be there, I tended to find fulfillment too fast the first time each night. The second embrace of the evening was usually fine and the third, if there was one, could be positively enjoyable, but I was distressed by the inevitable prematurity of the initial intercourse. These repeated attempts to communicate what could have been communicated more elegantly the first time—I'd been in this bind before. Once, after I'd finished too quickly for Gretchen to have much fun, she said, "So what are you going to do? See a sex counselor as well as a speech therapist? Don't throw your money away. Don't worry about it. That's just your Ur-pattern: the second or third time around on everything you're t-t-terrific."

On her birthday, December eleventh, I treated her to a good restaurant, a bad play, and a hookers' convention hotel in Hollywood. I took her hand and tried to get her to imitate wild, youthful abandon by racing across Sunset Boulevard, but she stayed put on the curb, watched me nearly get hit by, of all things, a boy on a bicycle, then walked two blocks south to a stoplight, where "for

Chrissake, Jeremy, any sane person would cross." I wanted to walk away from the sun, toward big buildings and the promise of Paramount Studios. After returning from her expedition to the stoplight, Gretchen started stocking up on every kitschy item she could get her hands on—star maps, free tickets to daytime TV shows, Krishna roses; she stuffed an astonishing amount of this stuff into the purse which I always told her was too big and bulky but which came in handy for her on this birthday bash in the variously inclined city.

The rest of the afternoon consisted of Gretchen consulting her maps and saying, "No, no, we take a left here, a left," while I ran around buying thick slick sick skin magazines. I was always half a block ahead of her, looking back, and she was always waving, rattling her maps, calling out, "Have we passed Cahuenga?" We were two well-dressed children lost in a neighborhood we both could have sworn we knew better than this. We'd taken this little vacation to "find out why we're together," as Gretchen said, and all we found out was that neither of us had much sense of direction. During appetizers I used my napkin, which had been sticking out of the empty water glass like beautiful white ears, to suppress a sneeze, which Gretchen thought was such a "primitive display of bad table manners" she left the restaurant with her sweater and bulky purse in one hand and her half-eaten piece of quiche Lorraine in the other. I grabbed her just as she was getting in the car to head, I supposed, home.

At night in the hotel room she fell asleep the second I touched her and then rain was general all over Los Angeles. Because it was still raining the next morning and the road was slippery, Gretchen asked me to buckle up. It was one of those shoulder straps that lock into place in your lungs. She kept asking me to strap myself in, I kept looking at the coil of black plastic, and I kept saying no until Gretchen said if I was going to be like that she was happy to stop the car and wait for me to come to my senses. She pulled off Santa Monica Boulevard onto a side street and something in me snapped. I just started shaking her against the fake-wood paneling of her parents' sedan. Cars passed, rain fell. I just kept shaking her. She said, "I don't know why we're together. I really don't, Jeremy. I have no idea why we're together." In times of trouble, in the face of fear, I've never really found language very useful. I tossed her umbrella into a tree, shrugged, turned, and waited in the falling rain for the 3:20 back to Westwood.

That was the lowest of the low points, but there were others. I'd already been to the bathroom and was sitting in the middle seat of the middle row, holding a large Coca-Cola, a box of popcorn. Gretchen was feeding me her least favorite flavors of Jujyfruits, licorice and lime, while we were waiting for the curtains to part. Gretchen said, "What are you doing?"

I stopped stroking her shoulder and said, *"Lo siento, señorita.* I was just stroking your shoulder."

The lights dimmed. Gretchen said, "You were stroking my shoulder, but there's a big difference, don't you think, between lovers making out in a dark movie theater and a little boy pawing his mother's blouse." No question mark.

I swigged my Coke, poured the rest into her lap, and left as the first trailer screamed on.

At a Christmas party Gretchen tried to teach me the mambo. It was a very sophisticated party. Her thesis adviser was there. The chairman of the English department. Some people from the chancellor's office. A candidate for Santa Monica city council. The *femme fatale* of the comparative literature program. When the music began I sat down and out. Gretchen, who had an ardent admirer wrapped around her arm, came up to me and said, "O wazza mazzer with Jeremy poo? He no like to choreograph?" I ignored her by pretending to spot a long lost friend on the far side of the dance floor but, later, dead drunk, she dragged me into the bedroom and attempted to demonstrate. She could hardly stand up and I couldn't learn when to lean forward, when to lean back, when to snap her wet little wrist, so we wound up wrestling on the waterbed while everyone else was singing Christmas carols and motioning toward the mistletoe.

26

FOR OUR FINAL meeting of the semester, Sandra pulled out all the stops. Once we got a lot of hand-holding and teary hugging out of the way, it was quite the informative session. As a kind of hortatory prologue, she asked if I knew why American Indians didn't stutter and, before I could guess, she explained that there's no pressure upon Indian children to speak and very little tension in the culture as a whole. I saw myself running away to join the Iroquois—shooting buffalo, raindancing, sending smoke signals, and finally asking Yellow Feather, "What's my nickname going to be, Yellow Feather?"

"We call you," Yellow Feather says, smiling wide, adjusting his headdress, "Chattering Teeth."

"Oh yeah? Well, you can take your bow-and-arrow and your leather m-m-moccasins, too," I say, sprinting down the mountain to civilization.

Sandra then launched a quick survey of the principal attempted cures. Guy DeChauliac, a French doctor, recommended embrocations to desiccate the brain—an advance for which the Academy of Science gave him an award. Sir Francis Bacon thought the tongue was too cold and dry and suggested hot, steaming wine. Thomas Dieffenbach, a German surgeon, thought a triangular wedge should be excised completely across and nearly through the tongue. A Pythian princess urged emigration south to Libya. Emile Coué, a nineteenth-century physician, invited stutterers to join him on stage, where he shouted into their ears: "You can talk! I know you can! Believe me! You can talk!"

What was the point of these pathetic anecdotes? To get hope hanging in the atmosphere like low-flying smog? To hear the sound of one word flapping? The window was open, for once, in the clinic room. Air circulated. Light did whatever it does: collect dust motes, whatever. I took my notebook out of my backpack and handed my hierarchy of feared situations to Sandra, who said she assumed I'd ultimately overcome every anxiety on the list. She looked straight at me and asked, "Is that your goal, too?"

"Sure," I said. "But it's not a very realistic one. At least right now."

She rubbed my hands together, like she was trying to start a fire, and said, "Why not?"

"Because it just isn't. In at least ten of those situations, I can hardly talk."

"Well, what makes, say, providing information over the phone a tough task and talking to your father in person a relatively easy one?"

"I-i-it's hard to explain."

"Try it again."

"It's hard to explain."

"Good."

"Sometimes I feel happy, relaxed, and confident, while other times I feel like I-I-I'm throwing words down a well."

"Again."

Sandra reiterated her favorite theme that, while it was perfectly natural to be more nervous and self-conscious in certain situations than others, it wasn't at all natural to let these emotions interfere with speech. As brutal proof she wasn't kidding, she took out of a deep desk drawer a plastic skull which, half the size of a human head, she held easily in her hand. On both sides of the skull was a square cutout so you could see gray and white matter, but Sandra wasn't interested in the interior of the brain. She pointed with her pencil to the levels through which language passed on the way outside. With a pull on the lever she could make the mouth open wide and suddenly contract or make the jaw bounce or make the teeth clench. It had no eyes.

"Do you see what happens?" she said. "It's all interconnected. Tension in your abdomen produces tension in your thorax, which produces tension in your neck, which produces tension in your glottis, which produces tension in your articulators, stopping airflow at the larynx." She shut the skull's mouth. "You fixate your thorax, glottal, and mandibular areas." She shook its jaw. "You increase your subglottal air pressure until your glottis is forced open." She opened the skull's mouth. "You reduce tension. You reinitiate voicing." The skull relaxed.

Sandra manipulated the mock-mini-mind as well as Beth ever used to operate her marionette. Who or what, I wondered, is pulling me every which way at once? Why can't I do what I want with my mouth?

"We can do good work with this," she said, making the skull form a smile, "if you'll stop pushing this into overdrive." Pointing to the gray matter.

Next, for several minutes, I had to practice saying feared words by "bouncing," which necessitated neither the rubber room nor the trampoline. Instead, I softly repeated the first letter of words I otherwise would trip over. *S-S-Sandra* to circumvent *SSSSSSSSSSSS-Sandra,* with the implication that I'd slowly decrease the number of times I bounced until I wasn't bouncing at all. I'd be talking. We role-played a couple of situations in which I pretended to introduce Sandra to someone else or called stores to inquire about camera prices. These exercises went so much better than expected that she handed me an intrainstitutional phone number.

"What's this?" I said, turning over the page but recognizing the extension of Dr. Driessen, my Latin professor.

"Your final exam."

"What are you talking about? This isn't a class. I don't—"

"Jeremy. Sweetheart. Relax. I just want to show you or, better, have you show yourself that you can control your speech, at least a little, even when your heart's racing."

"That's easy," I said. "I never stutter when I'm playing sports." Having answered her trick question with a trick answer, I got up to go.

"Whoa, cowboy."

"What?"

"I want you to call somebody."

"Who?"

"Dr. Driessen. Talk to him about your final grade or something."

"I already know how I did."

"This is what we in America call a telephone," Sandra said, sliding the communications system over toward my side of the table. "See these little square buttons? Push them." While I practiced picking up and putting back down the receiver, she kept up her pep talk: "Try to bounce on five feared words in the course of the conversation. And especially try to get a couple in right at the beginning to get you going."

"Yes, ma'am."

"Come on. I have someone else coming in in two minutes. Give me a Christmas present, Jeremy. Call."

Dr. Driessen's extension was composed entirely of odd numbers and possessed the potential, it seemed to me, for being busy during the next two minutes. In his absence the classics department secretary answered, a matronly white-haired lady to whom I had no trouble conveying a long if somewhat vague message about my Petronius paper. I hung up all flush with fluency.

"You forgot to bounce. You didn't bounce once," Sandra said, kicking open the door to the null but noxious smell of Christmas in L.A.

27

I WAS RELIEVED to have a holiday from school and speech and sex and sentences. Neither, though, was home haven. Father had been fired from his job as city housing inspector for spending too much time in the magazine room of the public library and was now studying all day in the library for his realtor's license. Beth had moved to Oakland to be out of whimpering distance from Michael, who "has decided he doesn't love me. His feelings don't go beyond 'caring.' Nothing can interfere with his Work." I suspected Mother's illness of being just another career move; she was now bragging that Linus Pauling ("a real scientist," as opposed to her brother Gil, who was one more atom exploder) looked in on her at Stanford to discuss the acidity of her urine. As with most of the other crucial events of her life, Mother sought escape from pain by seeing it as part of some sort of crusade: Dr. Pauling's lionization of vitamin C. In this case, though, the escape route wasn't appropriate or even possible, since the pain was physical and the pain was so bad. She had simultaneous chills and fever, and her right foot and leg swelled into elephantiasis until five days' I.V. of penicillin brought her home from the hospital woozy, sore, a bit dim in the brain, but at least diagnosed. Phlebitis, Nixon's disease. She lay on the den couch with her leg propped on three huge pillows, snuggling with that wrinkled, ridiculous excuse for a dog, listening to KKHI, becoming a one-woman phone bank for the California Council on Health Plan Alternatives. Mother's friends adored her in a purer light than her family did, and hardly a day of vacation passed without one of them dropping off dinner to listen to Mother's evidence that the American Cancer Society funded only research that couldn't possibly lead to a cure.

On New Year's Eve Father was attending a party thrown by Price, Finch, Poole, and Fenimore, the real estate company he hoped to join; Beth was volunteering as an usher in order to see *Butley* Off-Geary; and Mother and I were alone in the living room, watching the city below celebrate the cessation of '76. She couldn't walk on her swollen leg. I fluffed and piled pillows behind her head and under her ankle. Her eyes closed. She sipped pink champagne, waiting for better luck next year.

Guy Lombardo babbled in the background while Mother and I played cards. It hurt her to sit up or even turn on one side and she had trouble holding onto her hand. I sat in a chair next to her and dealt. I won consistently, as Mother's mind wasn't on Seven-Card Draw.

"So tell me about this girl you're dating," she said.

" 'Girl'?" I said. " 'Dating'? Mother, we're not talking about the senior prom."

"Oh, then, what are the proper Bicentennial terms for romance?"

"First of all, she's not a girl. She's a woman."

"What, she's thirty-seven and has two kids?" Mother was fifty and soon would look sixty.

"She's twenty-four, a *summa cum laude* graduate of Stanford, a doctoral student in American literature, and the editor of *West-words.*"

"Well, la-di-da."

"And I believe the correct phrase is: I'm s-s-seeing her."

" 'S-s-seeing her'?" Mother said, trying to gather into a neat deck the cards that spilled under her body into the crevices of the couch.

"Yes."

"Just how much of her are you s-s-seeing, Jeremy?"

"I'm seeing all of her all the time," I said as Guy Lombardo chronicled for us on tape delay what had long passed into aftermath at the site of transmission.

"Is it permissible to ask what you see in her other, of course, than all of her?"

This was silly, self-conscious dialogue, like the worst of the Hamlet-Gertrude exchanges. Mother was usually not that prone to wordplay. She was interested in what words meant, not how they sounded; but this was New Year's Eve, she was slightly tipsy, and the last eighteen months of her life she made a self-conscious attempt to be wiser and wittier than she had ever been before. She shuffled the cards and shifted her weight on the sofa, then said, "You're trying to play the reluctant source of information. But tell me—what's this girl like?"

I removed from my wallet a wrinkled black-and-white photograph of Gretchen staring into space with one less shirt button than usual buttoned. So vulgarly masculine, so impotently possessive, I held the picture in the backlight of the reading lamp for Mother to see. Mother prided herself on her ability to "psych out" photographs and she looked at it for the longest time, looked at it again for the longest time but with her glasses on, and finally said, "She doesn't love you."

"Mother, please."

"She doesn't."

"What's that supposed to mean?"

"Just what I said: she doesn't love you."

"What a dumb thing to say. I'm not even in the picture."

"Jeremy, please. She doesn't. Any mother could see that. She loves herself first and only." This last formulation devolved into a long lecture about the inevitability of a bad marriage, the insubstantiality of physical beauty, and the ephemeral quality of love, at the end of which—her lecture, not love—she said, "Promise me you'll never marry this girl."

"Marry her? We're not even going steady."

Mother sat up on one hip to lean over and say, in a voice halfway between whispering and talking, "Promise."

I promised.

Mother and Guy Lombardo let out a happy yell.

28

HAVING VOWED never to marry Gretchen, I'm afraid I avoided her a little when I returned to Los Angeles. In an attempt, I suppose, to recapture the scholastic purity of my sophomore year, I started spending all my time in the last carrel on the southwest side of the fourth floor stacks of Powell Library. Gretchen would study at home, then come get me to give her a backrub or help make dinner or go into Beverly Hills with her to buy a dress. I enjoyed it more when she stayed for a while rather than drew me outside, when she sat with her chair to my chair, her toes on my toes, and I could almost hear her difficult mind at work. I'd always whisper too loud for the fourth floor isolationists to tolerate, and Gretchen and I would wind up at the bottom of the stairwell, eating oatmeal cookies she'd baked, drinking chocolate milk she'd bought, laughing at the silly library.

I sat in my carrel twelve hours a day and wrote grandiloquent

essays on purely formal matters: "Style in *Troilus and Cressida:*
Infecting the Myths"; " 'I Laid the Ghost of His Gifts at Last with
a Lie': The Problem of Language in *Heart of Darkness";* "Poem as
Passion: Rhetorical Strategies and Seduction Techniques in Ovid's
Amores"; "The Echo Chamber of 'Time Passes': Language as Metaphor of Memory." When I was trying to write an exegesis of "Time
Passes," the short middle section of *To the Lighthouse,* I contracted
urethritis—the honeymoon disease—from Gretchen. I'd lie awake,
itching, scratching, tossing, turning, moaning, applying a gooey
ointment, visualizing a white box in which Virginia Woolf bounced
hundreds of letters and sounds against one another, for "Time
Passes" is a cacophonous twenty-six pages. I couldn't think about
"Time Passes" without thinking about bouncing sounds inside a
white box, so I wrote this as a thesis:

> She presents a verbal surface that, in its alliterative and rhym-
> ing schemes, its punning, its inverted syntax, its broken-
> record repetitions, its ceaseless metamorphosis, parallels the
> chaos of time received by memory. Her metaphor for con-
> sciousness haunted by the past is language that stresses loud
> sound rather than literal sense and produces a superficial re-
> ality for the reader that is incomprehensible and absurd until
> he acknowledges there exists no meaning other than scattered
> sounds, and enters—as reader, as historian of the self—the
> rhythms of reprise.

I refer to the writer as "she," the reader as "he," and if that isn't
commentary upon the weird effect of growing up under Mother's
semantic shadow I don't know what is. The prose, as the professor
herself typoed, "doesn't violate Virgin's own prose," which might
tell us less about Virgin or me than Dr. Kerr. Most interesting to
me, though, were phrases such as "inverted syntax," "broken-
record repetitions," "language that stresses loud sound rather than
literal sense," "the rhythms of reprise"—what I was trying to talk
about here, without even knowing it, was the repeater gun in my
mouth. That's the subtext of this explication. That's the UCLA
Speech and Hearing Clinic reading of "Time Passes."

I was so excited by this discovery that, although I wasn't scheduled for an appointment, I ran down into Westwood Village to see Sandra, but when I told her she only swiveled in her chair and said, "Well, of course, Jeremy. We've been trying to get you to see that for a full year now. The Nowness of Forward Moving Speech. If you're ever going to gain complete control of your communicative skills, you have to pay attention to each successive moment of utterance—*now* and *now* and *now;* in other words, the continuously moving present, not previous moments of poor performance and certainly not upcoming feared words."

Mother had a different reaction to my interpretation of *To the Lighthouse.* She said she'd always regarded "Time Passes" as a powerful if abstract evocation of the First World War and wondered why I hadn't discussed "primary questions of content rather than secondary questions of form." Gretchen, who could be so harsh on everyone else's efforts but had a blind spot to any defects in my work, said she admired the essay's "empathy between the male critic and female writer, its pretty rhetoric, its (for you) uncharacteristically tight structure, its subtitle, its elaboration of metaphor into metonymy," and printed it on pages 1–7 of the Winter '77 issue.

Gretchen worked hard on *Westwords*—it's the only thing I've ever seen her devote herself to with any discipline—and transformed one more college rag into a readable quarterly. The superiority of *Antony and Cleopatra* to undergraduate luv-poetry notwithstanding, she'd always have piles of manuscripts scattered over the bedspread like so many white islands in a blue-green sea. Some of the submissions were so bad they were fun to read, but for the most part I tried to avoid my duties as assistant editor and persuade Gretchen to perform the act that gave me the deepest pleasure: reading aloud my favorite passages from my favorite books. The epilogue to *The English Reformation,* Beth's birthday present; the ending of *Call It Sleep,* Father's bible; the "Eumolpus" fragment of *Satyricon;* the last ten pages of *The Unnameable,* supposedly understood by Gretchen; Pandarus' speech concluding *Troilus and Cressida.* I lived for the endings of things, when life turned into coda.

Gretchen would always read with unfaltering fluency but without a millimeter of emotion. One night when she was going over galleys in bed, she was appalled at the number of mistakes the previous proofreader had missed. The second side of Jean-Pierre Rampal's jazz album, which I've never much liked but to which Gretchen genuflected, was playing over and over again on the stereo in the living room. The only light in the apartment was the pale pool of the reading lamp.

"Gretchen," I said, "are you awake?"

Though it was midnight, she was obviously awake. She was correcting proof sheets. I just wanted to get her attention. She didn't answer. I shook her shoulders, wiggled her toes, and said, "Gretchen, honey, it's true, isn't it, that in the next issue you're publishing a newly discovered letter of 'Pep' West's that casts new—"

"Hnnn?" she said, completely preoccupied with her galley slaves, I mean galley sheets. She still hadn't heard me. She was turned on her side, with a cigarette in one hand and a red pen like an arrow in the other.

I had to do it to get her to look at me. She had a spot of skin just above her right hip that was about as ticklish a four-by-four-inch area as I've ever tickled, and I let my fingers frolic until she giggled, slapped my hand away, sat up and said, "What? What do you want?"

I wanted her to read aloud the only full paragraph on page 192 of "Time Passes." Gretchen put away her proofs, dragged on her cigarette, capped her pen, pressed her glasses to her nose, increased the crease between pages 192 and 193.

But what after all is one night? A short space, especially when the darkness dims so soon, and so soon a bird sings, a cock crows, or a faint green quickens, like a turning leaf, in the hollow of the wave. Night, however, succeeds to night. The winter holds a pack of them in store and deals them equally, evenly, with indefatigable fingers. They lengthen; they darken. Some of them hold aloft clear planets, plates of brightness. The autumn trees, ravaged as they are, take on the flash of tattered flags kindling in the gloom of cool cathedral caves where gold letters on marble pages describe death in battle and how bones bleach and burn far away in Indian sands. The autumn trees gleam in the yellow moonlight, in the light of harvest moons, the light which mellows the energy of labour, and smooths the stubble, and brings the wave lapping blue to the shore.

She read these words with an astonishing perfection of almost British enunciation and an equally amazing atonality, as if she were trying to underline the dichotomy that divided us: the control of which she was capable and the helplessness to which I was prone. She closed the book, turned out the light, and under the covers, in the madness of the post-midnight dark, intertwined my chest hairs, of which I have six, and said, "I like reading to you, sort of, but you should read to me sometimes, Jeremy. Do you really s-s-stutter that bad when you r-r-read aloud?"

"Fuck you. Yes, I stutter that bad when I read aloud."

I would have died if I had stuttered on that sentence. The bedroom was a black mouth, the pillow was hot and sweaty, her sheets scratched. I wanted to go run in the March wind until I caught cold.

"You know that paragraph by heart, don't you?"

"Which paragraph?" I said, stalling.

"The paragraph I just read."

"I know how it goes."

"Well, you're here with me now. You're happy, right? You're sleepy, you're relaxed. If you lie back and close your eyes and let me massage your mind while you recite your little paragraph, I bet you'll be as articulate as I am."

"Heaven forfend."

"I didn't mean it like that."

I explained to her what Sandra had explained to me: tension's travel from the stomach to the teeth. She rubbed my loins while I stared at the ceiling, feared the dark, and asked, "But what after all is one night?"

The answer—as Virgin, Sandra, Gretchen, Mother, and I knew—was not an easy one. "A short space," though neither correct nor incorrect, seemed coy. "Night succeeds to night," though inarguable, seemed evasive and obvious. The answer, as with all true answers, was in the words themselves. Just as the sounds seemed to stutter out successive nights ("cool cathedral caves," "bones bleach and burn"), I stuttered out the sentences. It was the first time Gretchen had ever heard me mumble for more than a moment. It was worse than I'd feared. It was much worse than she'd anticipated. It was like the mimesis of an imitation of a parody of bad behavior.

I stuttered on every *S*, of which there were seven in the second sentence. I didn't stutter on the *L*s or I might never have made it to morning. I faltered so long on *fingers* that Gretchen, with reluctance, had to say it for me. I never got in the vicinity of *sands,* and the sentence that concluded the paragraph wasn't within my purview. I backed up all the way to "Some" to get a running start, which succeeded only in raising my pitch. I gulped, shook my head, tried to say *Indian. Ih-Ih-Ih-Ih. Ih-Ih-Ih-Ih.* By now our eyes had become adjusted to the darkness. She could see me wince, see me raise my right eyebrow with each attempt to implode my Adam's apple; could see, swimming on my face, the gaudy mix of sweat and tears. Finally, from me, silence, then my tired tongue rolled back into my mouth. It seemed like about time for someone to do something. She covered my lips with hers.

29

GRETCHEN WOULDN'T let me wallow in my woes and by the end of the week she'd planned, organized, and publicized:

A Fiction Reading!
3 Up-and-Coming, Soon-to-be-Famous Student Writers!
Crystal Room, Sproul Hall, 4 PM, March 23!

This poster was tacked to every bulletin board in the department, taped to every elevator wall and glass door. It was in the window of every Westwood Village bookstore, every restaurant, every cute little clothes shop, It was in at least two places on every floor of every library. It was so prominent in the cafeteria it disrupted the color coordination of Ackerman Union.

I went to the *Westwords* office to congratulate Gretchen on the excellence of the idea as well as ubiquity of the blitz. She was seated at her desk, typing happily, when I walked in and asked: "Who are the three up-and-coming, soon-to-be-famous student writers?" I knew and I didn't know.

She back-spaced, pulled out her little packet of Ko-Rec-Type, and said, "George Hall, Mimi Hammer, and. . . ." She was concentrating upon positioning the white tab of opaquing film. The sun flashed off the floor; her typewriter twinkled. An advertisement for the upcoming issue was tacked to the front door, covers of back issues were spread across the walls, a submissions poster was taped to the ceiling, dozens of different editions filled bookshelves, all over were manuscripts, order forms, form rejections. She stood, hugged me, and whispered, "You."

The office was on the third floor of the oldest building on campus. I stood near a window, looking out at the lucky, mechanical swimmers in the pool. The window was large and round and could be swung open from the inside. I had a deep, jittery urge to jump. I was certain I could get someone, anyone, to substitute for me, but Gretchen said she'd already mailed announcements to the *Bruin*, KCRW, the *Evening Outlook*.

"You can't violate an expectation that's already been aroused," she said. "As a writer, even a beginning one, you can appreciate that."

The clear, round window looked inviting again. I tipped over a rickety table as I chased Gretchen around the room and asked her why she had done this to me. Arrested for streetwalking, she could have explained the high heels, the black hose, the hand-held purse in such a way that she would be given a citation for exemplary citizenship. I knew any attempt at inquiry was useless, but, still, I was curious what was going through that amazing mind of hers when she conjured up this fiasco. She said she'd never heard me babble that bad before and was so determined to erase my feelings of failure that she decided to orchestrate a triumphant night of eloquence. Gretchen was certain that once I was wearing a three-piece suit, speaking into a microphone, and looking out only at friends and admirers, my trembling difficulties would die a quick death. I had, of course, heard previous versions of this remedy: Mrs. Sherfey's suggestion that I play Iago, Mother's hope that I'd become fluent through the forensic society. This time, though, for reasons that remain a little fuzzy—deluded about the transformative properties of art? weary of my own despair? who knows?—I was weirdly sanguine about the solution. I avoided Gretchen's kiss and trotted off to my afternoon class, which was, if I remember right, Moral Problems in Philosophy: Kant, who languished in limbo between noumenon and phenomenon, to Camus, who got all chilly inside when Maman dropped dead.

This was a moral problem, and I approached it very philosophically. With Camus in my pocket and Kant in my mind I realized I'd probably be able to read if I read under the influence, and I could get back at Gretchen if I wrote and read a story about her. I told Gretchen I was writing a story based on my grandfather—the pawn shop, the bowl of pennies, the ancient clock, the white whiskers, the glass of bourbon, the Sunday paper open to the obituaries—and needed the entire weekend to myself.

My ambition was to write about someone I hadn't grown up with, to make someone else matter. It didn't help a lot to receive a flurry of calls and letters all weekend from my family. Mother photocopied a publisher's dismissal of her book about "civil liberties for young people." The editor said that "if, instead of answering your own questions yourself, you developed a series of inquiries through which you led the student to arrive at the proper conclusions, you'd have a more marketable product. Unless you involve the students in each of the episodes, you run the risk of losing their interest; let them uncover for themselves the facts and principles that underlie each unit." I felt like maybe he was onto something. Beth passed along a joke that passed right over my head:

—Was Ben Franklin a Puritan?
—No. He never went to church.

Father sent me a two-sentence, homemade postcard that said: "If a shirt comes to you from Macy's it's from me, Dad. The shirt is from Dad." On the front was a photograph he'd taken of the Transamerica Building, never a good omen with Father. Then Beth called and got caught on her favorite complaint: "Sometimes I wish people didn't have to look at me at all. I don't know who I feel more sorry for—them or me." I wrote twelve hours a day; slept six; ate two; read three; masturbated, in anger at Gretchen, one. She, and everybody else, and even I at first, thought the story was about her, but it wasn't. Not really. All I've ever fixed on is my nonfictional family in its perfect righteousness.

Gretchen thought I'd written about my grandfather's drinking habits and untimely (at ninety-six, he was guiding one of his best customers through the back room of his junk shop when his heart suddenly hurt) death. She invited Charles to come to the reading, and Sandra, and a number of classmates whose language I'd declined when I was helping Gretchen with *Westwords*. All these people were sitting in the most comfortable chairs of the Crystal Room in Sproul Hall when I entered, drunk as a skunk. I'd been drinking pure gin in a plastic cup since mid-morning and it was now four, I grabbed the arms of couches; I didn't recognize Gretchen or Sandra (Beth couldn't come, though Charles was a surprise witness); I took a thin blue pattern in the rug for a river and leapt away from it; I thought the top of my head was going to twirl off; I had the pleasant sensation of a gauzy veil separating me from everyone else as I made my way to a seat up front. The Crystal Room had that gorgeous, riverlike rug wall-to-wall, velvet-covered chairs, foot rests for important people, unfathomably deep cushions, color portraits of past presidents, and one immense crystal chandelier that refracted everything.

While Gretchen stood at the podium, giving some sort of benediction, I kept seeing the crystals convert into snow, ice, falling glass. The room had a maximum capacity of seventy-five, but there must have been a hundred and fifty people there, standing, sitting on the floor, leaning against lamps, listening to Gretchen, who was urging everyone to subscribe to or join *Westwords* and emphasizing beyond common decency the coincidence that all three up-and-coming, soon-to-be-famous student writers had published first in her magazine. She got a big hand at the end of her subscription drive, then sat down. I haven't the faintest idea whether the first act of George Hall's screenplay was any good because I wasn't listening, and I can remember only the two totally explicit tableaux in what Mimi Hammer called a "cruel pastiche of shy pornography."

When Mimi was finished most of her friends left, but everyone else stayed and watched me take my manuscript out of my coat pocket, watched me clip the recording microphone to my tie, watched me grip the podium with both hands. The room twirled. The chandelier kept shattering. People's faces lost integrity.

"Good afternoon," I said and the microphone screeched a little. "I think we should all be grateful to Gretchen Noyes for organizing this very successful event." I motioned for Gretchen to rise, and she rose, and the audience applauded. "To those of you who know either me or the organizer of this very successful event, the story I'll be reading might appear to be somewhat autobiographical in origin." Gretchen gasped. "Whereas, actually, it's completely made up." A few scattered skeptics. "I've never gone hiking with the organizer of this very successful event. I'm not a sadist or a photographer. I'm no nature buff. None of this happened. I dreamed the whole thing."

I said the title—which occurred to me at that very moment—was "Deep Breathing" and began to read:

We hiked and hiked and hiked. The moon hung above us like a floater in the eye. Thin, lighted disc; electric lamp; perfectly circular moon—I hated it. I didn't want to see her face. I didn't want her to see mine. The moon seemed accessible to me, bothersome and ceaseless, and I hated it. I wanted darkness and earth. Clouds, if possible. Not the moon. I craved eclipse.

I imagined I was a harlequin, danced about, told jokes. Charla said she'd heard the stories before: they weren't funny.

I disagreed. We looked into each other's glasses, saw ourselves, and waved. We exchanged glasses and stumbled.
Charla was nearly blind. I wore glasses to feel detached and
look intelligent. She thought I was brilliant. She told me so. I
wasn't brilliant. The moon was brilliant.

The path narrowed. Tree limbs shook at us like parents'
fingers. Bushes jumped out at us like animals. We were lost.
Lost, Charla said. I was wearing jeans, a torn green lumber-
jack shirt, boots. I was carrying a sleeping bag, a backpack.
Let's go back, she said. I had no idea how to get back. I had
no intention of going back. I didn't want to go back, I wanted
to hike. Charla wanted to sleep. She was tired. I offered to
carry her backpack for her. Her sleeping bag. Her head. The
moon. She walked ahead of me, moving her arms like pistons.

My eyes focused on her ass. I thought that was vulgar and
tried to avert my attention. I stared at her backpack, her head
bobbing up and down. I looked up at the moon, down at the
dirt. Moon like an attenuated traffic light, dirt like waves. I
squinted toward the treetops, peered into labyrinths of entan-
gled tree limbs. They were all of only passing interest. My
eyes were riveted on her ass.

She asked me if I thought her ass was too large. I couldn't
decide. With my tongue I took her temperature. I was worried.
She seemed feverish. Her ass stared me in the face like bal-
loons. She lay face down on the mattress on the floor. She
chewed the pillow case. Her shirts hung like straitjackets above
us on the backs of chairs, from the lightless chandelier. She
asked me if I thought her ass was too large. I rubbed balloons
until they squeaked. I licked them until they shined. I pulled
the balloons apart, rubbed them some more. I took her tem-
perature: 98.6 was obliterated. I untied the knots in the bal-
loons, let the air out. Charla turned on her side, away from
me. She asked me if I thought her ass was too large. I told her
no. I lied. I accommodated.

She asked me to promise we would stop at the first clearing
to which we came. I promised. I'm tired, she said, you have
to respect that. I told her I did. I was tired, too—sleep was

inevitable and natural, like the moon. I wanted to remove the moon, rebel against sleep. I wanted to hike until the moon faded, until the sun rose, until my backpack slipped off my shoulders.

We walked into a black meadow that was dominated by plants taller than we were. The plants dwarfed Charla. We walked in wet soil and whipped whorls of long, pointed leaves out of our way. Culver's Root, she said. I disagreed. I hate displays of knowledge. Charla slipped and pulled clusters of leaves with her. The moon surveyed the field, withheld comment. We turned our hands into scythes, trampled Culver's Root, tore off leaves.

The meadow curved upward. We used plants like walking sticks. The meadow straightened its back, stood straight up. The meadow became a hill, became a 70-degree angle. Our backpacks hung on our shoulders like vaults. Charla's sleeping bag slipped out of her hand, unrolled into mud, opened flat like a mattress. I suggested we stop hiking, take advantage of the mattress. She rolled up the sleeping bag like a tongue. She stood and walked ahead of me. I quoted a passage of Camus's so banal it is the text of a fairly popular poster: do not walk ahead of me, do not walk behind me, walk next to me and be my friend, et cetera. She hurried away from me. I ran after her. Climbing the hill, carrying my backpack and sleeping bag, I ran after her and overtook her.

Until I was twelve years old I was the fastest person I knew. I ran to the store, around the block, to school, up the stairs, around town, across highways, away from people, with people, toward people, on dirt, on sand, on asphalt, on the beach, in bare feet, in sneakers, in sandals, in boots, in good thin tight shiny laced black shoes. I was twelve and had no hair on my legs, had legs hard as rubber, tanned as an Indian. My girlfriend was twelve and ran, too. We ran together. We ran into each other, into trouble, around lakes. We raced. She won. I thought, perhaps, she got a false start. I demanded a rematch. She said no. I took off my sneakers, threw them into the lake, stepped on twigs, rocks, glass in my bare feet. She ran away

*from me. She started smoking cigarettes, lost her wind, became
a cheerleader.*

The top of the hill curved toward us like a lip. The moon
flashed off the plants like lightning. We made crunching
sounds, snapped twigs, stepped on snails. We kissed the hill's
lips. We . . .

The podium rocked, the rug curled up, the chandelier crashed to
the floor, everyone turned upside down, and I fell backward with a
cold thud. My skull was bleeding, the microphone was wrapped
around my neck like the umbilical cord at my birth. The next thing
I knew I was in a high bed surrounded by metal railing in a white
room decorated with plastic flowers, staring at Sandra.

I sat up and said the expected.

Sandra, who was sitting in a chair on the other side of the metal
railing, put her finger to her lips and said, "Shhh. Lie back down.
You need to rest. You're in Student Health."

Curtains, sheets, floor, table: everything in the room was white.
I could feel a bandage on the back of my head and that, I assumed,
was also white.

"What happened to me?"

"Well, you were obviously somewhat inebriated at the reading,"
she said. "Just as you were really getting into your story, which
sounded like it was going to be quite exciting, you fell over and hit
your noggin on, it looked like, the front leg of a chair. Gretchen
and I and George somebody carried you out, and I drove you over
here last night."

"Last night?"

"It's Thursday morning, Jeremy. They gave you some sedatives
and you slept sixteen hours. Gretchen told me to tell you she figured you passed out from 'sheer embarrassment over the autobio-
graphic cannibalization.' "

"Tell her I told you that's not funny."

"She also said even those few pages were a revelation to her.
She had no idea how angry you were; she feels kind of shy and
confused right now." I looked glum. "Don't look so glum. You're
being released the day after tomorrow."

When Sandra thought I was physically and emotionally prepared to hear her harangue she said, "I hope you realize you nearly killed yourself yesterday afternoon. It probably seems very romantic to you to be self-absorbed and self-destructive, but what you're engaged in is so obviously slow suicide. You have to face the problem frontally—rationally. Won't you take the big step and try, at least for a while, voluntary stuttering?"

I couldn't take any big steps, at least for a while, since I was confined by the metal railing and still felt woozy from all the pills and spills, but I consented to Sandra's proposal; I hardly had the strength to do otherwise. Thursday, Friday, Saturday afternoon she came in with her tape recorder and told me to establish tension in my upper articulators on unfeared sounds at progressively higher levels of tension.

"What are my upper articulators again?" I asked, turning on my side so I could see her on the other side of the bars.

"Teeth, tongue, mouth, and lips."

"What are my unfeared sounds?"

"Jesus, Jeremy, that fall must have really thrown you for a loop. You've forgotten everything." The tape recorder was on. The light failed. "I've never heard you have any real problems on *B, D, G, J, K, L, M, N, P, R, T, V,* or *Y.*"

I rattled the metal bars and attempted to suppress a strong, sudden insight that if I kept going I'd assume permanent occupation of the basement in the tower of Babel. Why create dissonance I didn't need? I felt absurd bouncing my lips like a bumblebee on *B* when I no longer stumbled on *B.* Where was *S* now that I wanted it?

"I just wish all these tools and techniques and concepts had some real impact on my speech other than making me abnormally self-conscious about it. When I was a little kid I didn't think that much about stuttering. It wasn't that bad. It didn't mean that much to me."

"Is that true?"

No, Sandra, you know that isn't true. You know everything. You can read my mind. You know I wouldn't be writing this if that were true.

She suggested I list a hundred unfeared words, then "we" would voluntary stutter our way through them. Unlike all of Sandra's other voodoo, voluntary stuttering wasn't a technique to talk. It was a style of stuttering. She had at her disposal a lot of paradoxical aperçus to the effect that stuttering is the attempt not to stutter, you stutter because you're afraid you might stutter, you remain a stutterer as long as you pretend not to be one.... The basic idea was consciously to practice your bad habits, thus eliminating them. It scared me because I knew it would work if I wanted it to.

All through April and May she'd instructed me to use, for instance, "goose" as the last word in a sentence, prolonging the g smoothly. In the empty clinic room, looking straight into Sandra's sympathetic eyes, I said, "Last night I went into the woods and shot a gghhoose." This wasn't strictly true. Last night I'd neither gone into the woods nor shot a goose. Which wasn't the point. The point was that I had, at least for a moment and in special circumstances, controlled the act of communication.

I flew from goose to dogwood to jonquil to Mesopotamia with such surprising confidence and success that Sandra thought I should now attempt to stutter voluntarily on *feared* words in real life, for instance, with Gretchen. My relationship with my editor was now barely cordial—from what little she'd heard (and neither she nor anyone else ever actually read the rest), "Deep Breathing" wasn't true to how anything happened, she simply didn't talk like that, the staccato sentences proved the story was a rape fantasy—and this would be only one more pressure upon our crumbling alliance, but Sandra explained that I'd never rise out of the linguistic ghetto if I didn't test my private triumphs out on the road. It was near-impossible to deny her anything since she always asked so nicely and you hated to hurt her feelings. I promised to float, when arguing with Gretchen, through five feared words a day.

WHILE SHE WAS turning up the volume on the Jupiter Symphony, I said, "Ah, the Jupiter Sssymphony!" and she turned the volume down. While she was cutting cucumbers, I said, "Don't you ever get tired of sssalad?" and she threw a tiny tomato at me. After dinner, after dessert, Gretchen washed dishes and I dried them. The kitchen was too small, cold, and dark: an ideal boxing ring. I dried a dish and tried to voluntary stutter on my third feared word of the day. My listener's back was to me; my luck left.

"Do you want to go to the beach on S-S-S . . . ?"

Maybe she didn't want to go to the beach on Saturday. Maybe that was what she was trying to tell me. She wiped clean the face of the toaster and ran the rag over the knobs of the gas stove. Then she threw the rag into the sink, spun around, and said, "I think Sandra has got you so hyper-aware of your mouth you hardly know where to put your lips anymore when you kiss. What's happening to you, sweetheart? You've become so childishly shy, so involuted. So self-self-self. Blah-blah-blah. I think I need someone who's a little stronger and more certain of himself."

July Fourth weekend we rented a boat on a bay near Newport Beach. In the distance sand dunes rose up out of the backshore and farther away the sun burned the water white out at the horizon. It was low tide. The ocean rocked softly, coughing up moss and seaweed. Sea gulls, gliding over the water and looking for food and trouble in large fluttering packs, did tricks in the air. We couldn't have been more than fifty yards afloat when Gretchen started telling me how to row. "Stop feathering," she said, for she wanted to remind me she'd once been the star student at the most exclusive boarding school in Santa Barbara. "We're drifting left."

Quite frankly, I let us drift left. Direction didn't matter to me. It mattered to Gretchen, as it seems to for all the women in my life. Her doctoral dissertation was a kind of complicated map reading of *The Dream Life of Balso Snell*. At the other end of the bay were some sailboats we were in no danger of disturbing. Sea gulls spread their pearl gray wings and soared up into the air toward those hulking sand dunes. Gretchen said we should definitely stop drifting and pull right. She used numerous nautical terms I didn't quite catch. I squirmed on the seat with my arms folded, refusing to row, while Gretchen in angry silence brought us back to the beach, where we hit each other across the arms with the oars.

from Father, and it said: MOTHER IN HOSPITAL FOR BONE SCAN. CANCER HAS SPREAD TO SPINE, LUNGS, SKULL. ADRENAL GLANDS BEING REMOVED. COME HOME IMMEDIATELY. IS THERE NO END TO ALL THIS DARKNESS?

30

WEARING SANDALS and shorts, apparently the proper uniform of enlightenment, Beth met me in Baggage, then drove me to Stanford Hospital, where Father was completing the *Chronicle*'s kindergartensque crossword puzzle and Mother was asleep in a bed of gold bars. Oxygen was being pumped into her nostrils; some sugar solution, into her main vein. Her head was gray and her skin was splotchy and purple, like a grandmother's. She was turned on her side, wrapped in a white sheet. Her left foot was caught between two bars. Chocolate melted in the setting sun.

When she was well Mother's distinguishing feature was her incontestable authority and now here she was, snoring beneath the fluorescent lights, helpless as a hurt pup. Through her diction, dress, and attitude, Mother prided herself on being mistaken for Beth's older sister; now, without even trying, she looked easily as old as Father.

When the nurse woke her up for a second to give her a sleeping pill, I said, "Hi, Mom. It's Jeremy. Nice to see you. Go back to sleep if you're tired. I'll see you in the morning."

Beth dog-eared a middle page of the book of Baba quotes she was reading and said, "She's obviously very tired. Too many visitors wore her out. We should all go home and let her rest." In the back seat of the car Beth meditated, while Father and I explored the topic of property, for he was now a real estate agent and unpersuasively preoccupied with lot space, the coherence of blocks, the abiding beauty of two and a half baths.

The things in my room were like speech clinic furniture. I couldn't get my knees under the desk. I had to hunch to get my head under the shower faucet. The bed was a full foot shorter and narrow, narrow. I awoke at five a.m. to Father howling. Beth slept right through the noise; she must have incorporated it into the assemblage of her nightmare. I donned bathrobe and slippers and padded upstairs to find Father buck naked in the breakfast room, screwing in and unscrewing a low light bulb, shaking his head, and saying between screams: "Memory goes and I forget what the other thing is. Ha ha. . . . Reporter races into the city desk of the *Jerusalem Post*, shouting, 'Hold the back page!' . . . The food is terrible and such small portions! . . . Oh, oh, the Einstein joke— . . . 'and from this he makes a living?' You always loved that one, Jeremy. . . . 'Why would an insignificant person like me carry such things and, besides, who can read?' . . . Why do Ukrainians live so long? They eat oatmeal for eighty years. Ha ha. Okay, maybe that's not one of the best. . . . How do you make a hormone? You know that one. . . . Oh, oh—'*Still*, two slices of bread?' . . . Rabbi, dying: 'Will somebody please say something about my humility?' It doesn't always get a laugh. . . ."

Maybe it hit Father suddenly in the middle of the night. If so, I envy him. He got it all out in one lifetime of sorrow, whereas I've never had even a good long cry and have had to organize these sentences to try to experience some sort of major emotion. Father loved Mother. More than that, he needed her. He desperately needed her and when, for once, she needed him he collapsed on the breakfast room linoleum, announcing, "I need the juice again, Jeremy. I can't stand it any more."

He couldn't do it. He couldn't impersonate the part of the good guardian. I didn't argue or attempt to reason with him. I packed his bags and drove him to Montbel, which, ten miles east, was rather pretty: sycamore trees, parking spaces, teenage boys with bandages on their heads. Father's room even had a view of a little river. He jumped from wall to wall like a jai alai player, altering his mood every minute—exuberant, bashful, distressed, disgusted, tormented, tickled, grave, bemused, scared, dead, delirious—and I didn't know what to do, so I kept hugging him, saying he'd be all right. A nurse knocked and said I had to leave now.

"Well, goodbye, then, Dad. I have to go, but Dr. Skolnick will come see you in a second. You know how much you like him."

"Skolnick?" he said. "Don't know him. What's he going to do, nick my skull? Get it, Jeremy? *Skolnick: nick my skull?*"

I got it, Father, I got it, but didn't dare laugh, since the nurse was still standing in the doorway. *The schizophrenic mind, in its depressive state, focuses upon form to the virtual exclusion of content.*

"You remember Dr. Skolnick, don't you, Dad? You saw him the last time you were here and the time before that, too, I think. He's a good man. You liked him. You talked tennis together. You always ask for him."

"Will he give me the juice?" Father asked, bouncing up and down on his bed. There was very little else in the room other than a bureau and that unbeatable view of the river.

Despite the nurse's stagy protestations, I said, "Yes, of course he will. He'll give you whatever you want."

"I'm thirsty for the juice," he said, making obscene sounds with his lips.

Dr. Skolnick entered the room, waving sphygmomanometer and stethoscope like party favors. More jai alai acrobatics from Father. I was told to leave and return tomorrow. I left, but halfway down the hall I could still hear Father weeping.

I drove from Montbel to Stanford, from Stanford back to Montbel, comparing my parents' problems. Sometimes I was accompanied by Beth, whom I tried to talk back to the wonderful world of books while we ministered to the diseased and dying. The first day after Thanksgiving I gave Mother an oversize Kodacolor postcard of boats and birds and the beach going to amber in the Balboa sunset.

"It's so beautiful," Mother said, crying and placing the card in the most privileged position at the edge of her portable table. She further flouted her scary new serenity by laying across her lap a long, thin piece of wood that she was sanding into maybe a letter-opener for Gargantua. "There's a certain logic and reason in it all that I find very comforting," she lectured an incredulous Beth and Jeremy, "even a kind of purity to bringing out the best in the grain."

I don't know whether Mother thought she should recover her strength if Father was going to be weak again or whether, in some not-so-secret chamber of her heart, she was cheered by the news— I don't know how to explain it other than to say she briefly rallied when she heard Father was at Montbel. She was encouraged to come home, where she lay quietly in a gray gown, listening to operatic radio, breathing borrowed oxygen, asking often for Father of all people. She rang a gold bell, which was tied to her wrist, whenever she needed one of us to feed her, wash her, push pills past her mouth, lift her onto the commode.

While I was getting ready to go back to school, Gretchen flew up one Sunday morning to visit before flying back with me to L.A. Beth was reading most of the major soliloquies to a sleepy Mother; somehow I got talked into giving Gretchen a guided tour of the basement.

Although it was adjacent to my bedroom, I hadn't been down there for years. I hadn't wanted to go crawling around in cesspools. The basement ran the length of the house, beginning with dull light and a water heater and ending with low beams, cracked cement, complete darkness. I guided Gretchen through the alcove where Beth and her friends had once held secret meetings of the Monkees' club and where a sign still read MICKY LIVES. Maybe Micky lived, maybe he didn't, but everything else was ruined: corroded thermoses and canteens and broken garden equipment, an abandoned workbench, busted boxes of dead language written by Mother and Father. Gretchen kept hitting her head on the low beams. I held her hand and exhibited suitcases without handles, wicker baskets without wicker, year after year of Puppa's junk shop account books, and my leg brace. I probably would have stumbled over the brace if Gretchen hadn't noticed its rusted steel, moldy leather, locked buckles, its knotted laces. I held it high and clanked it about a little like half a Halloween skeleton, tried to strap it to my leg to recall the past.

Gretchen, who was sitting on a box of old tax forms, said, "Don't, Jeremy. Please. Really. Don't do that. It's positively ghoulish."

"You're right," I said, folding up the brace and putting it away. "I'm sorry."

"What is that thing, anyhow?"

"What thing?"

"That steel contraption that squeaks."

"My old leg brace."

"You mean you actually used to hobble around with that wrapped around your knee?" she asked.

I detected the small curve of a smile and wondered what, if anything, was so funny. "All junior year everyone thought I was crippled," I said. "Not until the middle of senior year did I destroy their deepest hopes."

Gretchen, giggling, said, "I never realized it was that bad." Confronted with tragic facts, we occasionally laugh when we don't know what else to do. "It sounds absolutely awful," she continued, massaging my right leg as if it were still in traction. The massage led us from the basement to my bedroom, where I, as always, peaked too early and Gretchen, as always, didn't peak at all.

31

The conversation occurred in the basement. I was talking to Gretchen. We were talking about my leg brace. It was a medium-stress situation. Tension occurred in my right leg. Tension was within normal limits. Speech kept moving forward. Airflow stopped at the basement door. It was very stuffy. Tension increased on feared words, but I didn't avoid *S* or *F*. On the other hand, I didn't voluntary stutter very much. A leg brace is only a leg brace until I remember the pause when I brought my feet together, swung the crutches from behind, and gathered myself to go nowhere. Stuttering is just excessive tension in the lower articulators until I see myself, at four, flipping flash cards on the living room couch. I haven't been stuttering that much recently or, if I have, I haven't noticed it because it hasn't seemed that important. Me and Gretchen, Beth with her body, Father at Montbel, Mother on her deathbed. We're all so afraid, Sandra. We're all so alone.

Dear Jeremy,

The enclosed is one of the very few things I wrote for the *West Bay Sun* that's worth a damn.

Love,
Dad

For the past three years I was the guardian and guru of this enlightened corner of tennis intelligence and incidentals. It has been a labor of profound and requited love. Now the time has come for others to take over. The January issue of the *West Bay Sun* will carry the byline of another member for "Net Set." What I attempted to do in these monthly dispatches was to stimulate interest in tennis: for the novice as well as the NCTA-ranked player, for those of ample girth and feeble forehands as well as the mercurially swift thirty-year-olds with their 120 mph serves.

Employing my own distillation of drollery and hyperbole, I tried to de-emphasize the winning at all costs syndrome. My message, delivered subliminally at times, more pointedly at other times, was that tennis was the open sesame to a lifelong, wholesome recreational outlet; a wondrous way to have fun with your clothes *on*, with incalculable benefits to psyche and sinew; an endurable bridge to friendships on and off the court.

What was of overriding importance, I felt, was not merely reporting who won what major tournament, but the number of players who participated, especially the names of newcomers trying their wings and Wilson large-sized rackets for the first time. I don't know how well or how often I got the message over, but the thrust of these columns—forgetting my paraphrastic penchant—was that no matter whether you won or lost a casual weekend mixed-doubles match or a major championship final the earth would continue to rotate on its axis around the sun; the stars would take their assigned places in the firmament; and lovers, strolling where the woodbine twineth, would plight their troths as they had since the dawn of time.

The gospel according to St. Theodore was that tennis is just a game. To be played for fun under the sun. The rest, the who-won-what-big-match, was secondary and commentary. The stuff of seared and yellowing newspaper—you, dear reader, will have trouble remembering the name of this ink-stained wretch who wrote the "Net Set" column for three years. And that is how it should be. Time marches on. The graves are filled with indispensable men and women. Even editors and columnists.

To those members of the club who stopped me occasionally to tell me how much they enjoyed a particular column of mine or a turn of phrase, my sincere gratitude. I shall miss—more than these chaste, inadequate words can convey—writing this column each month. I'll be seeing you around West Bay soon, I hope, but not in the columns of the *Sun*.

Dear Jeremy,   December 16

I started doing it about six months ago sort of by accident and since then have gone through constant feelings of guilt, mostly centered around the idea that you should love some-one else and not yourself. I've never failed to regret it right afterward, even while recognizing the imperiousness with which I felt I had to do it at the time. It varies from twice to several times a week. I always thought it would stop once I'd "gotten over" Michael and, while I do it less now, I haven't stopped completely. Is it adolescent to be still doing it at my age? What do people do when they're not involved with some-one? Is it possible to suppress sexual tension? The reformation makes us turn not only inward but to those around us who can help.

Love,
Beth

Ethan couldn't believe how sick his mother was. He'd read all the letters his sister had written, in purple ink to imply pain; on wide-ruled, blue-lined notebook paper to suggest innocence; and in infinitesimal illegibility to suggest a mind so involuted as to be incapable of registering anything other than its own agenda. He'd looked at the last photographs his father had taken of his mother: black-and-white snapshots of her sitting up in bed and trying to smile as an invisible wind blew white curtains around in the background. And he had listened to his mother's voice vibrate over the phone, had heard it crack, had heard her hang up in mid-sentence. He hadn't let any of the letters, photos, or phone calls touch him, though, hadn't really let the catastrophe get conveyed. He'd been under the impression his mother was recovering but, standing now at the foot of her bed in cool morning light, wearing a little boy's terry cloth bathrobe for which he was now rather too big, watching her sleep flat on her back on top of the sheets, Ethan couldn't believe how sick she was. Through her diaphanous smock he saw blue bones. . . .

32

WHILE A NURSE babysat Mother and Father received his fifth of eight shock treatments, Beth and I played basketball at the appealingly low hoop a few blocks down the hill. It was Beth's idea and she was extremely excited for some reason about shooting a few baskets, as we'd done when we were kids. She was wearing her inevitable black tennis shoes and blue jeans with a Giants cap. I didn't tell her this was probably not proper attire for playing basketball; I let her wear what she wanted to wear. I tried not to interfere with her happiness and freedom. We ran a few laps around the playground to get loose, passing the ball back and forth. She wanted to play Around the World, a game at which she'd never beaten me, but she thought she could win now that I was out of practice. Getting in shape was part of her new regimen whereas I never recovered the speed and agility I possessed before I broke my leg and had pretty much abandoned athletics. In Around the World each person tries to travel from one end of the court to the other and back again. Beth adjusted the bill of her cap, rolled up the sleeves of her sweatshirt and cuffs of her jeans, double-knotted the laces of her shoes, and in general concentrated upon the action with a seriousness and determination she once reserved only for absurdist drama in translation.

She knocked her knees together, held the ball with two hands, put some backspin on her shot, and followed through. She used the same techniques Father had once taught me, and hardly missed. On your first trip across the court you were allowed two attempts from any one position, but if you missed both you had to start over. This was what was happening to me while Beth, cautious but consistent, was moving around the world. She won when her last shot, a layup, hit the front rim, kissed the backboard, and fell straight through the net. When I tried to congratulate her she ran away from me, sat on a bench near the fence, and started crying. I didn't ask what was wrong. I just sat next to her, bouncing the ball, brushing the dirt off her face, winding and unwinding her ponytail. Trivial victory often rings empty and releases a sadness so deep there's no conceivable comfort. You just stare and smile and hope it vanishes, but there's absolutely nothing you can say.

CHRISTMAS EVE Mother was in such excruciating pain we had to carry her body above us like a virgin sacrifice to the bathroom. . . . "Tell her what you've always wanted to tell her," Gretchen telephoned, knee-deep in Kübler-Ross. . . . Beth cheer-led epigrams: "So lett us choose life that wee and our posterity may live." John Winthrop, 1630 . . . looking straight at me down at the other end of the bed with eyes as cold and gray and still in the sockets as old dimes caught in coin slots . . . the crown of her head nearly bald and what was left along the sides and in back falling out . . . wilted white rose petals caught beneath the bureau glass . . . grieving for the agony of not grieving, learning too well what Mother had taught me: how to take notes.

Father sat quietly in a dark corner of the Montbel game room, wearing plastic slippers and a robe. The game room was done in orange. Maybe that was the reason no one else was in it except me, Father, and Dr. Skolnick. Father's face was empty of all emotion, brown and red like a burnt field. I looked into his eyes, I held his hand, I squeezed his thin arms, I slapped him across the knee. Abruptly he stood, ran in an insane circle, and said, "I'd walk all night on the shoulder of 101 to see Annette again."

As if Father weren't there, I turned to Dr. Skolnick and said, "I c-c-can't trust him to behave properly. He might trip over an oxygen tank or spill some pills. He'd upset my mother. I c-c-can't take him home." I turned and walked away. The door shut on Father's face. This is the worst thing I've ever done in my life.

That night Mother looked at me and said, "I'm all pickled up." I'd never heard this phrase before, but it sounded old-fashioned and I assumed her mind was moving across memories of childhood in Steubenville, Ohio. She awoke only to be lifted onto the commode. She breathed faster and faster, in lunging convulsions, then slower and slower, in little kisses of air through the space in her teeth, then hardly at all.

Ethan put the logs and some newspapers in the fireplace and unfolded the screen to cover the hearth. He'd never been much good with matches—he couldn't light a candle or a cigarette—but he quickly struck the match on the floor and flicked it into the fireplace and another and another until the paper burned and a log fell and the fire started. His mother wrapped a blanket around herself and sank down into the chair and blanket. All he could see of her was the wrinkled half-moon of her forehead and white hair, which gathered in a knot at her shoulder. She reached out her hands to receive the fire's heat. The fire hissed and crackled, and smoke swirled up the chimney. The flame shapes danced and flickered and vanished and then recurred again. The fire was at once unchanged and completely transformed every second. The fire was like snow. . . .

Beth and I watched a color cartoon in a shopping mall, and I laughed at everything. The odd, purplish night in the movie filled with hundreds of narrow, jazzy, yellow-orange blocks, which meant: Lady and the Tramp were in a very big city, and Lady was probably pretty scared. Beth said, "How can you laugh at this? It's not in the least amusing." I kept laughing. She said, "I don't see how you can laugh like a goddamn hyena when Mom's so sick." I kept laughing like a goddamn hyena. She said, "I don't see much love in your heart any more, Jeremy, do you? I don't see any real concern." I couldn't help it. I kept laughing.

I pressed from the wrist to the elbow along both arms, trying to find it. Beth, still in her pajamas, couldn't find it, either. We stood at the foot of Mother's bed, squinting into the sun. The sun, white sheets, a gray strand of Mother's hair; maybe now I'd be able to talk. While Beth drank red wine for breakfast, I jingled car keys and said, "I'm going to tell Dad."

In unlaced business shoes on bare feet, in swimming trunks, a wool cap, and a Jewish Welfare Fund T-shirt, Father ran around the high school track adjacent to Montbel. I stood in the shade of sycamore trees, watching, then suddenly I was running alongside him, breathing hard. Even with his unlaced shoes, he was running as well as he ever had. I was in the outside lane, I hadn't run around a track for years, and I had trouble keeping up with him. As we came into a straightaway, I grabbed his arm and said, "I have something to tell you."

Father stopped and turned around. "Are we running the wrong way?" he asked.

"We're going the right way," I said. "But I have something very important to tell you. I have some very bad news."

"They want me back at Montbel. Well, you can tell them I'm staying right here."

"Listen to me. I have something very terrible to tell you. I want you to be prepared. I don't want you running into the fence or banging your head against the water fountain. I came here to tell you Mother died early this morning."

I don't know how I said these words so calmly, but I must have felt the need for some rational force to offset Father. He didn't respond unreasonably, though. He didn't do anything. He just kept running right along.

"Do you hear me? Mother died. My mother. Your wife. Annette. *Kaput, capisce?"*

I thought a little wordplay might wake him up—he always loved language games—but he kept bobbing his head up and down, he kept on kicking. The toe of my right shoe was starting to pinch. We came into the last bend of the backstretch, I wanted to stop and rest and get things straight, then Father stepped quite literally out of his shoes, leaning into the turn. The rest was a mad run. He sprinted the final hundred and fifty yards in world-record time with his swimming trunks falling off and his hands raised over his head. He was screaming: "Annette! Annette! Annette!"

By the time I caught up with him he was sitting in the stands, picking pebbles and tiny pieces of glass out of his feet, still screaming Mother's name. It seemed to me he was saying, "A net! A net! A net!" The poor man wanted a net. I took him back to Montbel.

I examined every photograph of her as a little girl, every article she'd ever written, every letter ever written to her. I read back to front, right to left, like beginning with conclusions. I opened every desk and dresser drawer, looking . . . looking for what? Sentences I could criticize.

She made the sharp truth ring, like golden spurs, but it sounded on ears deafened by fear and evil.

Seductively dressed in nondenominational, nonpolitical, nonprofit colors, Spiritual Mobilization and its donors thereby enjoy tax exemption; it is not surprising that the décolletage has attracted patrons from both sides of the street.

Winding up a four-year investigation of Communism in the film industry, the House Committee on Un-American Activities departed from Hollywood in the manner of carefree picnickers who, having enjoyed the sunshine and the flowers, feel no concern about the mess they leave behind.

In her closet I came upon a pair of shiny new shoes still in the box. Beth can't get those shoes out of her mind. At Mother's desk, in her high style, I wrote her obituary.

No funeral, though. No nothing, despite my fantasy of standing before the mourners with my mouth open, trying to do the seemingly simple thing of saying one word and then another but, instead, getting escorted offstage by Gretchen to the compassionate acclaim of the crowd. Just a party, as Mother's will specified, "to celebrate life rather than mourn death." Some celebration. A folk guitarist upon whom Mother had always had a crush played poorly. Father wept in the den. She'd been carried out of the bedroom in a plastic bag. Her body was burned. The ashes were scattered at sea. Whenever I cross the Golden Gate Bridge, I think not of suicide, as Father does, but of Mother, swimming.

I analyzed rather than swooned over all the sincerely sincere condolences. I wanted to feel famous feelings but couldn't get past difficulties in construction. "The last time I talked to your mother must have been the middle of December. She still sounded so extraordinarily plucky, although for the first time she had lost the lilt in her voice that she somehow managed each previous time that I'd called. What a brave and plucky woman she was." "I hope these words will comfort you a little. Words were the tool your mother used so well. She was a fine craftsman in her profession. Perhaps more importantly, she was a fine human being." *Perhaps?* I love that. Where did my family and their friends ever get the idea language could eclipse life?

I talk the way I talk, I write the way I write, I live the way I die because of Mother. Everything I've ever done I did to win her admiration. She always used to say, "You may not love me, but you must respect me." We loved her from afar.

Father came home walking slowly. He no longer has any memory of the last few months, but he does have a real estate license. Ten days out of the hospital, he insisted upon serving as realtor for the sale of our house. He walked through the rooms, giving guided tours to families of four, saying, "This was where my beautiful wife slept with a smile, this was where she soaked in the tub for entire afternoons, this was where she cooked delicious dinners, this was where she wrote the finest articles in American journalism. . . ."

In sixth grade everyone in Mrs. Gradinger's homeroom had to

build a balsa wood miniature of the family manse, which our mothers were supposed to be exhilarated by when they came for parent-teacher-student conferences. My replica was painted black and yellow, and featured bushes everywhere like broccoli. Although our actual house had an open-sided carport, I constructed a square, detached garage, without doors or windows or a very well applied roof. Mother greeted Mrs. Gradinger, looked at my model for the longest time, then looked at me for the longest time.

"Jeremy," she said, "Jeremy, sweetheart, are you ever just going to come inside with everyone else and get warm?"

She touched his nose and cheeks, tousled his hair, kissed his forehead with dry lips. Ethan's mother smelled like laundry mixed with buttermilk. She leaned forward and he held her in his arms but was afraid of hurting her with too hard a hug, so he set her back down against the pillow and let go, moving away.